THE
HUNTER
AND
OTHER STORIES

DASHIELL HAMMETT

THE HUNTER

and

OTHER STORIES

Edited by Richard Layman and Julie M. Rivett

SCHAUMBURG TOWNSHIP
DISTRICT LIBRARY
130 SOUTH ROSELLE ROAD
SCHAUMBURG, ILLINOIS 60193

Printed in the United States of America
Published simultaneously in Canada

ISBN: 978-0-8021-2158-5
eBook ISBN: 978-0-8021-9295-0

The Mysterious Press
an imprint of Grove/Atlantic, Inc.
154 West 14th Street
New York, NY 10011

Distributed by Publishers Group West

www.groveatlantic.com

CONTENTS

Introduction   1

CRIME

Commentary   11
"The Hunter" (unpublished)   13
"The Sign of the Potent Pills" (unpublished)   21
"The Diamond Wager" (1929, uncollected)   36
"Action and the Quiz Kid" (unpublished)   57

MEN

Commentary   65
"Fragments of Justice" (unpublished)   68
"A Throne for the Worm" (unpublished)   72
"Magic" (unpublished)   76
"Faith" (2007)   89
"An Inch and a Half of Glory" (unpublished)   100
"Nelson Redline" (unpublished)   113
"Monk and Johnny Fox" (unpublished)   121
"The Cure" (2011, uncollected)   125

MEN AND WOMEN

Commentary 139

"Seven Pages" (2005) 142

"The Breech-Born" (unpublished) 146

"The Lovely Strangers" (unpublished) 148

"Week--End" (unpublished) 166

"On the Way" (1932, uncollected) 173

SCREEN STORIES

Commentary 187

"The Kiss-Off" (unpublished, story for *City Streets*,
     Paramount 1931) 190

"Devil's Playground" (unpublished and unproduced) 201

"On the Make" (unpublished, story for
     Mr. Dynamite, Universal 1935) 208

APPENDIX: THE LOST SPADE

Commentary 279

"A Knife Will Cut for Anybody" (unpublished) 281

Afterword 287

THE
HUNTER
AND
OTHER STORIES

INTRODUCTION

Call this volume Hammett Unplugged. It includes seventeen short
stories and three screen stories, none previously collected and most
previously unpublished, that stand in significant contrast to the work
for which he is best known while exhibiting the best qualities of his
literary genius. The earliest of the stories in this collection seem to date
from near the beginning of Hammett's writing career, and the latest
might well mark the end of it. In the stories included in this volume
Hammett was breaking boundaries. This collection includes no stories
from *Black Mask* magazine, the detective pulp where Hammett made
his reputation as a short-story writer; it includes no stories featuring
the Continental Op, Hammett's signature short-story character; and
it includes only one story narrated by the main character, which was
Hammett's preferred approach in most of his best-known short fiction. Here he addresses subjects, expresses sentiments, and explores
ideas that would have fit uneasily in the pages of *Black Mask*. In these
stories Hammett displays his fine-tuned sense of irony and explores the
complexities of romantic encounters. He confronts basic human fears
and moral dilemmas. He is sometimes sensitive and more often stonily
objective. He caricatures prideful men, draws sympathetic portraits of

strong women, and parodies pulp-fiction plots. And violence takes a back seat to character development.

The story of Hammett's career as a writer is well-known. He published his first story in October 1922 at the age of twenty-eight, after his career as a Pinkerton's detective had been cut short by tuberculosis. He wrote to survive. Severely disabled during most of the 1920s, he was unable to provide for his wife and family in any other way. After a brief attempt to break into the slick-paper (which is to say middle-class) short-story market, he found his home as a writer in the pages of the detective pulps, aimed at blue-collar, primarily male readers. He drew on his five years as a Pinkerton operative to write stories that had the authority of experience, and soon he became the most popular writer for the most popular of the detective-fiction pulps. He came to regard that distinction as a mixed blessing; he had broader interests. Of forty-nine stories Hammett published before June 1927, half neither feature a detective nor are about crime. Of the eleven new stories that appeared after *The Maltese Falcon* was published in 1930, five are about noncrime subjects.

With the April 1, 1924, issue, which carried Hammett's fourteenth *Black Mask* story, the sixth featuring the Continental Op, a new editor took over at the magazine. Phil Cody had been circulation manager for *Black Mask*, and though he described himself as primarily a businessman, he took an aggressive stance as an editor. Cody insisted that the quality of the writing in his pages be elevated, championing Hammett as a model for his other writers and imposing what might be called the *Black Mask* editorial formula on his authors. Cody encouraged longer, more violent stories, and he insisted on action and adventure in the fiction he published rather than simply what the previous editor called "unusual subject matter." The main characters of the stories Cody published were masters of their world, offering readers vicarious triumph over the threats and frustrations of modern urban life. Cody the businessman set about cultivating a dedicated readership who knew what to expect issue after issue. From Hammett, *Black Mask* readers expected the Continental Op.

Hammett flourished under Cody's editorship. But as he began to take his editor's compliments to heart, as he developed a surer confidence in his writing ability, and as his financial situation became more stressed when his wife became pregnant with their second daughter, he asked for more money and was denied. Hammett didn't take "no" well. By the end of 1925, he decided that he had had enough of Cody and his magazine, and he said so before quitting. In November of that year he wrote a letter to *Black Mask*, apparently a response to Cody's solicitation of his opinion about the most recent issue. Hammett warned him, "Remember, I'm hard to get along with where fiction's concerned." He then offered perceptive criticism of each story in the issue, concluding with the comment that three of the stories "simply . . . didn't mean anything. People moved around doing things, but neither the people nor the things they did were interesting enough to work up a sweat over." Hammett was busy by that time writing stories for other markets in which interesting people from various walks of life do interesting things. Those stories are in this volume.

In fall 1926, Cody became circulation manager and vice president of *Black Mask* parent company Pro-Distributors, and Joseph T. Shaw was named the new editor of the magazine. Shaw's first move was to attempt to lure Hammett back into the fold. He offered more money and promised to support Hammett's literary ambitions. Hammett, who needed the money to help support his growing family, capitulated. Over the next two years he focused on *Black Mask* with stories that were longer and more violent than ever before. When the editors at Knopf, Hammett's hardback publisher, read his first two novels, *Red Harvest* (1929) and *The Dain Curse* (1929), both of which had first appeared serially in *Black Mask*, they responded in both instances that "the violence is piled on a bit thick." With that, Hammett turned to tough-minded dramatic confrontation rather than violence as a means of advancing his plots. As he famously told Blanche Knopf in 1928, he was trying "to make literature" of his work. These stories document his efforts to that end.

He was also trying to make more money from his work. Perhaps because his health was improving a bit, clearly because of his pressing financial needs, Hammett began promoting his writing career with renewed energy in 1928. He sent his first novel to Knopf, unagented, and they accepted it for publication. The same year, he traveled south to Hollywood to try to sell his stories for adaption as movies. By that time the new sound movies were clearly about to transform the movie industry, and Hammett wanted in on the action. He began writing fiction in a form that could be easily filmed—paying attention to restrictions of time, place, and action. It is fair to say that by the end of 1929, Hammett's fiction was shaped by an intent to make not just literature, but movies of his work. By 1930, he had sold *Red Harvest* (the unrecognizable basis for *Roadhouse Nights* [1930] featuring Helen Morgan, Charles Ruggles, and Jimmy Durante in his first movie role) and "The Kiss-Off," which was the original story for *City Streets* (1931, starring Gary Cooper and Sylvia Sidney), to Paramount. Warner Bros. released the first of what would be three film versions of *The Maltese Falcon* in 1931. During the early 1930s he worked for Howard Hughes's Caddo Productions, Universal Studios, and MGM, among others. "The Kiss-Off" and two other of Hammett's original screen stories—"Devil's Playground," which was not produced, and "On the Make," which became *Mr. Dynamite* (1935, starring Edmund Lowe)—are included in this volume.

After publication of his most successful novels, *The Maltese Falcon*, *The Glass Key*, and *The Thin Man*, when *Black Mask* couldn't afford him any longer, Hammett turned again to the slick-paper market during his breaks from movie work. He published stories in *Collier's*, *Redbook*, and *Liberty*—"On the Way," which appeared in the March 1932 *Harper's Bazaar*, is included here because it has not been collected previously—and he wrote others that were not placed, but his primary interest was the movies by that time. He was under contract to MGM, writing the original stories for their Thin Man series published in our *Return of the Thin Man* (2012).

To our minds, this volume includes some of Hammett's finest short fiction, and there is strong evidence that he valued these stories. Hammett was not a hoarder. He disposed of books, magazines, and manuscripts as soon as he was done with them. But he saved the typescripts and working drafts of stories in this book for more than thirty years, moving from coast to coast, hotel to hotel, and among several apartments. They were important to him. While many of these stories were clearly prepared for submission, with a heading on the typescript giving Hammett's address, the word count, and the rights offered, there are only two pieces of evidence that he actually sent any of them out. A sheet is attached to "Fragments of Justice" with a note in Hammett's hand, "Sold to the *Forum*, but probably never published." *Forum* magazine published three book reviews by Hammett between 1924 and 1927, but not "Fragments of Justice." In a letter to his wife, Jose, Hammett remarks that one story sent to *Blue Book* in 1927 "came sailing back"; the story he referred to is unidentified, but a good guess is "The Diamond Wager," published in *Detective Fiction Weekly* in 1929 under the pseudonym Samuel Dashiell. *Blue Book*, distinguished at the time for their publication of Agatha Christie's Hercule Poirot stories, was among the highest-paying detective-fiction pulps, the kind of market Hammett would have been trying in 1927, and "The Diamond Wager" seems tailor-made for them.

After publication of *The Maltese Falcon* established Hammett as one of the finest writers in America, he could easily place his fiction in most any market he chose, but before that he was typed as a genre writer, a hard tag to overcome. His primary readership was mystery fans interested in realistic fiction about crime. Before publication of *The Maltese Falcon*, a story submission to the slicks by Dashiell Hammett would have gone into the slush pile with hundreds—more likely thousands—of other submissions. It would have been a hard sell. With two exceptions, "The Hunter" and the light satire "The Sign of the Potent Pills," the stories in this volume are not detective stories. They are Hammett's attempts to resist and then to break out of the mold that came to define him as a writer.

After 1934, when *The Thin Man* was published and Hammett began devoting his full energies as a writer to screen stories, he stopped publishing his work. For the next twenty-seven years remaining in his life he published no new fiction. For the first sixteen years of the period, until

1950, he didn't need the money and had other interests; for the last ten he seemed to lack the energy and the spirit to write. After Hammett died, in January 1961, his literary properties fell under the complete control of Lillian Hellman, who set about carefully and expertly reviving his literary reputation—as a detective-fiction writer. There is evidence that she began editing some of the stories in this volume for publication—her light edits appear on a couple of typescripts—but she restricted her efforts to republishing what she regarded as his best detective fiction, because that was where the market lay. Hellman sold Hammett's literary remains—or most of them, one assumes—to the Harry Ransom Center, University of Texas, from 1967 to 1975, and guarded access to the archive carefully. These stories were first discovered in the Ransom Center archive in the late 1970s, but publication was restricted. Over the last thirty-five years, Hammett's unpublished stories have been regularly "rediscovered," but for practical reasons, having to do primarily with licenses to publish and the indifference of the trustees who held sway until they were replaced at the end of the last century, these stories remained unpublished. Make no mistake: the stories in this book are not newly discovered; they are made newly available to a wide readership.

This book is arranged into four broadly defined sections—with a special appendix. Within each section stories are arranged into roughly chronological order, sometimes on the basis of guess and instinct, though the headings, paper, and typographical arrangement offer reliable clues in most cases. The texts are essentially as Hammett left them. We have resisted editing and modernizing his style: compound words, for example, are hyphenated as Hammett wrote them, and his old style of forming possessives is retained. In some cases punctuation has been judiciously standardized. In one instance an untitled story, which we call "The Cure," has its title supplied, with the advice and consent of the people best positioned to judge what title Hammett might have chosen—his daughter and granddaughter.

The appendix deserves special attention. Provided courtesy of a generous private collector, it is the elegant beginning of a Sam Spade story or novel, perhaps. It alone among the several fragments Hammett left behind was chosen for inclusion in this print edition of *The Hunter and Other Stories*. Interesting though they may be, literary fragments are of primary interest to a limited audience. A selection of Hammett's unfinished starts is included as a feature of the e-book edition of this collection.

R. L.

CRIME

COMMENTARY

The four stories in this section provide a prismatic view of Hammett's experiments over a decade with the treatment of crime. These stories show Hammett trying different forms—from a standard *Black Mask*–type story, to parody, to Golden Age models, to the type of hard modernism associated with Hemingway—and varying types of narration. Three of the stories are narrated in the third person, though each in a different variety, and the other is told in the first-person voice of a wily and affected dilettante with a keen interest in fine jewels, suggesting a more famous Hammett villain.

"The Hunter" is a detective story in the mold of the *Black Mask* Continental Op stories, but with an important difference. Here the detective, named Vitt, is as hard-boiled as a detective gets. He has a job to do, and he does it with neither distraction nor emotional involvement, and then he turns ironically to his own mundane domestic concerns at the end. Judging from the return address on Eddy Street, where Hammett lived from 1921 to 1926, it was likely written about 1924 or 1925, when Hammett wrote six stories published in magazines other than *Black Mask* and introduced two new protagonists in stories told in the third person, as "The Hunter" is—Steve Threefall in "Nightmare

Town" (*Argosy All-Story Weekly*, December 27, 1924) and Guy Tharp in "Ruffian's Wife" (*Sunset*, October 1925).

"The Sign of the Potent Pills" is a farce that builds on the depiction of the detective as something less than a heroic crime fighter. The return address is 891 Post Street, where Hammett lived from 1927 to 1929. In January 1926, Hammett published "The Nails in Mr. Cayterer," a satirical story about a writer-detective named Robin Thin similar in tone to "The Sign of Potent Pills." (Another Robin Thin story, "A Man Named Thin," was published shortly after Hammett's death in 1961.) In this typescript someone crossed out the first two paragraphs of the story. They have been restored here, because they provide the only mention of the billboard that gives the story its name and identify Pentner, who calls the police at the end. Lillian Hellman edited the story, and the first paragraphs seem to have been cut by her. Hellman's edits have been accepted only when they corrected clear typographical errors or undeniable infelicities.

"The Diamond Wager," a clear imitation of the Golden Age mystery stories popular at the time, was, by our guess, written in 1926 and rejected by the pulp *Blue Book*, though not published until 1929 in another pulp, *Detective Fiction Weekly*. There is no known typescript. The story is told in the first person by a master criminal and was published while *The Maltese Falcon* was being serialized in *Black Mask*.

"Action and the Quiz Kid" is possibly the last story Hammett completed. It is set in New York and refers to Joe DiMaggio's home run–hitting prowess. DiMaggio was a star for the minor-league San Francisco Seals in 1932 and 1933. He was bought by the New York Yankees in 1934, but sat out a season with a knee injury. When he played his first season for the Yankees in 1936, he hit twenty-nine home runs; in 1937, he had forty-six homers, the most in his career. A reasonable guess is that this story was written early in 1936, after Hammett was released from the hospital in January and then spent the rest of the year recuperating in and around New York City. A so-called slice-of-life story, "Action and the Quiz Kid" is typical of Hammett's late interest in character as opposed to plot.

THE HUNTER

There are people who, coming for the first time in contact with one they know for a detective, look at his feet. These glances, at times mockingly frank, but more often furtive and somewhat scientific in purpose, are doubtless annoying to the detective whose feet are in the broad-toed tradition: Fred Vitt enjoyed them. His feet were small and he kept them neatly shod in the shiniest of blacks.

He was a pale plump man with friendly light eyes and a red mouth. The fortunes of job-hunting not guided by definite vocational training had taken him into the employ of a private detective agency some ten years ago. He had stayed there, becoming a rather skillful operative, although by disposition not especially fitted for the work, much of which was distasteful to him. But he liked its irregular variety, the assurances of his own cleverness that come frequently to any but the most uniformly successless of detectives, and the occasional full-tilt chase after a fleeing someone who was, until a court had decided otherwise, a scoundrel of one sort or another. Too, a detective has a certain prestige in some social divisions, a matter in no way equalized by his lack of any standing at all in others, since he usually may either avoid these latter divisions or conceal his profession from them.

Today Vitt was hunting a forger. The name of H. W. Twitchell—the Twitchell-Bocker Box Company—had been signed to a check for two hundred dollars, which had been endorsed Henry F. Weber and cashed at the bank. Vitt was in Twitchell's office now, talking to Twitchell, who had failed to remember anyone named Weber.

"I'd like to see your cancelled checks for the last couple of months," the detective said.

The manufacturer of boxes squirmed. He was a large man whose face ballooned redly out of a too-tight collar.

"What for?" he asked doubtfully.

"This is too good a forgery not to have been copied from one of 'em. The one of yours that's most like this should lead me to the forger. It usually works out that way."

Vitt looked first for the checks that had made Twitchell squirm. There were three of them, drawn to the order of "Cash," endorsed by Clara Kroll, but, disappointingly, they were free from noteworthy peculiarities in common with the forgery. The detective put them aside and examined the others until he found one that satisfied him: a check for two hundred and fifty dollars to the order of Carl Rosewater.

"Who is this Rosewater?" he asked.

"My tailor."

"I want to borrow this check."

"You don't think Rosewater—?"

"Not necessarily, but this looks like the check that was used as a model. See: the *Ca* in Carl are closer together than you usually put your letters, and so is the *Ca* in Cash on this phoney check. When you write two naughts together you connect them, but they're not connected on the forgery, because whoever did it was going by this two-hundred-and-fifty-dollar check, where there is only one. Your signature on the Rosewater check takes up more space than usual, and slants more—written in a hurry, or standing up—and the forged one does the same. Then the forgery is dated two days after this check. This is the baby, I bet you!"

*　*　*

Only two men in the Rosewater establishment had handled Twitchell's check: the proprietor and his bookkeeper. Rosewater was heavy with good eating. The bookkeeper was manifestly undernourished: Vitt settled on him. The detective questioned the bookkeeper casually, not accusing him, but alert for the earliest opportunity: he was so distinctly the sort of idiot who would commit a low-priced crime that could be traced straight to him, and, if further reason for suspecting him were needed, he was the most convenient suspect at hand.

This bookkeeper was tall and concave, with dry hair that lay on his scalp instead of growing out of it. Thick spectacles magnified the muddle in his eyes without enlarging anything else the eyes may have held or been. His clothing tapered off everywhere in fine frayed edges, so that you could not say definitely just where any garment ended: a gentle merging of cloth and air that made him not easily distinguished from his background. His name was James Close. He remembered the Twitchell check, he denied knowledge of the forgery, and his handwriting bore no determinable resemblance to the endorsed Henry F. Weber.

Rosewater said Close was scrupulously honest, had been in his employ for six years, and lived on Ellis Street.

"Married?"

"James?" Rosewater was surprised. "No!"

Posing, with the assistance of cards from the varied stock in his pockets, as the agent of a banking house that was about to offer the bookkeeper a glittering if vague position, Vitt interviewed Close's landlady and several of his neighbors. The bookkeeper unquestionably was a man of most exemplary habits, but, peculiarly, he was married and the father of two children, one recently born. He had lived here—the third floor of a dull building—seven or eight months, coming from an address on Larkin Street, whither the detective presently went. Still a man thoroughly lacking in vices, Close had been unmarried on Larkin Street.

Vitt returned briskly to the Ellis Street building, intent on questioning Close's wife, but, when he rang the bell, the bookkeeper, home for luncheon, opened the door. The detective had not expected this, but he accepted the situation.

"Got some more questions," he said, and followed Close into the living- and dining-room (now that the bed was folded up into the wall) through whose opposite door he could see a woman putting, with thick pink arms, dishes on a kitchen table. A child stopped building something with blocks in the doorway and gaped at the visitor. Out of sight a baby cried without purpose. Close put the builder and his materials into the kitchen, closed the door, and the two men sat down.

"Close," the detective said softly, "you forged that check."

A woodenness came up and settled on the bookkeeper's face. First his chin lengthened, pushing his mouth into a sullen lump, then his nose thinned and tiny wrinkles appeared beside it, paralleling its upper part and curving up to the inner corners of his eyes. His eyes became smaller, clouded behind their glasses. Thin white arcs showed under the irides, which turned the least bit outward. His brows lifted slightly, and the lines in his forehead became shallower. He said nothing, and did not gesture.

"Of course," the detective went on, "it's your funeral, and you can take any attitude you like. But if you want the advice of one who's seen a lot of 'em, you'll be sensible, and come clean about it. I don't know, and I can't promise anything, but two hundred dollars is not a lot of money, and maybe it can be patched up somehow."

Though this was said with practiced smoothness—it being an established line of attack—Vitt meant it honestly enough: so far as his feelings were affected, he felt some pity for the man in front of him.

"I didn't do it," Close said miserably.

Vitt erased the denial with a four-inch motion of one plump white hand.

"Now listen: it won't get you anything to put us to a lot of trouble digging up things on you—not that it'll need much digging. For instance, when and where were you married?"

The bookkeeper blushed. The rosiness that so surely did not belong in his face gave him the appearance of a colored cartoon.

"What's that got to—?"

"Let it go, then," Vitt said generously. He had him there. His guess had been right: Close was not married. "Let it go. But what I'm trying to show you is that you'd better be wise and come through!"

"I didn't do it."

The repetition irritated Vitt. The woodenness of the bookkeeper's face, unlivened by the color that had for a moment washed it, irritated him. He stood up, close to the bookkeeper, and spoke louder.

"You forged that check, Close! You copied it from Twitchell's!"

"I didn't do it."

The kitchen door opened and the woman came into the room, the child who had been playing with the blocks holding a fold of her skirt. She was a pink-fleshed woman of perhaps thirty years, attractive in a slovenly way: sloppy was the word that occurred to the detective.

"What is it, James?" Her voice was husky. "What is it?"

"I didn't do it," Close said. "He says I forged a check, but I didn't do it."

Vitt was warm under his clothes, and his hands perspired. The woman and child made him uncomfortable. He tried to ignore them, speaking to Close again, very slowly.

"You forged that check, Close, and I'm giving you your last chance to come through."

"I didn't do it."

Vitt seized the irritation that the idiocy of this reiteration aroused in him, built it up, made a small anger of it, and his discomfort under the gazes of the woman and child grew less.

"Listen: you can take your choice," he said. "Be bull-headed, or be reasonable. It's nothing to me. This is all in my day's work. But I don't like to see a man hurt himself, especially when he's not a crook by nature. I'd like to see you get off easy, but if you think you know what you're doing—hop to it!"

"I didn't do it."

A suspicion that all this was ridiculous came to the detective, but he put it out of his mind. After he got a confession out of his man he could remember things and laugh. Meanwhile, what had to be done to get that confession needed an altogether different mood. If he could achieve some sort of rage . . .

He turned sharply to the woman.

"When and where were you folks married?" he demanded.

"None of your business!"

That was better. Against antagonism he could make progress. He felt the blood in his temples, and, his autogenetic excitement lessening the field of his vision, everything except the woman's moist pink face became blurred.

"Exactly!" he said. "But, just so you'll know where you stand, I'll tell you that you never were married—not to each other anyway!"

"What of it?" She stood between her man and the detective, hands on broad hips. "What of it?"

Vitt snorted derisively. He had reared by now a really considerable rage in himself, both weapon and anesthetic.

"In this state," he said, nodding vigorously, "there's a law to protect children's morals. You can be arrested for contributing to the delinquency of minor children! Ever think of that?"

"Contributing to— Why, that's foolish! I raise my children as decent as anybody. I—"

"I know! But in California if you're living with a man not your husband, then you're guilty of it—setting them a bad example, or something like that."

The bookkeeper appeared from behind the woman.

"You stop that!" he ordered. "You hear me, you stop that! Amy hasn't done anything!"

The child began to cry. The woman seized one of Vitt's arms.

"Let me tell you!" Defiance was gone out of her. "My husband left me when he found I was going to have another baby. He went out on a

Sunday night in the rain and didn't ever come back. Not ever! I didn't have anybody to help me but James. He took me in, and he's been as good a man as there ever was! The children are better off with him than they ever were with Tom. He's better to them. I—"

The detective pulled his arm away from her. A detective is a man employed to do certain defined things: he is not a judge, a god. Every thief has his justification, to hear him tell it. This hullabaloo just made his work that much harder, without doing anybody any real good.

"That's tough!" He put into word and feature all the callousness for which he was fumbling inside. "But the way it stands is that if you're going to fight me on this check business, I'm going to make the going as tough as I can for the pair of you."

"You mean," Close cried, "that if I don't say I forged that check you'll have Amy and me arrested for this—this delinquency thing?"

"I mean that if you'll be reasonable I'll not make any more trouble than I have to. But if you want to be hard-boiled, then I'll go the limit."

"And Amy'll be arrested?"

"Yes."

"You—you—" The bookkeeper clawed at Vitt with hands fashioned for grappling with pens and ledger-pages. Vitt could have handled him without especial difficulty, for, beneath his plumpness, the detective was strong enough. But the passion for which he had groped with affectation of face and voice had at last become actual.

He made a ball of one fist and drove it into the bookkeeper's hollow belly. The bookkeeper folded over it and writhed on the floor. Screaming, the woman knelt beside him. The child who had come into the room with the woman and the baby Vitt had not seen yelled together. The doorbell began to ring. From the kitchen came the stench of scorched food.

Presently Close sat up, leaning against the kneeling woman, his spectacles dangling from one ear.

"I forged it," he said into the clamor. "I didn't have any money to pay the bills after the baby came. I told Amy I borrowed the money from Rosewater." He laughed two sharp notes. "She didn't know him, so she believed me. Anyway, the bills are paid."

Vitt hurried his prisoner down to the city prison, had him booked and locked in, and then hastened up to the shopping district. The department stores closed at half past five, and his wife had asked him to bring home three spools of No. 60 black thread.

THE SIGN OF THE POTENT PILLS

The house was large and austerely symmetrical in the later Bourbon fashion. Its pilastered façade, factually of a light gray stone, was dully whitish in the morning sun. Level grassplots cut by sharp-edged paths spread around the house, holding it apart from its neighbors and from the street. The grassplots in turn were guarded from the outer world by a fence of iron pickets, unfriendly as so many tall black pikes. Just inside the fence's eastern line the billboard stood. Its wide back was to the house. Its edge was to the street. It faced, with an outrageous red and green face advertising a forgotten cure-all—Pentner's Potent Pills—a porticoed house of red brick behind tidy hedges some twenty yards away.

Hugh Trate, walking up from the car-line with that briskness which young twenty-two need not temper to moderate hills, stared at the billboard's ugly discordance until he was nearly abreast it and its edge had become too meager to hold his attention. Then his attention passed on to the stone house, his destination.

In front of the house a high grilled gate interrupted the black fence. It was a gate designed for shutting out rather than admitting, a gate wrought in lines as uninviting as the upright sharp pickets, but it was not locked. The young man closed it behind him and went up the walk to the house.

The young man shut the gate behind him and went up the walk to the house. The door was opened in response to the bell by a stolid red-faced man of genial cast whose footman's clothes did not fit him very well.

"What do you want?" he asked.

"I should like to see Miss Newbrith."

"She ain't home. Sorry."

"Wait a moment," the young man insisted as the door began to close. "I've an appointment. She phoned me. My name is Trate."

"That's different," the stolid man said cheerfully, opening the door again and stepping to one side. "Why didn't you say so? Come on in." He closed the door behind the young man and started up a broad flight of stairs. "Up this way."

On the second floor landing the stolid man halted to face Trate again.

"You don't happen to be carrying a gun, now do you?" he asked pleasantly.

"Why no."

"You see, we can't take no chances," the man explained, and, stepping close, ran swift hands over Trate's hips, chest, and belly. "We got to be mighty careful in a spot like this." He stepped back and moved toward a broad closed door on the right, throwing a friendly "Come along" over his shoulder.

Eyes wide in surprise, Trate followed obediently to the door, which the man opened with a flourish.

"A young fellow to see Miss Newbrith," he shouted merrily, bowing low with an absurd outflinging of his arms. When he straightened up he added, "Ha-ha-ha!"

Hesitantly Trate advanced into the room wherein was nothing to set him immediately at ease. It was a drawing-room in gold and white, quite long, elaborate with the carved, inlaid, and stuccoed richness of the fourteenth Louis' day. Opaque blinds and heavy curtains hid the windows. A glittering chandelier lighted the room. From the farther end a dozen faces looked at Trate with indefinite expectancy.

The owners of these faces had divided themselves into two groups. The larger numbered eight. They, no matter how comfortably established on chairs in this gold and white room, were unmistakably servants. Across the floor from them the smaller group occupied more space. The eldest of these four sat upright in the middle of a sofa. He was small, slight, old, and well preserved except that his mustache, white as his hair, was ragged at one end with recent gnawing. To his right a full-bodied woman of forty-something in a magenta frock leaned forward on her gilded chair and held a *champlevé* vial near her thin nose. Beside her a middle-aged man sat in a similar chair. He resembled—in younger, plumper mould—the man on the sofa, but was paler, more tired than the elder.

The fourth member of the group stood up when Hugh came in. She derived from both the sitting men: a girl of less than twenty, small with a daintiness of bone-structure and fleshing which, however delicate, had nothing to do with fragility. Her face was saved from the flat prettiness of mathematically proportioned features by her mouth: it was red, too narrow, full and curiously creased. She took four steps toward Trate, stopped, looked past him at the door through which he had come, and at him again. "Oh, Mr. Trate, it was nice of you to come so quickly!" she said.

The young man, still a dozen paces away, approached smiling somewhat stiffly, a little pink, looking at her with brown eyes that seemed uneasily aware of the concerted stare of the eleven other persons watching him with ambiguous hopefulness. He made a guttural gargling sound, in no way intelligible, but manifestly polite in intention. The girl took his hand, then his hat and overcoat, and turned with him to face the others.

"Grandad," she said to the old man on the sofa, "this is Mr. Trate. He—" She stopped, indicated something behind her by a swift sidewise jerk of her eyes, and nodded significantly.

"Say no more." The old man's glance darted for a fleeting instant past Trate. A dry whisper crept from behind his white mustache. "We are in your hands."

Trate said something like, "Uh," and shifted his feet uncertainly.

The girl told him that the tired man and the woman in magenta were her parents, and now the woman spoke, her voice nasally querulous. "The stout man is by far the most odious and I do wish you would secure him first." She gestured with the *champlevé* vial toward the door.

Two men stood in that end of the room. One was the stolid man who had opened the door. He nodded and grinned amiably at Trate. His companion scowled. The companion was a short man in shabby brown, with arms too long hanging from shoulders too broad. Red-brown eyes peered malignantly from beneath the pulled-down visor of his cap. His face was dark, with a broad nose flat on his long and prominent upper lip above an outthrust chin.

Trate looked from one Newbrith to another. "I beg your pardon?" he asked.

"It's nothing," the old man assured him. "Your own way."

Trate frowned questioning puzzlement at the girl.

She laughed, the creases in her red mouth multiplying its curves. "We must explain it to Mr. Trate. We can't expect him to guess the situation."

Old Newbrith's ragged mustache blew out from his mouth in a great blast of air.

"Explain! Didn't you—?"

"There was no time," said the girl. "It took me nearly five minutes to get Mr. Trate on the wire, and by then they were hunting for me."

The old man leaned forward with bulging eyes. "And you've no assistance? No men outside?"

"No, sir," Trate said.

The elder Newbrith looked at the girl's father and the girl's father looked at him, each looking as if he found the sight of the other amazing. But the amazement with which they regarded one another was nothing to that with which they looked at the girl. The old man's small fingers crushed invisible things on the sofa beside his legs.

"Precisely what did you tell Mr. Trate, Brenda?" he asked.

"Why, I simply told him who I was, reminded him I had met him at the Shermans', and asked him if he could run up here immediately. That was all. There wasn't time for anything else, Grandad. They were already hunting for me."

"Yes, they would be," said the old man, softer of voice, his face angrier. "So instead of giving the alarm to the first voice you heard, you wasted five minutes getting this—ah—young gentleman on the wire, and then hadn't time to do more than—ah—casually invite him to join us?"

"Oh, but really," his granddaughter protested, "Mr. Trate is very clever. And I thought this would be such a wonderful chance for him to make a reputation at the very beginning of his career."

"Ah!" the old man cooed while wild lights twinkled in his eyes, "so our young friend is at the very beginning of his career, is he?"

"Yes. I met him at the Shermans' reception. He was guarding the presents, and he told me that was his first case. He had only been a detective for three days then. Wasn't that it, Mr. Trate?"

Mr. Trate said, "Uh—yes," without taking his eyes from the old man's face.

"So then our Mr. Trate has had by this time"—Newbrith was lisping with sweetness now—"no less than ten days experience?"

"Eleven," Trate said, blushing a little.

Old Newbrith said, "Ah, eleven, to be sure!" and stood up. He smiled and his face was swollen and purple. He plucked two buttons from his coat and threw them away. He found a yellow scarf to tear into strips and a handful of cigars to crunch into brown flakes. He took the *champlevé* vial from his daughter-in-law's hand and ground it under his heel. While thus engaged he screamed that his granddaughter was an idiot, a fool, a loon , a moron, a dolt, an ass, a lunatic, a goose, a simpleton, a booby, a numbskull, an imbecile, and a halfwit. Then he relapsed on the sofa, eyes closed, legs out, while daughter-in-law and granddaughter strove with loosening, fanning, chaffing hands to stop the bubbling in his upturned open mouth.

"What's the old boy up to now?" a very thin squeaky voice asked. Its owner stood with the two men by the door. He was ridiculous. Well over six feet in height, he was a hill of flesh, a live sphere in loose gray clothes. His features were babyish—little round blue eyes, little lumpy nose, little soft mouth—all babyishly disposed, huddled together in the center of a great round face, between cheeks like melons, with smooth pink surfaces that seemed never have needed shaving. Out of this childish mountain more piping words came: "You oughtn't to let him carry on like that, Tom. First thing you know he'll be busting something and dying on us before we're through with him."

"The young fellow did it," replied the cheerful man in the footman's ill-fitting dress. "Seems like he's a detective."

"A detective!" The fat man's features gathered closer together in a juvenile pout, blue eyes staring glassily at Trate. "Well, what does he come here for? We mustn't have detectives!"

The long-armed brutish man in brown took a shuffling step forward. "I'll bust him one," he suggested.

"No, no, Bill!" the fat man squeaked impatiently, still staring at Trate. "That wouldn't help. He'd still be a detective."

"Oh, he ain't so much a one that we got to worry about him," the cheerful man said. "Seems like he ain't been at it only for eleven days, and he comes in not knowing no what's what than the man in the moon."

But fat pink fingers continued to pluck at the puckered baby's mouth, and the porcelain eyes neither blinked nor wavered from the young man's face. "That's all right," the fat man squeaked, "but what's he doing here? That's what I want to know."

"Seems like the kid got to the phone that time she slipped away from us in the mixup before we brought 'em down here, and she gives this young fellow a rumble, but she's too rattlebrained to smart him up. He don't know nothing until he gets in."

The mountainous man's distress lessened to a degree permitting the removal of his stare from Trate, and he turned to the door. "Well, maybe it's all right," his treble came over one of the thick pillows that were his shoulders, "but you tell him that he's got to behave himself."

He lumbered out, leaving the cheerful man and the malevolent man standing side by side looking at Trate cheerfully and malevolently. The young man put his back to those parallel but unlike gazes and found himself facing old Newbrith, who was sitting up on his sofa again, his eyes open, waving away his ministering womenfolk.

Looking at Trate, the old man repeated the burden of his recently screamed complaint, but now in the milder tone of incomplete resignation: "If she had to pick out one detective and bring him here blindfolded, why must she pick an amateur?"

No one had a direct reply to that. Trate mumbled an obvious something about everybody's having been a novice at one time. The old man readily, if somewhat nastily, conceded the truth of that, but God knew he had troubles enough without being made Lesson II in a How To Be A Detective course.

"Now, Grandad, don't be unreasonable," Brenda Newbrith remonstrated. "You've no idea how clever Mr. Trate really is! He—" She smiled up at the young man. "What was that awfully clever thing you said at the Shermans' about democracy being government with the deuces wild?"

The young man cleared his throat and smiled uncomfortably, and beyond that said nothing.

The girl's father opened his tired eyes and became barely audible. "Good Lord!" he murmured. "A detective who amuses the guests with epigrams to keep them from making off with the wedding presents!"

"You just wait!" the girl said. "You'll see! Won't they, Mr. Trate?"

Mr. Trate said, "Yes. That is— Well—"

Mrs. Newbrith, raising her eyes from the ruins of her vial on the floor, said, "I don't understand what all this pother is about. If the young man is really a detective, he will arrest these criminals at once. If he isn't, he isn't, and that's the end of it, though I grant that Brenda might have exercised greater judgment when she—"

"Go ahead, young fellow," Tom called encouragingly from the other end of the room, "detect something for the lady!"

The man with the brutish muzzle also spoke. "I wish Joe would leave me take a poke at him," he grumbled.

"You *can* save us, can't you, Mr. Trate?" the girl asked pointblank, looking up at him with blue eyes in which doubt was becoming faintly discernible.

Trate flushed, cleared his throat. "I'm not a policeman, Miss Newbrith, and I have no reason to believe that Mr. Newbrith wishes to engage my services."

"None at all," the old man agreed.

The girl was not easily put aside.

"I engage you," she told him.

"I'm sorry," Trate said, "but it would have to be Mr. Newbrith."

"That's silly! And besides, if you succeeded in doing something, you know Grandad would reward you."

Trate shook his head again.

"Ethical detectives do not operate on contingent fees," said he as if reciting a recently studied lesson.

"Do you mean to do nothing? Are you trying to make me ridiculous? After I thought it would be such a wonderful opportunity for you, and gave you a chance any other man would jump at!"

Before Trate could reply to this, the fat man's treble was quivering in the room again. "Didn't I tell you you'd have to make him behave himself?" he asked his henchmen.

"He's just arguing," the stolid Tom defended Hugh. "There ain't no harm in the boy."

"Well, make him sit down and keep quiet."

The brutish Bill shuffled forward. "He'll sit down or I'll slap him down," he promised.

Hugh found a vacant gilt chair in a corner half behind the elder Newbrith's sofa. Bill said, "Ar-r-r!" hesitated, looked back at the fat man and returned to his post by the door.

The mountain of flesh turned its child's eyes on old Newbrith, raised a hand like an obese pink star, and beckoned with a finger that curved rather than crooked, so cased in flesh were its joints.

Old Newbrith caught the unchewed end of his mustache in his mouth, but he did not get up from his sofa.

"You've got everything," he protested. "I haven't another thing that—"

"You oughtn't to lie to me like that," the fat man reproved him. "How about that piece of property on Temple Street?"

"But you can't sell that kind of real estate by phone like stocks and bonds," Newbrith objected. "Not for immediate cash!"

"*You* can," the fat man insisted, "especially if you're willing to let it go for half of what it's worth, like you are. Maybe nobody else could, but *you* can. Everybody knows *you're* crazy, and anything *you* do won't surprise them."

Newbrith held his seat, stubbornly looking at the floor.

The fat man piped, "Bill!"

The brutish man shuffled toward the sofa.

Newbrith cursed into his mustache, got up, and followed the waddling mountain into the hall.

There was silence in the drawing-room. Bill and Tom held the door. The servants sat along their wall, variously regarding one another, the men at the door, and the four on the other side of the room. Mrs. Newbrith fidgeted in her chair, looking regretfully at the fragments of her vial, and picked at her magenta frock with round-tipped fingers that were pinkly striped with the marks of rings not long removed. Her husband rested wearily beside her, a cigar smoldering in his pale mouth. Their daughter sat a little away from them, looking stony defiance from face to face. Hugh Trate, back in his corner, had lighted a cigarette, and sat staring through smoke at his outstretched crossed legs. His face, every line of his pose, affected an introspective preoccupation with his own affairs that was flawed by an unmistakable air of sulkiness.

Twenty minutes later the elder Newbrith rejoined his family. His face was purple again. His hair was rumpled. The right corner of his mustache had vanished completely. The fat man, stopping beside his associates at the door, was forcing a thick black pistol into a tight pocket.

"You!" the old man barked at Trate before sitting on his sofa again. "You're hired!"

"Very well, sir," the young man said with so little enthusiasm that the words seemed almost an acceptance of defeat.

The fat man departed. The red-faced man grinned at Hugh and called to him with large friendliness, "I hope you ain't going to be too hard on us, young fellow."

The brutish man glowered and snarled, "I'm gonna smack that punk yet!"

After that there was silence again in the gold and white room, though the occasional sound of a closing door, of striding, waddling, dragging foot-falls, came from other parts of the house, and once a telephone bell rang thinly. Hugh Trate lit another cigarette, and did not restore the box of safety matches to his pocket.

Presently Mrs. Newbrith coughed. Old Newbrith cleared his throat. A vague stuffiness came into the room.

Trate leaned forward until his mouth was not far from the white head of the old man on the sofa. "Sit still, sir," the young detective whispered through immobile lips. "I've just set fire to the sofa."

Old Newbrith left the burning sofa with a promptness that caught his legs unprepared, scrambled out into the middle of the floor on hands and knees. His torn mustache quivered and fluttered and tossed in gusts of bellowed turmoil. "Help! Fire! Damn your idiocy! Michael! Battey! Water! Fire! You young idiot! Michael! Battey! It's arson, that's what it is!" were some of the things he could be understood to shout, and the things that were understood were but a fraction of the things he shouted.

Tumult—after a moment of paralysis at the spectacle of the master of the house of Newbrith yammering on all fours—took the drawing-room. Mrs. Newbrith screamed. The line between servants and served disappeared as the larger group came to the smaller's assistance. Flames leaped into view, red tongues licking the arm of the sofa, quick red fingers catching at drapes, yellow smoke like blonde ghosts' hair growing out of brocaded upholstery.

A thin youth in a chauffeur's livery started for the door, crying, "Water! We've got to have water!"

Stolid Tom waved him back with a pair of automatic pistols produced expertly from the bosom of his ill-fitting garments. "Go back to your bonfire, my lad," he ordered with friendly firmness, while the brute called Bill slid a limber dark blackjack from a hip pocket and moved toward the chauffeur. The chauffeur hurriedly retreated into the group fighting the fire.

The younger Newbrith and a servant had twisted a thick rug over the sofa's arm and back, and were patting it sharply with their hands. Two servants had torn down the burning drape, trampling it into shredded black harmlessness under their feet. The elder Newbrith beat a smoldering cushion against the top of a table, sparks riding away on escaping feathers. While the old man beat he talked, but nothing could be made of his words. Mrs. Newbrith was laughing with noisy hysteria beside him. Around these principals the others were grouped: servants unable to find a place to serve, Brenda Newbrith looking at Hugh Trate as if undecided how she should look at him, and the young man himself frowning at the charred corpse of his fire with undisguised resentment.

"What in the world's the matter now?" the fat man asked from the door.

"The young fellow's been cutting up," Tom explained. "He touched off a box of matches and stuck 'em under a pillow in a corner of the sofa. Seemed like a harmless kind of joke, so I left him alone."

The brutish man raised a transformed face, almost without brutality in its eager hopefulness. "Now you'll leave me sock him, Joe," he pleaded.

But the fat man shook his head.

Mrs. Newbrith stopped laughing to cough. The elder Newbrith was coughing, his eyes red, tears on his wrinkled cheeks. A cushion case was limp and empty in his fingers: it had burst under his violent handling and its contents had puffed out to scatter in the air, thickening in an atmosphere already heavy with the smoke and stench of burnt hair and fabric.

"Can't we open a window for a second?" the younger Newbrith called through this cloud. "Just enough to clear the air?"

"Now you oughtn't to ask me a thing like that," fat Joe complained petulantly. "You ought to have sense enough to know we can't do a thing like that."

Old Newbrith spread his empty cushion cover out with both hands and began to wave it in the air, fanning a relatively clear space in front of him. Servants seized rugs and followed his example. Smoke swirled away, thinning toward the ceiling. White curls of fleece eddied about, were wafted to distant parts of the room. The three men at the door watched without comment.

"I'm afraid this young man is going to make a nuisance of himself," the fat man squeaked after a little while. "You'll have to do something with him, Tom."

"Aw, leave the young fellow alone," said Tom. "He's all—"

A white feather, fluttering lazily down, came to hang for a moment against the tip of Tom's red nose. He dabbed at it with the back of one of the hands that held his pistols. The feather floated up in the air-current generated by the hand's motion, but immediately returned to the nose-tip again. Tom's hand dabbed at it once more and his face puffed out redly. The feather eluded his hand, nestling between nose and upper lip. His face became grotesquely inflated. He sneezed furiously. The gun in the dabbing hand roared. Old Newbrith's empty cushion case was whisked out of his hands. A hole like a smooth dime appeared in the blind down across a window behind him.

"Tch! Tch!" exclaimed the fat man. "You ought to be carefuller, Tom. You might hurt somebody that way."

Tom sneezed again, but with precautions now, holding his pistols down, holding his forefingers stiffly away from the triggers. He sneezed a third time, rubbed his nose with the back of a hand, put his weapons out of sight under his coat, and brought out a handkerchief.

"I might of for a fact," he admitted good naturedly, blowing his nose and wiping his eyes. "Remember that time Snohomish Whitey gunned that bank messenger without meaning to, all on account of being ticklish and having a button bust off his undershirt and slide down on the inside?"

"Yes," fat Joe remembered, "but Snohomish was always kind of flighty."

"You can say what you want about Snohomish," the brutish man said, rubbing his chin reflectively with the blackjack, "but he packs a good wallop in his left, and don't think he don't. That time me and him went round and round in the jungle at Sac he made me like it, even if I did take him, and don't think he didn't."

"That's right enough," the fat man admitted, "but still and all, I never take much stock in a man that can't take a draw on your cigarette without getting it all wet. Well, don't let these folks do any more cutting up on you," and he waddled away.

Hugh Trate, surrounded by disapproval, sat and stared at the floor for fifteen minutes. Then his face began to redden slowly. When it was quite red he lifted it and looked into the elder Newbrith's bitter eyes.

"Do you think I started it because I was chilly?" he asked angrily. "Wouldn't it have smoked these crooks out? Wouldn't it have brought firemen, police?"

The old man glared at him. "Don't you think it's bad enough to be robbed without being cremated? Do you think the insurance company would have paid me a nickel for the house? Do you—?"

A downstairs crash rattled windows, shook the room, put weapons in the hands of men at the door. Feet thumped on distant steps, scurried overhead, stamped in the hall. The door opened far enough to admit a pale hatchet-face.

"Ben," it addressed the cheerful man, "Big Fat wants you. We been ranked!"

Two shots close together sounded below. Ben, recently Tom, hurried out after the hatchet-face, leaving the brutish Bill alone to guard the prisoners. He glowered threateningly at them with his little red-brown eyes, crouching beside the door, blackjack in one hand, battered revolver in the other.

Another shot thundered. Something broke with a splintering sound in the rear of the house. A distant man yelled throatily, "Put the slug to him!" In another part of the building a man laughed. Heavy feet were on the stairs, in the hall.

Bill spun to the door as the door came in. Gunpowder burned diagonally upward in a dull flash. Metal buttons glistened against blue cloth around, under, over Bill. His blackjack arched through the air, twisted end over end, and thudded on the floor.

A sallow plump man in blue civilian clothes came into the room, stepping over the policemen struggling with Bill on the floor. His hands were in his jacket pockets and he nodded to Newbrith senior without removing his hat.

"Detective-sergeant McClurg," he introduced himself. "We nabbed six or seven of 'em, all of 'em, I guess. What's it all about?"

"Robbery, that's what it's all about!" Newbrith stormed. "They seized the house at daybreak. All day they've held us here, prisoners in our own home! I've been forced to withdraw my bank balances, to sell stocks and bonds and everything that could be sold quickly. I've been forced to make myself ridiculous by demanding currency for everything, by sending God knows what kind of messengers for it. I've been forced to borrow money from men I despise! I might just as well live in a wilderness as in a city that keeps me poor with its taxes for all the protection I've got. I haven't—"

"We can't guess what's happening," the detective-sergeant said. "We came as soon as Pentner gave us the rap."

"Pentner?" It was a despairing scream. The old man's eyes rolled frenziedly at the bright round hole in the curtained window that concealed his neighbor's residence. "That damned scoundrel! I hope he waits for me to thank him for his impudence in meddling in my business! I'd rather lose everything I've got in the world than be beholden to that—"

The detective-sergeant's plumpness shook with an inner mirth. "You don't have to let that bother you," he interrupted the old man's tirade. "He won't like it so much either! He phoned in saying you had taken a shot at him while he was standing in his room brushing his hair.

He said he always expected something like that would happen, because he knew you were crazy as a pet cuckoo and ought to have been locked up long ago. He said that, since you had missed him, he was glad you had cut loose at him, because now the city would have to put you away where you belonged."

"So you see," came the triumph of Brenda Newbrith's voice, "Mr. Trate *is* clever, and he *did* show you!"

"Eh?" was the most her grandfather could achieve.

"You know very well," she declared, "that if he hadn't set fire to the sofa you wouldn't have burst the cushion, and the feathers wouldn't have tickled that man's nose, and he wouldn't have sneezed, and his gun wouldn't have gone off, and the bullet wouldn't have frightened Mr. Pentner into thinking you were trying to kill him, and he wouldn't have phoned the police, and they wouldn't have come here to rescue us. That stands to reason. Well, then, how can you say that Mr. Trate's cleverness didn't do it?"

Detective-sergeant McClurg's plumpness shook again. Old Newbrith snorted and fumbled for words that wouldn't come. The younger Newbrith murmured something about the house that Jack built.

The young man who had been clever turned a bit red and had a moment of trouble with his breathing, but the bland smile his face wore was the smile of one who wears honestly won laurels easily, neither over-valuing nor under-valuing them.

"I think it's wonderful," the girl assured him, "to be able to make plans that go through successfully no matter how much everybody tries to spoil them from the very beginning."

Nobody could find a reply to that—if one were possible.

THE DIAMOND WAGER

I always knew West was eccentric.

Ever since the days of our youth, in various universities—for we seemed destined to follow each other about the globe—I had known Alexander West to be a person of the most bizarre, though not unattractive, personality: At Heidelberg, where he renounced water as a beverage; at Pisa, where he affected a one-piece garment for months; at the Sorbonne, where he consorted with the most notorious characters, boasting an acquaintance with Le Grand Raoul, an unspeakable ruffian of La Villette.

And in later life, when we met in Constantinople, where West was American minister, I found that his idiosyncrasies were common topics in the diplomatic corps. In the then Turkish capital I naturally dined with West at the Legation, and except for his pointed beard and Prussian mustache being somewhat more gray, I found him the same tall, courtly figure, with a keen brown eye and the hands of generations, an aristocrat.

But his eccentricities were then of more refined fantasy. No more baths in snow, no more beer orgies, no more Libyan negroes opening the door, no more strange diets. At the Legation, West specialized in rugs and gems. He had a museum in carpets. He had even abandoned his old practice of having the valet call him every morning at eight o'clock with a gramophone record.

I left the Legation thinking West had reformed. "Rugs and precious stones," I reflected; "that's such a banal combination for West." Although I did recall that he had told me he was doing something strange with a boat on the Bosporus; but I neglected to inquire about the details. It was something in connection with work, as he had said, "Everybody has a pleasure boat; I have a work boat, where I can be alone." But that is all I retained concerning this freak of his mind.

It was some years later, however, when West had retired from diplomacy, that he turned up in my Paris apartment, a little grayer, straight and keen as usual, but with his beard a trifle less pointed—and, let's say, a trifle less distinguished-looking. He looked more the successful business man than the traditional diplomat. It was a cold, blustery night, so I bade West sit down by my fire and tell me of his adventures; for I knew he had not been idle since leaving Constantinople.

"No, I am not doing anything," he answered, after a pause, in reply to my question as to his present activities. "Just resting and laughing to myself over a little prank I played on a friend."

"Oho!" I declared; "so you're going in for pranks now."

He laughed heartily. I could hardly see West as a practical joker. That was one thing out of his line. As he held his long, thin hands together, I noticed an exceptionally fine diamond ring on his left hand. It was of an unusual luster, deep set in gold, flush with the cutting. His quick eye caught me looking at this ornament. As I recall, West had never affected jewelry of any kind.

"Oh, yes, you are wondering about this," he said, gazing into the crystal. "Fine yellow diamond; not so rare, but unusual, set in gold, which they are not wearing any longer. A little present." He repeated blandly, after a pause, "A little present for stealing."

"For stealing?" I inquired, astonished. I could hardly believe West would steal. He would not play practical jokes and he would not steal.

"Yes," he drawled, leaning back away from the fire. "I had to steal about four million francs—that is, four million francs' worth of jewels." He noted the effect on me, and went on in a matter-of-fact way: "Yes, I stole it, stole it all. Got the police all upset; got stories in the newspapers. They referred to me as a super-thief, a master criminal, a malefactor, a crook, and an organized gang. But I proved my case. I lifted four million from a Paris jeweler, walked around town with it, gave my victim an uncomfortable night, and walked in his store the next day between rows of wise gentlemen, gave him back his paltry four million, and collected my bet, which is this ring you see here."

West paused and chuckled softly to himself, still apparently getting the utmost out of this late escapade in burglary. Of course, I remembered only recently seeing in the newspapers how some clever gentleman cracksman had succeeded in a fantastic robbery in the Rue de la Paix, Paris, but I had not read the details.

I was genuinely curious. This was, indeed, West in his true character. But to go in for deliberate and probably dangerous burglary was something which I considered required a little friendly counsel on my part. West anticipated my difficulty in broaching the subject.

"Don't worry, old man. I pinched the stuff from a good friend of ours, really a pal, so if I had been caught it would have been fixed up, except I would have lost my bet."

He looked at the yellow diamond.

"But don't you realize what would have happened if you had been caught?" I asked. "Prank or not, your name would have been aired in the newspapers—a former American minister guilty of grand larceny; an arrest; a day or so in jail; sensation; talk, ruinous gossip!"

He only laughed the more. He held up an arresting hand. "Please don't call me an amateur. I did the most professional job that the Rue de la Paix has seen in years."

I believe he was really proud of this burglary.

West gazed reflectively into the fire. "But I wouldn't do it again— not for a dozen rings." He watched the firelight dance in the pure crystal of the stone on his finger. "Poor old Berthier, he was wild! He came to see me the night I lifted his diamonds, four million francs' worth, mind you, and they were in my pocket at the time. He asked me to accompany him to the store and go over the scene.

"He said perhaps I might prove cleverer than detectives, whom he was satisfied were a lot of idiots. I told him I would come over the next day, because, according to the terms of our wager, I was to keep the jewels for more than twenty-four hours. I returned the next day, and handed them to him in his upstairs office. The poor wretch that I took them from was downstairs busy reconstructing the 'crime' with those astute gentlemen, the detectives, and I've no doubt that they would eventually have caught me, for you don't get away with robbery in France. They catch you in the end. Fortunately I made the terms of my wager to fit the conditions."

West leaned back and blinked satisfyingly at the ceiling, tapping his fingertips together. "Poor old Berthier," he mused. "He was wild."

As soon as West had mentioned that his victim was a mutual friend, I had thought of Berthier. Moreover, Berthier's was one of those establishments in which a four-million-franc purchase or a theft of the same size might not seem so unusual. West interrupted my thoughts concerning Berthier.

"I made Berthier promise that he would not dismiss any employee. That also was in the terms of our wager because I dealt directly with Armand the head salesman and a trusted employee. It was Armand who delivered the stones." West leaned nearer, his brown eyes squinting at me as if in defense of any reprehension I might impute to him. "You see, I did it, not so much as a wager, but to teach Berthier a lesson. Berthier is responsible for his store, he is the principal shareholder, the administration is his own, it was he and it was his negligence in not rigidly enforcing more elementary principles of safety that made the theft possible." He turned the yellow diamond around on his finger. "This thing is nothing, compared to the value of the lesson he learned."

West stroked his stubby beard. He chuckled. "It did cost me some of my beard. A hotel suite, an old trunk, a real Russian prince, a fake Egyptian prince, a would-be princess, a first-class reservation to Egypt, a convenient bathroom, running water and soapsuds. Poor old Armand, who brought the gems—he and his armed assistants—they must have almost fainted when, after waiting probably a good half hour, all they found in exchange for a four-million-franc necklace was a cheap bearskin coat, a broad brimmed hat, and some old clothes."

I must admit that I was growing curious. It was about a week ago when I had seen this sensational story in the newspapers. I knew West had come to tell me about it, as he had so often related to me his various escapades, and I was getting restive. Moreover, I knew Berthier well, and I could readily imagine the state of his mind on the day of the missing diamonds.

I had a bottle of 1848 cognac brought up, and we both settled down to the inner warmth of this most friendly of elixirs.

II

"You see," West began, with this habitual phrase of his, "I had always been a good customer of Berthier's. I have bought trinkets from Berthier's both in New York and Paris since I was a boy. And in getting around as I did in various diplomatic posts, I naturally sent Berthier many wealthy clients. I got him the work on two very important crown jewel commissions; I sent him princes and magnates; and of course he always wanted to make me a present, knowing well that the idea of a commission was out of the question.

"One day not long ago I was in Berthier's with a friend who was buying some sapphires and platinum and a lot of that atrocious modern jewelry for his new wife. Berthier offered me this yellow diamond then as a present, for I had always admired it, but never felt quite able to buy it, and knowing at the same time that even if I did buy it he would have marked the price so low as to be embarrassing.

"However, we compromised by dining together that night in Ciro's; and there he pointed out to me the various personalities of that international crowd who wear genuine stones. 'I can't understand,'

Berthier said, after a comprehensive observation of the clientele, 'how all these women are not robbed even more regularly than they are. Even we jewelers, with all our protective systems, are not safe from burglary.'

"Berthier then went on to tell me of some miserable wretch who, only the day before, had smashed a show window down the street and filched several big stones. 'A messy job,' he commented, and he informed me that the police soon apprehended this window burglar.

"He continued, with smug assurance: 'It's pretty hard for a street burglar to get away with anything these days. It's the other kind,' he added, 'the plausible kind, the apparently rich customer, the clever, ingenious stranger, with whom we cannot cope.'"

When West mentioned this "clever, ingenious stranger," I had a mental picture of him stepping into just such a role for his robbery of Berthier's; but I made no comment, and let him go on with his story.

"You see, I had always contended the same thing. I had always held that jewelers and bankers show only primitive intelligence in arranging their protective schemes, dealing always with the hypothetical street robbery, the second story man, the gun runner, while they invariably go on for years unprotected against these plausible gentlemen who, in the long run, are the worst offenders. They get millions where the common thief gets thousands.

"I might have been a bit vexed at Berthier's cocksureness," West continued by way of explanation, "but you see, I am a shareholder in a bank that was once beautifully swindled, so I let Berthier have it straight from the shoulder.

"'You fellows deserve to be robbed,' I said to Berthier. 'You fall for such obvious gags.'

"Berthier protested. I asked him about the little job they put over on the Paris house of Kerstners Frères. He shrugged his shoulders. It seems that a nice gentleman who said he was a Swiss," West explained, "wanted to match an emerald pendant that he had, in order to make up a set of earrings. Kerstners had difficulty in matching the emerald which the nice Swiss gentleman had ordered them to purchase at any price.

"After a search Kerstners found the stone and bought it at an exorbitant price. They had simply bought in the same emerald. Of course, the gentleman only made a mere hundred thousand francs, a simple trick that has been worked over and over again in various forms.

"When I related this story, Berthier retorted with some scorn to the effect that no sensible house would fall for such an old dodge as that. I then asked Berthier about that absurd robbery that happened only a year ago at Latour's, which is a very 'sensible' house and incidentally Berthier's chief competitor."

West asked me if I knew about this robbery. I assured him I did, inasmuch as all Paris had laughed, for the joke was certainly on the prefect of police. On the prefect's first day in office some ingenious thief had contrived to have a whole tray of diamond rings sent under guard to the prefect, from which he was to choose one for an engagement present for his recently announced fiancée.

The thief impersonated a clerk right in the prefect's inner waiting room, and, surrounded by police, he took the tray into the prefect's office, excused himself for blundering into the wrong room, slipped the tray under his coat, walked back to the waiting room, and after assuring the jeweler's representatives that they wouldn't have to wait long, he disappeared. Fortunately, the thief was arrested the following day in Lyons.

West laughed heartily as he talked over the unique details of this robbery. I poured out some cognac. "Well, my genteel burglar," I pursued, "that doesn't yet explain how you yourself turned thief and lifted four million."

"Very simple," West replied. "Berthier was almost impertinent in his self-assurance that no one could rob Berthier's. 'Not even the most fashionably dressed gentleman nor the most plausible prince could trick Berthier's,' he asserted with some vigor. Then he assured me, as if it were a great secret, 'Berthier never delivers jewels against a check until the bank reports the funds.'

"'There are always loopholes,' I rejoined, but Berthier argued stupidly that it was impossible. His boastful attitude annoyed me.

"I looked him straight in the eye. 'I'll bet you, if I were a burglar, I could clean your place out.' Berthier laughed in that jerky, nervous way of his. 'I'd pay you to rob me,' he said. 'You needn't; but I'll do it anyway,' I told him.

"Berthier thought a bit. 'I'll bet you that yellow diamond that you couldn't steal so much as a baby's bracelet from Berthier's.'

" 'I'll bet you I can steal a million,' I said.

" 'It's a go,' said Berthier, shaking my hand. 'The yellow diamond is yours if you steal anything and get away with it.'

" 'Perhaps three or four million,' I said.

" 'It's a bet. Steal anything you want,' Berthier agreed.

" 'I'll teach you smart Rue de la Paix jewelers a lesson,' I informed him.

"Accordingly, over our coffee, we arranged the terms of our wager, and I suppose Berthier promptly forgot about it."

West sipped his cognac thoughtfully before restoring the glass to the mantel, and then went on:

"The robbery was so easy to plan, yet I must admit that it had many complications. I had always said that the plausible gentleman was the loophole, so I looked up my old friend Prince Meyeroff, who is always buying and selling and exchanging jewels. It's a mania with him. I had exchanged a few odd gems with him in Constantinople, as he considered me a fellow connoisseur.

"I found him in Paris, and soon talked him into the mood to buy a necklace. In fact, he had disposed of some old family pieces, and was actually meditating an expensive gift for his favorite niece.

"I explained to the prince that I had a little deal on, and asked him to let me act as his buyer. I had special reasons. Moreover, he was one of my closest friends back in St. Petersburg. Meyeroff said he would allow me a credit up to eight hundred thousand francs for something very suitable for this young woman who was marrying into the old French nobility.

"I told the prince to go to Berthier's and choose a necklace, approximating his price, but to underbid on it. I would then go in and buy it at the price contemplated.

"I figured this would give them just the amount of confidence in me that would be required to carry off a bigger affair that I was thinking of.

"Meanwhile I bethought myself of a disguise. I let my beard grow somewhat to the sides and cut off the point. I affected a broad-brimmed, low-crowned hat, and a half-length bearskin coat. I then braced up my trousers almost to my ankles. Some days later—in fact, it was just over a week ago—I went to Berthier's, after I ascertained that Berthier himself was in London. I informed them I wanted to buy a gift or two in diamonds, and it was not many minutes before I had shown the clerks that money was no object with me.

"They brought me out a most bewitching array of necklaces, tiaras, collars, bracelets, rings. A king's ransom lay before my eyes. Of course, I fell in love with a beautiful flat stone necklace of Indian diamonds with an enormous square pendant. I fondled it, held it up, almost wept over it, but decided, alas, that I could not buy it. Four million francs, the salesman, Armand, had said. I shook my head sadly. Too expensive for me. But how I loved it!

"I finally decided that a smaller one would be very nice. It was the one with a gorgeous emerald pendant, *en cabochon*, which Prince Meyeroff had seen and described to me. I asked the price.

"Armand demurred. 'You have chosen the same one that a great connoisseur has admired. Prince Meyeroff wanted it, but it was a question of price.'

"'How much?' I asked.

"'Eight hundred thousand francs.'

"Of course, I was buying for the prince, so with a great flourish of opulence I arranged to buy the smaller necklace, though I continued flirting with that handsome Indian string. I assumed the name of Hazim, gave my home town as Cairo, and my present address a prominent hotel in the Rue de Rivoli.

"I ordered a different clasp put on the necklace, and departed for my bank, declaring I was expecting a draft from Egypt. I then went to my apartment, sent to the hotel an old trunk full of cast-off clothes, from which I carefully removed the labels. My beard was proving most disciplined, rounding my face out nicely. Picture yourself the flat hat, the bulgy fur coat, my trousers pulled up toward the ankles!"

III

"I returned to Berthier's next day and bought the necklace for Meyeroff. I paid them out of a bag, eight hundred thousand francs, and received a receipt made out to Mr. Hazim of Cairo and the Rue de Rivoli. I again looked longingly at the Indian necklace. I casually mentioned what a delight it would be for my daughter who was engaged to an Egyptian prince.

"'I must get her something,' I told Berthier's man. He tried all his arts on me. Four million was not too much for an Egyptian princess, and in Egypt, where they wear stones. He emphasized the last phrase. I hesitated, but went out with my little necklace, saying I'd see later.

"I had a hired automobile of enormous proportions waiting outside which must at least have impressed the doorman at Berthier's, whom I had passed many times in the past, but who failed to recognize me in this changed get-up. You see, Egyptians don't understand this northern climate, and are inclined to dress oddly.

"I then went to my hotel and made plans for stealing that four-million-franc necklace. In the hotel I was regarded as a bit of an eccentric, so no one bothered me. I had two rooms and a bath. Flush against the wall of my salon, toward the bath, I placed a small square table. I own a beautiful inlaid Louis XVI glove box which, curiously, opens both at the top and at the ends. The ends hinge onto the bottom and are secured by little gadgets at the side, stuck in the plush lining. It makes an admirable jewel case, especially for necklaces; and moreover, it was just the thing needed for my robbery. I placed this box on the little table with the end flush against the wall.

"It looked simple. With a hole in the wall fitting the end of the glove box, I could easily contrive to pull down the shutterlike end and draw the contents through the wall into the bathroom.

"Being a building of modern construction, it would not require much work to punch a hole through the plaster and terra cotta with a drill-bit. I decided on that plan, for the robbery was to take place precisely at three o'clock the following afternoon and in my own rooms.

"That afternoon I decided to buy the Indian necklace. I passed by Berthier's and allowed myself to be tempted by the salesman Arnold. 'I can't really pay so much for a wedding gift,' I said, 'but the prince is very rich.' I told Armand that naturally I felt a certain pride about the gift I should give my daughter under such special circumstances.

"Armand held up the gorgeous necklace, letting the lights play on the great square pendant. 'Anyway, sir, the princess will always have the guarantee of the value of the stones. That is true of any diamond purchased at Berthier's.'

"And with that thought I yielded. I asked for the telephone, saying I must call my bank and arrange for the transfer of funds. That also was simple. I had previously arranged with Judd, my valet, to be in a hotel off the Grands Boulevards, and pretend he was a banker if I should telephone him and ask him to transfer money from my various holdings."

West interrupted his narrative, gulping down the remainder of the cognac. The wrinkles about his eyes narrowed in a burst of merriment.

"It was really cute," he continued. "I telephoned from Berthier's own office, asking for this hotel number on the Élysée exchange. Naturally no one remembers all the bank telephone numbers in Paris, and when Judd answered the telephone his deferential tones might have been those of an accredited banker.

"'Four million tomorrow,' I said, 'and I'll leave the transfer to your judgment. I want the money in thousands in a sack. I'll come with Judd, so you won't need to worry about holding a messenger to accompany me. I am only going as far as Berthier's. It's a wedding gift for my daughter.'

"Judd must have thought me crazy, although it would take a lot to surprise him.

"Armand listened to the conversation. Two other clerks heard it, and later I was bowed out to the street, where my enormous hired car awaited. My next job was to get a tentative reservation on the

Latunia, which was leaving Genoa for Alexandria the following day. Prince Hazim, I called myself at the steamship office. This was for Berthier's benefit, in case they should check up my sailing. Then I went to work.

"I went to the hotel and drew out a square on the wall, tracing it thinly around the end of the box. I slept that night in the hotel. In the morning I arose at nine o'clock, paid my bill, and told the hotel clerk I was leaving that evening for Genoa.

"I called at Berthier's still wearing the same bearskin coat and flat hat, and assured myself that the necklace was in order. Armand showed it to me in a handsome blue morocco case, which made me a bit apprehensive. He was profoundly courteous.

"I objected to the blue box, but added that it would do for a container later on, as I had an antique case to transport both the necklaces I was taking with me. I told him of my hasty change of plans. Urgent business, I said, in Egypt.

"Armand was sympathetic. I promised to return at three o'clock with the money. I went to the hotel and ordered lunch and locked the doors. I had sent Judd away after he had brought me some tools. It was but the work of fifteen minutes to cut my square hole through the plaster. I wore out about a dozen drills, however, getting through that brittle terra cotta tile.

"At one o'clock, when the lunch came up, I had the hole neatly through to the bathroom. I covered it with a towel on that side, and in the salon I backed a chair against it over which I threw an old dressing gown.

"I quickly disposed of the waiter, locked the door, and replaced the table at the wall. Taking out the necklace I had bought for Prince Meyeroff, I laid it doubled in the glove box. It was a caged rainbow, lying on the rose-colored plush lining. The box I stuck flush with the square aperture.

"I had provided myself with a stiff piece of wire something like an elongated buttonhook. A warped piece of mother-of-pearl inlay provided a perfect catch with which to pull down the end of the box.

"I tried the invention from the bathroom. I had overlooked one thing. I forgot that when the hole was stopped up by the box it would be dark. Thanks to my cigarette lighter, I could see to pull down the hinged end and draw out the jewels. I tried it. The hook brought down the end without a sound. I could see the stones glowing in the flickering light of the briquette. I began fishing with the hook, and the necklace with its rounded emerald slid out as if by magic.

"I fancied they might make a grating sound in the other room, so I padded the hole with a napkin. I'll cough out loud, or sing, or whistle, I said to myself. Then I thought of the bath water. I turned on the tap full force; the water ran furiously. I walked into the salon swinging the prince's necklace in my hand; the water was making a terrific uproar. Satisfied as to this strategy, I turned off the water.

"But what to do to disguise the box at the close-fitting square hole still bothered me. My time was getting short. I must do some important telephoning to Berthier's. I must try the outer door from the bedroom into the hall. I must have my travel cap ready and my long traveling coat across the foot of the bed. I must let down my trousers to the customary length. I must get ready my shaving brush.

"It was five minutes to three. They were expecting me at Berthier's with four million francs. Armand was probably at this moment rubbing his hands, observing with satisfaction that suave face of his in the mirrors.

"Still there was that telltale, ill-fitting edge of the hole about the box. I discovered the prince's necklace was still hanging from my hand. It gave me quite a surprise. I realized this was a ticklish business, this robbing of the most ancient house in the Rue de la Paix. I laid the necklace in the box closing the end. The hole was ugly, although the bits of paint and plaster had been well cleaned up from the floor.

"I had a stroke of genius. My flat black hat! I would lay it on its crown in front of the hole, with a big silk muffler carelessly thrown against it shutting off any view of the trap. I tried that plan, placing the box near the side of the hat. It looked like a casual litter of the objects. My old trunk was on the other side of the table to be sacrificed with its old clothes necessary stage properties.

"I then tried the camouflage, picked up the box, walked to the center of the room. The hat and muffler concealed the hole. I then walked to the table and replaced the box, this time casually alongside the hat, deftly putting the end in the hole. The hat moved only a few inches and the muffler hung over the brim, perfectly hiding and shadowing the trap, though most of the box was clearly visible. It looked perfectly natural. I then placed the box farther out, moved the hat against the hole, and the trap was arranged.

"Now to try my experiment in human credulity. I telephoned Berthier's. Armand came immediately. 'Hazim,' I said. 'I wish to ask you a favor.' Armand recognized my voice, and inquired if I were carrying myself well. 'My dear friend,' I began in English, 'I have found that the Genoa train leaves at five o'clock, and I am in a dreadful rush and am not half packed. I have the money here in my hotel. Could you conceivably bring me the necklace and collect the money here? It would help me tremendously.'

"I also suggested that Armand bring someone with him for safety's sake, as four million in notes, which had to be expedited through two branch banks, was not an affair to treat lightly. Someone might know about it. I knew Berthier's would certainly have Armand guarded, with one or perhaps two assistants.

"Armand was audibly distressed, and asked me to wait. It seemed like an hour before the response came. 'Yes, Mr. Hazim, we shall be pleased to deliver the necklace on receipt of the funds. I shall come with a man from our regular service and will have the statement ready to sign.'

"I urged him to hurry, and said I would be glad to turn over the money, as the presence of such an amount in my rooms made me nervous.

"That was exactly three fifteen. I quickly arranged the chairs so two or three would have to sit well away from the table. I laid my bearskin over the chair nearest the table. I opened the trunk as if I were packing. I telephoned the clerk to be sure to send my visitors to the salon door of my suite.

"My cap and long coat were ready in the bedroom. The door into the hall was almost closed, but not latched, so I would not have to turn the knob. I quickly removed my coat and vest, and laid them on a chair in the bedroom, ready to spring into. I wore a shirt with a soft collar attached. I removed my ready-tied cravat and hung it over a towel rack and turned my collar inside very carelessly as if for shaving purposes.

"In the bowl I prepared some shaving lather, and when that was all ready I was all set for making off with the prince's necklace and that other one—if it came.

"I'll admit I was nervous. I was considering the whole plot as a rather absurd enterprise, and all I could think of was the probably alert eyes and ears of the two or more suspicious employees on the glove box."

IV

"They arrived at twenty-five minutes to four. There were only two of them. I hastily lathered the edges of my spreading beard, and called out sharply for them to enter. The boy showed in Armand and a dapper individual who was evidently a house detective of Berthier's. Armand was all solicitude. I shook hands with him with two dry fingers, holding a towel with the other hand, as I had wished to make it apparent that I was deep in a shaving operation.

"'Just edging off my beard a little.'

"The two men were quite complacent.

"'And the necklace?' I asked eagerly.

"Armand drew the case from inside his coat and opened it before my eyes. We all moved toward the window. I was effusive in my admiration of the gems. I fluttered about much like the old fool that I probably am, and finally urged them to sit down.

"I then brought the glove box and showed the prince's necklace to both of them, and continued raving about both necklaces.

"We compared the two. The Indian was, of course, even more magnificent by contrast. The detective laid the smaller necklace back in the box, while I asked Armand to lay the big one over it in the box into which I was going to pack some cotton. My glove box was smaller and therefore easier and safer to carry, I said. I held the box open while Armand laid the necklace gingerly inside. I was careful to avoid getting the soap on the box, so I replaced it gently on the table near the hat, getting the end squarely against the hole. It seemed I had plenty of time.

"I even lingered over the box and wiped off a wayward fleck of soapsuds. The trap was set. I could not believe that the rest would be so easy, and I had to make an effort to conceal my nervousness.

"The two men sat near each other. I explained that as soon as I could clear the soap off my face I would get the sack of money and transact the business. I took Armand's blue box from Berthier's and threw it in the top tray of the trunk. They appeared to be the most unsuspecting creatures. They took proffered cigarettes and lighted up, whereupon I went directly into the bathroom, still carrying my towel. I dropped that towel. My briquette was there on the washstand. I hummed lightly as I turned on the hot water in the tub. It spouted out in a steaming, gushing stream. Quickly I held the lighted briquette at the hole, caught the gleam of the warped mother-of-pearl, and pulled at it with the wire.

"It brought the end down noiselessly on the folded napkin in the hole. The jewels blazed like fire. My hand shook as I made one savage jab at the pile with the long hook and felt the ineffable resistance of the two necklaces being pulled out together. I was afraid I might have to hook one at a time, but I caught just the right loops, and they came forward almost noiselessly along the napkin to where my left hand waited.

"I touched the first stone. It was the big necklace, the smaller one being underneath. My heart leaped as I saw the big pendant on one side of the heap not far from the *cabochon* emerald. I laid down the wire and drew them out deftly with my fingers, the gems piling richly in my spread-out left hand, until the glittering pile was free. I thrust them with one movement of my clutching fingers deep into the left pocket of my trousers. The water was churning in my ears like a cascade.

"I shut off the tap and purposely knocked the soap into the tub to make a noise, and walked into the bedroom, grabbing my cravat off the rack as I went. That was a glorious moment. The bedroom was dark. The door was unlatched. The diamonds were in my pocket. The way was clear.

"I pulled up my shirt collar, stuck on the cravat, and fixed it neatly as I reached the chair where my coat and vest lay. I plunged into them, buttoned the vest with one hand, and reached for my long coat and cap with the other. In a second I was slipping noiselessly through the door into the hall, my cap on my head, my coat over my arm.

"I had to restrain myself from running down that hall. I was in flight. It was a great thrill, to be moving away, each second taking me farther away from the enemy in that salon. Even if they are investigating at this moment, I thought, I should escape easily.

"I was gliding down those six flights of steps gleefully, released from the most tense moments I had ever gone through, when suddenly a horrible thought assailed me. What if Berthier's had posted a detective at the hotel door. I could see my plans crashing ignominiously. I stopped and reflected. The hotel has two entrances; therefore the third person, if he is there, must be in the lobby and therefore not far from the elevator and stairway.

"I thought fast, and it was a good thing I did. I was then on the second floor. I called the floor boy, turning around quickly as if mounting instead of descending.

"'Will you go to the lobby and ask if there is a man from Berthier's waiting? If he is there, will you tell him to come up to apartment 615 immediately?'

"I stressed the last word and, slipping a tip into the boy's hand, started up toward the third floor. With the boy gone, I turned toward the second floor, walked quickly down to the far end, where I knew the service stairway of the hotel was located. As I plunged into this door I saw the boy and a stout individual rushing up the steps toward the third floor. I sped down this stairway, braving possible suspicion of the employees. I came out in a kind of pantry, much to the surprise of a young waiter, and I commenced a tirade against the hotel's service that must have burned his ears. I simulated fierce indignation.

"'Where is that good-for-nothing trunkman?' I demanded. 'I'm leaving for Genoa at five, and my trunk is still unmoved.' Meanwhile I glared at him as if making up my mind whether I would kill him or let him live.

"'The trunkmen are through there,' said the waiter, pointing to a door. I rushed through.

"Inside this basement I called out: 'Where in hell is the porter of this hotel?'

"An excited trunkman left his work. I repeated fiercely the instructions about my trunk, and then asked how to get out of this foul place. I spotted an elevator and a small stairway, and without another word was up these steps and out in a side street off the Rue de Rivoli.

"I fancied the whole hotel was swarming with excited people by this time, and I jumped into a cruising taxicab.

"'Trocadero,' I ordered, and in one heavenly jolt I fell back into the seat while the driver sped on, up the Seine embankment to a section of quiet and reposeful streets.

"I breathed the free air. I realized what a fool I was; then I experienced a feeling of triumph, as I felt the lump of gems in my pocket. I got out and walked slowly to my apartment, went to the bath and trimmed my beard to the thinnest point, shaving my cheeks clean. I put on a high crown hat, a long fur-lined coat, took a stick, and sauntered out, myself once more, Mr. West, the retired diplomat, who would never think of getting mixed up in such an unsightly brawl as was now going on between the hotel and the respected and venerable institution known as Berthier's."

West shrugged his shoulders.

"That's all. Berthier was right. It was not so easy to rob a Rue de la Paix jeweler, especially of four million francs' worth of diamonds. I had returned to my apartment, and was hardly through my dinner when the telephone rang.

"'This is Berthier,' came the excited voice. He told me of this awful Hazim person. He asked if he might see me.

"That night Berthier sat in my library and expounded a dozen theories. 'It's a gang, a clever gang, but we'll catch them,' he said. 'One of them duped our man in the hotel lobby by calling him upstairs.'

"'But if you catch the men, will you catch your four millions?' I asked, fingering the pile of stones in my pocket.

"'No,' he moaned. 'A necklace is so easy to dispose of, stone by stone. It's probably already divided up among that bunch of criminals.'

"I really felt flattered, but not so much then as when I read the newspapers the next day. It was amusing. I have them all in my scrapbook now."

"'How did you confess?" I asked West.

"Simple, indeed, but only with the utmost reluctance. I found the police were completely off the trail. At six o'clock the next afternoon I went to Berthier's, rather certain that I would be recognized. I walked past the doorman into the store, where Armand hardly noticed me. He was occupied with some wise men. I heard him saying: 'He was not so tall, as he was heavily built, thick body, large feet, and square head, with a shapeless mass of whiskers. He was from some Balkan extraction, hardly what you'd call a gentleman.'

"I asked to see Berthier, who was still overwrought and irritable.

"'Hello, West,' he said to me. 'You're just the man I want. Please come down and talk with these detectives. You must help me.'

"'Nothing doing,' I said. 'Your man Armand has just been very offensive.'

"Berthier stared at me in amazement.

"'Armand!' he repeated. 'Armand has been offensive!'

"'He called me a Balkan, said I had big feet, and that I had a square head, and that I was hardly what one would call a gentleman.'

"Berthier's eyes popped out like saucers.

"'It's unthinkable,' he said. 'He must have been describing that crook we're after.'

"I could see that Berthier took this robbery seriously.

"'I thought you never fell for those old gags,' I said.

"'Old gags!' he retorted, his voice rising. 'Hardly a gag, that!'

"'Old as the hills!' I assured him. 'The basis of most of the so-called magic one sees on the stage.' I paused. 'And what will you do with these nice people when you catch them?'

"'Ten years in jail, at least,' he growled.

"I looked at my watch. The twenty-four hours were well over. Berthier had talked himself out of adjectives concerning this gang of thieves; he could only sit and clench his fists and bite his lips.

"'Four million,' he muttered. 'It could have been avoided. That man Armand—'

"I took my cue. 'That man Berthier,' I said crisply, accusingly, 'should run his establishment better. Besides, my wager concerned you, and not Armand—'

"Berthier looked up sharply, his brain struggling with some dark clew. I mechanically put my hand in my trousers pocket and very slowly drew out a long iridescent string of crystallized carbon ending in a great square pendant.

"Berthier's jaw dropped. He leaned forward. His hand raised and slowly dropped to his side.

"'You!' he whispered. 'You, West!'

"I thought he would collapse. I laid the necklace on his desk, a hand on his shoulder. He found his voice.

"'Was it you who got those necklaces?'

"'No. It was I who stole that necklace, and I who win the wager. Please hand over the yellow diamond.'

"I think it took Berthier ten minutes to regain his composure. He didn't know whether to curse me or to embrace me. I told him the whole story, beginning with our dinner at Ciro's. The proof of it was that the necklace was there on his desk.

"And I am sure Armand thinks I am insane. He was there when Berthier gave me this ring, this fine yellow diamond."

West settled back in his chair, holding his glass in the same hand that wore the gem.

"Not so bad, eh?" he asked.

I admitted that it was a bit complicated. I was curious about one point, and that was his make-up. He explained: "You see, the broad low-crowned hat reduces one inch from my height; the wide whiskers, instead of the pointed beard, another inch; the bulgy coat, another inch;

the trousers, high at the shoes, another inch. That's four inches off my stature with an increase of girth about one-sixth my height—an altogether different figure. A visit to a pharmacy changed my complexion from that of a Nordic to a Semitic."

"And the hotel?" I asked.

"Very simple. I had Berthier go around and pay the damages for plugging that hole. He'll do anything I say now."

I regarded West in the waning firelight.

He was supremely content.

"You must have hated to give up those Indian gems after what you went through to get them?"

West smiled.

"That was the hardest of all. It was like giving away something that was mine, mine by right of conquest. And I'll tell you another thing—if they had not belonged to a friend, I would have kept them."

And knowing West as I do, I am sure he spoke the truth.

ACTION AND THE QUIZ KID

Lots of kids used to hero-worship Action. At eighteen, he could never navigate the sidewalks without a coterie of awestruck ten year olds swarming around him. They worshipped him for his round black derby and the fat cigar that left a wavering trace of smoke over the route to the poolroom. But none of them had the great crush of Vittorio Corregione.

Action had entered the City College Business School. His high school marks had been poor and he had been forced to take an entrance exam to make the college. I drilled and coached him for a solid two-week period and his voracious brain devoured and held everything I fed it. He passed the exam with highest marks.

The successful entrance was only the beginning of his troubles. To pick out a course that would lead to a money-making profession was the real problem. Uncle Myron volunteered the advice. Having stashed away the most loot in the family, Uncle Myron was entitled to offer advice to young college entrees.

"Take a course in accounting," pontificated Uncle Myron, "and when you get out you'll find a wide-open field. I personally will guarantee you placement in an accounting job."

The money man had spoken, so Action followed through. Years later, when Action had staggered past the course without having cracked a single book, he came to Uncle Myron for the promised job. Myron told him to enlist in the army. Our uncle always held patriotism above all.

Action found the business administration course a complete bore. The usual shortage of cash at home forced him to get a job delivering dog medicine to Park Ave. homes but he grew tired of seeing the dogs wearing finer sweaters than he had and he quit. He had refrained from betting for a couple of months after starting school, but the old lure was too strong and after he located a bookmaker and ticker near the college he was back in the old-time groove. He hung around the Board, noting scores and getting in an occasional small bet when he met the kid.

Vittorio Corregione was a skinny little runt of fourteen with snapping black eyes, and a hungry wet red mouth that puckered in a perpetual pout. He was a bright bundle of brain and attended the honor school that was housed in the college building. Action failed to discover why he shunned his home and the kid wouldn't volunteer the information, but the kid never did want to return at night. He adored Action and saw in the little schemes and plots that my brother wove, the manifestations of genius.

Action had noted the kid hanging around the poolroom but had never bothered to say too much to him until one day, when the runt came over with a five-dollar bill and asked Action to wager it for him. He placed the bet as per the request and the money rode safely home. Thereafter, Vittorio would seek out Action for all of his wagers and even allow him to hold the cash winnings.

The following term the kid was moved to the afternoon session and couldn't make the poolroom during the action hours. He'd hand my brother a small roll and give him carte blanche to pick winners for him, phoning later in the afternoon to discover how he had made out. I was spending the afternoon with Action one day when the kid called. Action eyed the incomplete scores on the Board and rattled off some names. Each one was a stiff and the kid was sure to drop some twenty bucks.

"What's the pitch here," I asked, after he had hung up the phone. "You grabbed the boy a bundle of blanks."

Action looked out the window and his ruddy face took on an even darker shade of red.

"I didn't pick any blanks," he muttered, half to himself. "Things haven't been breaking right for me lately and I've been dipping into the kid's dough. As a matter of fact, I didn't make any bets at all today."

"You mean," I gasped, "you're suckering the kid out of his dough?"

"If not me, some other sonova bitch." He turned on his heel and walked away.

Action was not always as brutal as on this day. If he was doing well, he'd give the kid a fair shake. But somehow he didn't make out too often and the kid suffered. A wide swath was cut in the kid's roll but he never complained and he took it regularly on the chin. One day the apparently limitless wad began to thin out and the kid dropped the play.

"Action," he said, "I want your advice on a business venture."

"What kind of business, kid?"

Vittorio blushed. "I know you'll laugh at me but I'll tell you anyway. I want to book small bets like laying ten to one against a guy hitting a homer in a particular game. Herb Roddes has been drawing a fat take with that pitch in my math class."

Action smiled gently, "It's your dough, Vit, and your life. To show you I have no ill will towards you, call me tomorrow and I'll feed you a bet."

The kid almost purred at Action's gesture and floated out of the poolroom on an inflated cloud of if-money. He called Action at three the following afternoon, right after the ticker had announced a homer for J. DiMaggio.

"At ten to one, Vit, I'll put a deuce on J. DiMag to hit a homer today. Thank you kid and good luck."

The kid didn't make out too well on his venture and went bust after the first day. Action took his twenty-dollar payoff and roughed the kid's hair with his fingers.

"You're wasting your time, Vit, when you work with a small roll. You've got to begin fat or you just can't make it."

The kid's big black eyes had grown bigger and more desperate looking. His gestures had become quicker and reflected an overwrought inner tension that threatened to consume him.

"I can get dough, Action," he offered. "At least I can get stuff that's worth dough. If I do, Action," he pleaded, "would you hock it for me, old friend?"

The old friend hocked the kid's books and when the books began to run out, little items that came from the home. But tie clasps and confirmation rings don't bring in much. The kid laid a big turnip of a gold watch on the table one evening. Action hefted it and gasped.

"It's a ton weight, Vit, for sure. It'll bring in at least ten or fifteen for the gold alone."

"Not the gold, Action. Just hock it. I got to get it back later on. Get me fifteen for it and you can keep five."

The pawnbroker offered twenty on a loan and commented happily on the weight of the gold case. Action was upset over what he had to do but he did it. The Frammis-We-Pay-Highest-Prices-for-Old-Gold Company gave him forty bucks for the gold and tossed the unwanted works into a trash basket.

The kid accepted his ten with delight and ran through it in a day. He was feverish when he left that evening and Action solicitously made him bundle up against the autumn winds. He phoned Action that night.

"I just got to get the watch back tomorrow, Action. Something has come up and I just got to return it. Lend me fifteen bucks old pal and I'll return it to you first chance I get."

"I ain't even got the five you gave me," muttered Action.

"You don't understand," half screamed the kid, "I got to get it back. It ain't a maybe situation anymore!"

"Must or maybe, I ain't got the dough."

"I'll get it somehow and give it to you tomorrow so that you can get it back for me."

Action wrestled inside for a bit.

"Did you hear me, old friend, I'll get the dough to you somehow."

"No use, kid, the watch ain't hocked. I sold the gold and the works were scrapped. There's no way of ever getting it back."

The kid gasped. A sick despairing whine came wailing over the wire in a heartrending keen and the phone clicked off.

Action didn't show at the poolroom the next day, but it didn't matter. Neither did the kid. In a few days, Action seemed to have forgotten that Vittorio had ever existed.

I mentioned the kid to him a year or so later and he told the story of the watch. I sat down on the nearest curb and tried to hold down a cantankerous stomach. Action drew his cigar out of his mouth, slowly bubbled bolls of smoke in a gray, upward spiralling arch.

"One thing bothers the hell out of me," he said, "what in hell ever became of the kid?"

MEN

COMMENTARY

Dashiell Hammett's long-standing interest in the ways in which men struggle to find their places among each other and in the world is reflected in the eight stories collected here. The pulp magazines of the post-WWI era had provided an ideal marketplace for Hammett's hard-boiled crime fiction—"real, honest-to-Jasper he-man stuff" in the words of *Black Mask* editor Phil Cody—satisfying blue-collar readers with triumphant tales of working heroes who were both shrewd and strong. The explorations of masculinity featured here, however, all of which were unpublished during Hammett's lifetime, seem targeted to broader audiences. Hammett had his earliest sights set on tony literary periodicals and later, as his reputation developed, on the more lucrative slick magazines. The first three tales were completed no later than 1926. The last two were written perhaps a decade later. In the span of those years Hammett's ambitions expanded, his standpoint shifted, and his writing evolved—yet his attention to core tensions remained fixed, sharp, and wryly irreverent.

"Fragments of Justice"—one of the earliest pieces of Hammett's unpublished work—was sold to *Forum* magazine, but never released. It was likely submitted sometime in 1922, when Hammett's references to the Jack Dempsey–Georges Carpentier fight of July 1921 and Roscoe (Fatty) Arbuckle's acquittal in February 1922 would have been fresh in readers' minds. As in "Seven Pages" (in the Men and Women section that follows), Hammett uses a series of vignettes to mock private conceits and public conventions.

"A Throne for the Worm" was suited to and probably intended for publication in the *Smart Set*, "The Aristocrat among Magazines," edited by H. L. Mencken and George Jean Nathan. *Smart Set* debuted Hammett's first published fiction in October 1922, and featured five additional contributions in the year that followed. Hammett explores one of his favorite early topics in this story—the struggle of a man who suffers daily humiliation while yearning for a modicum of respect.

In "Magic," Hammett melds his concern for professional obligation with his enthusiastic interest in the supernatural. Among his favorite writers on the mystical arts was Arthur Edward Waite, who wrote the classic work on Rosicrucianism, *The Brotherhood of the Rosy Cross* (1924), mentioned by Hammett in his second novel, *The Dain Curse* (1929). Waite also wrote *The Book of Black Magic and Pacts* (1898) revised as *The Book of Ceremonial Magic* (1911), apparently used as a reference source for this story. As in the tale of the Maltese falcon, Hammett informs his fiction with scholarly accuracy. *The Black Pullet* manuscript, including its protracted title and subtitle, is genuine, first published, according to Waite, in Rome in 1740.

"Faith" was probably completed in 1926, the year the Hammett family moved from Eddy to Hyde Street. Its dark conflict is consistent with Hammett's personal viewpoints. Although raised as a Catholic, he was zealously critical of the Church, which he considered a political troublemaker and exploiter of the poor. Reference to Wobbly songster Joe Hill's "The Preacher and the Slave" also points to an early aware-ness of progressive labor causes. Hammett's sympathies in the contest between workmen are never in question.

"An Inch and a Half of Glory" was written shortly after "Faith," listing first the same Hyde Street address, then Post Street, where Ham-mett lived between 1927 and 1929, while writing his first three novels— *Red Harvest*, *The Dain Curse*, and *The Maltese Falcon*. Unlike the novels, however, there is no crime involved in the short story. Questions of valor and identity drive the narrative, evidence that even during Hammett's *Black Mask* heyday, he strove for more mainstream expressions of his talent. The influence of two young daughters on Hammett's life during this period may have heightened his sensitivity to a man's duty to vulnerable youth.

The first page of "Nelson Redline" is missing from Hammett's archives, lost at some point between the writing and the saving. The title is penciled in Hammett's hand on the second sheet. The setting is almost certainly San Francisco and the tension, much like in "Inch and a Half of Glory," stems from choices, social expectations, and questions of character revealed in response to the threat of fire.

"Monk and Johnny Fox" marks a break in the short-story sequence. There is no header, no address, fewer clues to time and place. But the text suggests a shift from San Francisco to New York, where Hammett lived, off and on, beginning in late 1929. The style and subject matter link the story to "His Brother's Keeper" (*Collier's*, February 1934), likewise narrated in the first person by a troubled young fighter called Kid. The storyteller in "Monk" is more wary and self-aware than in "Brother's Keeper" and it is unclear whether the two are discrete characters who share a commonplace nickname or a single youth who (much like Effie in *The Maltese Falcon*) has been forced to abandon hopeful innocence. While several of Hammett's works feature cameo appearances from the fighting world, only these two stories focus on its extreme masculine turf and agonizing, untenable options.

"The Cure" explores the tenets of courage—a hallmark of male identity—as both man against environment and man against man. In "Nelson Redline" and "Inch and a Half of Glory," defining challenges stemmed from fire, one of humankind's primordial adversaries. In "The Cure," the issue is water, a less volatile but equally intractable foe. The conflict is set at an unidentified lakeside, amplified by the taunts of a braggart, and complicated (as often happens in Hammett's fiction) by the presence of a woman. Although Hammett's draft typescript lacks date or address, the story is markedly subtle and sophisticated in its treatment of social interactions, suggesting that the tale dates to at least the early 1930s.

FRAGMENTS OF JUSTICE

I

When his stiffening legs began to propel the lawnmower so waver-
ingly that the lawns were often irregularly marked by thin curving lines
of unclipped grass—like raw recruits in their first "company front"—
and the hedges often went untrimmed for days while he waited for
weather favorable to the wrapping of his fingers around the handle of
the pruning-shears, the Park Board pensioned Tim Gurley. His pen-
sion was just large enough to pay for meals and a bed at a very modest
boarding-house, with a little left over for tobacco. Some day he would
need clothes, but not many, and not for some months. His failing sight
and hearing obviated the necessity of any expenditures for amusements.

Within a week Tim Gurley had settled into the habits of his new
life. He would get out of bed at six or six-thirty in the morning, and
putter around his room until seven-thirty, when breakfast was ready.
After the meal he would leave the house for the public square—two
blocks away—that had been his charge until now. There, he would sit
on a bench—preferably one facing the sun; or, on very warm days, he
would sit on the grass itself—sometimes talking to other old men who

were almost indistinguishable from him both in appearance and history, but more often sitting silent and alone, neither wholly awake nor wholly asleep. On cool days he would leave the square for the ledge that ran around the Public Library, where he could sit on the sunny side, with the broad building behind him fending off the wind. When it rained, he stayed at home.

One day when he returned to his boarding-house for dinner, he found a summons to jury duty there. After that life was different.

He served on many juries; he liked serving. There was the two dollars a day—later raised to three—that it brought in; and two dollars would buy a lot of tobacco and of the sticky taffy he was beginning to enjoy so much despite its malignant effect upon his remaining teeth. But the money wasn't the only consideration, nor even the most potent one. He liked the feeling of importance that came to him in the jury-box, the knowledge that all these attorneys and their clients and their witnesses were here for but one purpose: to convince him, Tim Gurley, of the justice of their cases; that he was having a hand in the world's graver work, helping make weighty and important decisions, doing justice.

Neither his eyes nor his ears were very responsive now, and at first he found himself frequently being excused from service after the attorneys' preliminary questions; but he soon learned what was expected of him. By straining his attention to the utmost he could catch the substance of the lawyers' queries—sufficient to tell him whether a yes or a no was expected of him.

He would have liked to have heard more clearly the testimony of some of the witnesses, especially when he could see that the other jurymen were leaning forward in their chairs with attentive expressions upon their faces; but a man can't have everything, and now and then a witness would take the stand and speak clearly enough for Tim Gurley to hear every word he said. But, even at the worst, Tim Gurley was never wholly at loss for knowledge of what was going on: the attorneys, while delivering their closing arguments, almost invariably stood close to the jury-box and reviewed the salient points of their cases in language that was loud and impassioned and easily audible.

II

Born into a family whose adherence to the principles of the Democratic Party dated from the 1830s, Elton Bemis, by shunning all political doctrine that did not spring from Democratic sources, had kept his heritage unsullied. His reading was confined to two Democratic newspapers—one in the morning and one in the evening—and, while professing a worldly skepticism, he really believed everything he read therein; not excepting the vague, but nonetheless stirring, stories of abductions by gaudy villains and incarcerations in unknown prisons told by young women who return to their families after protracted absences. He had, on the strength of their representative war records as advertised in the same papers, bet $10 on Carpentier to defeat Dempsey; he had denounced the acquittal of Roscoe Arbuckle as a flagrant miscarriage of justice; and he never trusted a man who parted his hair in the middle.

He had forbidden his daughter to see or communicate with the young man of her choice on the grounds that, although otherwise unexceptionable, the young man was a Roman Catholic; and had he known that his daughter had cultivated a mild appetite for Egyptian tobacco it is quite likely that he would have put her out of the house, though he himself burned black tobacco in a black pipe to the stimulation of his salivary glands.

In his youth he had resigned from a pleasure and social club upon the admittance of a Jew to its membership; and notwithstanding that economic expediency had induced him to assume a less rigorous attitude in later years, he still got a definite pleasure from the memory of that act. He firmly believed that his country could, in either one pitched battle or a campaign of any length whatsoever, defeat the other nations of the world all together; and he had nothing but contempt for all foreigners, were they Swedes, Limies, Harps, Heinies, Bohunks, or any of the dozen or more varieties of Dagoes. He admitted, with suitable reservations, the existence in the Negro of a soul.

One day Elton Bemis sat in the jury-box, in Department 4 of the Superior Court, and counsel for the plaintiff asked him:

"If you are selected to serve on this jury, Mr. Bemis, do you think that you can give both parties to this action a fair and impartial hearing? Will you be guided by the evidence submitted and the instructions of the Court, and not allow your mind to be influenced by personal feelings or prejudices?"

And Elton Bemis replied:

"Yes, sir!"

III

He was undersized and faded and with the face of an unhealthy rodent. From the corners of a thin-lipped and colorless mouth whose looseness had erased everything of expression but a pusillanimous cruelty, lines, deep but nevertheless not clearly defined, ran up to a little crafty, twitching nose. His forehead and chin were negligible: twin slantings away into soiled collar and unkempt hair. Furtive eyes of a dark and dull opacity were set as close together as the sunken bridge of his nose would permit; the eyes moved with an uneasy jerkiness and were seldom focused upon anything higher than a man's shoulder. His dirty fingers, with their chewed nails, scratched nervously at each other, his face, his legs.

He sat slumped down in his chair, listening with manifest disgust to the arguments with which his fellow jurors had been engrossed since the bailiff had locked them in the jury-room. Presently there came a lull in the discussion.

He spat inaccurately at a distant cuspidor, and spoke with whining plaintiveness:

"What's the use of arguing? That guy's guilty: you can look at him and see he's a crook!"

A THRONE FOR THE WORM

"Are you going to be all morning? Your breakfast is on the table?"

"I'll be down in a minute now."

Elmer Kipp's reedy voice wavered like an uncertain ghost down the stairs that had resounded to his wife's ululant contralto. Hastily finishing his shaving, he got into the rest of his clothes while descending to the dining-room, where his wife and daughter were eating, and where his own meal was cooling on a cold plate.

"Good morning," the head of the Kipp family said indistinctly.

His wife said nothing; Doris' inattention was even more deliberate, and when she spoke presently to her mother she spoke as one who complains without hope of relief—for the purpose of having the records show that an objection has been made, as the lawyers say.

"I do wish papa would use a little judgment. He came in the parlor last night, and I thought he was never going to bed. He staid until almost time for Lloyd to go. I should think a girl who earns her own living and pays her own board might be allowed to entertain her own company."

Kipp looked at his daughter without raising his head: a turning up of faded eyes that made him resemble not so much an abject man as a cartoon of an abject man.

"I didn't think that— We got talking and—" He brightened with foolish guile. "That Lloyd is a mighty clever young fellow."

Doris did not seem to have heard her father.

"Just because Lloyd has to be polite, papa seems to think Lloyd comes to see him."

Mrs. Kipp sighed with exaggerated resignation.

"Your father will never be any different. I never knew such a man for not considering other people. I've talked to him enough, goodness knows. But you can't do anything with him."

At the office Kipp found something wrong with his chair. When he attempted to lean back in it the superstructure came out of its socket and slid him off to the floor. An examination convinced him that this was not his chair at all, that his chair now served Harry Terns. But the chairs were all of the same model and age; and for the recovery of his own chair conclusive proof of proprietorship, as well as some skill in repartee, would be essential. So Kipp merely called the chief clerk's attention to the broken one, and brought in a straight-backed chair from the outer office.

For half an hour Kipp's world was six sheets of paper, each divided into little squares that either held inked numerals or yawned for them. Then a gust of air flung the sheets into swirling anarchy. He closed the window beside his desk and rearranged his world.

"Good gracious, Mr. Kipp!" Miss Propson's syllables clicked as monotonously from between her thin lips as the keys of her typewriter clicked under her thin fingers. "Don't you think we should have *some* ventilation?"

From their desks farther away Eells and Bowne looked up with annoyance, and the rustling of papers in the chief clerk's hands stopped.

"A little fresh air won't kill you," Harry Terns said.

Just as this window was beside Kipp's desk, there were windows beside Eells and the chief clerk, and they were closed. But Kipp did not denounce the manifest injustice of this; he capitulated before the unanimity of his colaborers' protests, and disposed his two paperweights, a box of pins, a metal ruler, and an extra inkwell so that his papers were not blown around enough to prevent his working.

An hour passed, and a harsh buzzing broke out: the signal that summoned Kipp to his employer's office. Lucian Dovenmichle was fat beyond the fatness that gives a body many curves. His curves were few, but gigantic in sweep. Kipp came softly into this mountainous presence.

"Finish the National accounts?" The Dovenmichle voice was fat with a husky pinguidness.

"Yes, sir. That is, the recapitulation will be ready by noon."

"All right."

Then, Kipp's hand on the door-knob.

"My shoe-lace is undone. Can't tie it with all these damned clothes on. Tie it, will you?"

Kipp bent deferentially over the Dovenmichle foot—a leather-enveloped thing as large as a healthy baby—and tugged at the ends of the inadequate black strings. The Dovenmichle leg jerked in what was nearly a kick.

"Damn it, Kipp, are you trying to choke me?"

Kipp got the lace knotted in place and went back to his desk.

With eleven o'clock, this being the fifteenth of the month, came the chief clerk with Kipp's salary. After that Kipp worked erratically, with a trembling of the pen in his fingers, a feverish lip-licking trick of tongue, and a careless spattering of ink about the mouth of his ink-well. When the noon gong sounded he was the first man through the Dovenmichle door.

Ignoring the establishment where he usually ate, he plunged through the mid-block traffic to where a barber's sign revolved brilliantly against a white building front.

Very leisurely—while four barbers stood at attention behind their chairs and a negro held ready hands for each garment—Kipp removed his coat, his vest, his collar and tie, and last of all his hat. His face now was not the one with which his familiars were acquainted. His jaw had advanced, his lips had reared up, his sallow skin had acquired pinkness, his shoulders were almost straight, and what chest had survived twenty years of crouching over desks did its best to arch. The unhurried disrobing completed, he turned—very deliberately—and strutted to the farthest vacant chair.

"Fairly close. Not too high with the clippers."

His voice achieved depth with unostentatious authority. The first Napoleon, ordering a brigade or two of dragoons forward, may have spoken thus.

A nod summoned a bootblack. Another a manicure. With two men and a woman hovering attentively, obsequiously, over his head, his feet, his hands, Elmer Kipp sat looking with rapt eyes at the picture he made in the wall mirror opposite.

MAGIC

It was late on the ninth day of Straït's fasting that Simon, his talmid, brought the jeweler Buclip into the room where the magician sat reading a tattered manuscript titled, adequately enough, *The Black Pullet, or the Hen with the Golden Eggs, comprising the Science of Magic Talismans and Rings, the Art of Necromancy and of the Kabalah, for the Conjuration of Ærial and Infernal Spirits, of Sylphs, Undines and Gnomes, serviceable for the acquisition of the Secret Sciences, for the Discovery of Treasures, for obtaining power to command all beings and to unmask all Sciences and Bewitchments. The whole following the Doctrines of Socrates, Pythagoras, Zoroaster, Son of the Grand Aromasis, and other philosophers whose works in MS escaped the conflagration of the Library of Ptolemy. Translated from the Language of the Magi and that of the Hieroglyphs by the Doctors Mizzaboula-Jabamīa, Danhuzerus, Judahim and Eliaeb.*

The room was large, white-floored, its tall walls hidden behind dark velvet glitteringly embroidered with occult insignia. In a corner the boy who had not yet got back the speech lost in awe at being apprenticed to the magician, some two months ago, squatted on his heels, and with a rumpled square of silk polished the silver ring of Raum, graved with his seal that was like the deck-plan of an eccentric small boat.

Straït was a plump man who may have been forty years old, though with magicians you cannot tell. His shrewd face was transparent of skin and sagging of mouth-corner, for this was the ninth day of his fasting. When he marked his place with a clean pudgy finger and raised his face to Simon, a reversed five-pointed star in a Hebraic-legended circle on the velvet behind him made a gay nimbus for his round pink head.

For a fidgeting moment the jeweler Buclip tried to catch the magician's gaze, then he too looked at Simon, waiting for him to speak. But when the talmid would have spoken Buclip burst into sudden babblement.

"It's— I want— If you can—I know you can," he tumbled his incoherence at the magician, "if you will. I want—" His words degenerated further into unintelligible low sounds directed at the limp hat his hands worried.

Above these low sounds Simon said, "He wants the love of a woman, Master."

The jeweler Buclip shuffled his feet and cracked his knuckles and looked at nothing, but he nodded manfully. He was a large nervous man whose naked head was as grey as grey hair could have made it.

"An especial woman?" Straït's brown eyes that were tired from abstinence turned to the jeweler for the first time. "Or any woman?"

Buclip shook his head until his collar creaked.

"An especial one!"

"Is she wife or maid?"

"Mai— She is not married."

"And there's no trinket in your shop to catch her with?"

"I've got the finest stock in the city!" The jeweler's mercantile glibness died with a gulp in his burly throat. "My gifts don't seem to make her any more—don't seem to give her any more—" Anxiety succeeded shame between the grey pads encompassing his eyes. "You'll help me? You'll help me again?"

Elbows on table beside the manuscript of *The Black Pullet*, face in hands, Straït rolled flaccid cheeks in cushioned palms and made the jeweler wait while the only sound in the room was the whisper of silk to silver in the hands of the squatting boy.

"You shall have her," the magician said when the jeweler's twisting fingers had spotted his hat with damp prints. "You will tell Simon what we need to know."

Buclip stepped jubilantly forward.

"You will—?"

Simon caught his arm, sh-h-hed in his ear, led him out.

"Always," said Straït, leaning back in his chair, when the talmid had returned to put a handful of gold coins and a written paper beside his master. "Always," Straït the magician complained when he had swept them over the edge into an open drawer, "it is love and wealth they want, no matter which variety of those things may be popular for a while. Twice perhaps in twenty years I have been asked for wisdom, twice it may be for happiness, once I can remember for beauty. For the rest, come fad, go fashion, there is love and there is wealth. Train your mountebankery on those targets, my Simon, and you need never want clients."

"Mountebankery?"

"Charlatanism."

The talmid chewed his red mouth and fear harassed his eyebrows crookedly.

"I will not get beyond that?"

When Straït had shaken his head, muscles writhed dismally in the talmid's white young face, and the working of his mouth was out of all proportion to the volume of sound that came out, but he held his master's gaze, however forlornly.

"I am too stupid, then," he achieved, "to really learn the Art?"

Straït puffed his cheeks out, blew them empty, and reproached his pupil.

"Tch! Tch! What I meant was I have nothing else to teach."

"Master! The things you do!"

"Yes," Straït confessed with an indifferent shrug. "I grant you the queer monsters riding wolves I bring out of nowhere or Hell, as the case may be, and the wolves riding queerer monsters, and the bulls with men's heads, and the men with snakes' heads. I grant you all those, if they mean anything. What with all the nonsense I go through, what with fasting and poring over weird rituals and smelling unlikely odors, what with confusing my eyes with intricate symbols and chanting complicated conjurations, wouldn't it be funny, Simon, if I didn't see the things, however monstrous, I point my bewildered mind at?"

Simon was respectful, but Simon was triumphant.

"But I have seen those things too, Master, and the boy!"

"You have?" The magician's tired brown eyes taunted the talmid with his youth. "And why shouldn't you? Because I am a mountebank must I be an altogether incompetent one? Is it so great a trick to make you see and hear and smell phantasmata? Must I be less adept than politicians and recruiting sergeants and the greenest of girls?"

Simon, thus taken in conceit, flushed and looked down. Nevertheless he shook his head confidently.

"But the things you have done! The Wengel girl, the General, Madame Reer! And all the others, and all the things you have done for them!"

Straït snorted at the idea that the authenticity of his work was to be measured by its consequences.

"Equal results, far greater results," he pointed out, "have been achieved by wizards whose methods were the nadir of idiocy. Indubitable marvels have been worked at one time or another by means of almost anything you can name, so long as it was a thing offensive or ridiculous enough of itself. Guts of a sort or another have more than held their own in the long run, of course, but there are few things in our world that have not had their goetical properties soon or late."

He leaned forward to tap with derisive finger the tattered manuscript of *The Black Pullet*.

"This childish hocuspocus, whose fraudulent absurdities are known even to men who write books—haven't magicians used it successfully? Haven't such asinine formulas as the *Grimoire of Honorius*, the *Verus Jesuitarum Libellus*, and the *Praxis Magica Fausti* been effectively applied to the disarrangements of natural things' balance? Haven't simpler sorcerers perpetrated like wonders without any tools at all?"

"Yes, Master," Simon said, tight-lipped, his back to the wall of his faith, "but you have shown me things that could not be unless a true magic was behind them."

Straït put his face in his hands and fell to rolling his cheeks in his palms again. A wistfulness was behind the tired shrewdness of his pink face, perhaps because he could not now contradict his talmid.

"There is that thing in back of these things, Simon, in back of our toying, behind even the explorations of the elder cabalists. That thing, almost corporate, perhaps, in the knowledge and experience of the Magi's sanctuaries in the distant years, is a wisdom, a mystic science of knowledge behind and beyond and above known knowledge. It hasn't, it can't have anything to do with our trickeries, our juggling. All this"—he flicked a hand from his cheek to indicate the room and its appointments and everything that had happened or could happen in the room, and in the world because of the room—"is a twisted false shadow of that thing's possible shadow. And because that thing is almost certainly back there, this theurgic sleight-of-hand of ours would be all the more shabby for being valid.

"On a day, Simon, perhaps you will go through this playing to a perception of that thing in back. But it is not likely. What is likely is you'll try and fail and fall back into this legerdemain in which you daily gain facility. Maybe you'll try again, but it is not likely anything will come of it. In this nonsense you've learned you'll find the satisfaction a man has in doing what—however silly—he can do skillfully. There will be days when you'll find a pleasure in the thought of things you have done for your clients, though that will come only on optimistic days. You'll have the flavor of your power over our thin Procels and Hagentis, and of your romantic, even important, place in your world. Intelligent people will have small use for you, true enough, knowing your work is as futile when it succeeds as when it fails. But that won't worry you greatly: the intelligent won't be, really, citizens of your world.

"You'll have your skill, and your craftsman's pride in that skill, and the money it brings you, and presently you will be middle-aged and old. Some nights the thought of the True Magic you mock with your trickery will be a torment in your bed, but, in the end, your brain addled by fasting, by immersion in symbolism and formula, and by the rest of the business, you will become—as I hope—a simple-minded sorcerer with childish pride and faith in your utility."

"Yes, Master." A pleasantly indifferent smile colored the talmid's face. "Just the same, I'll be perfectly satisfied if I can ever do half the things you do."

Straït looked at his talmid with eyes wherein pity and amused contempt and a certain pleasure in the compliment were curiously blended. He grunted away the matter so unsatisfactorily discussed and turned to the immediate.

"I can't use Raum for this Buclip business, though he would have served nicely for the other," he said. "But, since I can raise one demon to handle both, there's no need of fasting another nine days. What we need, then, is one who is a reader of minds and a reconciler for the one, and a kindler of love for the other. There is Vaul, the camel, agreeable enough if it were not for his persistence in talking Egyptian, a devilishly confusing language for me. Dantalian would be best, I think, especially as the morning should be fair." He spoke to the boy who still rubbed Raum's ring. "Put up that ring, my son, and look to Dantalian's. You will find it near the top of the cabinet, a copper ring with a sprawling seal of crosses and small circles."

The morning's dawning, fair as the magician had foretold, was barely accomplished when, white and large in linen cap and robe, belted with the broad skin girdle that was marked with the Names, Straït came into the room where his assistants were in their proper garments. When he gave them good-morning they answered with nods only: they might not speak until the business was done. From the open west windows the velvet hangings had already been gathered back, and the four candles—the red, the white, the green, and the greenish black—stood on the table beside the silken roll in which the tools of the Art were bundled.

When he had seen that these things were ready, Straït drew on the white floor, still damp from the lustral water, a wide circle, and, within it, another, less wide. Into the space between the circles he copied, to the rhythm of an inarticulate mumbled chant, and writing always toward the west, the Names that were on his girdle, spacing them with the astrological signs of sun, moon, Mars, Mercury, Jupiter, Venus, and Saturn. In the inner circle's centre he drew a square whose angles terminated in crosses. Between that square and the circle he drew four five-pointed stars. In the centre of each he put the Tau, and, in the proper places, the proper letters. Outside the circle, close to its curve, he repeated the astrological signs, and, in the prescribed places, the four five-pointed stars with their centred Taus, but in each point of these stars he wrote a syllable of the Name Tetragrammaton. Last of all, he drew a triangle that lay partly outside the circle and partly over its western rim.

All this while Straït's chant had purred oppressively out of his throat to hang heavily about him, so that, by the time he had finished his mystic architecture and had gone to the table to unroll the silken bundle, the room's atmosphere was thick, repressive of movement: the talmid, carrying the brazier of virgin charcoal into the triangle, moved sluggishly, and the dumb boy's hands, setting the candles in the stars that were outside the circle, moved clumsily, stiffly, as if they needed the eyes' help to tell when they held the candles and when not. When the candles and the charcoal in the brazier had been lighted, Straït took the hazel rod inscribed Tetragrammaton and the sword whose legend was Elohim Gibor from the table and stepped into the circle's square. At their master's heels, one holding each of the lesser swords with their lesser legends—Panoraim Heamesin and Gamorin Debalin—Simon and the boy knelt.

Straït planted his feet firmly apart, looked to Dantalian's ring on his left hand that its bezel was out, shrugged his shoulders for greater ease under the heavy robe, hitched his girdle, freshened his grip on rod and sword, cleared his throat, and lifted his face to the west.

"I invoke and conjure you, O Spirit Dantalian, and, fortified with the power of the Supreme Majesty, I command you by Baralamensis,

Baldachiensis, Paumachie, Apoloresedes and the most potent princes Genio, Liachide, ministers of the Tartarean Seat, chief princes of the Seat of Apologia in the ninth region; I exorcise and command you, O Spirit Dantalian, by Him Who Spake and it was done, by the most holy and glorious Names Adonai, El, Elohim, Elohe, Zebaoth, Elion, Escherce, Jah, Tetragrammaton, Sadai: do you forthwith appear and show yourself to me, here before this circle, in a fair and human shape, without any deformity or horror; do you come forthwith, from whatever part of the world, and make rational answers to my questions; come presently, come visibly, come affably, manifest that which I desire, being conjured by the Name. . . ."

And so, on and on, the mystic rigmarole rose and fell in carefully cadenced strain, on through its tedious length, now contradictory, now tautological, now repetitious, but not ever in its emptiest phrase to be escaped. When it was done, except for the more rosy light of fuller risen sun, there was nothing in the room that had not been there before.

"Um-hmmm," Straït hummed briefly. "We shall see."

And he swung into the second conjuration, less restraint in his voice, loosing a gong-like resonance in his broader vowels. He called now on the Name Anehexeton which Aaron spoke and was made wise, the Name Joth that Jacob learned, the Name Escerchie Ariston which Moses named and the rivers and waters of Egypt were turned into blood, and others. And when he was done there was a vague flickering between brazier and window, a distortion of the air that was gone as soon as it was come.

Straït's face was bleak and Straït's eyes were hard and Straït's knuckles were white on rod and sword hilt.

"So?" he said softly, and softness went out of his voice. The third conjuration was a brazen song that beat the velvet walls, beat back on itself, beat the candle-flames to dim sparks, beat dark dampness out on the linen garments of the kneeling apprentices from armpit to hip. Besides the Names he had already invoked, Straït now called on Eye and Saray, and the Name Primematum, and others.

When he had done that, something was in the room without having come there in any manner: a soldier in russet, a narrow band of yellow metal around his brows, sat a sorrel horse between brazier and west window. If you chose to think he had materialized there, or had whisked himself there from another place, you were welcome, but it was certain you could not say when.

Straït's lids crept closer around his mad eyes, and there was no favor in the face with which he faced the soldier.

"O Spirït Berith, transmuter of metals, revealer of the past and the present and the future, giver of dignities, liar: because I have not called you, do you at once depart, without injury to man or beast. Depart, I command you and be you. . . ."

Here the soldier Berith, fingers toying with red mane, leaned over his charger's neck and sought to stem the dismissal. His scarred face was bland, and his harsh voice counterfeited bluff friendliness.

"But since I am here, Straït, you may as well make use of me."

". . . ready to come whensoever, and only when, duly exorcised and conjured," the magician's voice went heedless on. "I command you to withdraw peaceably. . . ."

The soldier urged the sorrel nearer, and leaned farther over its neck.

"But, Straït, what is the—?"

With "and quietly, and may the peace of God continue forever between me and you," Straït had finished, and the russet soldier was no more in the room than his russet mount.

The magician rubbed the back of one hand over his forehead that was wet and shiny, and with camphor and brandy he revivified the brazier's weakening flame, while the apprentices shifted their knees on the floor behind him and breathed with unguarded noisiness through open mouths.

The charcoal burning afresh, Straït put away his vials, braced himself on his short legs, lifted his face once more to the west, and became an iron horn through which thunder trumpeted the invocation of King Corson of the West. That invocation completed to no effect save the shivering of the two behind him, Straït hunched his shoulders, smiled a basilisk's smile, and the Chain Curse came cruelly out of his mouth.

The dumb boy tried to stop his ears with his fingers, but Simon struck his arm down.

When the last hard black word of the Chain Curse had been uttered, and no thing had come into the room, Straït took a small black box from under his robe, and held his other hand behind him. Into that hand the talmid put the virgin parchment inked with Dantalian's seal. Into the box, among the assafetida and brimstone that was there, went the parchment, the lid closed, iron wire went thrice around the box, Straït's sword found purchase in a loop of the wire, and the box dangled down in the charcoal's flame.

The jagged, crackling phrases of the Fire Curse dulled the walls' embroidery into colorlessness, made a cringing small heap of the boy, painted the talmid's chin with blood beneath the sob-checking cut of his teeth. Straït's face was a cold, dry, white blur as the box slid off his sword and nestled among the hot coals.

Between fire and window stood a man-shape. The face atop his neck was not ugly even in its sullen endurance of agony. Some of his other faces grimaced hideously in their pain. The faces that were his right hand's finger-tips were smeared into shapelessness by the book they held.

Straït plucked the box from the fire, dropping in its stead a pinch of incense that clouded the room with pungent sweetness. He spoke politely to the man by the window, but he held aside the fold of his robe that bared the Seal of Solomon until that man had come into the part of the drawn triangle which lay outside the circle.

"I am here, Straït," that one said meekly enough, however confusing it was to have each word in turn come from another of his faces. "Command me."

The magician wasted no time in recrimination, in railing against the obstinacy the spirit had shown. Into the hand Straït held behind him Simon put two written slips of paper. From the first of these Straït looked up at the demon.

"There is a man Eton who had some ships with another man Dirk. A while ago they divided their ships and each took his portion to himself. Now I must know does Dirk prosper more than Eton, who seems to prosper little?"

Dantalian raised the book in his right hand while his finger-tip faces turned the leaves with their tiny white teeth. Dantalian nodded with all his faces.

"Dirk prospers more," three of his mouths affirmed.

"So? Now you will put it in Dirk's mind that he should return to Eton, that they should pool their boats again, share and share alike."

The woman's face on Dantalian's left shoulder smiled slowly and heavily through her weight of seductiveness, and took the answering from the other heads:

"Will it serve to put the idea first into the head of Dirk's wife?"

Straït shrugged his linened shoulders.

"I have heard the gossip. So the matter is arranged, you may suit yourself how. Now there is another thing; there is a jeweler Buclip who wants the love of a woman"—Straït bent his head to the second slip in his hand and clicked his teeth together—"named Bella Chara. You will—"

"Wait!" Dantalian called deafening, discordantly, with all his mouths at once. "Don't do this foolish thing!"

Though there was nothing yielding in his cold eyes, Straït withheld his words and looked at the demon.

"Why should you do this foolish thing?" the vocal change-ringing went on. "You have—"

Now Straït checked the demon's words with upraised rod in the hand on which the demon's seal glowed, looking meanwhile for an uneasy instant over his shoulders at his kneeling assistants.

"We will take all that for granted," he said. "You and I know what we know. Let us only say what needs to be said from that point, if anything."

"Then why should you give her away?" some of Dantalian's voices were asking while the courtesan's head on his shoulder leered knowingly. "Is it any fairer to herself than to you to bind her by these means in a place she has not gone of her accord? She is yours—keep her."

"What of the jeweler's gifts?"

The courtesan sniggered, but a fair face elsewhere on Dantalian spoke softly:"Weren't you away for weeks at a time with your abstinences and your fastings? Was she, knowing nothing, to sit in her house and twiddle her fingers and wait for you to find time to visit her? And what of the jewelry? Does not Buclip's coming to you show that he needs more than jewelry?"

Straït frowned and said, "I made a bargain. I set my theurgy to do a thing. You will—"

"Wait!" Dantalian cried again, and tried scoffery. "You made a bargain, yes. But what of your bargain with her? That, of course, is nothing where your silly vanity is concerned! That is not enough to balance the fear that this dolt Buclip might tell his neighbor Straït's sorcery failed him. Are you a child, Straït, to toss away that which you value for the sake of a traffic in which you have no belief? Does being pointed out as Straït the magician mean that much to you?"

Scowling, Straït replied, "You will give—" and he stopped to look at the book whose pages spun swiftly to the click of Dantalian's snapping finger-mouths. The white whir of the leaves became less a whir, less a book, and into the demon's hand came a woman's face.

This face was the first thing to come eerily into the room. For a demon to materialize, however abruptly, however trickily, can be nowise genuinely weird, for such is the nature of spirits. But the matter is different when a face of ripe pink flesh comes out of a book, a warm oval of compact meatiness and creased lips and merry eyes that so awfully do not belong apart from a soft pulsing body.

"This is what you will pay for the privilege of showing off," Dantalian accused the magician. "This is what, in your empty vanity, you will throw to a baldly grey jeweler."

Straït swallowed and wet his lips and looked away from the delectable face held up in a hand whose finger-ends were tiny faces that kissed and ran red tongues over the round throat they held. Straït looked at the floor and wrinkled his forehead under his linen cap and seemed in every way ashamed.

And Straït said, "You will give the jeweler Buclip the love of this woman so she will never see any other man with love."

Dantalian was a pandemonium of voices that barked and growled and screamed, a horrible gallery of rage-masks that snarled and spat.

Straït said, "O Spirit Dantalian, because you have diligently answered my demands, I do hereby license you to depart, without injury to man or beast. Depart, I say, and be you willing and ready to come, whensoever duly exorcised and conjured. I conjure you to withdraw peaceably and quietly, and may the peace of God continue forever between me and you."

Straït flourished sword and rod and copper ring, and there was not anything in the room but the magician and his paraphernalia, and white Simon swaying up from his knees, and the boy fainting across the floor, his face all smudged by the charcoal with which the mystic circle had been drawn.

Simon the talmid touched his master's sleeve.

"Oh, Master, if I had only known when the jeweler gave me her name!"

Straït said that was nonsense. He said it did not matter; Dantalian had made much of little. He said he was a middle-aged man who should not be trifling with love.

"But, Master, isn't the jeweler at least ten years older than you? And she herself—she's twenty-five if she's a day!"

Straït smiled sidewise then into the talmid's pale face, and asked if Simon had considered her ancient hag's face not at all desirable.

Simon blushed contritely and tried to wipe out the slight.

"No, Master!" he protested. "She was—if she had been mine, I would never have—" and there he floundered, for that way lay another slight.

But Straït did not seem to mind. He confessed he had not played the man's part. He said Simon would understand, when his day came, that to the extent one becomes a magician one ceases to be a man. And he added that this same thing might hold true of sailors and jewelers and bankers, and the boy seemed to be stirring, and Simon might let the cleaning of the room wait while he went out to market for a fat goose and whatever else they would need for the evening meal, now the fasting was over.

FAITH

Sprawled in a loose evening group on the river bank, the fifty-odd occupants of the clapboard barrack that was the American bunk-house listened to Morphy damn the canning-factory, its superintendent, its equipment, and its pay. They were migratory workingmen, these listeners, simple men, and they listened with that especial gravity which the simple man—North American Indian, Zulu, or hobo—affects.

But when Morphy had finished one of them chuckled.

Without conventions any sort of group life is impossible, and no division of society is without its canons. The laws of the jungles are not the laws of the drawing-room, but they are as certainly existent, and as important to their subjects. If you are a migratory workingman you may pick your teeth wherever and with whatever tool you like, but you may not either by word or act publicly express satisfaction with your present employment; nor may you disagree with any who denounce the conditions of that employment. Like most conventions, this is not altogether without foundation in reason.

So now the fifty-odd men on the bank looked at him who had chuckled, turned upon him the stare that is the social lawbreaker's lot everywhere: their faces held antagonism suspended in expectancy of worse to come, physically a matter of raised brows over blank eyes, and teeth a little apart behind closed lips.

"What's eatin' you?" Morphy—a big-bodied dark man who said "the proletariat" as one would say "the seraphim"—demanded. "You think this is a good dump?"

The chuckler wriggled, scratching his back voluptuously against a prong of the uptorn stump that was his bolster, and withheld his answer until it seemed he had none. He was a newcomer to the Bush River cannery, one of the men hurried up from Baltimore that day: the tomatoes, after an unaccountable delay in ripening, had threatened to overwhelm the normal packing force.

"I've saw worse," the newcomer said at last, with the true barbarian's lack of discomfiture in the face of social disapproval. "And I expect to see worse."

"Meanin' what?"

"Oh, I ain't saying!" The words were light-flung, airy. "But I know a few things. Stick around and you'll see."

No one could make anything of that. Simple men are not ready questioners. Someone spoke of something else.

The man who had chuckled went to work in the process-room, where half a dozen Americans and as many Polacks cooked the fresh-canned tomatoes in big iron kettles. He was a small man, compactly plump, with round maroon eyes above round cheeks whose original ruddiness had been tinted by sunburn to a definite orange. His nose was small and merrily pointed, and a snuff-user's pouch in his lower lip, exaggerating the lift of his mouth at the corners, gave him a perpetual grin. He held himself erect, his chest arched out, and bobbed when he walked, rising on the ball of the propelling foot midway each step. A man of forty-five or so, who answered to the name Feach and hummed through his nose while he guided the steel-slatted baskets from truck, to kettle, to truck.

After he had gone, the men remembered that from the first there had been a queerness about Feach, but not even Morphy tried to define that queerness. "A nut," Morphy said, but that was indefinite.

What Feach had was a secret. Evidence of it was not in his words only: they were neither many nor especially noteworthy, and his silence held as much ambiguity as his speech. There was in his whole air—the cock of his round, boy's head, in the sparkle of his red-brown eyes, in the nasal timbre of his voice, in his trick of puffing out his cheeks when he smiled—a sardonic knowingness that seemed to mock whatever business was at hand. He had for his work and for the men's interests the absent-minded, bantering sort of false-seriousness that a busy parent has for its child's affairs. His every word, gesture, attention, seemed thinly to mask preoccupation with some altogether different thing that would presently appear: a man waiting for a practical joke to blossom.

He and Morphy worked side by side. Between them the first night had put a hostility which neither of them tried to remove. Three days later they increased it.

It was early evening. The men, as usual, were idling between their quarters and the river, waiting for bed-time. Feach had gone indoors to get a can of snuff from his bedding. When he came out Morphy was speaking.

"Of course not," he was saying. "You don't think a God big enough to make all this would be crazy enough to do it, do you? What for? What would it get Him?"

A freckled ex-sailor, known to his fellows as Sandwich, was frowning with vast ponderance over the cigarette he was making, and when he spoke the deliberation in his voice was vast.

"Well, you can't always say for certain. Sometimes a thing looks one way, and when you come to find out, is another. It don't *look* like there's a God. I'll say *that*. But—"

Feach, tamping snuff into the considerable space between his lower teeth and lip, grinned around his fingers, and managed to get derision into the snapping of the round tin lid down on the snuff-can.

"So you're one of *them* guys?" he challenged Morphy.

"Uh-huh." The big man's voice was that of one who, confident of his position's impregnability, uses temperateness to provoke an assault. "If somebody'd *show* me there was a God, it'd be different. But I never been showed."

"I've saw wise guys like you before!" The jovial ambiguity was suddenly gone from Feach; he was earnest, and indignant. "You want what you call proof before you'll believe anything. Well, you wait—you'll get your proof *this* time, and plenty of it."

"That's what I'd like to have. You ain't got none of this proof *on* you, have you?"

Feach sputtered.

Morphy rolled over on his back and began to roar out a song to the Maryland sky, a mocking song that Wobblies sing to the tune of "When the bugle calls up yonder I'll be there."

> *You will eat, by and by,*
> *In that glorious land they call the sky—*
> *'Way up high!*
> > *Work and pray,*
> > *Live on hay.*
> *You'll get pie in the sky when you die.*

Feach snorted and turned away, walking down the river bank. The singer's booming notes followed him until he had reached the pines beyond the two rows of frame huts that were the Polacks' quarters.

By morning the little man had recovered his poise. For two weeks he held it—going jauntily around with his cargo of doubleness and his bobbing walk, smiling with puffed cheeks when Morphy called him "Parson"—and then it began to slip away from him. For a while he still smiled, and still said one thing while patently thinking of another; but his eyes were no longer jovially occupied with those other things: they were worried.

He took on the look of one who is kept waiting at a rendezvous, and tries to convince himself that he will not be disappointed. His nights became restless; the least creaking of the clapboard barrack or the stirring of a sleeping man would bring him erect in bed.

One afternoon the boiler of a small hoisting engine exploded. A hole was blown in the store-house wall, but no one was hurt. Feach raced the others to the spot and stood grinning across the wreckage at Morphy. Carey, the superintendent, came up.

"Every season it's got to be something!" he complained. "But thank God this ain't as bad as the rest—like last year when the roof fell in and smashed everything to hell and gone."

Feach stopped grinning and went back to work.

Two nights later a thunderstorm blew down over the canning-factory. The first distant rumble awakened Feach. He pulled on trousers, shoes, and shirt, and left the bunk-house. In the north, approaching clouds were darker than the other things of night. He walked toward them, breathing with increasing depth, until, when the clouds were a black smear overhead, his chest was rising and falling to the beat of some strong rhythm.

When the storm broke he stood still, on a little hummock that was screened all around by bush and tree. He stood very straight, with upstretched arms and upturned face. Rain—fat thunder-drops that tapped rather than pattered—drove into his round face. Jagged streaks of metal fire struck down at ground and tree, house and man. Thunder that could have been born of nothing less than the impact of an enormous something upon the earth itself, crashed, crashed, crashed, reverberations lost in succeeding crashes as they strove to keep pace with the jagged metal streaks.

Feach stood up on his hummock, a short man compactly plump, hidden from every view by tree and undergrowth; a little man with a pointed nose tilted at the center of the storm, and eyes that held fright when they were not blinking and squinting under fat rain-drops. He talked aloud, though the thunder made nothing of his words. He talked into the storm, cursing God for half an hour without pause, with words that were vilely blasphemous, in a voice that was suppliant.

The storm passed down the river. Feach went back to his bunk, to lie awake all night, shivering in his wet underwear and waiting. Nothing happened.

He began to mumble to himself as he worked. Carey, reprimanding him for over-cooking a basket of tomatoes, had to speak three times before the little man heard him. He slept little. In his bunk, he either tossed from side to side or lay tense, straining his eyes through the darkness for minute after minute. Frequently he would leave the sleeping-house to prowl among the buildings, peering expectantly into each shadow that house or shed spread in his path.

Another thunderstorm came. He went out into it and cursed God again. Nothing happened. He slept none after that, and stopped eating. While the others were at table he would pace up and down beside the river, muttering to himself. All night he wandered around in distorted circles, through the pines, between the buildings, down to the river, chewing the ends of his fingers and talking to himself. His jauntiness was gone: a shrunken man who slouched when he walked, and shivered, doing his daily work only because it required neither especial skill nor energy. His eyes were more red than brown, and dull except when they burned with sudden fevers. His finger-nails ended in red arcs where the quick was exposed.

On his last night at the cannery, Feach came abruptly into the center of the group that awaited the completion of night between house and river. He shook his finger violently at Morphy.

"That's crazy!" he screeched. "Of course there's a God! There's got to be! That's crazy!"

His red-edged eyes peered through the twilight at the men's faces: consciously stolid faces once they had mastered their first surprise at this picking up of fortnight-old threads: the faces of men to whom exhibitions of astonishment were childish. Feach's eyes held fear and a plea.

"Got your proof with you tonight?" Morphy turned on his side, his head propped on one arm, to face his opponent. "Maybe you can *show* me why there's *got* to be a God?"

"Ever' reason!" Moisture polished the little man's face, and muscles writhed in it. "There's the moon, and the sun, and the stars, and flowers, and rain, and—"

"Pull in your neck!" The big man spit for emphasis. "What do you know about them things? Edison could've made 'em for all you know. Talk sense. Why has there got to be a God?"

"Why? I'll tell you why!" Feach's voice was a thin scream; he stood tiptoe, and his arms jerked in wild gestures. "I'll tell you why! I've stood up to Him, and had His hand against me. I've been cursed by Him, and cursed back. That's how I know! Listen: I had a wife and kid once, back in Ohio on a farm she got from her old man. I come home from town one night and the lightning had came down and burnt the house flat—with them in it. I got a job in a mine near Harrisburg, and the third day I'm there a cave-in gets fourteen men. I'm down with 'em, and get out without a scratch; I work in a box-factory in Pittsburgh that burns down in less'n a week. I'm sleeping in a house in Galveston when a hurricane wrecks it, killing ever'body but me and a fella that's only crippled. I shipped out of Charleston in the *Sophie*, that went down off Cape Flattery, and I'm the only one that gets ashore. That's when I began to know for sure that it was God after me. I had sort of suspected it once or twice before—just from queer things I'd noticed—but I hadn't been certain. But now I knew what was what, and I wasn't wrong either! For five years I ain't been anywheres that something didn't happen. Why was I hunting a job before I came up here? Because a boiler busts in the Deal's Island packing-house where I worked before and wiped out the place. That's why!"

Doubt was gone from the little man; in the quarter-light he seemed to have grown larger, taller, and his voice rang.

Morphy, perhaps alone of the audience not for the moment caught in the little man's eloquence, laughed briefly.

"An' what started all this hullabaloo?" he asked.

"I done a thing," Feach said, and stopped. He cleared his throat sharply and tried again. "I done a thi—" The muscles of throat and mouth went on speaking, but no sound came out. "What difference does that make?" He no longer bulked large in the dimness, and his voice was a whine. "Ain't it enough that I've had Him hounding me year after year? Ain't it enough that everwheres I go He—"

Morphy laughed again.

"A hell of a Jonah you are!"

"All right!" Feach gave back. "You wait and see before you get off any of your cheap jokes. You can laugh, but it ain't ever' man that's stood up to God and wouldn't give in. It ain't ever' man that's had Him for an enemy."

Morphy turned to the others and laughed, and they laughed with him. The laughter lacked honesty at first, but soon became natural; and though there were some who did not laugh, they were too few to rob the laughter of apparent unanimity.

Feach shut both eyes and hurled himself down on Morphy. The big man shook him off, tried to push him away, could not, and struck him with an open hand. Sandwich picked Feach up and led him in to his bed. Feach was sobbing—dry, old-man sobs.

"They won't listen to me, Sandwich, but I know what I'm talking about. Something's coming here—you wait and see. God wouldn't forget me after all these years He's been riding me."

"Course not," the freckled ex-sailor soothed him. "Everything'll come out all right. You're right."

After Sandwich had left him Feach lay still on his bunk, chewing his fingers and staring at the rough board ceiling with eyes that were perplexed in a blank, hurt way. As he bit his fingers he muttered to himself. "It's something to have stood up to Him and not give in. . . . He wouldn't forget. . . . Chances are it's something new. . . . He wouldn't!"

Presently fear pushed the perplexity out of his eyes, and then fear was displaced by a look of unutterable anguish. He stopped muttering and sat up, fingers twisting his mouth into a clown's grimace, breath hissing through his nostrils. Through the open door came the noise of stirring men: they were coming in to bed.

Feach got to his feet, darted through the door, past the men who were converging upon it, and ran up along the river—a shambling, jerky running. He ran until one foot slipped into a hole and threw him headlong. He scrambled up immediately and went on. But he walked now, frequently stumbling.

To his right the river lay dark and oily under the few stars. Three times he stopped to yell at the river.

"No! No! They're wrong! There's got to be a God! There's got to!"

Half an hour was between the first time he yelled and the second, and a longer interval between the second and third; but each time there was a ritualistic sameness to word and tone. After the third time the anguish began to leave his eyes.

He stopped walking and sat on the butt of a fallen pine. The air was heavy with the night-odor of damp earth and mold, and still where he sat, though a breeze shuffled the tops of the trees. Something that might have been a rabbit padded across the pine-needle matting behind him; a suggestion of frogs' croaking was too far away to be a definite sound. Lightning-bugs moved sluggishly among the trees: yellow lights shining through moth-holes in an irregularly swaying curtain.

Feach sat on the fallen pine for a long while, only moving to slap at an occasional pinging mosquito. When he stood up and turned back toward the canning-factory he moved swiftly and without stumbling.

He passed the dark American bunk-house, went through the un-used husking-shed, and came to the hole that the hoisting engine had made in the store-house wall. The boards that had been nailed over the gap were loosely nailed. He pulled two of them off, went through the opening, and came out carrying a large gasoline can.

Walking downstream, he kept within a step of the water's edge until to his right a row of small structures showed against the sky like evenly spaced black teeth in a dark mouth. He carried his can up the slope toward them, panting a little, wood-debris crackling under his feet, the gasoline sloshing softly in its can.

He set the can down at the edge of the pines that ringed the Po-lacks' huts, and stuffed his lower lip with snuff. No light came from the double row of buildings, and there was no sound except the rustling of tree and bush in the growing breeze from southward.

Feach left the pines for the rear of the southernmost hut. He tilted the can against the wall, and moved to the next hut. Wherever he paused the can gurgled and grew lighter. At the sixth building he emptied the can. He put it down, scratched his head, shrugged, and went back to the first hut.

He took a long match from his vest pocket and scraped it down the back of his leg. There was no flame. He felt his trousers; they were damp with dew. He threw the match away, took out another, and ignited it on the inside of his vest. Squatting, he held the match against the frayed end of a wall-board that was black with gasoline. The splintered wood took fire. He stepped back and looked at it with approval. The match in his hand was consumed to half its length; he used the rest of it starting a tiny flame on a corner of the tar-paper roofing just above his head.

He ran to the next hut, struck another match, and dropped it on a little pile of sticks and paper that leaned against the rear wall. The pile became a flame that bent in to the wall.

The first hut had become a blazing thing, flames twisting above as if it were spinning under them. The seething of the fire was silenced by a scream that became the whole audible world. When that scream died there were others. The street between the two rows of buildings filled with red-lighted figures: naked figures, underclothed figures—men, women, and children—who achieved clamor. A throaty male voice sounded above the others. It was inarticulate, but there was purpose in it.

Feach turned and ran toward the pines. Pursuing bare feet made no sound. Feach turned his head to see if he were being hunted, and stumbled. A dark athlete in red flannel drawers pulled the little man to his feet and accused him in words that had no meaning to Feach. He snarled at his captor, and was knocked down by a fist used club-wise against the top of his head.

Men from the American bunk-house appeared as Feach was being jerked to his feet again. Morphy was one of them.

"Hey, what are you doing?" he asked the athlete in the red drawers.

"These one, 'e sit fire to 'ouses. I see 'im!"

Morphy gaped at Feach.

"You did that?"

The little man looked past Morphy to where two rows of huts were a monster candelabra among the pines, and as he looked his chest arched out and the old sparkling ambiguity came back to his eyes.

"Maybe I done it," he said complacently, "and maybe Something used me to do it. Anyways, if it hadn't been that it'd maybe been something worse."

AN INCH AND A HALF OF GLORY

Out of the open doorway and an open second-story window thin curls of smoke came without propulsion to fade in the air. Above, a child's face—a young face held over the sill with a suggestion of standing tiptoe—was flat against the glass of a window on the third floor. The face held puzzlement without fear. The man on Earl Parish's left saw it first.

"Look!" he exclaimed, pointing. "There's a kid up there!"

The others tilted their faces and repeated: "There's a kid up there."

"Did anybody turn in the alarm yet?" a man who had just arrived asked.

"Yes," several voices assured him, one adding, "The engines ought to be here any minute now."

"He's all right, that kid," the man who had first seen the child praised his discovery. "Ain't crying or nothing."

"Most likely he don't even know what's going on."

"The firemen will be here in a second. Ain't much use of us trying to do anything. They can get him out with their hook'n'ladders quicker than we could."

Feet shuffled on the sidewalk and gazes left the upper window to fasten on the smoking doorway. No one answered the man who had spoken last. After a moment, his face reddened. Earl Parish found his own cheeks warm. Looking out of the corners of his eyes at the faces around him, he saw more color than before. His glance met another man's. Both looked quickly across the street again.

A woman's voice came from a house behind the men.

"Somebody ought to get that child out of there! Even if it ain't burnt up, it's liable to get scared into convulsions or something."

Earl Parish tried to take his gaze away from the upstairs window, and failed. It was terrible, and it held him: a stupid flat face into which panic must come each instant—and did not. If the child had cried and beat the pane with its hands there would have been pain in looking at it, but not horror. A frightened child is a definite thing. The face at the window held its blankness over the men in the street like a poised club, racking them with the threat of a blow that did not fall.

Earl Parish wet his lips and thought of words he did not say. The child was not in real danger. No great heat was behind the smoke that came from the house. To leave these men and bring the child down from its window would seem a flaunting of inexpensive courage. To suggest a rescue—if he could have explained his wish to save the child from consciousness of danger rather than from danger itself, he would have spoken. But he distrusted his ability to make the distinction clear.

"The engines ought to be here any minute now," the man who had made that prediction twice before was repeating. He scowled up and down the red-brick street. "Where in the hell are them engines?" he demanded.

The man who had discovered the face at the window cleared his throat, his eyes focused somewhat rigidly on the window.

"Maybe she's right," he said. "The kid's liable to be scared into fits. I had a nephew that got scared into St. Vitus's dance just by having a cat jump up on him."

"Is that so?" the fire department's herald asked with extraordinary interest.

"Maybe we better—" Earl Parish suggested.

"Maybe we better."

The group swayed indecisively. Then eight men crossed the street, their pace quickening as they approached the smoking doorway. Going up the four wooden steps they jostled one another, each trying to get ahead of the others. All were going into the house: such risk as attended them would be shared. But he who went first would bring the child down: the others would constitute a not especially important chorus.

Inside the door a gust of smoke blew on them, shutting out the light, scorching eyes and throats. Gongs and sirens clamored in the street.

"There's the engines now!" their prophet cried. "They'll have the kid down in no time!"

Out of sight, the suspended blow in the child's face was without power. Seven men went back into the street with nothing apologetic in the manner of their going. Earl Parish remained in the house.

Through the smoke that clouded but did not fill the hallway brass lines gleamed on a flight of steps. He hesitated. He wanted to climb those steps and either bring the child down or stay with it until the fire had been extinguished. But to do so seemed a breach of faith with the men who had gone back to the street. Had he told them he was going through with the venture, they would have accompanied him. Having stayed silently behind, if he came out now with the child, or was found upstairs with it when the fire had been put out, they would think he had tricked them so he might pose as one who had gone alone through something that had daunted them.

He took a step toward the street, and stopped. To go out without the child now would be no better. The men in the street, who no doubt had missed him by this time, would think he had lost courage after breaking faith with them.

Earl Parish went up the brass-striped steps. The smoke thickened as he mounted, but was never dense enough to make advance difficult. He saw no flames. On the third floor a rickety door barred him from the front of the building until he remembered this was an unusual occasion, an emergency, strictly speaking. He thrust the door in with his shoulder.

He found little smoke in the room with the child, though a thin fog came in with him. The child came to him.

"'Moke," it pronounced gravely.

"You're all right, sonny," Earl Parish said, picking the child up. "I'll have you out of here in a jiffy."

He draped a red and green cloth from the table lightly about its head, leaving a corner loose for his own possible use. He took pains not to show himself at the window, and went down the way he had come up.

In the street again, someone took the child. He was faintly giddy from the smoke, the effort of groping his way down with the child, and the excitement that had grown in him as he descended—the nervousness that is inseparable from even the most orderly of retreats. He stood very erect, avoiding curious stares. The eyes of the seven men who had crossed the street with him reproached him from twenty paces.

He walked away, down the street with a stiff affectation of nonchalance: a short, sturdy man of thirty or so in a stiffly pressed double-breasted coat that made him as rectangular as a shoe-box standing on end.

At his desk the next morning Earl Parish searched the day's papers. In the *Morning Post* he found an inch and a half of simple news that a fire of unknown origin had been subdued with slight damage after a child had been carried to safety by Earl Parish. He folded the account into the center of the newspaper and put it out of sight.

Between the departure of No. 131, southbound, and the arrival of No. 22, a train announcer came to Earl Parish's window and grinned at him over the sign that said, INFORMATION.

"Where's the medal?" the train announcer asked.

Earl Parish grinned foolishly back, blood came into his face, he perspired.

The news went around the station: Earl Parish had rescued a child from a blazing building—two children. The station employees with whom he was intimate joked about his deed. The more important employees—baggage master, stationmaster, chief dispatcher—congratulated him solemnly, as if on behalf of the company. At noon, the general passenger agent himself, on his way to a convention in St. Louis, stopped to commend

Earl Parish's bravery. Earl Parish listened to his words, answered his questions, kept his gaze fixed on the general passenger agent's watch chain, and perspired. The general passenger agent's train was finally announced. He shook Earl Parish's hand and went away.

Earl Parish did his day's work in an emotional muddle, avoiding eyes, mopping his moist face incessantly with his handkerchief. Looking up to find the most casual glance turned in his direction, his face would go crimson, and a desire to drop on his knees out of sight below the window would come to him. Between the necessary contacts with fellow employees and inquiring travelers he pretended business with guidebooks and folders in the rear of his cubbyhole, and there was exaltation in him.

That night he lay for a long while across his bed, studying the printed inch and a half he had cut from the *Morning Post*. There had been nothing heroic—except perhaps in a negative way—about his going into the smoking building: he had brought the child down not as one would snatch it from peril, but as one would protect it from awareness of peril. Nevertheless, it was pleasant to lie across his bed knowing that people throughout the city had read of what he had done, that his acquaintances thought him a man of courage and perhaps were mildly boasting that they knew this Earl Parish.

Lying across the bed, these things he found pleasant. To listen to praise, even if thickly overlaid with banter, was not pleasant. It was embarrassing to be studied by eyes that tried to estimate the familiar Earl Parish in terms of the new development. But that was his self-consciousness, his shyness, and would pass. It was a transient annoyance. The joy that had come to him out of this affair would not wear away, however: that was a fixed thing in him.

He went rosy-faced to work the next morning, creeping out of the house to avoid his suddenly too-tender landlady. The day was less uncomfortable than the previous one. To the same extent that he was becoming accustomed to his new position among his fellows he was drifting back to last week's position. The ticket sellers, opposite his window, still threw jests through their grilles: "The next time you save any women and children, save me a blonde!" But now he could smile back at them without perspiring.

Occasionally he met acquaintances who had seen the *Post*'s story and spoke of it. He blushed and was uncomfortable at these times, but he enjoyed the later thoughts of them. He never went into the street without a wish for one of these meetings. The next issue of the railroad company's *Employees' Magazine* contained his photograph and an elaborated account of his feat.

Then the fire was as if it had never happened.

No one ever mentioned it. He brought it casually into his talk once or twice, but no one showed any interest. At first he thought this coldness sprang from boredom. Later he decided envy was truly responsible.

He began to keep to himself. After all, what had he in common with the people around him? An uninteresting lot: the lesser inhabitants of the world, unimportant cogs in not especially important machines. He himself was a cog, true enough, but with the difference that on occasion he could be an identity. The last drop of ancestral venturesomeness had not been distilled from his blood. He experimented with this thought, evolving a sentence he liked: "All their ancestral courage distilled by industrialism out of their veins." He would look at the world over his sign that said, "Information," and repeat the sentence to himself.

People who passed his window or brought their questions to it were sorted. Did they retain some part of their ancestral courage? Or did they not? The first class was small.

Complaints went uptown to the general offices: the man at the information window had been unobliging, had been rude, had been insulting. Earl Parish received a formal letter, calling his attention to a number of these complaints and to the purple slogan on the company's advertising matter: Courtesy All-Ways. Such important departments as the information bureau, the letter insisted, had great influence on the public's attitude toward the company, and on that attitude depended not only the road's income but also its success in securing favorable legislation.

Earl Parish did not like this letter. With a pencil and a pad of paper he began framing a reply, not such a reply as might be expected of a cog. A testy old man came to his window with an unanswerable question. The Earl Parish of a while ago would have led the old man around to a point where the answer to an altogether different question would have satisfied him. The Earl Parish who was busy with the draft of his reply to the general offices told the old man point-blank that his question was silly. The testy old man was a personage of some sort. The next day Earl Parish was given two weeks' notice. He left within ten minutes.

Ten days later he found a place in a steamship agency. A month later he was looking for work again. He had sat dreaming over his desk one afternoon and his employer, a little fat man with a fat sneering mouth, had asked him if he was afraid of work. Had asked *him*—a little fat man who would have buried his face in his arms at the first sign of danger. He had told the little fat man exactly what he was afraid of and exactly what not, and in the end had found himself walking down the street with his wages in his pocket.

His next position was in the basement of a wholesale drug house, but he quit this place after two weeks. He was done with working at a desk. He had reasoned things out. Desk jobs were well enough for a man who could not rise above them. But nowadays there was a scarcity of—hence must be a demand for—men whose ancestral courage had not been distilled out of their veins. He meant to find and fill such an opening.

Three months of searching exhausted his savings and persuaded him he had been mistaken. It seemed there was no place for venturesomeness in the modern world. Courage was the one thing for which business had no use—not only could not use it, but did not want to have it around. If your employer learned you were not a sheep or a worm—a timid, docile sheep or worm—he immediately got rid of you.

Earl Parish was working temporarily in a soap factory when he read one day in a newspaper that the city fire department was dangerously undermanned. He deserted the soap factory at once, amazed that he needed the newspaper to point out his path: the city fire department was so obviously the one place in the world for him!

He submitted his application and a doctor surveyed his body. Days passed, and he was told he had failed the physical examination—a matter of defective kidneys. In the office of a fire commissioner that same afternoon Earl Parish created a diversion. An inch and a half of cut newspaper was brandished before the commissioner's eyes. The commissioner was called an old fool. Presently Earl Parish was hustled to the sidewalk.

He went then to the offices of the *Morning Post*, where he found someone to listen to his story. The *Post* happened to be an opposition paper at the time. It gave half a column to the tale of the man who once had "dashed into a blazing building to rescue a little child," and who now, unable to find other employment, was barred from the Fire Department by "the same red tape which is responsible for the department's inability to get and keep an adequate force."

Out of this advertisement Earl Parish got—besides a new clipping —employment as night watchman in a packing plant. He was paid four dollars a night and soon learned that two men who had divided the work had been discharged to make a place for him. It was the watchman's duty to make a tour of the building once an hour, registering at fifteen little boxes hung on the walls. After the first week Earl Parish began to skip boxes, those in distant corners. There were complaints, of course, but he ignored them. He had been hired, he reasoned, because of his known courage, and he trusted that to overbalance minor irregularities. He was mistaken. He was discharged at the end of the third week.

Returning to the *Post*, he could find no one to listen to his story. The other papers were as indifferent. He found several positions within the next few months. Sometimes he resigned, sometimes he was discharged. He earned enough to pay for meals and a place to sleep. He spent much time in a public square just out of the business district. Sitting on a bench, or sprawling on the grass, he would sort passersby according to his habit. Fewer and fewer were those whose ancestral courage had not been distilled by industrialism out of their veins. Now and then, he would write a letter to the *Post's* Open Forum, commenting bitterly on this failing of the race.

Sometimes he would go down to the waterfront, pretending he was going to make his way to some virile land where the courageous still prospered and sheep were eaten. He never put his foot on a deck, never asked a question that could lead to a place aboard a boat. The periods of halfhearted search for work grew longer. The intervals of employment shrank. Some days he was hungry.

One of these days he went to the house from which he had carried the child. The child's family had moved from the neighborhood to nobody knew where. Another morning when hunger was a hard lump in his stomach he walked the streets studying the faces of the people he passed, classifying them, but not in his familiar fashion. He sought now to pick out the probably liberal from the probably not liberal.

Three times, he approached faces that bespoke generosity. Three times, last-minute timidity and the too-near presence of others in the street kept him silent, sent him hurrying on as if a pressing engagement awaited him at the end of the street. The fourth face that attracted him was very old, and years had washed it clean of all color, of all expression save a meek friendliness. Its owner walked alone and slowly with the help of a silver-knobbed cane. His shoes were black mirrors.

Earl Parish turned around and followed the old man. Other pedestrians passed and repassed them. Earl Parish kept half a block behind his man, and as he walked he took his three finger-worn clippings out of their envelope and put them loose in his pocket, where they would be readily available if his request for "a dime or so" needed documentary bolstering.

Presently the old man turned into a street where people were few. Earl Parish quickened his pace and the distance between them shrank. Hurrying thus, he came to a corner where a bareheaded man was breaking the glass front of a fire-alarm box with a fist wrapped in a handkerchief.

Earl Parish forgot his kindly faced quarry.

"Where is it?" he asked the bareheaded man in a curt professional tone.

"Around in the back street."

Earl Parish ran around the corner. Three men were converging on the opening of a narrow street that split the block. He hurried after them. From a red-and-white house in the middle of the block spongy smoke rolled out to gray the street.

In front of the house a man tried to grab Earl Parish's arm. He struck aside the interfering hand and sprang up the front steps.

"Hey! Come out o' there, you!" the man called after him.

Earl Parish pushed open the front door and plunged into the murky interior. A blow on his chest stopped him, jarred him back on his heels, emptied his lungs of the clean air they had carried in from the street. Smoke stung his throat, chest. His hands found the thing that had struck him—a newel. He clung to it while he closed his eyes against the scorching smoke and coughed.

A foot found the bottom of a flight of steps. He went up, one hand fumbling along the railing, the other clenched over nose and mouth. The platform of an interfloor landing came under his feet. His hand on the rail guided him around the turning in the stairs. He started to climb again.

A boiling hiss, the beat of hotness on his face jerked his eyes open. In front of him nimble red blades of fire poked up at the ceiling.

Earl Parish cried out—a smoke-garbled protest against this trickery, this betrayal. In that other house had been no visible fire. Nothing had been there but smoke, and a child to be carried out. Here was live flame and—he was a fool!—perhaps nobody to be carried out. How did he know anyone was upstairs? Was it likely?

A limber bright sword bent down at him. He turned and scurried down the stairs. The landing tripped him with its break in the step-after-step descent, tumbled him down on hands and knees. Red light sizzled down the rail after him. Its flare was mauve on a small piece of paper that lay close under his nose as he huddled there.

He stared at the paper with curious intentness. It was somehow familiar, this small rectangle of soiled wood pulp, so altogether unimportant, so trivial a thing here in a burning house. And when he recognized the paper he continued to stare, seeing now for the first time in its true size his cherished clipping from last year's *Post*: an inch and a half of simple news that a fire of unknown origin had been subdued with slight damage after a child had been carried to safety by Earl Parish.

Seeing the clipping truly, he saw its significance, and he saw other things: he saw himself with a clearness that mottled his face beyond power of smoke and fire. He stood up on the landing and faced upstairs with the bit of paper crunched in his fist.

"I had my fun, you—" he personified the clipping in a compound invective and flung the clipping to the fire. "Now I'm going to earn it!"

Smoke swirled in the stairs, red light sizzled, and living flame blades poked up at the ceiling. Earl Parish went through them to the second floor. Not all of him went through. Some hair, a patch of one hand's skin, parts of his clothing that were frayed into ready kindling disappeared. The rest of Earl Parish gained the second story, slammed a door between him and the stairs, and beat out the points of light that dotted his clothes.

On the other side of the door fire seethed and crackled. He laughed at the noise as well as he could with smoke strangling him, and began to explore the fumid gloom.

He found no one in the room with him, nor in the other rooms that made up the house's top story. He swayed as he walked back to the first room. His head was hollow and buoyant, and he breathed in choking gulps. He staggered toward the front window.

A small sneeze came out of a corner.

Earl Parish dropped down on hands and knees and peered under the chair there. A cinnamon kitten stopped rubbing paws on nose to sneeze again. Earl Parish laughed hoarsely as he scooped the kitten out of its retreat and stuffed it into a coat pocket.

He had trouble in getting himself erect again, but managed it finally. The window slid up easily, to create a draft that swung open the room's door and swept in flame bulky out of all semblance to sword blades.

Earl Parish clambered up on the windowsill and looked into the upturned faces down in the street.

A policeman waved an arm.

"Stick it out, brother," he called. "Here's the wagons now!"

"Look out!" Earl Parish yelled back, and jumped.

There was a shock, but not of the expected hard pavement. He was on a sort of blue cushion: the policeman had run to stand under him. Men dragged them out of the arriving firemen's way, helped them to their feet. The policeman's face was bleeding.

"You're a lunatic!" he said.

Earl Parish was busy with his coat pocket, disentangling the cinnamon kitten from the torn lining. Someone took the kitten. Voices said things, asked things. One of the questions had to do with Earl Parish's name and address.

"Earl—" He coughed violently to cover up the halt, and repeated: "Earl—John W. Earl," and gave a street and number, hoping they didn't belong to any of the people around him.

He was insisting that he was all right, that he didn't need medical attention. He was sneaking through the crowd. He was hurrying away from the fire, down an alley. He turned three corners before he stopped. Out of his pocket he took two clippings—from a railroad employees' magazine, the other from a newspaper.

He tore them into very small bits and tossed them up in a flurry of artificial snow.

In Howard Street, sandwiched between a secondhand clothing store and a lunch counter, there is an establishment whose large front room is bare and unfurnished except for shabby desk, chair, table behind a battered counter in the rear and a blackboard that occupies one sidewall. You will find listed in chalk on this board such items as "Laborers, company, country, $3.75; Wood Choppers, 4 ft. and stove wood, $2.50–4.50 cord; Choremen, country, $45–65, fd.; Lead Burner, company, $8." Beneath some of these items "Fare paid" will appear.

Into this establishment one afternoon came a short sturdy man of thirty or so, inordinately dirty-faced and shabby. He had no hat, and some of his hair seemed to have been eaten off. A smudge was where one eyebrow should have been. He walked unsteadily. His red eyes had the inward hilarity of a drunken philosopher. But he did not smell of alcohol—rather of fresh wood smoke. He learned over the battered counter and grinned jovially at the establishment's proprietor.

"I want," he said, "a job. Any kind of job you've got, if only it'll get me away from town before the morning papers come out."

NELSON REDLINE

Nelson Redline was as ruddy and as plump as our employer, but more pompous than sleek—not sleek at all, in fact—and his cuffs, flamboyantly exposed to half their lengths on Mondays, day by day crept back into the sleeves of his coat until, by Friday, not even their edges could be seen.

Martin Karbo was without annoying peculiarity and therefore, in such a company as ours, colorless; and he drew pictures at night.

Myself: two months before, I had ceased being associated with a workers' paper that had killed itself by a shortsighted policy of specialization upon the case of the unemployed, who couldn't give it the material support it needed.

Such we were. Irene Vickery's shoes were comparatively new; Karbo's brown hat was still undeniably glossy. Those were our show pieces. Beyond them we were shabby, and patched where we weren't frayed. And our jobs were good for exactly one month, Thurner having divided the work into thirty precisely proportioned lots. And he saw to it that each day's quota was accomplished to the final syllable. But his mathematics had this to our advantage: it was a rigid thing, and each day's task equaled each other day's task, with no allowance for our becoming more expert with practice, so that toward the end of our term, by carefully concealing our increased proficiency, we had rather an easy time of it.

We were established on the top floor of a ramshackle building far down on Garden Street; a building that had been—according to the wit who tended the one tired elevator—the first four-story structure erected in the city, and owed its ricketiness in large measure to its builders' fears that so dare-devil a venture would fail, and to their desire that not too much valuable material be involved in the failure. Our particular room still had the air of a bedroom, in spite of the buff paint that years before had replaced the roses with which the walls must once have been papered, and in spite of the scant and battered office equipment Thurner had provided us with.

But our month was up on a Wednesday, and by the Monday of that last week we thought this erstwhile bed-chamber, with its rented desks, chairs, typewriters, and table, not a bad sort of place at all.

We were sitting idle late that afternoon, the day's assignments completed, except for the bits we habitually saved so that we might have something to be busy with when Thurner arrived. Karbo was studying the Help Wanted Male columns of an evening paper. Irene Vickery and I were listening to Redline, who, with his usual malapropos quotations from political speeches—for which he had a remarkable memory—was elaborating fancifully upon an already fanciful theory that he had come upon somewhere with wholehearted acceptance, whereby the elimination of all international differences was to be brought about by an interchange of children—only orphans, I think, until the system was perfected—between neighboring nations for periods of ten or fifteen years.

In the middle of this the door opened and the elevator man said: "You people better get out. It's burning pretty bad downstairs."

He said it calmly, even flatly, with no emphasis anywhere: an unnatural diction, under the circumstances, what could be accounted for only by supposing that he had rehearsed it. But, delivered thus, it was undoubtedly more impressive than any stressing could have made it.

Karbo, across the desk from me, was nearest the door. With a single revolving motion he whirled himself around in his chair, to his feet, past the elevator man, and through the door. His feet sounded noisily on the wooden floor of the corridor, the elevator door slammed, and the elevator groaned downward.

It was Monday. Redline's cuff showed broad and white as he ruffled his mustache with the back of a forefinger, a little theatrically.

"The damned coward!" he said, also a little theatrically.

Irene Vickery and I were for the next little while only slightly less stagy than Redline. The elevator man had gone. We three, with elaborate courtesy and consideration each toward the others, and a great display of leisureliness, gathered our belongings—pointedly and a little childishly ignoring Karbo's still glossy hat on its nail—and walked down the stairs. The other compartments on our floor were used only for storing goods, and the people below had already left the building, so the dignity of our procession was undisturbed by alien influence. Even when the smoke became thicker and more pungent we quickened our steps but slightly.

Out in the street we saw Karbo immediately. He was standing in the front rank of onlookers on the opposite sidewalk, watching the lazy curls of smoke that wound out of the second-story windows; and I couldn't see wherein his face differed in expression from the faces around him.

Straight across to him Redline marched, with Irene Vickery and me—still held by the parts we were playing—at his heels.

"Never, sir, have I seen such a contemptible action!" Redline hurled at Karbo; and heretofore Redline's "sirs" had been reserved for our employer. "You are a dirty cur!"

Karbo's muddy eyes widened questioningly. Then he shrugged with slight impatience and returned his attention to the upper windows of the building we had just left, where firemen were visible now. But Redline's denunciation hadn't been low-voiced; and the people around us were forming a circle, turning away from the fire—manifestly a failure as a spectacle—toward this more promising and more intimately displayed show. Redline wasn't a man to disappoint an audience. He struck an attitude and cleared his throat; and I, feeling foolish and uncomfortable, pushed through the crowd and went for a walk around the block.

I walked around several blocks, thinking of Karbo and his dash for the elevator that had left us on the fourth floor of a supposedly blazing building with only a winding wooden stairway to get out by. I had liked Karbo, in a casual way. Undersized, frail, with a pale pinched face that had not one significant feature, he was, by virtue of an utter simplicity and never-varying unobtrusiveness, decidedly agreeable to work with, especially when viewed in contrast with the pompous Redline and the ridiculous Vickery.

We happened to luncheon together occasionally. He was not very articulate, but neither reticent nor garrulous. He told me that he drew pen-and-ink pictures; just simply that. I didn't know whether he attached any importance to them or not. He had spent two years in the army during the war: first in a Maryland training camp and then in an English one. The uniform, except for the blouse, was the most comfortable sort of clothing he had ever worn. That was the war to him. He was as simple throughout. After his discharge from the army he had not gone back to the poverty-ridden family that had bred him in a West Virginia mining town. There seemed to have been no particular reason for it. He was now about thirty years old, and only once had he ever received a salary of more than thirty dollars a week, and that for but a short while. Except when he was discharged from the army he had never had so much as two hundred dollars at one time. He was neither humble nor resentful. Life, as he knew it, was like that.

For him to have shown the sort of cowardice that makes self-preservation a thing to be accomplished at all costs wouldn't have been, then, either surprising or especially blameworthy. Such courage as poverty breeds is usually the courage that faces danger for the sake of large reward: not—except in unusual cases, and only then when other factors are present—that which makes for sacrifice of life for another. And it couldn't very well be otherwise. A man who throughout his whole life is face to face with the threat of starvation, whose life hangs always insecurely upon the thread of his own none-too-productive day-by-day efforts, whose whole life, in short, is devoted to the business of preserving itself, can't be expected to fling it aside on some sudden chance occasion.

That sort of thing is all very well for the comparatively well-to-do, for the man whose condition has permitted him to cultivate other habits than one of the struggling for his life. . . .

But this was beside the point. Karbo hadn't been afraid—not desperately. He had believed, of course, that he was in very real danger. But his face and manner in the street a few minutes later had certainly not been those of a man who had recently experienced a great fear.

Then what? I wondered, finding no answer, and coming back by this time to Garden Street, now empty of crowd and firemen.

Redline and Irene Vickery were up in the office, with Karbo's hat still upon its nail. He had not returned, and Redline was of the opinion that we would not see him again. The affair in the street had been even worse than I had feared. After being subjected to an onslaught of Redline's oratory—in which, more likely than not, the women and children, and perhaps the flag, had been featured prominently—Karbo had been knocked about by the orator and volunteers from the audience, until the police had broken up the game. Irene Vickery had refrained from participating in the assault as she now refrained from echoing the vituperation that Redline still spouted—chiefly, I imagined, because she didn't wish to be suspected of thinking her sex had entitled her to preference in time of danger.

Redline was wrong about not seeing Karbo again. He was at his desk when I came down the next morning. Around one eye his face was swollen and dark; his nose was buried under adhesive tape and more tape lay in little squares on forehead and cheek; one wrist was bandaged; and one of his coat's shoulder-seams was puckered with amateur tailoring.

Irene Vickery and Redline were already there, so I missed the meeting. But, in view of the totality with which they ignored him all that day and the next—when our association ended—I came to believe that his entrance had struck them surprisingly dumb, and that, in lieu of a more satisfactory weapon, they had nursed that momentary speechlessness into deliberate ostracism. Fortunately, Karbo's work and mine were linked together and did not touch that of the other two, and so the rift made no difference in a business way. Then, too, Karbo had never shown much interest in what either of them said or did, and so this new situation was not obtrusively noticeable. He seemed to accept it as a matter of unimportant fact.

Thus we worked through the last two days of our employment. Thurner was with us all of the final day, having taken the day off from his place of employment to supervise the winding up of the work. We finished in mid-afternoon, left our addresses with Thurner—in case he should succeed in filching another contract—and went our separate ways.

At least, I thought our ways were separate until, at the corner below, I found Karbo at my elbow.

"Have you got an hour to spare?" he asked.

I don't know exactly why I went to his room with him. I knew it was going to be an uncomfortable, even a painful, hour—that he was going to say things that having to listen to would embarrass me. But I went with him. Perhaps I thought it the part of fairness that I should give him an opportunity to explain, to defend himself. My former casual liking for him had, I think, nothing to do with it. That was gone now. I felt sorry for him, in a vague way that made me try to conceal from him my present repugnance. Perhaps that is why I went. . . . There had been nothing in his manner since the fire to indicate that he regretted his actions; and it could easily be that he had sufficient, or even excellent, reasons for so behaving that day. Then, too, there was the undeniable fact that all philosophic justification is with him who runs. So, in justice, I couldn't condemn him. But that sort of thing—if you could live up to it—would complicate life beyond reasonable bounds. These men who refuse to—or for one reason or another are unable to—conduct themselves in accordance with the accepted rules—no matter how strong their justification may be, or how foolish the rules—have to be put outside. You don't know approximately what they will do under any given set of circumstances, and so they are sources of uneasiness and confusion. You can't count on them. They make you uncomfortable. . . .

His room was what is known as a housekeeping room. Besides the bed with its iron peeping out through chipped enamel, the yellow bureau, the table, and the chairs, there were, huddled in one corner, a sink, a two-burner gas stove, and some shelves of pans and dishes.

Leaving me to close the door, he went immediately to the bureau and took out an armful of paper, which he put on the bed. Then he motioned me toward it. I looked at the drawings while he stood silently beside me. I don't know whether there was anything in them or not. Figures, mostly, more men than women, and the hands. . . . But I don't know enough about that sort of thing to pass judgment. They were all simple lines.

He spoke after I had looked through about half the pile.

"You've seen enough to know what they're like. They don't count. Nothing I've done so far does. But I wanted you to see them before I— It's about the fire I wanted to talk."

I continued looking at the pictures to avoid his eyes: a glance had shown them appealing, childishly.

"You weren't nasty about it," he went on, his voice husky and uneven. "You weren't nasty like Redline and that Vickery woman; but I know you got a pretty low opinion of me out of it, and you can't be blamed for that. About them and what they think I don't care. They're— they don't matter. But you're—you're more of—you're different. And I wouldn't want you to— I'd want to be sure that you understood, if I can make it plain."

I was fidgeting by this time, and I knew my face was blazing. He kept on talking, his voice more broken, trying to look into my eyes; and I had my eyes desperately fixed upon the drawings that I couldn't see clearly, and upon whose margins my hands were leaving sweaty marks.

"I tried to make myself think that I didn't care what anybody thought. But a man's got to have some—I've always been a lonely kind, and you're the first— This was my last chance. If I didn't get hold of you today I'd probably never see you again. And I didn't want to— Those things you are looking at: they aren't anything. Nothing I've done is. But I've got it inside me and some day— A man can't be wrong on a thing like that. I know. I've got it in me. I know. It isn't a thing that can be argued about or proved, but it's a fact. It's a fact, all right. And, knowing that, I can't afford to—"

He had stopped and was waiting for me to say something. But what could I say? Suddenly he went on, talking faster.

"It's not myself. If I could do them now I'd be willing to die tomorrow. But I can't. Tomorrow, maybe, or next month, or next year. But I can't do them now. I'm not equipped. But I will be. I've got the things in me. I can't die with them undone. It's more important than people, or obligations to people. A thing like that can't be killed for— Listen! I haven't been on a boat or a train or a street car or even an automobile for a year—not since I learned this. I don't go out at night: anything can happen to a man at night! I haven't done a thing that had the slightest danger attached to it. And I'm not a coward. I swear I'm not! You saw me after the fire. Was I scared? Trembling? No. I'm not a coward. It isn't for my own sake. This thing isn't me—isn't even a part of me—it's just something that I'm guardian of. I can't—just can't until the things are done! I wanted to tell you. I wanted you to understand, if you could, but—"

I don't like to think of the next five minutes. They were like nothing I had ever gone through before; and what wasn't too hazy for remembrance was indescribably unpleasant. My feelings: irritation, contempt, pity, but dominated by an agony of unreasonable self-consciousness. My arm for a while, I know, was around his shoulders. I gave him promises, assurances. And when I stumbled down the stairs there were dark spots of moisture on my coat where he had leaned his head.

I saw him once after that, on the street, and went into a cigar store until he had passed.

MONK AND JOHNNY FOX

I was pretty tired. When Monk came over to my table I didn't see him until he put a hand on my shoulder, and then his face was fuzzy. He said, "I'm sliding, Kid. Why don't you?"

"Listen, Monk," I said, "I only had three drinks. I'm all right."

He smiled along one side of his mouth. "Sure, Kid sure, I know. It ain't that. But use a little sense. You're walking on your heels right now. I'm not trying to pull you out. All I'm asking is don't make it all night."

I said, "All right, all right," and he went away.

The blonde on my right asked, "What's the matter with that guy?"

"There's nothing the matter with that guy," I explained carefully. "He's a swell guy. He don't give a damn for you and he don't give a damn for me and he don't give a damn for anybody but himself. He's a swell guy."

"I don't see anything swell about that," she said.

"Sometimes I don't either," I said, "but it's there. Listen, let's scram out of here, let's go some place where we can talk, take a ride or something."

She said, "I don't know about the fellow I'm with."

"All right. Forget it."

"Don't be like that," she said. "Wait till I see what I can do." She got up and went around the table.

Johnny Fox came over from the bar to shake hands with me. "What a fight, Kid!" he said. "Did you walk to and fro through that mug!"

I said I was glad he liked it, or something like that. If he—if none of them but Monk and me—didn't know it wasn't a good fight I wasn't going to argue.

I introduced Johnny to the others, waving a hand at the ones whose names I couldn't remember, and he said he would like to buy a drink.

The blonde came back to her chair, saying, "Yes, sir," to me as she sat down.

I said, "Swell. We'll break away after this drink."

We had to wait a little longer than that because Johnny was telling me a long story about something and then everybody said it was still early, but I told them I was all in—"Those pokes I stopped with my chin didn't harden me up any"—and we finally got away.

My car was around the corner on Fifty-Third Street. "Anywhere?" I asked. She said, "Sure," so I turned the car over towards the river.

She lit a cigarette, gave it to me, lit another for herself, slid down comfortable in the seat, and asked, "When do you fight again?"

"First of the month, in Boston."

"Who?"

"Pinkie Todd."

"I never saw him fight."

"Neither did I," I said, "but I hear he's all right."

She laughed. "He'll have to be a lot better than all right to—"

"Yes," I said, "I'm great, I'm marvelous, I'm the toughest, gamest, cleverest middle-weight since some guy whose name I forget. Now shut up."

"What's the matter with you?" she asked.

"Nothing," I said, "except I'd like to bust out crying."

We were riding over the bridge then. She put her face close to mine, staring at me, and said, "Listen, Kid, I don't care how fast you drive if you're sober. Are you?"

"I'm sober."

She said, "OK," and made herself comfortable again.

I said, "But I don't see why you take my word for it."

She sat up straight. "And I don't see why you brought me out here just to pick a fight with me. I never did anything to you. You never saw me before tonight. You don't know me from Adam."

"That's just it," I said. "Why do I have to pick up some girl I don't even know her name and might be any kind of tramp and go—"

"You didn't pick me up," she said. "We were introduced by Fred Malley and my name's Judith Parrish and I'm not any kind of tramp and you can let me out right here at the end of the bridge."

"Stop it. I didn't mean anything personal. I'm just trying to—"

She laughed and said, "You must be a honey when you get personal." Her laugh was nice.

"I'm just trying to get something straight, for myself I mean."

She put a hand in the crook of my arm. "It's that fight tonight that's worrying you, isn't it?"

I nodded.

"Fixed?" she asked.

"No. That's happened without bothering me, but tonight was on the level."

"Well, then, what's the matter with you? It was a swell fight. You were swell."

"I know better," I said, "and Monk knows better."

"That's what's the matter with you. That guy's got you buffaloed."

"You talk too much—what's your name?—Judith, about things you don't know anything about."

She took her hand away from my arm and said, "Listen, Kid, this was your idea. You said, 'Let's go for a ride where we can talk,' and now every time I open my mouth you jump all over me."

"Well, lay off Monk. He's a swell guy. He don't give a damn for anybody but himself."

"You said that before, but you didn't say how that made him such a swell guy."

"It makes him a swell guy for me," I said, "because he's my manager."

She stared at me again. "Could a girl ask what that's supposed to mean without getting jumped on?"

"I mean he's smart and he gets thirty percent of my take."

She whistled. "I'll say he's smart if he's collecting a third of your money. You must be in love with that guy."

"You're being a cluck again. Light me a cigarette? Listen, did you—"

She interrupted me. "Listen, Kid, this way you talk to me doesn't mean anything? That you don't like me or something? It's just your way of talking, isn't it?"

"I like you fine," I said. "I'm just dead tired."

She gave me the cigarette I had asked for. "Go ahead," she told me. "I won't mind any more."

"I'm scared," I said and I didn't know I said it out loud until she jumped and asked, "What?" in a sharp voice. I wouldn't lie about it then. "I'm scared stiff," I said.

She put her hand back in the crook of my arm, her head against my shoulder. "You're just tired, Kid, and no wonder. Eight rounds of the kind of fighting you did tonight is enough to—"

"I'm scared too."

"Scared of what?"

"I don't know how to say it," I said, really talking to myself, "except it's Monk."

THE CURE

"So I shot him."

Rainey screwed himself around in his chair to see us better, or to let us see him better.

I was sitting next to him, a little to the rear. Above the porch rail his profile stood out sharp against the twilight gray of the lake, though there was nothing sharp about the profile itself. It had been smoothly rounded by thirty-five or more years of comfortable living.

"I wouldn't have a dog that was cat-shy," he wound up. "What good is a dog, or a man, that's afraid of things?"

Metcalf, the engineer, agreed with his employer. I had never seen him do anything else in the three days I had known them.

"Quite right," he said. "Useless."

Rainey twisted his face farther around to look at me. His blue eyes—large and clear—had the confident glow they always wore when he talked. You only had to have him look at you once like that to understand why he was a successful promoter.

I nodded. I didn't agree with him, but I was there to put him in jail if I could, not to pick arguments with him. And with Rainey you had to agree or argue: he always treated his audience like a board of directors to be won over one by one to some project.

Satisfied with my nod, he turned to the fourth man on the porch, Linn, who sat on the other side of Metcalf. That—saving Linn till last—was another promoter's trick. Rainey never forgot his profession. He had turned first to Metcalf, his personal yes-man, then to me, who had managed to agree with him in most things during the three days of our acquaintance, and then, with our votes in his pocket, had turned to the one of whose agreement he was least sure.

Linn didn't say anything. He was staring thoughtfully down the lake, down where Rainey's and Metcalf's dam was not hidden by the dusk.

Rainey leaned toward him, trying to catch his eye, didn't succeed, settled back in his chair again, and asked: "Well, am I right, Linn?"

Linn cleared his throat and, still staring down at the dusky lake, replied: "I don't know." He said it as if he really did not know. "It's possible, isn't it, that a dog might run from a cat and not from a wolf? There are things—"

"Nonsense." Rainey's easy tone made his words sound more polite than they really were. "Either you're afraid or you're not. You can't pin fear on one form of danger. The things to be afraid of are pain and death. Either you have the nerve to do things that might bring them, or you haven't. That's all there is to it. Eh, Metcalf?"

"Quite right, I think," the engineer agreed without much interest. He was a lank sandy-haired man, hard and sour of face, who seldom spoke unless spoken to, and then, even when coming up with a yes for his employer, made no attempt to hide his indifference.

Linn turned his face slowly from the lake to the promoter. His face seemed a little pale under its sunburn, and a little tense, as if the conversation was of importance to him. Light from one of the hotel windows behind us made shiny ripples on his smooth black hair when he shook his head.

"You may be right," he said hesitantly, "about pain and death being the things men fear, but in one form they might frighten him beyond reason, while in other forms he might be able to face them quite calmly. Fear isn't a reasonable thing, you know."

Rainey clapped a hand on his thick knee and thrust his ruddy face—full-blooded and round-muscled under curly light hair—forward.

"I've heard of that," he said, "but I've never seen it. I've banged around some. The men I've seen that were afraid of one thing were afraid of others. All of them."

"I've seen it," Linn insisted quietly.

"Yes?" Rainey's deep-chested voice was openly skeptical. "Can you give us a specific instance?"

"I could."

"Well?"

"Myself," Linn replied, so low that the word was barely audible.

Rainey's voice was loud and challenging: "And you're afraid of—?"

Linn shivered slightly and turned his face from the promoter to nod simply at the dark water in front of us.

"Of that," he said, still speaking very low. "Of water."

Rainey made a little puffing noise with his mouth and looked with proprietary contemptuousness at the broad lake that had been little more than a pond before the organization of the Martin E. Rainey Development Company. Then he smiled with little less contemptuousness at the man who was afraid of the thing he had built.

"You mean," he suggested, "that being on the water makes you a little nervous, perhaps because you're not sure of your swimming?"

"I mean," Linn said, speaking rapidly through tightened, thinned lips, looking Rainey straight in the eye, "that I'm afraid of water as a rat is of a cat. I mean that I am not a little nervous when I am on the water, because I do not go on it. I mean that to cross a bridge even leaves me useless for hours afterwards. I mean, in short, that I am afraid of water."

I looked at Metcalf. The engineer was looking, without moving anything but his eyes, from Linn to Rainey. He looked disgusted with the pair of them, as if he wished they would shut up.

I was enough interested in what was going on that I didn't light my cigarette because I was afraid the flare of light would bring them, or at least Linn, back to normal.

Rainey made a circle in the air with the pink end of his cigar.

"You're exaggerating, of course," he said. "Swim?"

"Swim?" Linn repeated with an angry sort of softness. "How in hell can I swim when more water than a bath-tub will hold drives me into lunacy?"

Rainey chuckled.

"Ever try to cure yourself?"

Linn laughed, a low laugh with an insulting purr in it.

"Try to cure myself?" Excitement blurred his words, but he kept his voice pitched very low. "Do you think I like being this way? Oh, yes, I've tried—and succeeded in making myself worse."

"Nonsense," Rainey said, and now the professional mellowness of his voice couldn't hide a sharp-edged undertone of annoyance. "A thing like that can be cured—if its owner is sound at bottom."

Linn's face flushed in the deepening twilight, and then paled again. He didn't say anything.

"I'll bet you," Rainey said, "one thousand dollars I can cure you."

Linn laughed in his throat, without enjoyment.

"It would be worth that and more," he said, "but—" He shrugged and asked: "Do you know what time the last mail goes out?"

"It's simple as can be," Rainey said. "Naturally you're afraid of water if you can't swim. Why shouldn't you be? It's a real enemy if you're help-less in it. But if you learn to swim, then where will your fear come from?"

Linn laughed again.

"Fair enough," he said softly, "but how in hell can a man learn to swim when more than a tubful of water turns him into a lunatic? Do you think I've gone all these years without trying to learn? Do you think I like burying my head under Pullman blankets when I hear the roar of a bridge under my train?"

"You've tried to swim, then, and couldn't?" Rainey insisted.

"Of course," Linn said wearily.

"How?"

"How? In the water, of course, going into the water."

"Going slowly in, with fear climbing up into your neck with each step?"

"Something of the sort."

"Exactly the wrong way," Rainey said triumphantly. "No wonder you're still scared silly."

"And how"—Linn's voice was tauntingly mild—"would you suggest going about it in the right way?"

"In the simplest, most sensible way, the way I learned. Listen, Linn, I'll cure you, absolutely, if you'll do what I say. I'll put five hundred dollars against your hundred that I can do it. Or if you don't want to bet I'll put a hundred dollars in either of these gentlemen's hands—yours if it doesn't work."

"How?"

"In the only sensible way. Go out with me in a boat tomorrow, and jump over in the middle of the lake. If you can't jump, let me throw you. You'll swim, no fear."

"My God," Linn said in an awed tone, "I believe you mean it."

"Certainly I mean it. Why shouldn't I mean it? And it'll work, too. You needn't be afraid of drowning. I'll be there to pull you out if necessary: I'm not exactly an infant in the water. But it's ten to one you won't need pulling out. Swimming isn't a mysterious thing: it's something that all animals do naturally and that a man can do naturally too when he needs to. You'll find yourself somehow moving back to the boat. Are you game?"

The corner of my left eye caught a movement. I turned my head to that side, but saw nothing now except the dark angle of the porch eight or ten feet from us, where it turned to run down the side of the building. I had the impression that somebody had looked, or had started to come, around the corner, and then, seeing us, had withdrawn.

"It isn't a question of gameness," Linn was protesting evenly. "It's simply that I know myself and my terror in water. I'm supposed to be resting just now. It seems foolish that I should tear my nerves to pieces—that's what it would amount to—just to disprove an old theory."

"Well, of course, if you're afraid to take a chance." Rainey shrugged his big shoulders.

"It's not that I'm afraid to." Linn's voice was thin and higher pitched than it had been. "But it's so useless. I've tried everything, and—"

"And you're used to being afraid," Rainey finished for him, bluntly. "Did it ever occur to you that everybody is more or less afraid of nearly everything, and that courage isn't a damned thing but a habit of not dodging things because you're afraid of them?"

Linn started to jump up out of his chair, and then sat there very erect. In the dim light from the window his face showed pale and shiny with sweat. He was trembling from foot to mouth.

"But," the promoter said, and yawned showily, "if you're really too scared to take a first-rate chance of curing yourself, I suppose there's nothing to be done about it."

Linn jumped up out of his chair now and cried angrily: "I tell you, it's more complicated than that. It's not simply a matter of driving myself to do something. That can be done. But it's the after-effect—whether it's worth it or not."

Rainey said, "Oh, hell!" and threw the remains of his cigar away. He stood up and looked contemptuously down at Linn. "It's all right with me," he said. He turned his broad back to Linn and addressed Metcalf and me: "Let's see if we can find a billiard table."

Linn put out a hand to Rainey's arm and turned the big man around.

"I'll take you up, Rainey," he said through lips that barely moved. "When shall we try it?"

Rainey grinned down at him and put a hand on his shoulder.

"That's sensible," he said. "That's damned sensible of you, Linn. Tomorrow's Sunday. Suppose we try it first thing in the morning."

Linn nodded without saying anything. His face was still angry.

Rainey said: "I don't suppose you've got a swimming suit. Well, I'll get you one, and we'll go off a little after breakfast. Don't worry about it. You'll see it'll be all right."

Linn nodded again.

Footsteps approached from the end of the porch. Metcalf and I stood as Mrs. Rainey came up. Her face was white at Linn's.

"Please, Mr. Linn," she said earnestly, "I wish you wouldn't. I don't think it's safe to tamper with yourself that way. I wish you'd think it over first, anyway. I honestly think you'd be wiser to let well enough alone."

There was an uncomfortable pause during which nobody could think of anything to say. Then Linn bowed awkwardly at Mrs. Rainey and said: "I think perhaps your husband is right, Mrs. Rainey." He spoke stiffly, and his face was flushed: he was embarrassed. "We'll see tomorrow. I'm—I'm really anxious now to try it." He bowed again. "You'll excuse me? I've some letters to get off." He turned toward the door.

Mrs. Rainey went with him, her hand on his arm, saying as she went: "Please, don't, Mr. Linn. I'd never—"

"My dear," Rainey called after her, not succeeding in altogether keeping the snarl out of his voice, "you mustn't intrude. It wasn't nice of you to eavesdrop."

She paid no attention at all to him.

He jerked himself up tall and straight, and took a step forward.

"Pauline," he called, and there wasn't anything in his tone except authority.

Mrs. Rainey turned her head over her shoulder as Linn opened the door. The light fell on her blonde hair and handsome face with its very tired blue eyes.

"Yes, dear," she said to her husband, smiled politely, and went into the hotel with Linn.

Rainey said: "Well, how about billiards?"

His game was terrible that night.

II

A little to the left of the hotel, a short concrete pier stuck out into the lake like a stubby finger pointing at the other shore. Fifteen or twenty of us—guests of the hotel, a hotel employee or two, a few men from the development company's camp, and some from the village—were on hand to watch the Rainey-Linn experiment the next morning.

The promoter, in red bathing suit and light overcoat, was on the pier when I got there. He was sitting on the railing, smoking a cigar and talking to Metcalf and some of his other hired men.

"Good morning," he said. I had missed him at breakfast. "A swell day, eh?"

"Yeah. Looks like you're going to have plenty of audience."

He chuckled in a satisfied way.

Presently Linn came out of the hotel, in a tan rep bath-robe that hung around his heels. Close behind him came Mrs. Rainey. She caught up with him and began talking to him, walking close to his side. Linn spoke stiffly to her as they came down the pebble walk to the pier. It was plain that she was still trying to persuade him to call the experiment off, and that her interest in it embarrassed him.

I looked at her husband. He was smiling jovially toward the approaching pair, but his blue eyes weren't as jolly as his mouth.

Linn and the woman came up to us. Linn's face was wan, with lines from nose-corners past mouth corners. His mouth was thin and so were his eyes. He kept his eyes on the pier in front of him, never letting them look either right or left, where he might see the water.

"All set?" Rainey greeted him in a loud, too hearty voice.

Linn said: "Yes."

Rainey took off his coat and handed it to Metcalf. In the red swimming suit he seemed larger than ever, a big sun-brown athlete. He had a little too much meat on him everywhere, but under that outer soft covering of flesh he had plenty of muscles everywhere.

Linn dropped his bath-robe on the pier. The suit he wore was a little too loose around the waist and beside Rainey's ruddy bulk he looked almost puny. Nevertheless he was compact and wiry, better set up than he had seemed in his clothes.

Rainey went down first to the boat tethered at the foot of a landing ladder.

"Come on," he called heartily.

That wasn't necessary, because Linn was already following him, but that was like Rainey.

Linn went down the ladder slowly. His knuckles showed tight and white on each rung. His eyes were open very little if at all. His lips moved in and out with his breathing. His face was sallow and damp.

Rainey took the oars. Linn sat in the stern facing him. When Rainey pulled the boat clear of the pier I saw Linn's ghastly frightened face bent toward the bottom of the boat. His eyes were screwed tight.

Rainey rowed the boat farther from the pier than was necessary, building up his act, of course. Linn did not once raise his head. His back was bent, tense, and small in comparison with the rowing promoter's bulk.

Mrs. Rainey was standing beside me, shivering. Twice she muttered something. The second time I thought it polite to say: "I beg your pardon?"

She laughed nervously.

"Talking to myself," she said. "Oh, I wish—"

She didn't finish her wish. She was staring with desperate eyes at the men in the boat, working her fingers together with a force that made one of her knuckles crack sharply.

The others of the audience had been standing around cracking jokes, trying to guess whether the experiment would be a success or not. The postmaster's son—a fidgety slim youth with a bright-eyed, cheerful, pimply face—had bet one of his companions a dollar that Linn would have to be dragged out of the lake. Nobody took the affair very seriously until it became apparent that Mrs. Rainey was so highly wrought up over it. Then the others began to catch her nervousness, so that by the time the boat stopped we were all quite tense.

Rainey shipped his oars and stood up. He looked like a living statue against the dark trees that bounded the lake on the other side, and I suppose he knew it. The lake was smooth and shiny.

Rainey said something to Linn. The smaller man stood up, facing the pier. His eyes were still shut, with a tightness that drew his brows down and wrinkled his forehead.

Rainey spoke again.

Linn nodded but did not move otherwise.

Rainey laughed and went on talking.

No sound of this came to us. All I could hear was the lapping of the water against the pier, the shuffling of feet among the audience, and Mrs. Rainey's breathing.

Linn bent forward quickly, and as quickly straightened himself again. His knees didn't look very steady.

He put his hands together in front of his chest, rubbing the back of his left nervously with the palm of his right. His eyes were clenched shut.

Rainey spoke again.

Linn nodded emphatically.

Rainey came up behind Lynn, and, in a confusion of flailing arms and legs, the smaller man went out over the side of the boat into the lake.

Mrs. Rainey screamed.

Standing with his legs far apart, Rainey steadied the violently rocking boat and looked down at the turmoil Linn was making in the lake.

The man in the water seemed to have a dozen arms and legs, and all of them working, beating the lake into white froth.

The man in the boat called some laughing thing down to the man in the water.

Linn's head, wet and black as a seal's, came up high out of the water and went down again in an upflung shower of white drops. His arms beat the lake into a whirlpool.

The man in the boat stopped laughing and called sharply to him, the words *head down* coming clear to us on the pier.

Mrs. Rainey had begun to pace up and down the edge of the pier, muttering to herself again. I heard her say something with the name of God in it.

Rainey called again into the lake, but with no effect on the boiling confusion there.

Linn's head came up high again, and he seemed to be trying to climb up into the air.

Then he plunged down and the water closed over him.

Mrs. Rainey had stopped running up and down the edge of the pier. She was standing beside me. Her fingers were digging into my arm. She was saying, "Oh, Oh, Oh!" softly and foolishly.

The black head of the man in the lake showed on the surface like the snout of a fish, and vanished, his white face not showing at all.

Rainey went out of the boat, into the lake in a short clean arc, as smoothly as if he had been poured into the water.

The next few seconds seemed like a lot of minutes—before the two heads came to the surface again.

They came up side by side.

Linn's arms came out of the water, flailing, beating the lake as if it was something he was fighting. They knocked spume high over his head.

Rainey caught Linn, let him go, caught him, let him go again.

They maneuvered around in the water, one smoothly, skillfully, the other crazily, violently.

Rainey was trying to get behind Linn, and failing.

Twice it looked as if Rainey had tried to hit Linn with a fist, to quiet him. Linn was twisting and turning and beating up too much water for the blows to be clearly seen, but if they landed they didn't do much good.

Linn was fighting now for a hold on Rainey.

Rainey's attempts to get a safe hold on Linn failed.

Rainey seemed to be tiring, moving slower around Linn now.

Mrs. Rainey's digging fingers had my arm sore by now. She was babbling excitedly, incoherently.

I turned my head to the others and asked: "Hadn't somebody better go help him?"

The postmaster's son jumped across the pier and disappeared down a ladder. Others, including Metcalf, followed him.

I remained with Mrs. Rainey, watching the two men in the water.

There was less confusion there now, and their heads were close together, but it didn't look as if Rainey had secured a very good safe-hold on Linn. However they were moving, if very slowly, in the direction of the empty boat.

The roar of a motor broke out below us, and a blunt boat carrying the postmaster's son, Metcalf, and two other men dashed away from the pier.

Mrs. Rainey screamed again and her fingers ground painfully into the bone of my arm. I looked quickly from the motor boat to where the men had been struggling in the water.

Neither Rainey nor Linn could be seen. The surface of the lake was smooth and shiny except where the motor boat cut it.

Then, after what seemed too many minutes to justify any guess except that both men had gone under for good, the water was broken close to the deserted boat, almost in the path of the motor boat. It was just a queer hump in the surface, as if something had struggled up almost to the top.

The motor boat sheered off. Men leaned over the side of it where the hump had showed. The boat and the men hid the spot from us.

The boat twisted again, slowing up, and bumped into the empty boat, lying far over into the water under the weight of the leaning men.

Presently we could see that they were lifting Linn aboard.

Rainey did not appear.

Metcalf took off his coat and shoes and went overboard, came up after a while, rested for a moment with one arm on the gunwale of the rowboat, and dived again.

One of the other men began diving.

The postmaster's son brought Linn to the pier in the motorboat. The others stayed in the rowboat, taking turns diving. Men from the pier in other boats joined them out there.

Linn was carried up to the hotel, and a doctor was called.

I took Mrs. Rainey up to the hotel and got rid of her by turning her over to the proprietor's wife. My arm was sore as hell.

Three-quarters of an hour later, when Linn had been drained of water, restored to semi-consciousness, and put to bed, the divers brought Rainey's body.

Nothing the doctors knew could bring him to life again.

He was dead.

MEN AND
WOMEN

COMMENTARY

The stories in this section treat what Hammett called "the relation between the sexes," a topic of particular interest to him throughout his writing career. In these stories, all told in the third person, his sympathies generally seemed to lie with women, whose emotional intelligence most often surpassed that of the men in their lives, who were often self-consumed and boastful in the early stories, independent and unwilling to commit to a permanent relationship in the later ones. In summer 1924, Hammett engaged in a debate on the merits of what he called the "sex story" with H. Bedford-Jones, a popular and prolific Canadian writer of adventure stories and science fiction, who wrote some ninety novels in addition to earning the title King of the Wood Pulps from Erle Stanley Gardner. Bedford-Jones wrote to *Writer's Digest* complaining about those authors who used sex to sell their stories. Hammett replied that he had written "altogether three stories that are what is sometimes called 'sex stuff' and two—or possibly three—that might be so-called if you stretched the term a bit." He refused to be cowed by Bedford-Jones's moralizing: "If you have a story that seems worth telling, and you think you can tell it worthily, then the thing for you to do is tell it, regardless of whether it has to do with sex, sailors, or mounted policemen."

"Seven Pages" exists in at least two original typescripts, one at the Ransom Center at the University of Texas, and the other in the private collection of the family of a Hammett girlfriend whom he worked with at Albert Samuels Jewelers from March to July 1926 and to whom he gave an early draft. The form of this apparently autobiographical piece is like that of two of his publications in the *Smart Set*—"The Great Lovers" (November 1922) and "From the Memoirs of a Private Detective" (March 1923)—seemingly disconnected vignettes. The references are to Hammett's adolescence in and around Baltimore in vignettes 3, 4, and 7; his days in 1920 as a detective in the Northwest in vignette 6; his early days in San Francisco, circa 1922, in vignettes 1 and 2. The woman in vignette 5 is a mystery.

"The Breech Born" also has all the characteristics of one of Hammett's *Smart Set* pieces from the early 1920s, but there is some evidence that it may have been written a couple of years later. The two-page typescript has crumbled at the top edges, so a few words, supplied here in brackets, are missing from the end of the story, and there is no return address. On the back of the typescript are pages from a heavily edited working draft of "The Big Knockover," published in *Black Mask* in February 1927. "The Breech Born" features a goofy self-absorbed poet not unlike Robin Thin, the amusingly sensitive poet-detective who appeared in two Hammett stories, "The Nails in Mr. Cayterer" (*Black Mask*, January 1926) and "A Man Named Thin," apparently written about the same time but not published until March 1961, after Hammett's death. Hammett himself tried his hand at light verse. Three of his poems were published, first in the *Lariat* in November 1925 and later in *The Stratford Review* in March and June 1927.

Both "The Lovely Strangers," and "Week--End," which follows, seem to have been written for the slick-paper magazine market. Hammett's standard caption at the top for the pulps "First American Serial Rights Offered" has been crossed out in both instances. "The Lovely Strangers" is a rare attempt by Hammett to write the sort of romance comedy associated with the *Saturday Evening Post*. The characters are more or less sophisticated, and the plot, at least as old as Shakespeare, involves a couple of destined but reluctant lovers, he a news reporter and she a wealthy industrialist, who spar verbally to mask their feelings toward one another. Love outs, true to formula, as the reporter saves his lady from a predator interested only in her money.

"Week--End," which dates from late 1926, features a young unmarried woman traveling to San Francisco to meet and share a room with her boyfriend, who treats the situation with disturbing familiarity. The subject matter would have been considered daring at the time. In the typescript the title words are suggestively separated by two hyphens, providing added weight to the word "End." It is the type of story associated with Hemingway, with much of the narrative implied rather than explicitly stated, though it predates "Hills Like White Elephants," for example, by a year. Like most of Hammett's "sex stories" his sympathies are with the woman, though his depiction of Harry as a man unwilling to commit to a typical domestic relationship is characteristic.

"On the Way" is one of two stories in this collection published during Hammett's lifetime (the other is "The Diamond Wager"), and it is one of his most poignant. Set in Hollywood among the moviemaking community, where Hammett was spending much of his time in the early 1930s, "On the Way" is about a man who realizes that relationships are impermanent, especially in Hollywood, and who is strong enough to face the truth of his situation. It can be paired with "This Little Pig" (*Collier's*, 1934), his only other story about Hollywood moviemakers.

SEVEN PAGES

One

She was one of the rare red-haired women whose skins are without blemish: she was marble, to the eye. I used to quote truthfully to her, "Thou art all fair, my love; there is no spot in thee." She was utterly unpractical. One otherwise dreary afternoon she lay with her bright head on my knee while I read Don Marquis' *Sonnets to a Red-Haired Lady* to her. When I had finished she made a little purring noise and stared dreamily distant-eyed past me. "Tell me about this Don Marquis," she said. "Do you know him?"

Two

I sat in the lobby of the Plaza, in San Francisco. It was the day before the opening of the second absurd attempt to convict Roscoe Arbuckle of something. He came into the lobby. He looked at me and I at him. His eyes were the eyes of a man who expected to be regarded as a monster but was not yet inured to it. I made my gaze as contemptuous as I could. He glared at me, went on to the elevator still glaring. It was amusing. I was working for his attorneys at the time, gathering information for his defense.

Three

We would leave the buildings in early darkness, walk a little way across the desert, and go down into a small canyon where four trees grouped around a level spot. The night-dampness settling on earth that had cooked since morning would loose the fragrance of ground and plant around us. We would lie there until late in the night, our nostrils full of world-smell, the trees making irregular map-boundary divisions among the stars. Our love seemed dependent on not being phrased. It seemed if one of us had said, "I love you," the next instant it would have been a lie. So we loved and cursed one another merrily, ribaldly, she usually stopping her ears in the end because I knew more words.

Four

He came into the room in brown stocking-feet, blue policeman's pants, and gray woolen undershirt. "Who the hell moved that pi-ano?" he demanded, and grunted and cursed while wheeling it back into the inconvenient corner from which we had dragged it. "It's my pi-ano, and it stays where I put it, see," he assured us before he went out again. His daughters were quite embarrassed, since Jack and I had bought the whisky that was in him, so they didn't object when, just before we left, we took all the pictures down from the walls and stacked them behind the pi-ano. That was in the part of Baltimore called Pig Town, a few blocks from another house where we had found one night two in the

company who would not drink alcohol. We gave them root beer into
which had been put liberal doses of aromatic cascara.

Five

I talked to her four times. Each time she complained of her husband.
He was ruining her health, he was after her all the time, this supergoat,
he simply would not let her alone. I supposed he was nearly, if not
altogether, impotent.

Six

The fat cook and I huddled to the fire that had thawed him out of his
vomiting blue cold-sickness. Behind us the Coeur d'Alene mountains
rose toward Montana, down below us a handful of yellow lights marked
a railway stop. Perhaps it was Murray: I've forgotten. "You're crazier
than hell, that's what!" the fat cook said. "Any lousy bastard that says
Cabell ain't a romantycist is crazier than hell!" "He's not," I insisted. "He's
anti-romanticist: all he's ever done for romance is take off its clothes
and laugh at it. He's a romanticist just like Mencken's a Tory, which is
just like the wooden horse was a Trojan." The fat cook bunched his lips
and spat brownly at the fire. "Grease us twice, Slim!" he complained.
"If you ain't a son-of-a-gun for damn-fool arguments!"

Seven

In Washington, D.C., I worked for a while in a freight depot. On my
platform were two men who worked together, sweeping out cars, re-
pairing broken crates, sealing doors. One of them was a man of fifty-
something with close-clipped gray hair on a very round head. He was a
small man but compact. He boasted of the hardness of his skull and

told stories of butting duels, head-top crashed against head-top until blood came from noses, mouths, ears. His mate told me privately he thought these combats degrading. "It's being no better than animals," he said. This mate of the butter was a younger man, a country-man, brown-skinned and awkward. He who boasted the hard gray head told me this country-man had a fly tattooed on his penis. Gray-head thought this disgusting. "I'd think it'd make his wife sick to her stomach," he said.

THE BREECH-BORN

He came backward out of the womb, causing a great deal of trouble to himself, his mother and the attending medical craftsmen. And that was the curse on him, not, as his father, a barber eternally irritated because in the twenty years of barbering he had learned no practicable way of keeping short hairends from sifting through his clothes, said, his becoming a poet. This was merely a manifestation of it. He toiled conscientiously at his verse, sitting day and night over dictionary, thesaurus, rhyming dictionary—that invaluable book in which one finds so readily that there is no acceptable rhyme for the word one has in mind. His poetry was not bad poetry, nor was it good—and that of course is the sort of poetry that makes most trouble for everyone, especially for the poet. After the first of it was published he left his home, thoughtlessly, and went to New York.

There, in keeping with the curse on him, he met a girl. He loved her quite passionately, and wrote her long and fervent poems, which painted her in such gay colors that she resigned herself to holding his admiration by never letting him become intimate enough to know that she wasn't quite all he said. After some months of this self-defeating courtship, he sat down to write her a letter which should quite overwhelm her. He worked on the letter for eight days, though it was not a lengthy letter. He polished each phrase until it was perfect. The letter was so good that reading it he was tempted to narcissism.

Not having heard from him for eight days, the girl's love for him overcame her liking for his admiration, and she determined to go to his room one night, even if she had to break an engagement with her employer, an extremely wealthy hat manufacturer of no matrimonial connections or intentions. But that afternoon the poet's letter arrived. Reading it, she saw herself as something greater than she had ever supposed. Her already adequate beauty heightened by this letter, her confidence upholstered, she went forth to the engagement with the affluent employer, and not only convinced him that she had thought his intentions honorable, but convinced him that they might well be.

For a week the poet waited, for an answer to his letter, while what little money he had left dwindled. That week the girl was too busy accumulating a trousseau, though, to write the poet, which she finally did, inviting him to the house, meaning to thank him for the help he had given her. He walked the streets for that week, unable to write poetry because everything in him had gone in the letter. [He went] without food all day [spending] his last money [on a bouquet of flowers for her. The] emptiness of his stomach brought on hiccoughs as he entered [into her] presence. The fervent speeches with which he customarily greeted her were thus jumbled, so that he gave up talking as hopeless, presented his flowers, and knelt to kiss the toe of her shoe. Somewhat startled, thinking because of his hiccoughs that he was probably drunk, she jerked her foot in surprise, kicking his mouth, breaking out two front teeth, which, entangled in a hiccough, lodged in the neighborhood of his larynx and choked him quite to death. In falling he managed to upset the goldfish and to mash the flowers into the carpet.

THE LOVELY STRANGERS

They ran into one another in front of Parson's drug store, literally, with a violence that brought grunts from both of them and scattered every which way the photographs at which she had been looking as she stepped into the street.

"Good Lord, Joan!" Thus the young man exclaimed, putting his hat straight above a jovial round face, "if you can't look where you're walking, why don't you walk where you're looking?"

The young woman's green-brown eyes were of a height with his light ones. Her eyes were not in any way jovial.

"Oughtn't we dance now? Or sing a song?" she asked unpleasantly. "Tom Ware, I've heard that line at least a dozen times in vaudeville shows!"

"Uh-huh, that's where I got it. It would fit better if you were cockeyed, but it went pretty good at that, didn't it?"

The young woman looked at his cheerful pink face with that special feminine look whose synonyms are a slight sidewise shaking of the head or a heavily breathed "Such a man!" Then she shrugged and turned to the photographs on the street. He stooped to help her, but in his assistance there was a noticeable unwillingness to take unfair competitive advantage of her sex. When they straightened together from their task the damp and gritty pictures—for a twilight shower and tracking feet had begrimed the sidewalk—were quite equitably divided between them.

She frowned at her share, and of the seven clicks known to phoneticians the one she made with tongue and teeth was most eloquent of disapproval.

"The only picture I've ever been able to get of him!" she complained, holding up a print whose back and edges were stained with mud which, in the red glow from the druggist's window, had the complexion of half-dried blood. "And all the trouble I had getting it! And now, just because you're so clumsy—look at it!"

With that easy-going tolerance of feminine displeasure attained completely only by him who has had sisters of his own, the young man ignored all but the last three of her words, and took the photograph from her hand.

It was a snapshot of a personable dark man of forty-something, slender in loose tweeds, posed against a tree. He was looking down, this tall and graceful man, into the raised bright face of a small girl of perhaps eighteen who sat on a knobbed root at his feet.

"Ah, the handsome fiancé and his daughter!"

"Of course Maud had to tell you!" The young woman was irritable. "But didn't she tell you it wasn't to be bellowed out on street corners?"

The young man could have replied truthfully that he hadn't bellowed, but he seemed, despite his grinning amiability, not at all pacifically inclined.

What he said was: "If you're ashamed of it what are you engaged to him for?" And: "You needn't think you can mother-in-law me, even if you are going to marry him. I'm not in the Hannibal family."

"No?" It was not a question. "One might think you were, from the frequency with which one hears of your being up there."

"Oh, does one? Well, one might put another tally on one's list, because one is on one's way up there now. I'm like you, Joan: the home talent is nice enough in its way, but when lovely strangers come, then's when I polish the curling iron and reach for the beauty clay."

The young woman's eyebrows raised indifferent arcs over her decidedly not interested eyes. She put out a hand for the photographs he held. He grinned at her eyebrows and avoided her hand.

"The negatives are all right." He held up the yellow envelope that had protected its contents from the street. "I'll have fresh copies made for you."

"Thanks, but I'd rather you didn't. I'd rather be sure that none of them gets into your precious *Weekly Leader* under one of your quaint—is that the word?—captions."

"*My Leader*! Old Ahearn will tell you whose *Leader* it is! And he'll tell you what a fat chance you've got of ever seeing your picture in it as long as your brick plant, or whatever it is, has its printing done out of town!"

"The policy of the Robson Portland Cement Corporation has nothing—"

"Now don't make a speech! Old Ahearn wouldn't print it, even if I had a pencil. The trouble is, Joan"—the young man's voice sank into kindly, brotherly, key—"as I used to tell you when you were a kid whose stockings were always coming down and always trying to get into a ball game and making a nuisance of yourself generally just because you were a Robson of the Robson furniture factory, or whatever it is—the trouble is you're pig-headed! You think everybody ought to give you your own way all the time, and that's not good for you.

"Now I'm a poor boy who'll have to hock his etiquette guide and maybe miss a lunch to pay for these photos, but I'm going to do it. I don't care how many fertilizer works, or whatever they are, your father left you. No she-millionaire can jump me through hoops just because she—"

The majority stockholder of the Robson Portland Cement Corporation achieved the emphatic perpendicularity of a brown rep exclamation mark.

"Really, I didn't mean to provoke all this," she said into the middle —or, since he seemed in full course, perhaps only the beginning—of the young man's harangue. "You may do as you wish."

She smiled at him, a thin formal smile of parting, smiled across the street at Judge Eastwood raising his hat, and walked away from the young man. Watching her walk away, putting his half of the soiled photographs in his pocket, going into the drug store to leave the negatives, he carried himself as one who has no cause for dissatisfaction.

The Hannibal residence—too newly the Hannibal residence not to be still the Magruder place in local geography—occupied the top of China Hill. The house was large, of red brick. Its roof pitched sharply here, gently there, but each divergent green-slated plane ran finally into smooth agreement with the massed trees and bushes that gave house and grounds the British air of seclusion frequently found in California.

From the top of China Hill, in daytime, a river could be seen joining San Francisco Bay. At night, a cloudy night—with the moon a vague light hint among clouds that lagged behind the earlier shower—such as this one on which the young man who had so enjoyed an encounter in front of a drug store climbed the hill, nothing five feet away could be seen.

So when the young man was suddenly booed at from a bush, he jumped straight up off the clayey road, made an inarticulate sound, and flung both arms at the boo. A girl came laughing into his arms.

"That's one time you thought the devil had you, Mr. Thomas Ware!"

He found her face in the darkness, tilted it, kissed it, asked it: "Didn't she?"

A tap came out of the night to settle on his cheek, a laugh with it. "Impudent!"

They went on up the hill together, locked hands swinging between them, toward the cluster of jagged bright gold scraps that blind and trees made out of a window's light. Before they had reached the house she bore off to the left, leading him through a gap in the hedge.

"We're dodging the Papa tonight."

"What's the matter with him now?" There was no especial curiosity in the young man's voice, and what stress was there was on the "now."

"He's taking a fatherly interest in me again." Her tone deepened into mimicry of a precise male voice. "There was no point to our coming here, Maud, if you are not going to do your part. The climate alone will do little. If you are going to get no more rest, keep no earlier hours, we might as well have staid in Europe. Look out for the step," she added in her own voice.

The dim cube into which she led him materialized as a small summer house.

"That's nothing to what you'll be in for when your new step-mother is installed," he predicted genially as they sat down.

"The model Joan." The words were low-spoken, indecisively critical. "I don't know how I'm going to like her as a member of the family. She seems nice enough, but— Do you think we'll hit it off together, Tom?"

"I guess so. She's not a bad sort, considering. Spoiled, all right, but under that she's not so bad, I guess."

"Pretty, too," Maud suggested. "May I have a cigarette?"

The match he struck brought her out of the night: a small girl in rough tan sweater, dark eyes incredibly older than the dark face in which they glowed: the girl who had sat on the knobbed root in the snapshot.

The light went out, leaving only their voices and the metallic-red discs of their cigarettes.

"How is it you've never been in love with her, Tom? Or have you?"

The end of his cigarette burned bright under his laugh.

"You've never seen us together except in company where we had to behave. Joan and I fight fine—always did."

"That doesn't necessarily—"

A vibrant baritone called from the direction of the house: "Maud!"

Her cigarette raised a transitory tuft of small stars as it hit the floor, and was blotted out by her foot.

"Papa!" she whispered. "Now I'll catch it! I'll head him off, go up to my room, and sneak out again. Wait for me!"

"Maud!" The calling voice was nearer.

She was a shadow in the door and then only a crunching of gravel on the walk. The young man darkened his cigarette under his foot and sat still.

"Oh!" The syllable was sharp, startled. Then, glibly: "I was just coming in."

"I thought you had gone to your room, honey." The man's words were thick, tremulous with an excitement out of all reasonable proportion to their import. "But you weren't there when I went up, and. . . ."

His words ran down into a muttered crooning.

Above the crooning Maud cried out: "No! No!"

The young man in the summer house got up and went to the door. The moon eluded the last lingering cloud-fringe and spread down on China Hill a pallor that was as the light of noonday after the night's darkness.

A dozen feet from the door Hannibal held Maud to him with tight arms and beat kisses down on her whitely furious face and throat. Her fists pummeled his shoulders.

"Tom's there!" she screamed into his distorted face. "Tom's there, you fool!"

It was late morning in the *Weekly Leader* office. Tom Ware was condensing a National Geographic Society bulletin on the distinctions between, and proper uses of, coca, cacao, cocoa, and coco into an informative paragraph that would fill out an otherwise incomplete column in some future issue. The typewriter clicked irregularly under his fingers: his right hand was encumbered by a crisscross of adhesive tape. On the other side of the room, old Ahearn—stringy and colorless, even to the eyes that distrusted everything through spectacle lenses hardly larger than dimes—worked with scissors and paste-pot on a pile of the *Leader*'s contemporaries.

The street door opened and two strangers came in. One of them carried a camera, the other an overcoat.

"We want," this second one said without preliminary, "more dope on the prince—something to spread over a couple of pages in the Saturday magazine section."

The proprietor of the Robson *Weekly Leader* examined his visitors carefully, and when he spoke it was in the manner of one who engages a burglar in conversation while his fingers search under his pillow for the police whistle.

"The prince? H-m-m. What prince? Be definite."

"What prince?" the man with the overcoat repeated blankly. "Why the Russian—the one you sent in the story about."

He pulled a newspaper from his pocket—a San Francisco afternoon paper's early edition—and spread it on the desk, thumping a certain part of it with his forefinger.

"If you're drunk," old Ahearn threatened, "I'll see that your city editor hears about it."

He stabbed his paste brush into the inkwell, adjusted his too-small glasses to the indicated news item, and read it slowly and thoroughly.

"H-m-m," he said when he was through. "And I sent that in?"

"Absolutely!"

Old Ahearn said, "H-m-m," again, and his chair squeaked as he twisted around to look at the young man who was applying himself to his work just now with ostentatious devotion.

"Mr. Ware, can I take you from your work for a moment?"

The young man rattled his typewriter irregularly to the end of the immediate sentence, tapped the period smartly in place, and got up saying, "Certainly, Mr. Ahearn," with all the urbanity befitting one who for the first time had been mistered by his superior.

"Read this," old Ahearn commanded, thrusting the newspaper at him.

Tom Ware read the newspaper with as wholehearted an attention as had his employer, and with some additional thing that might have been fondness in his eyes.

The newspaper told of Prince Grigori Rostopchin, cousin to no less a personage than that Grand Duke Kyrill, or Cyril, who claimed the vacant czardom, or tsardom, of Russia. It told of Prince Grigori's separation from his cousin's court in Coburg and of his coming to America, to Robson, intent on using his considerable remaining millions to create in the new world an estate that would be so far as humanly possible a duplicate of the ones he had lost in the old. It told of the many acres he had bought and was buying, of the game he had imported to stock his forests, of the castle he was building. It told of the twenty Russian peasants who had arrived in Robson the previous day, forerunners of many more to come as speedily as the United States immigration restrictions would permit.

There was no photograph of the faithful muzhiks who had followed their hereditary lord to his new home, but there was one—apparently an enlarged snapshot—of Prince Grigori Rostopchin and his daughter. He was a tall man slenderly erect against a tree. She was a small girl who sat on a knobbed root at his feet.

"Pretty nice," Tom said as he returned the paper to his employer. "You get tired of all the time reading about dukes sweeping streets and countesses working in laundries."

Old Ahearn smiled the smile of a Borgia out of Dumas.

"Then you like it, Mr. Ware?"

The young man's face was bland. He gestured depreciatively with his bandaged hand.

"Of course, modesty— But I really don't think it's so awfully bad."

"A fake, huh?" the man with the overcoat demanded. "There isn't any prince?"

"I got the last name out of the back of the dictionary," Tom confessed. "He wasn't a prince, and anyway he's dead."

"And the picture?" the man with the overcoat went to the bottom of the hoax.

Old Ahearn slapped one hand down on his desk and recognition was in the colorless eyes with which he glared through small lenses at the photograph.

"That's Hannibal!" he declared. "That's exactly who it is!"

The man with the camera, hitherto silent, made a strangling noise deep in his throat and his face turned red.

"Aren't you ashamed of yourself?" he reproved his companion. "Not recognizing dear old Hannibal! I suppose," he yelled savagely at old Ahearn, "the girl is Queen Dido! Come on, Gus, let's get the hell out of here."

They went out, banging the door behind them.

Old Ahearn took a limp roll of paper money out of his pocket. He counted off some bills and recounted them carefully, though they were too few to make error likely.

"Here's what's coming to you. Now get!"

As the young man took his wages the door opened again and another man who was not of Robson and who carried a copy of a San Francisco afternoon paper came in. He was short and fat, his eyes were blue and placatory, his jaw was pugnaciously undershot.

"Where'll I find this Ro-stop-chin fellow?" he asked. "Nobody seems to know much about him."

"You've come to the right place, brother," old Ahearn told him cordially, "you certainly have. You'll find your Ro-stop-chin fellow right in this office." He aimed a stringy finger at Tom Ware. "Right in that fellow's head. He can tell you all you want to know about His Imaginary Highness, but he'll tell you outside, because I'm not going to have him hanging around here another second."

"Kind of peeved," the stranger remarked when he and Tom were on the sidewalk.

"You notice it, too?" Mirth went out of the young man's eyes and he looked dubiously at the other. "He's right, though, about that story being all in my head."

The fat man seemed neither disappointed nor surprised.

"I knew it was in somebody's," he said, "but the photo's not phoney."

"No." Eagerness came into the young man's light eyes. "That's Vincent Hannibal. You want to see him?"

"Yeah, if I can find him without wasting too much time."

"It won't take any time at all. He lives up on China Hill. You can't miss the house—a big red one on the top of the hill. Go straight up Broadway to the end of the paving and then take the left-hand road up the hill. Are you—?"

"I think maybe I can do business with him. Now where could I find you if I wanted to talk something over with you?"

"I live around the corner on Second Street—215. I'll wait there for you, if you want. Do—?"

"Yeah, do that. I won't be long."

The little fat man climbed into a black touring car, flicked a stubby hand at Tom, and turned the car up Broadway.

At the window of his boarding-house room Tom Ware sat for a while, smoking cigarettes and grinning at the spire of the Methodist church across the street. After a while he stopped grinning, and when he had returned his watch to his pocket for the sixth time he began to fidget in his chair. A little later he got up to walk around the room. He was definitely pacing the floor when he heard his landlady's thin voice on the stairs.

She brought the little fat man whose eyes and chin disagreed to Tom's door. The young man welcomed him warmly, insisted on his taking the rocking chair, and asked: "Did you find him?"

"Better close the door," his visitor suggested. Then: "Didn't have any trouble at all finding the place. Now what can you tell me about this Hannibal?"

Tom hesitated, looking at the man and away from him. The man said, "Oh!" and gave Tom a white card, which read:

William F. Roth
Roth-Radford Detective Agency
420 Carney Building
San Francisco, California

"Maybe I ought to give you a little dope on what's what," the detective said when the young man looked up from the card. "This fellow that you know as Hannibal has been known to marry women that had a dollar or two put away. One of 'em died in an accident. Some folks say one thing and some another, but it's a fact that the district attorney back there would like to see him, and the woman's relations are spending good money trying to find him."

The detective's card was a mangled thing in the young man's hand, and his young man's eyes were hot things in his face.

"So that's what he's up to! He— You got him, did you?"

"Whoah!" Roth ordered over an upheld thick hand. "You haven't spoken your little piece yet—what you know about him and why you wrote that piece for the papers."

"I was up there last night. I go up there now and then." The words were tumbling out of the young man's mouth before he sat down on the bed facing his guest. "We were sitting out in the summer house, because she was supposed to be in bed. And he came out there, not knowing I was there, and—"

The stream of words stopped. He squirmed on the bed, his face boyish with pink puzzlement.

"He kissed her, Mr. Roth, but it wasn't like a father would kiss a daughter. It was—"

"You surprise me," the detective said placidly. "But I get you. Go on. What happened next?"

"Next he saw me—she told him I was there. Then he got mad. He said some things and I guess I said some things, and anyway—" He stopped to look at his bandaged knuckles. "I was sorry afterward that I hit him, but now I'm glad of it. And then he had a gun, only Maud wouldn't let him use it, and she"—he flushed as if at a humiliating memory—"she sent me away. And that's all that happened up there."

The detective rubbed his undershot chin with stubby fingers and suggested: "And that led up to the newspaper story."

"Yes. I came down the hill thinking what a mess it was for Jo—for all of us to be mixed up in, and I got to thinking about his carrying a gun in his own home. And I remembered something else that—that I'd heard somewhere, about his not liking to have his picture taken and only having one taken since he came up here. And, putting those things together, it looked like he might be a crook or hiding something.

"So I thought that if I could get his picture published in some newspapers, maybe some of the people who were hunting for him—if anybody was—would recognize him. If they didn't, maybe he'd see the picture and think he'd better clear out.

"I happened to have that picture of him and his daughter. I got it— I picked it up off the sidewalk. So I came up here and lay across the bed and thought up that Russian prince story. Newspapers like that kind of stuff, and I had to have something that would be copied by other papers, with the photograph, in case the first paper didn't bring results. And I was afraid to take a chance on a wild story that would give Hannibal a come-back—libel or something of the sort—if I was wrong.

"So I wrote that Russian story. I went down to the *Leader* office and wrote it that night, and put it on the 3:50 train for San Francisco, sending it to the paper that old Ahearn is local correspondent for. I knew they'd swallow it, coming from the *Leader*."

"And why?"

"Why what?"

"Exactly why," Roth explained, "did you go to all that trouble to tip Hannibal's mitt?"

Tom Ware looked away from the questioning blue eyes, looked carefully at familiar things in the room.

"Well," finally and lamely, "I didn't want to see him get away with anything if he was a crook."

Amusement flickered in the detective's mild eyes.

"Well, what would you say, my boy, if I told you Hannibal cleared out early this morning?"

"Good riddance! But I wish you had caught him."

Roth leaned forward to put a hand on Tom's knee.

"And if I told you that the young lady whose name you've taken so much trouble not to mention went with them?"

"Joan!"

"Now there's no use tearing your collar," the little fat man protested as he stood up. "I tell you what: suppose you take a run into the city with me. Maybe I can use you, and maybe you'll be in on the finish."

"You think they're there?"

"Might be. Suppose your run-in last night stirred him up? Scared him into clinching his game with the young lady before you could tell her about the doings? Maybe he's been too busy with that to read any newspapers. Anyway, I got a couple of ideas I want to try out."

A thin man with a thin freckled nose joined them when the ferry from Oakland put them in San Francisco an hour and a half later. Roth introduced the thin man as Mr. McBride.

"Everything covered. Nothing stirring," McBride said as he climbed into the car.

They took Tom to the Roth-Radford offices, gave him a newspaper and a chair, and left him alone while the hands of a wall-clock exhausted their repertoire of angles.

Then McBride came in.

"Yup!" he said. "Let's go!"

In the street, Tom, Roth, and McBride got into Roth's car.

"Where are they? Is she with them?" Tom asked. "Have you found them?"

Roth patted his shoulder.

"Don't crowd us," he begged. "You'll see it all."

The car crept through the traffic of Market Street, turned off to the right for the greater speed of a side street, turned back to the left, and set them down at the Polk Street entrance of the Municipal Building. An elevator carried them to the third floor, where a sallow man stood among a litter of cigarette stubs.

"Your meat's in there."

He nodded at a frosted glass door, gold-labeled:

302

COUNTY CLERK

MARRIAGE LICENSE

D E P A R T M E N T

Roth opened the door, McBride at his shoulder, Tom and the sallow man close behind.

On opposite sides of a table, Joan and Hannibal worked with scratchy pens on printed forms. Maud Hannibal stood beside Joan, saying some laughing thing. Hannibal's back was to the door. He looked around when Joan and Maud, seeing Tom Ware, gasped together. But by then Roth was close to Hannibal on one side, McBride on the other.

"Hello, Allender!" Roth greeted him. "We're a committee of plenty to persuade you to go back to the old homestead in Nixon."

Hannibal stood up, tall and dark, facing Roth.

"I beg your pardon?" he said.

McBride's hands ran nimbly across Hannibal's hips. Hannibal spun around—too late. McBride was pocketing the square black pistol he had flicked out of the tall man's pocket.

"A tough break, Allender," McBride sympathized.

"Allender?" Restrained angry impatience was in Hannibal's voice. "My name is not Allender."

"Of course not," Roth agreed to his back. "But that's the name you used in Nixon, so that's the way the indictment reads, Ferguson."

Hannibal turned to face Roth again.

Tom Ware was looking at Joan. Joan's eyes were wide and dazed and not definitely focused on anything. One of her hands lay palm-down on the wet ink of the form she had been filling in. Beside her, Maud stood tense, watching Hannibal. On the other side of the room three clerks gaped over their counter.

"My name," Hannibal spoke deliberately, "is Vincent Hannibal. You need not take my word for it. I can furnish you—"

"Sure, you can prove it," Roth agreed again. "But that's nothing. I can prove you're Prince Grigori Ro-stop-chin. How do you like that?"

Hannibal frowned in sincere puzzlement.

Maud spoke: "This is ridiculous. The idea of—"

"Now! Now!" McBride protested, looking down his thin freckled nose at her. "We're only trying to break your husband of his marrying habits, Mrs. Ferguson."

Rage burned in her eyes, twisted her mouth viciously crooked.

"Why you big tramp!" she snarled. "You—"

"Maud!" Hannibal called sharply.

Her hands fell off her hips, her mouth straightened, and she became a small girl of perhaps eighteen again.

Joan Robson stood up, leaning over the hand that smeared her marriage license application, staring at Maud Hannibal with green-brown eyes wherein stupid incredulity was dying.

"Don't let this disagreeable affair alarm you, Joan," Hannibal said smoothly. "I shall see that someone pays for it."

She did not show that she had heard him. Her eyes were still on Maud, and her eyes were as if Maud's mask of girlishness had not been put on again.

Roth stepped back to put his mouth to Tom Ware's ear.

"Get her out of here," he whispered. "We want to take this guy back to Nixon. We don't want the local people holding him on any two-for-a-cent charges. Get her out and keep her quiet, and there'll be no need for her being mixed up in it."

Tom went around to Joan's side.

"Come on, Joan," he said. "Let's get out of this."

"Come on, Joan," he had to repeat. He took her arm and led her toward the door. She went with neither volition nor unwillingness.

"Wait, Joan!" Hannibal exclaimed, and started toward her.

Roth stopped him by the effective if painful means of a foot solidly down on his instep. Hannibal cursed as Tom and Joan went out of the room.

"I'd—I'd like to sit down," she said as they were going down the street steps.

He found a vacant bench facing a fountain across the street. She sat in the middle of the bench, upright, staring with round eyes just now peculiarly flat at the water tumbling in the shape of a white dwarfed weeping willow tree. He sat near one end of the bench, lighted a cigarette, and looked uneasily from cigarette to her profile. He had the nervous manner of a man who hopes there isn't going to be a scene.

"It's a wonder," she said presently, not at all in the properly grateful tone of delivered to deliverer, "you didn't wait until we were married! It would have been just like you! Letting me make a f-fool of myself all this time, and never saying a word!"

"Aw, Joan—" He broke off as she made a little swallowing sound. "How'd I know you were going to be in such a hurry to land him?" he growled.

"I believe you did know it! I believe you wanted me to marry him! I believe you made him do it!"

The young man thus undeservedly credited with Machiavellian cunning, in addition to early knowledge of the truth about Hannibal, blinked rapidly, but he kept quiet while she went on: "He—he came over early this morning and had Aunt Alice wake me, and he said he had a cablegram that his business associate in Vienna was dead, and he'd have to go there immediately, and couldn't get back for at least six months. And he insisted on my marrying him here today and going with him. And he talked so—so wonderfully about it that I gave in. We'd have to take a train for New York this afternoon, he said, so there wasn't time to think much about it, and I didn't tell Aunt Alice because she never liked him anyhow, and she would have raised Cain. And I believe you're at the bottom of it, Tom Ware. I believe you did something, or said something, to hurry him into it! You did, you know you did!"

Her eyes were no longer flatly dull. They were shiny with moisture that was beginning now to sparkle on the lashes.

Desperate truculence showed in the young man's face.

"Suppose I did know all about him," he demanded with unnecessary bitterness, "was there any good of my saying anything? You know how pig-headed you are!"

Anger whisked the moisture out of her eyes, and with the going of the moisture he seemed more at ease, more comfortable on the bench.

"Well, you can laugh at me as much as you like," she snapped at him, "and you can invite all Robson to laugh with you. But you needn't think I'll be there to see it."

"Now what are you up to?"

"You don't think I'm going back there to be the butt of the town, do you? You don't think I want to see your grinning face every time I put my head out of the house, do you?"

"Aw, don't be a chump!" he remonstrated. He sat up and took her arm. "Suppose we pretend you knew about him all the time? That both of us were stringing him along trying to get the goods on him?"

She pulled her arm away.

"That would be wonderful! I'd enjoy spending the rest of my life at your mercy, listening to your private jokes whenever I couldn't keep out of your way, and knowing that you could make me the laughing-stock of the town whenever the notion happened to strike you."

She stood up and smoothed her coat.

"And, besides, how many people would be fooled? No, thanks! I'm going to say good-bye to Robson. I've already said it. I'm away and I'm going to stay away. I'm sorry to spoil your little joke, but you know how contrary and pig-headed I am."

The young man held out a foot and looked at it, and as he looked, scowling a little, his face slowly reddened. His mouth jerked twice before words came out, but they came carelessly enough at last.

"If it'd do you any good, Joan, you could marry me and take me back to Robson."

She was standing with her face toward the Library, across the Civic Center. She looked at him without turning her head, a sidewise moving of the green-brown irises that crowded them into the corners of her eyes. He did not look up.

"That would serve both of us right," she said scornfully. "But exactly what possible good could it do me?"

He turned his foot so that more of the shoe's toe came into the field of his intent vision, and he spoke with an absence of enthusiasm that could hardly have been managed except consciously.

"Everybody knows that only lovers save maidens from villains." He chuckled here with mild derision. "Married to me, you'll be the rescued heroine of a romance—instead of a comic character." The second chuckle was harshly derisive. "And in a couple of days you'll have yourself believing the same thing. Then you'll have the advantage over me that a woman always has over a man who went to much trouble to get her. You'll be safely on top. Any joking I try to do about Hannibal will fall flat. You'll be firmly convinced that I turned myself inside-out trying to save you from him so I could win you for myself."

Her eyes burned darkly. She caught lip between teeth and jerked around to face him. He would not look up from his shoe. Her eyes narrowed. Coldness replaced the heat in them. She left off biting her lip and her mouth became straight and firm.

"You're sure it will work out that way?" she asked calmly.

"Sure!" He was studying the other foot now. "All these down-trodden husbands you see got that way from putting a high value on their wives in the early days, and letting their wives find it out. It's sure dynamite."

"Are you sure"—her voice was soft but her eyes were not—"that m-marrying me won't inconvenience you?"

"Hardly any." Now the young man looked up at her, and his face was without guile. "Old Ahearn fired me this morning, and I've got nothing special to do until I find another job."

"Well," her voice was pleasantly polite, and as free from any other expression as her face, "if you're sure it won't be a bother. . . ."

"Nothing to speak of," he assured her as he got up from the bench.

They went leisurely across Polk Street to the Municipal Building again.

In the lobby no elevator was immediately at their service. They did not wait the necessary few seconds, but began to climb the stairs, climbing quite breathlessly before they had gone six steps up. Both of her hands were on his forearm. His other hand held them there.

WEEK--END

On the bed Mildred had piled the things she intended taking with her: a mound of silks and crepes and laces, glowing under the room's one electric light, here pink and salmon, there flesh and cream, streaked irregularly by deeper ribbon-colors. Now Mildred, looking anxiously at her wrist watch, began moving the mound from bed to bag, packing with breathless care, with the infinite pains of a window-dresser.

The door opened and Mildred's mother came two steps into the room. She was a gaunt woman in her late forties. Ill-fitting teeth pushed her thin lips awry. Her pallid eyes protruded disapprovingly.

"A person would think you were going on your honeymoon," said she.

The pink in Mildred's face deepened. She bent low over the bag that the flush might seem to come from packing efforts. Envelopes, nightgowns, camisoles on the bed seemed confessions. The cream of several Christmases and birthdays, heretofore too fine for wear, they had an obscene eloquence. Their profusion underscored the confession: they exceeded two days' possible requirements, but they were soft and fine and would go easily into the bag; she had yielded to the temptation to take them all—a holiday gesture.

"No use letting them rot in the drawer." She did not look up. "I might just as well wear them and get some use out of them."

She went on packing, with exaggerated slowness now, hoping her mother would leave the room before she was done. The elder woman watched her daughter's preparations with severe pale eyes. When the last thing had gone into the bag and Mildred had looked through the bureau to make sure she had forgotten nothing, her mother spoke again.

"I'm sure I don't know what you're thinking of, running off after this Harry Kenney. Seems to me a young girl with any shame about her would wait for her young man to come see her." Her voice, aping resignation, achieved whining hostility. "And taking a day off from the office, and drawing two weeks' pay, when we need so many things. Fred has got to have shoes, and the dining-room couch is falling to pieces. I declare, I don't know what's got into you!"

"I don't care what we need. I'm tired of always scrimping and scraping and never having anything. I'm going to see Harry before he goes east if it's the last thing I do. I'm going to do something I want to do once."

"Oh, you'll have your own way, I know! There's no use of me talking. But I do hate to see you getting yourself talked about and doing things that a modest girl wouldn't do, after all the trouble I've gone to to bring you up right. Do you think your Harry will ever marry you with you running after him every time he crooks a finger? Likely!"

Mildred winced.

"How do you know I want to marry him?"

Her mother's lips writhed back between machine-trimmed teeth-edges.

"Look out you don't have to," she said harshly.

At a little after eight Mildred left the house, though her train did not go until half past nine. She stopped at the corner drug store for a box of someone's seasickness preventative. She never felt well on trains and the pills had been recommended by one of the girls in the office.

She reached the station a little before eight-thirty—an hour's wait. After taking two of the pills in the dressing-room she bought a magazine and sat on a bench near the iron gates that opened into the train shed. She was not so excited as she had expected to be, not nearly so much so as she had been the last two days. She looked at the pictures in the magazine, peering every few minutes at the clock across the concourse, comparing it with her wrist watch.

Presently hunger reminded her that she had not eaten since noon, had neglected the evening meal for dressing and packing. At the station lunch-counter she ordered a sandwich, a slice of pie, a cup of coffee. She had no appetite for them when they were set before her. She ate a mouthful of the sandwich and half the pie, washing the food down with coffee.

Excitement returned to her. When the gates were opened she was nervous, flustered, unreasonably afraid she would get aboard the wrong train. She asked three uniformed men for directions during her walk down the long platform. When she reached her car her berth was already made up. She got into it at once.

The night was interminable. The air was heavily odorous. She could not adjust her body comfortably to the berth. The other passengers were oppressively near. The rattling and rocking made her head ache. She was nauseated and from time to time took more of the pills, swallowing them difficultly without water. Switching on the light, trying to read, she found darkness preferable. When she dozed the jarring halts and starts at the frequent stations shook her into wakefulness. After dawn she lay looking out the window until the whirling country brought giddiness. She lowered the blind and tried to sleep until it was time to get up and dress.

The hurry and bustle from train to ferry in Oakland stimulated her. A light drizzle was falling. She felt unclean: the water in the train had been cold and she had been unable to do much with the small quantity the bowl held. But as she stood in the broad bow of the boat crossing the bay the damp salt wind washed away the taste and smell of cinders and smoke. The buildinged hills of San Francisco were gray in the rain, an inviting and cordial gray until she thought perhaps Harry wouldn't be there to meet her, then the approaching city was cold, hostile.

The crowd swept her through the ferry building toward the street. Harry, standing beside a flower stand, saw her, pushed through the crowd. He was short—barely an inch taller than Mildred—and, while he was not young for his thirty years, his mouth and eyes were boyish. He took her bag and led her toward a row of taxicabs, telling her the while how glad he was to see her, how fine it was of her to come all this distance to see him.

"Can't we walk, Harry?" she protested. "I'm tired of riding."

"Sure." He guided her across the Embarcadero.

The rain came down harder, but she did not mind. She had not eaten on the train, had eaten only a few mouthfuls since the previous noon. Now hunger came. In a restaurant in O'Farrell Street he smoked and talked over his coffee while she ate fried ham and waffles.

"We'll get a room and then I'll show you everything in the city," he promised. She had not been in San Francisco before.

"Now, listen, Harry," she said. "I know you're glad to see me and everything, but I came on my own account and I'm going to pay my own bills while I'm here. I mean it."

"Nonsense!" he laughed smokily. "But we'll fight that out after we get up to our room."

"Harry!" Mildred's face was suddenly rosy. "I couldn't!"

"Couldn't what?"

"We can't have a room together! That wouldn't be right!"

"Wouldn't be right? Nonsense! I'm going away and maybe we won't see each other again for months. I'm not going to fumble the only chance I've ever had of having you all to myself for two days. Be reasonable!"

"No, no! We couldn't." Mildred shook her head. Her eyes were frightened. "It wouldn't be right. You can come up to my room, but—"

"It'll be great," he insisted, "whether it's right or not, and I'll sit here and battle with you all day before I'll let you swindle me out of this chance."

They argued. The principle on which she based her refusal to share a room with him was too obscure for adequate defense: the objection did not extend to those intimacies to which that sharing would be a means. Her opposition presently was smothered by repetitions of "Nonsense," a favorite word of his.

They went to a hotel in Ellis Street, where she pretended interest in a framed map of California on the wall while he signed the register, *George Burns and wife, Los Angeles*. In their room she bathed and he made her lie down and try to sleep while he went out to see a fellow. Her headache returned. She tossed restlessly on the bed until Harry came back. Then they went out for luncheon.

The rain continued. She decided she would rather go to a matinee than sight-seeing. The music and lights made her head ache more violently. After the performance they returned to the hotel.

Later in the evening they went to a cabaret in Mason Street. She had never been in a cabaret before and momentarily expected some vague horror. The food was not bad and nothing exceptionable happened, but she was not comfortable, sat primly and disapprovingly straight on the edge of her chair. Harry looked disappointed, almost bored, though he talked gaily, volubly. Two tables away a woman lighted a cigarette. Mildred averted her face as from a shameful spectacle, and though Harry chaffed her good-naturedly about it she would not look in that direction again. They left early and went back to the hotel.

Harry had bought some magazines and the Sunday papers. He lay across the bed smoking and reading to her. She wondered with how many women he had spent days and nights like this. The matter-of-factness that made it bearable for her testified, she thought, to familiarity with the situation. But that, of course, was all right. He had never disguised his attitude toward this part of life. Perhaps that was why he had always had his way with her. She would have liked to have had him more ardent now, but that was not to be expected. He had never seriously said he loved her—not like that. He was not like that.

After a while he stopped reading and jumped into bed. She was long going to sleep. The street noises kept her awake. Her head ached, ached, ached. The thought that Harry had not wanted to see her before he went east came. She sat up in bed.

Harry rolled over, ran the back of a hand across his eyes, asked sleepily, "What's the matter?"

"Nothing," she said and kissed him.

Though the windows were wide the room was intolerably stuffy. She perspired. Accustomed to sleeping alone, every time she turned she bumped against Harry. He woke once or twice, talked drowsily, went back to sleep. The night dragged through.

Rain was still falling in the morning. Mildred fidgeted in bed until Harry opened his eyes. He grinned jovially under his tousled hair. The stubble on his chin scraped her face when he kissed her.

"Hell of a day," he said lazily, looking at the gray windows. "What say we eat up here?"

He telephoned for breakfast and got in bed again, to lie on his back with the ash from his cigarette sprinkling down on the sheets. She liked this, this lying beside him in the gray morning, with his rumpled hair and bearded cheek against her arm, smoke in little swirls overhead.

When breakfast came she had an appetite for it, and her head did not ache so much. The boat connecting with her train left at five. They staid in the hotel room until after two. Then, the rain having stopped, they went for a walk, had dinner, and went to the ferry. Harry kissed her good-bye.

Mildred took two of the pills on the boat and two more a little later. She had the porter make up her berth as soon as possible, got into it, and slept until daybreak. After she woke she took two more pills and tried to go back to sleep, but she could not lie still. A muscular pain in her side brought familiar fears. Crying a little, she tried to pray, but had to give it up: Harry's face, and the face of the woman who had smoked in the cabaret, intruded. She turned on her other side and the pain diminished.

She wondered what Harry was doing now, if she would ever see him again. She would get letters from him for a while anyway. The deception of the *George Burns and wife, Los Angeles* worried her. Hadn't Harry really wanted to see her before he went away, or hadn't he been able to come? But he had seemed glad. She had let him pay for everything after insisting on paying her own share. The miserable night on the

train going to San Francisco. . . . the sleepless night in the noisy hotel
room. . . . this night. . . . she cried softly until time to get up.

The train reached her station at seven-thirty, giving her time to go
home for breakfast before reporting at the office. Kissing her mother,
she found none of the elder woman's hostility gone.

"Well, I suppose you had a wonderful time," her mother said
bitterly.

Mildred halted with a foot on the stairs.

"Oh, it was lovely!" she cried.

Her mother sniffed.

Mildred changed into office clothes and went down to the kitchen
for breakfast. Her mother set dishes before her in silence that held until
Mildred began to eat.

"I only hope"—the elder woman's tone held nothing of hopefulness—"that you didn't do anything to bring shame on your family."

Mildred put down the piece of toast she had been about to bite.

"I should think you'd be ashamed to say such things to your own
daughter, or even think them. You talk as if a person couldn't have any
fun without being—being what you mean. I had more fun than I ever
had in my life before, and if you want to think things about me I can't
help it. Go ahead and think what you want. I'm glad I went. I had more
fun than I ever had in my life before."

Hurrying down Park Street toward the office, Mildred repeated to
herself, tentatively, "I had more fun than I ever had in my life before."

ON THE WAY

A Brief Cinematic Interlude Enacted under Western Skies

He lowered his newspaper and turned his browned lean face toward her. His smile showed white, even teeth between hard lips. "Click?" His voice was metallic, but not unpleasant.

"Clicked," she said triumphantly and took her hat off with a flourish and threw it at the green sofa. Her eyes were enlarged, glowing. "Two fifty a week for the first six months, with options."

"That's swell." He opened his arms to her, the newspaper dangling by a corner from one of his hands. "Up the ladder for you now, huh?"

She sat on his knees, wriggled back against his body, thrust her face up at his. Her face was happy. Her voice, after they had kissed, was grave, saying: "For both of us. You're as much a part of it as I am. You gave me something that—"

His eyes did not avoid hers, though they seemed about to. He patted her shoulder with his empty hand and said awkwardly, "Nonsense. You always had things—just a little trouble knowing what to do with them."

She squirmed in his lap, leaning back a little to peer more directly into his eyes. The slight puzzled drawing together of her brows did not lessen the happiness in her face. "Are you trying to back out?" she demanded with mock severity.

He grinned, said, "No, not that, but—" and cleared his throat.

She stood up slowly and stepped back from his arms curving out to enclose her. Playfulness went out of her face, leaving it solemn around dark questioning eyes. She stood in front of the man and looked down at him and uneasiness flickered behind his grin.

"Kipper," she said softly, then touched her lower lip with the end of her tongue and was silent while her gaze ran down from his eyes to his naked ankles—he was a long, raw-boned man in brown silk pajamas under a brown-striped silk robe—and up again.

He, somewhat embarrassed, chuckled and recrossed his legs. The movement of the newspaper in his hand caught her attention and she saw the "Shipping News" folded outside.

She looked levelly at him and asked levelly, "Getting restless?"

He replied slowly, "Well, you can get along all right now you've got a foot on the ladder and—"

She interrupted him sharply, "How much money have you got left?"

He smiled up at her, shook his head from side to side in answer to the question behind her question, and said, "I've got a grubstake."

She was speaking again before he had finished. Her words tumbled out rapidly, her tone was indignant. "If it's money, you're insulting me. You know that, don't you? You carried me long enough. We can get along on two hundred and fifty a week till you get something. You know yourself both F-G-B and Peerless have sea pictures coming up and you're a cinch for a technical job on—"

He smiled again and shook his head again. "Cross my heart it's not money, Gladys." He crossed his heart with a long forefinger.

She stared thoughtfully at him for several seconds before asking in a small flat voice, "Tired of me, Kipper?"

He said, "No," harshly and held out a hand. He scowled at the hem of her blue skirt. He looked up at her a bit shamefacedly, moved his shoulders, muttered, "You know what I am."

Presently she took his hand. "I know what you are," she said and let him draw her into his lap again. She leaned her head back against his shoulder and looked sleepily at the radio. She spoke as if to herself: "This has been coming up for a couple of weeks, hasn't it?"

He changed his position a little to make her more comfortable, but did not reply to her question. For a while the only sounds in the room came up ten stories from the automobile park below. Then he said: "Morrie's throwing a party tonight. Want to go?"

"If you do."

"We don't have to stay if we don't like it." He yawned silently over her head. "Let's go down to the Grove for dinner and dance a little first. I haven't been out of this joint all day."

"All right."

He stood up, lifting her in his arms.

In the Cocoanut Grove they stopped following a waiter down the edge of the dance-floor when a thick-chested, florid man in dinner clothes rose from his seat at a table and called, "Hey, people!"

They turned their faces in unison toward the thick-chested man, but Gladys's eyes jerked sidewise to focus on Kipper's profile before she smiled. Kipper was nodding and saying, "Hello, Tom."

Tom came between two tables to them. There was a prophecy of unsteadiness in his gait. "Well, well, here's the angel herself," he said, smiling hugely at Gladys, hugging her hand in both of his. The change in his eyes was barely perceptible as he turned his smile on the tall man. "How are you, Kipper? You people alone? Come on eat with us. I got Paula."

Gladys looked questioningly at Kipper, who said, "Sure. But it's our celebration. Gladys got a contract from Fischer today."

"Grand!" Tom exclaimed, squeezing the girl's hand again. "He putting you in *Laughing Masks*?" When she had nodded he repeated, "Grand!" and began to drag her toward his table. Kipper followed them.

Paula was a pale girl who extended beautiful slim arms toward Gladys and Kipper and asked, "How are you, darlings?" while they were saying together, "Hello, darling."

Chairs were brought to the table, places were rearranged, and they sat down. Tom had finished pouring whisky from a black and gold flask when the orchestra began. He rose and addressed Gladys, "We dance."

Kipper bowed them away from the table, sat down again, poured mineral water into his whisky, and asked, "Working hard?"

Paula was staring somberly at Gladys and Tom, not yet hidden by intervening dancers. "You're going to lose your girl to that bird if you don't watch him," she said unemotionally.

Kipper smiled. "Everybody likes Gladys," he explained. He stirred his drink very gently with a long spoon.

Paula looked gloomily at him. "You mean I do?"

"Why not?" He tasted his drink, set it down on the table, and, after a reflective pause, added, "I don't think she wants Tom."

A pair of dancers freed hands to wave at them from the floor. Paula waved back at the dancers. Kipper nodded and smiled.

Paula said wearily, "She's like the rest of us: she's trying to get somewhere in pictures."

He moved his shoulders a little. "Tom's not all Hollywood," he said indifferently: then, "She got a term contract out of Fischer today."

Paula said, "I'm glad," and with more emphasis, "I really am glad, Kipper. She earned it." She put an apologetic hand on his forearm and her voice lost spirit. "Don't pay too much attention to me tonight. I'm out on my feet. We worked till midnight and were back at it at nine this morning on retakes."

He patted her hand and they sat silent until Gladys and Tom returned from the floor and dinners had to be ordered.

At half-past eleven Gladys asked Kipper what time it was. He told her and suggested, "Shall we drift?"

"I think we'd better," she said.

"Where you going?" Tom asked, putting his face—now moist and more florid—close to hers.

"Down to Morrie's," she replied slowly while Kipper was holding a beckoning finger up at a waiter.

"We'll all go down to Morrie's," Tom decided loudly and put an arm around Gladys. "I don't like him and never did, but we'll go down there."

Paula said, "I'm dead tired, Tom. I—"

Tom released Gladys and leaned toward Paula to put his other arm around her. "Aw, come on, baby. The ride'll do you good. We won't stay long. You can—" He saw the waiter putting the check in front of Kipper, leaned across the table, pushed Kipper's hand aside, and snatched the check. "What makes you think I'd let you pay it?" he asked argumentatively.

Kipper said nothing. He put his billfold back in his pocket.

They rode to Santa Monica in Tom's car, a cream phaeton that he drove expertly. Kipper sat with Gladys in the rear. They sat close together and did not talk much. Once she asked, "When are you going?"

"I'm in no hurry, honey," he said. "Next week, the week after, any time." He drew her closer—one of his arms was around her. "Get me right on this. I'm not—"

"I know," she told him gently. "I know you, Kipper—at least I think I do." A little later she said, "You've been sweet tonight—I mean about him."

He clucked depreciatively. "He's not so bad."

They left the phaeton on the road-side by a white board fence, passed through a small wooden gate, and went in darkness down a narrow boardwalk between another fence and some buildings to a screened doorway through which light and noise came.

Tom opened the screen-door. There was a bright room with twenty or thirty people in it. A gangling dark-haired man wearing black-rimmed spectacles stopped scratching a dachshund's head and came over to them with welcoming words and gestures. They called him Morrie and went in.

Kipper moved around the room, speaking—at least nodding—to every one. The only one to whom he needed an introduction was a small blonde girl named Vale. She told him she had just arrived from England. He talked to her for a few minutes and then went downstairs to the bar.

The bar occupied one side of a small room in which there was a table, some stools and chairs, and a piano. Half a dozen people were there. Kipper shook all their hands, then leaned against the bar beside a pudgy gray-faced man he called Hank, and asked for a whisky-sour.

Hank said thickly, "It's a hell of a drink."

Kipper asked, "How's the picture coming?"

Hank said thickly, "It's a hell of a picture."

Kipper grinned, asked, "Where's Fischer tonight?"

Hank said thickly, "Fischer's a hell of a guy to work for." He asked the man behind the bar for some Scotch.

Kipper and Hank stood at the bar and drank steadily without haste for nearly an hour. People came in and went out. Paula came in with a big-shouldered blond youth who carried their drinks to the far end of the table and sat beside her talking incessantly in a low secretive voice. She sat with elbow on table, chin in hand, and stared gloomily at the table.

Gladys came in with Tom at her shoulder. There was a suggestion of timidity in her eyes, but it vanished as soon as Kipper grinned at her. She went over to him, ran an arm around his waist, and asked: "Is this professional drinking or can anybody get in it?"

Hank said, "'Lo, darling, I hear you made the riffle."

She gave him her free hand. "Yes, and thanks a lot, Hank."

He grimaced. "I didn't have much to do with it." He set his drink down on the bar and his bloodshot eyes brightened. "Listen," he said, "I got a new one."

Gladys squeezed Kipper's waist, smiled up at him, took her arm away from him, and followed Hank to the piano.

Kipper, turning to face the bar again, found himself shoulder to shoulder with Tom. He said, "This rye of Morrie's isn't any too good tonight."

Tom said low in his throat, "You're a heel, Kipper."

The corners of Kipper's mouth twitched. "You're a director, Tom," he said. He turned his head then to glance carelessly at the florid face beside him.

Tom was looking fixedly at the whisky glass he held on the bar with both hands. He spoke from the side of his mouth, "I'm damned near *the* director."

Kipper laughed, said, "That's one for *Variety*." He picked up his glass and turned away from the bar, going toward the outer door.

Morrie, coming in, stopped him and asked as if he actually wanted to know, "What's the matter with that guy?" He nodded at Tom's back.

Kipper shrugged. "Maybe he's not much worse than the rest of us."

Morrie looked sharply at him, growled, "Yes he ain't," and walked over to the piano.

Hank was playing the piano. Gladys was sitting on the bench beside him. Others were gathering around them. Paula and the blond youth had disappeared.

Kipper changed his course and started toward the group around the piano. Tom came up to him and said, exactly as before, "You're a heel, Kipper."

Kipper said, "I remember you. You're the fellow that said that a couple of minutes ago." The bantering light went out of his eyes, though he did not raise his voice. "What do you want, Tom?"

Tom said through his teeth, "I don't like you."

Kipper said, "I guessed that, but don't let me worry you too much, little man: I'm leaving town in a few days."

A forked vein began to come out in Tom's forehead. "Do you think I give a damn whether you go or stay?" he demanded. "Do you think you could get in my way?"

"Anyway, I thought you might like to know I'm going," Kipper said indifferently.

Tom drew his lips back and said, "A swell chance of you going away, now that your girl's working regular."

Every one else in the room, except the negro behind the bar, was grouped around the piano at the other end. The negro was washing glasses. Kipper glanced at the group hiding the piano, at the negro, and then down again at the angry face in front of him. His mouth twisted into a wry smile. His voice was wearily contemptuous. "Is this going to be one of those things where the guy that talks the loudest wins?"

Tom replied so rapidly he sputtered, "I can give you one of those things where the guy that hits hardest wins."

Kipper pursed his lips, nodded slowly, said, "Nice beach."

They went out together, up half a dozen steps to a paved walk, along it to a low gate and through the gateway and down six concrete steps to the clinging soft footing of the beach. There were stars, but no moon. The Pacific rustled sluggishly.

Kipper, walking beside Tom, turned suddenly to him and as he turned swung a fist from his hip to Tom's face. The blow flung Tom a couple of yards to the sand, where he lay outstretched and still. Kipper bent over him for a moment, looking, listening, then straightened up, turned, and went unhurriedly back to Morrie's house.

Hank had finished playing the piano and was at the bar again with Gladys. Kipper had a drink with them, then asked Gladys, "Want to go?"

She glanced curiously at him, nodding, saying, "Whenever you're ready."

"Going to stay awhile, Hank?"

"Until this guy locks up his bar. Or do you know a better place to go?"

"Borrow your car to get home? We'll send it right back."

Hank waved a hand. "Help yourself."

Kipper said, "Thanks. Be seeing you."

Upstairs he found Morrie, drew him aside, and told him, "I left Tom out on the beach. Give him a little while."

Perplexity gave way to comprehension and to delight on the gangling man's bespectacled face. He seized Kipper's hand and pumped it up and down with violence. "Say, that's marvelous!" he cried. "It's—it's—" He failed to find words and fell to pumping the hand again.

Kipper released the hand, said, "Good night—swell party," and joined Gladys at the door.

In Hank's car neither of them spoke until they were halfway up the grade to the boulevard. Then she said, "I'm going to miss you, Kipper." She was sitting erect, looking straight ahead, her profile blurred in the dark.

"I'm going to miss you," he said. "It's been swell." He cleared his throat. "I hope it's been as swell for you as for me."

"It's been as swell." She put a hand over on his without looking at him.

He said, "I had to slap Tom down."

"I thought there was something." Her voice was matter-of-fact as his.

Presently he spoke again. "It wasn't all his fault. I mean losing wasn't. I smacked him from behind."

She turned her face toward him and asked patiently: "Don't you ever fight fair?"

He said evenly, "I'm not a kid fighting for the fun of it any more. If I've got to fight I want to win and I want to get it over quick."

She sighed.

He said, "It was about you, I guess. He wants you."

She did not say anything.

They had ridden perhaps a mile when he said, as if thinking aloud: "Whatever else he is, it's a cinch he'll be one of the top-money directors this year."

She leaned against him, sliding down in the seat, resting her head on his shoulder, moving one of her shoulders to let him put an arm around her. She did not speak until they were entering Hollywood and then her voice was barely audible. "Will you do something before you go, Kipper, something for me?"

"Sure."

She stirred a little and said, "No. I don't want you to promise now. You've been drinking and I don't want it that way. Tomorrow when you're cold sober."

"All right. What is it?"

"I wish— Could you—could you marry me before you go?"

He blew breath out.

Abruptly she sat up straight, twisting herself around, taking the lapels of his coat in her hands. "Don't answer now," she begged, her face close to his. "Don't say anything till tomorrow. And listen, Kipper, I'm not trying to hold you. I know that wouldn't hold you, wouldn't bring you back. It'd—it'd be more likely to drive you away, but—but—" She took her hands away from his coat and rubbed the back of one across her mouth.

"But what?" he asked harshly.

She giggled and said, "And I'm not expecting a little one." Merriment went out of her face and voice. She put both hands on his leg, her face close to his again. "I don't know what it is, Kipper. I just would like it. Maybe I'm bats, but I would like it. I never asked you. I wouldn't ask you if you were staying—honest—but you're going and maybe you wouldn't mind. Maybe you would. I just thought I'd ask you. Whatever you say. I won't ask you again and I know it's silly, so I won't blame you the least little bit if you say, 'No.' But I would like it." She swallowed, patted his leg, said, "Anyhow, you're not supposed to answer me till tomorrow and if you just want to forget it then I'll let you—won't say a thing about it," and sat back on her portion of the seat.

Kipper's lean face was stony.

Five blocks passed. He said, "It's a go."

"No, no," she began, "you mustn't—"

He put his arm around her and pulled her over against his chest. "It'll be the same tomorrow." He cleared his throat harshly. "I'll do anything you say." He took in a deep breath. "I'll stay if you say so."

She began to tremble and tears came out. She whispered desperately, "I want you to do what you want to do."

His lower lip twitched. He pinched it between his teeth and stared through the window at street-lights they passed. He said slowly, "I want to go."

She put a hand up on his cheek and held it there. She said, "I know, darling, I know."

SCREEN
STORIES

COMMENTARY

Dashiell Hammett's earliest produced screen story was initiated with a memo sent by David O. Selznick to studio chief B. P. Schulberg, his boss at Paramount, on July 18, 1930. "Hammett has recently created quite a stir in literary circles by his creation of two books for Knopf, *The Maltese Falcon* and *Red Harvest*," wrote Selznick. "I believe . . . that he might very well prove to be the creator of something new and startlingly original for us." Schulberg was persuaded. Hammett accepted a contract with Paramount to write a screen story, moved from New York to Hollywood, and promptly turned out seven handwritten pages for "After School," soon after revised, expanded, and retitled "The Kiss-Off."

Hammett's treatment was adapted by Max Marcin, with a screenplay by Oliver H. P. Garrett, directed by Rouben Mamoulian. The film was released on April 18, 1931, as *City Streets*, starring Sylvia Sidney and Gary Cooper. It is a first-rate example of the period and genre, notable for its landmark use of voiceovers, what one reviewer called "phantom dialogue." Hammett had mixed feelings about the picture, though he was enamored of Sylvia Sidney (who was then romantically involved with Schulberg). "She's good, that ugly little baby," Hammett said, "and currently my favorite screen actress."

City Streets was in theaters and director Roy Del Ruth's adaptation of *The Maltese Falcon* was in postproduction on April 28, 1931, when Darryl Zanuck sent a letter to Hammett rejecting his final draft of "On the Make," a screen treatment he'd commissioned for Warner Bros. some three months earlier. The deal would later serve as evidence in a precedent-setting legal contest between Hammett and Warner Bros. over the ownership of character rights in the *Falcon*. "I had agreed," explained Hammett in his affidavit, "that I would write another original Sam Spade story for motion picture production by the defendant featuring the actor, William Powell." Warner Bros. paid a total of ten thousand dollars for the first two drafts, but in the end decided to cut its losses. "The finished story has none of the qualifications of *Maltese Falcon*, although the same character was in both stories," explained Zanuck.

Hammett and Zanuck's remarks notwithstanding, the Sam Spade in Hammett's novel and Gene Richmond in "On the Make" have little in common, not including geography. "On the Make" is a rare Hammett story set in Southern California. Sam Spade as portrayed by Ricardo Cortez in Warner's 1931 adaptation of the *Falcon*, however, does prefigure Richmond's rapacious tactics and unprincipled worldview. The two are greedy scoundrels, rather than existential antiheroes. It seems Hammett gave Zanuck what he'd asked for—a variation on his sleazy filmic detective, unctuous rather than cagey and grasping where the original (and later, Bogart) was reticent.

With Zanuck's rejection, the story reverted to Hammett, who again reworked the tale, as it is published here. It was sold to Universal in 1935. Gene Richmond's name was changed to T. N. Thompson—otherwise known as Mr. Dynamite—in a script liberally reworked by Doris Malloy and Harry Clork. *Mr. Dynamite* was released in 1935, starring Edmund Lowe as the corrupt detective and Jean Dixon as his girl Friday. Lively banter between the two would have echoed William Powell and Myrna Loy as Nick and Nora Charles in MGM's *The Thin Man*, still playing in theaters eleven months after its initial release. Universal's blend of comedy and crime drama was far less successful, however. *Mr. Dynamite* drifted into obscurity.

Despite occasional misfires and notoriously erratic work habits, Hammett's timely and unique talent was a magnet for Hollywood's early filmmakers. In 1931 and 1932 Hammett reported potential writing assignments for George Bancroft for Paramount, Wallace Beery for MGM, Ronald Colman for United Artists, for Gloria Swanson, and for Universal. Among the extant works in Hammett's archive are a handful of unfinished screen treatments that are likely products of those aborted negotiations.

Hammett's draft of "The Devil's Playground" dates to those heady years—when he was a hot property and current and cultural events had aroused Hollywood's interest in China. The Sino-Japanese War, Grace Zaring Stone's popular novel *The Bitter Tea of General Yen* (1930), and Pearl Buck's Pulitzer Prize–winning *The Good Earth* (1931) sent Hollywood's filmmakers scrambling for high oriental drama. It's easy to imagine Hammett's sweeping romantic adventure playing opposite *Shanghai Express*, *Red Dust*, *Roar of the Dragon*, or *War Correspondent*—all set in China and released in 1932. The typescript that follows is an amalgam of two overlapping drafts. Repetitious passages have been omitted and names have been regularized.

THE KISS-OFF

I

A high school is letting hundreds of youngsters out into a street. A girl of 16 waits for a boy of the same age. His clothes are old and neat; hers are newer and a bit gaudy. They are happy together in a quiet, casual way. They go to shooting gallery where boy works after school. Girl remains behind until the proprietor has left boy in charge, and then joins him. She shoots at targets with pistol; is a terrible shot. The boy shoots, seeming to pay little attention to what he is doing, but putting his bullets where he wants them. After a while she persuades him to show his skill again. Proprietor returns in middle of exhibition and gives boy hell for wasting cartridges. The girl runs away.

II

The girl goes home to a shabby furnished flat—not a tenement. Her mother—a frail woman with a weak once-pretty face—is in the kitchen cooking. The girl's step-father—Tom Cooley—is sitting with white-stockinged feet on the dining-room table, reading a newspaper. He is a fleshy man of forty-something with a round, good-natured face and a jovial manner. He looks at the clock and asks the girl where she has been since school let out. She won't tell him. He scowls, insists. The girl keeps quiet. Her manner isn't defiant—just spiritlessly stubborn. He twists her arm, threatens her with a fist (but keeps his feet on the table); she won't tell. He grins at her with paternal pride, pats her cheek, gives her a half-dollar, and praises her: "Good kid! Don't never tell nobody nothing!"

The girl helps her mother get the meal on the table. Cooley good-naturedly helps himself to the choicest and largest portion of each dish. After the meal he prepares to go out. The girl's mother puts his shoes on and laces them for him; the girl brings him collar, tie, and coat.

III

Tom Cooley goes to the building where Blackie lives, a large middle-class apartment building with dim corridors. Turning a corner of the corridor toward Blackie's apartment, Cooley stops, peeps. Agnes—Blackie's woman—is letting Jack Willis out of Blackie's apartment. Agnes is young, tall, hard, beautiful, reckless. Willis is a hard-faced, handsome, tall, debonair man in evening clothes. Cooley watches them. Willis draws Agnes through the door with him, pulling the door partly shut to screen them from inside, and puts his arm around her. The door is yanked open from the inside by Blackie. He is larger than Willis, tougher, and mad. His fist starts for Willis—and stops. Willis has stepped back, put a hand in an overcoat pocket, and is covering Blackie with the gun that is there. Willis says suavely: "You're making too much dough out of my booze to pick a fight with me, Blackie." Blackie says: "Yeah, but don't make me forget it." He puts out a big hand, takes Agnes by the neck, and pushes her indoors. Willis lifts the gun in his pocket again, hesitates, shrugs, and turns away. Blackie goes in and closes the door.

Cooley runs down the corridor a little distance and then comes back, whistling as he walks, looking innocent. He meets Willis at the bend in the corridor and greets him cheerfully. Willis speaks to him, goes on, turns to look thoughtfully at him, and then calls him back. "Tom," he says, "I've been thinking that if anything happened to Blackie, and you could hold his mob together, I'd be willing to do business with you. You could handle the customers better than he—your disposition's better." Cooley purses his lips, scratches his chin, and holds out a fat hand. "That's eggs in the coffee with me, chief," he says. They shake hands, and Cooley goes on to Blackie's apartment. Blackie opens the door. Agnes is getting up from the floor, holding her jaw with one hand. She goes into the bedroom to sulk and rage on the bed. Blackie and Tom Cooley go into the living room where Slim—Blackie's bodyguard—is sitting in front of a bottle. Both Blackie and Slim like Cooley—everybody does. Cooley encourages Blackie to drown his anger with the stuff in the bottle, and sees that Slim drinks with him. Slim doesn't need much urging. Blackie has to go out, to collect payment for a shipment from a cabaret owner. He asks Cooley to wait till he gets back, and keep an eye on Agnes, telling of his suspicion that she and Willis are cheating on him. Cooley pretends surprise. Black and Slim go away afoot, Slim strolling a little behind Blackie. Neither of them are drunk, but they've got fair edges on.

IV

As soon as they are gone Agnes comes out of the bed-room, takes a shot or two from the bottle, and walks the floor, cursing Blackie. Cooley eggs her on, until she says she's going to kill Blackie some day. "Suppose he don't live that long?" he suggests. She looks sharply at him, sees he means something, and they go into conference; and then he phones the girl—his step-daughter. The girl takes an automatic from a bureau drawer, puts it in a handbag—almost too small to hold it—and goes to meet her step-father in alley behind Blackie's apartment. Cooley takes the gun and tells her to wait. She waits submissively. He posts himself in court running from alley to street, beside apartment building.

While Blackie was conducting his business with the cabaret proprietor, Slim had taken more drinks, and now he's definitely tight. On the return trip he lags nearly a block behind Blackie. When Blackie passes the court where Cooley is hiding, Cooley shoots him down. A pedestrian on the other side of the street sees him, but it is too dark for the pedestrian to know anything except that a man did the shooting. Slim, staggering up, sees half a dozen men running down the court and shoots at and misses all of them—until a garbage-can trips him and he goes down.

Cooley runs down the court to the alley—where he has left the girl—and gives her the gun, saying: "Chuck it in the river. If you get nabbed, dummy up and I'll see you through." Then he runs behind apartment building, scrambling up the rear fire-escape to Blackie's apartment. The girl stuffs the gun into the too-small bag again, runs up to cross street, and then strolls down it. A policeman runs around the corner and asks her if she has seen a man. She says, "No." The policeman—having been told by the pedestrian and Slim that the killer was a man—hurries away hunting for him.

V

Agnes helps Cooley through the window from the fire-escape, fans him cool, gives him a cigar she has kept burning—with a long ash, as if it had been smoked peacefully by a man sitting still—and they sit down to a half-played pinochle game—a picture of peace when the police arrive. The police don't really suspect them, but they search them and the apartment, finding nothing. Outside, other police are searching alley and court with flashlight, hunting for clews, finding nothing except the empty shells Cooley's gun had ejected. Agnes, Cooley, and Slim are taken to headquarters for questioning, but purely as a matter of routine.

The girl with the gun has safely got through to the bridge over the river, but there she is picked up by two detectives returning from the scene of the shooting, who happen to spot the bulging outline of the gun in the too-small handbag when she passes under a street light. They take her to headquarters and give her everything they've got in the way of third-degrees; but she dummies up and stays dummied up, refusing to tell them who she is, refusing to open her mouth. The police bring Cooley, Agnes, and Slim into the room where the girl is, to see if any of them know her. Cooley cries: "My God, my little daughter!" and begs her to talk, to tell the police everything, not to break her dear mother's heart, and so on. He even weeps real tears; but he keeps two fingers of his right hand crossed where she can see them. He is shown the gun and instantly identifies it as his—kept in his bureau drawer.

They fail to get anything out of the girl. Cooley, talking the affair over with the police and an assistant district attorney, after they have left the girl, helps them arrive at a theory that some boy-friend of hers killed Blackie—they know it wasn't a girl—and slipped her the gun to chuck in the river. Cooley admits sadly that he hadn't been very strict with her—not as strict as if she'd been his daughter instead of his step-daughter—and she had probably got in with a bad crowd. "This younger generation," he says, "ain't got much respect for law and order." He agrees that the best thing for her would be a reform school till she's of age. He, Slim, and Agnes leave headquarters, Cooley jerking his head toward the building in which they have left the girl, and telling the others: "She's a good kid. It's all in knowing how to raise them."

VI

Blackie's mob meets—with Willis—in Blackie's apartment, and agree to string along with Cooley. They don't suspect him. They suspect Willis, but business is business and there's no profit in taking a dead man's part. Agnes packs her clothes and goes away with Willis.

Cooley goes away with Slim—*his* bodyguard now—strolling a little behind him. They come to the shooting gallery where the boy is—in the proprietor's absence—practicing. Cooley is impressed by the boy's skill. So, in another way, is the proprietor, who has just come around the corner on the other side of the street. Cooley, beckoning to Slim, goes to the gallery and has Slim try his marksmanship. Slim is a fair shot, sometimes scoring, sometimes not. Cooley offers the boy a drink from his flask. The boy doesn't drink. Cooley asks him: "Want a job?" The boy says: "Got one." The proprietor, who has arrived now, says: "No, you ain't. I've told you before, them cartridges cost money, and, besides, you showing off that-away makes people ashamed to shoot in front of you." (The boy doesn't look into anybody's face. The closest he comes to it is to look at their chests. He moves very deliberately, holding himself rather rigid, and has a cool, unsmiling, poker face.) The boy comes through the gate in the counter. Cooley holds out a couple of bills to him. The boy pockets them. Cooley, under cover of the counter and his coat, gives the boy an automatic. The boy pockets it. Cooley says: "All you got to do is go along behind me and see that nothing happens." Slim cuts in, protesting. Cooley tells him good-naturedly: "You drink too much and don't shoot enough, Slim. Look what you let happen to poor Blackie." Slim drops his hand to his pocket and glares at the boy. The boy looks at the handkerchief blossoming out of Slim's breast pocket, on the left side, over his heart; stares coldly at it. Slim looks from the boy to the handkerchief, to the target he and Cooley had watched the boy shoot at, back at the boy again, fidgets; rubs his lips with his tongue, and goes away. The boy follows Cooley down the street.

VII

After nearly five years in reform school, the girl—now of age—is turned loose, and comes home to Cooley's house. Cooley has prospered. His house is a large, ornate affair in a good neighborhood, expensively furnished, but never kept clean. Cooley still sits around collarless and shoeless; he scratches his matches on the wallpaper or the top of a mahogany table or whatever happens to be nearest; and he's as cheerful as ever. The boy, now the Roscoe Kid (it'll have to be explained to the customers, of course, that a "roscoe" is a gun), doesn't look any older than he did before. His clothes are better, but still very quiet and neatly worn; and he keeps pretty much to himself, holding himself apart from his associates. (Out of his skill with a gun, and his pride in it, has grown a self-respect that the others haven't.) The girl's five years in school have hardened her: in place of her former lack of spirit is now something that the Kid doesn't like. He looks into her eyes when she first comes in, sees the thing he doesn't like, and thereafter looks at her as he looks at the rest of the world—no higher than the chest. A frowsy plump woman in a soiled dressing gown is lying on a chaise longue eating chocolates and reading a magazine when the girl comes in. The girl looks inquiringly at her. Cooley says: "That's Pansy. Your Ma died on me."

The girl thinks the Kid is giving her the go-by because he considers her still a school-girl, and because of her clothes. She gets money from Cooley and goes shopping, returning to the house all gaudied up. Willis is there. He falls for her immediately and she cracks wise with him, trying to impress the Kid; but the wiser she acts, the more the Kid draws back into his shell. Willis suggests that Cooley ought to throw a party that night to celebrate the girl's being sprung, and Cooley agrees. Willis, leaving, asks Cooley if it's all right for him to make a play for the girl. Cooley says it's all right with him.

The girl goes upstairs, puzzled by her lack of success with the Kid. Passing his room, she hears him moving around, peeps in. He's sweeping the floor. She sees that his room is clean, neat, and orderly—the only one in the house that is. She sees, then, where she has gone wrong with him. She goes to her room, leaving the door open, and, after changing to quieter clothes, begins cleaning up the room. When he passes her door she asks him to lend her the broom, to help her move the furniture so she can sweep out the couple of years' accumulation of dirt that has been swept under bed, dressers, etc. She's quiet and demure now, and by the time they've finished with the room she has got him looking into her face again—they are once more as they were before she was sent over. She asks him about his shooting—reminding him of when they used to go to the gallery after school. He takes her down to the cellar where he has a private gallery laid out. She shoots, and is as bad a shot as ever. He shoots, and is as good as ever, or better. She's got him now: he puts down his gun as if he didn't like it, and says to her: "You and I don't belong here. This racket's all right for the rest of them, but not for us. Let's give it the kiss-off—get out of it—find something straight." The girl kisses him as Pansy calls down the stairs that it's time to dress for the party.

At the party that night the girl—between having her liberty and having the Kid—is too happy to be quiet: she's got to blow off. But the Kid is no good at celebrating: he doesn't drink; he's too quiet, reserved, especially among all these people he doesn't like very much. Willis is good at celebrating, and he's after the girl. Willis doesn't mean anything to her except somebody to blow off steam with, until she sees that the Kid has become sullenly jealous. He's stopped looking into her face when she talks to him. She begins to get angry with him; Willis leads her on; she starts drinking and playing up stronger to Willis to infuriate the Kid. The further she goes with Willis, the more the Kid draws back in his shell, and the angrier that makes her; until, finally, when she's had a few more drinks, she tells, as a swell joke, about the Kid asking her to give the racket the kiss-off and go straight with him.

Willis smiles, uneasily, when she tells it, but nobody else does. They know the Kid too well to laugh at him. Embarrassed and angered by the way her joke has flopped, the girl throws herself at Willis, putting her arms around his neck, putting her mouth up toward his. His mouth starts down toward hers, and stops. The Kid is standing close to them, staring at Willis's chest—at the left side. Willis tries to make himself go through with it—kiss the girl—but can't. He loosens her arms from his neck, smiling apologetically, and goes out of the room. The Kid, looking at nobody, goes upstairs.

Cooley follows Willis to the front door. Willis says: "Make the Kid lay off. You said I could have her." Cooley, smiling, tries to soothe

Willis, but refuses to interfere. Willis says, as he had said to Blackie: "You're making too much dough out of my booze to pick a fight with me, Tom." Cooley nods amiably, adding: "And with the Kid walking behind me—on good terms with me—I'll live to spend it." Willis leaves. The party breaks up. When the others have gone Cooley says to the girl: "What swell ideas you got—boobing the Roscoe Kid! Ever try patting an electric fan?" The girl, more sick than tight now, frightened at what she has done, goes up to the Kid's room.

He's packing his bag. She tries to apologize, but he cuts her off and goes down with his bag, telling Cooley he's through—leaving. Cooley tries to talk him out of it, fails, asks him to wait five minutes. Cooley goes up to the girl's room and tells her she'll have to square herself with the Kid. She says she tried, but it was no good. He insists that she can if she tries hard enough, but she sticks to it that it's hopeless.

Downstairs, the Kid waits till the five minutes are up, then starts for the street door. The noise of Cooley beating the girl stops him. He goes upstairs and tells Cooley he'll stay. Cooley goes out of the girl's room leaving them there together.

At his own apartment, Willis tells Agnes to get her stuff together and get out the next day. Then he phones Slim, who comes there. Willis tells him: "Slim, I've been thinking that if anything happened to Cooley, and you could handle his mob—hold them together—I'd be willing to do business with you." Slim says: "The Roscoe Kid would have to be taken care of first, and that ain't a job I'd want." Willis argues with him, dazzles him with the thought of the money that Cooley makes, that Slim could make in his place; and Slim finally agrees, on condition that Willis take part in the removal. They plan it together—with Agnes, in the next room, listening in. Willis phones a dive keeper, and has him phone Cooley and ask him to come to his place. Then Willis and Slim go out to collect some assistants and spring their trap.

The girl is trying, unsuccessfully, to square herself with the Kid when Cooley gets the dive keeper's summons, and calls the Kid down to go with him. They go in one of Cooley's cars, Cooley driving, the Kid beside him.

When Willis and Slim have gone, Agnes calls Cooley's number, and tells the girl, who answers the phone: "Tell Tom not to go out. It's a trap of Jack's and Slim's." The girl says: "They've gone." Agnes then goes to the police. The girl, knowing where her step-father and the Kid have gone, sets out to overtake them in another car. She arrives just as the trap is sprung—in a street that is half torn up by a sewer ditch. The girl gets there in time to jam her car between Cooley's and the attacking car, partially upsetting the latter. The Kid yanks her out of her car into his, shoots Slim—who was trying to take a crack at her—and has Willis and the others covered by the time they straighten up from the bump the girl's car gave them.

Cooley spots the police coming, from both sides. There's no getaway open. Cooley takes charge, giving orders. The Kid shoots the street light out, giving them darkness. The girl scrambles out and sticks the Kid's and Cooley's guns out of sight in the loose dirt along the ditch edge. They're all out of their cars when the first of the police arrive. Cooley pretends he's glad to see them, saying some men tried to stick them up. Asked which direction they went, he says, "That-away," making an almost complete circle with his arm. One of the police gets up from examining Slim, who is lying in the street. "Is this one of them?" he asks. "Is he dead?" Cooley asks, and is told that he is. "He's one of them," Cooley says.

Agnes comes up with the rest of the police, and laughs at Willis, boasting of having spoiled his plan. The police question Cooley. "Why, she must be goofy," he says, embracing Willis. "He's the best friend I got. He saved my life. If it hadn't been for him they'd of got me sure." Agnes, enraged at Cooley's attempt to rob her of her revenge, denounces him as the murderer of Blackie. A couple of policemen take hold of him. Then Willis suavely tells the police Agnes sent him and his friends into this trap where Cooley, the Kid, and the girl tried to shoot him down, just as Cooley and the girl had shot Blackie down five years ago.

The Kid grabs the girl and jumps backward into the ditch. The buried guns are close to his hands then. He gets them out and holds off the police for a moment, telling the girl to beat it down the ditch.

Everyone's attention is on him. Agnes picks up Slim's gun from the street and shoots Willis. The Kid and the girl take advantage of this break to get a running start down the ditch. Around a bend in it they find the opening of a small tunnel, boarded above to keep loose dirt from blocking the entrance. They go in. The Kid knocks the board loose. Earth has settled over the entrance by the time the pursuing police arrive.

Huddled in their sewer, the girl doesn't have much trouble squaring herself with the Kid, getting his forgiveness. At a little before daybreak they sneak out, brush off their clothes, and set out for the edge of town. When they are on the bridge where, five years ago, she had been picked up with Cooley's gun, she asks the Kid for his guns, kisses them goodbye and tosses them into the river.

Later in the morning they board a train at a small station some miles from the city, with a ticket reading still farther away. They're happy together. The Kid slumps comfortably down in the seat beside her, no longer holding himself rigid; nor has he a poker face now; and when he gives up his ticket he looks into the conductor's eyes with a friendly smile.

DEVIL'S PLAYGROUND

Guy Wayne, American soldier of fortune, is instructor in the army of the tuchun, or military governor, of a western Chinese province, holding a colonel's commission. With him are two white noncoms—Hank, a small, dried-up, heavily mustached, bowlegged oldish man, and Bingo Kelly, a big, slow-moving, good-natured husky.

Early one evening while Wayne is lying with his head in the lap of the tuchun's favorite wife, Hank climbs through the window to tell him a peeping servant has carried the news to the tuchun. Wayne tells the woman she will have to run away with them, but she has her own idea of how to take care of herself. She tears her clothes, disarranges her hair, and begins to scream rape. Hank wants to cut her throat, but Wayne, half-amused, says no. Hank throws her down on the floor, rolls her up in rug, and they stow her away, upside-down, out of sight. Wayne blows a kiss at her as he and Hank drop out the window.

Strolling through the streets, returning the salutes of Chinese soldiers, apparently chatting casually, with only the side to side shifting of their eyes denoting watchfulness, they go to where Wayne has left his car. Wayne gets into the car while Hank goes off afoot. Wayne rides outside the town, to where Bingo is drilling a machine-gun detachment. After a low-voiced conversation between the two white men Bingo marches his detachment over a hill, out of sight of the town, and spreads them out facing the town, their guns tilted high in the air.

By the time Bingo has his men placed, Hank appears around the hill, riding a horse, leading two saddled horses and a small pack train. Wayne nods to Bingo, who roars a command at his men. They begin firing, their bullets going high in the air over the hill and down on the sand between it and the town. Wayne and Bingo, slowly at first, then swiftly, move to join Hank, mount, and ride away without attracting the machine-gunners' attention.

When the tuchun's men, hurrying from town in pursuit of Wayne, see the barrage the machine-gunners are laying down, they halt in confusion. The machine-gunners cannot of course see them over the hill. By the time officers have made a wide detour and have stopped the machine-gun fire, the three white men are far away and night is falling.

For days Wayne and his companions travel northward through Mongolia, intent on reaching the Yenisei River and traveling down it to the Siberian Railroad. Their way lies through wild, windswept country; they have friendly encounters with native herdsmen, less friendly ones with roving bands of Chinese, Russian, Mongol horsemen, but Hank has brought along a couple of machine guns and plenty of ammunition, so they hold their own.

At length they come to the outskirts of a fairly large town. They bury their machine guns and most of their ammunition before entering it. As they approach the town they are overtaken by a large limousine, which bears down upon them with screaming siren and no slackening of speed, compelling them to scramble off the narrow road. As the limousine goes past, Wayne catches a glimpse of a beautiful woman's face looking haughtily out at him.

In the town, they have no sooner found lodgings than they are taken before the local authorities to explain their presence. Hank, acting as spokesman and interpreter, tells a straight story of their leaving the tuchun's service, and the authorities apparently are satisfied. The three men are allowed to go back to their lodgings.

There is a note brought to Wayne. Curtly worded, it summons him immediately to the house of a W. Ruric, by whom the note is signed. He resents the tone of the note, crumples it into a ball, tosses it into a corner of the room, and tells the messenger that is the only answer. Half an hour later the three men are arrested and thrown into a cell, where they spend the night. Hank, engaging one of their guards in conversation, learns that they have been arrested as deserters from the Chinese army and will probably be sent back to the tuchun.

Late in the morning, the woman they saw in the limousine visits them. She is accompanied by a dandified man whom she introduces as Mr. Verner. Speaking unaccented English, she says she is Wanda Ruric, and asks Wayne why he did not answer her note. He explains that he thought it was from a man and resented its tone. She apologizes for the note's curtness and explains what she wanted.

She has some mining concessions in the interior, inherited from her father, and some months ago had sent a Dutch engineer with laborers to begin operating the mines. Since then she has heard nothing of them. The country in which the mines are located is wild and peopled by fanatic natives who might easily resent strangers' presences there and refuse to recognize the authority of the government granting the concessions. She wants to know what happened to the engineer and his force. From what she has heard of Wayne and his companions she thinks them the men to find out for her. She will pay well. Will they take the job?

Wayne says, "Sure," but they are in jail and will probably be sent back to China. She assures them that is easily fixed, thanks them sweetly, and goes away. In a very few minutes the three men are released and go back to their lodgings. Wayne sends Hank out to learn what he can about Wanda Ruric.

Meanwhile, in her luxurious residence, Wanda is listening to Verner, who is arguing that she is making a mistake in trusting the three adventurers. She replies that there is nothing else she can do, since she can find no natives able to do the job and he—Verner—is too definitely a city man, as well as too ignorant of Mongolia, to be of much use. Verner persists in his objections until finally she says: "All right, I'll go too—to keep my eyes on them." Verner protests, but she is stubborn, so he says then he will go too, to which she agrees.

Hank returns to his companions with the information that Wanda Ruric inherited tremendous wealth from her father, a Russian engineer, and has been managing his various enterprises since his death; that she is through her wealth and influence practically the ruler of the town and surrounding country; and that Verner is a recent arrival from either London or New York, where he seems to have been her father's financial representative.

Wayne nods, says: "Uh-huh! I guessed that. When we didn't pay any attention to her note she had us thrown in jail, and only let us out when we promised to be good and to do what she told us. Now we'll go back to her and tell her what she can do with her job and let her throw us in the can again if she wants." The others are dubious, but they follow Wayne back to the girl's house.

There, before they can speak, she tells them she and Verner are going with them. Hank and Bingo are all against this, but Wayne, still angry at the means she had used to make them accept her offer, and knowing how tough the expedition will be, sees in it a chance to pay her back, and agrees readily. The three adventurers leave and begin to prepare their caravan, which will now be quite a large one, since Wanda must take along a maid and all sorts of things.

Verner leaves Wanda's house furtively and, speaking the native language with evident familiarity, sends some thugs he can depend on to join the expedition. Wayne and his companions, confident of their ability to handle men, are willing to hire any who seem tough and experienced enough, so Verner succeeds in packing the caravan fairly well with his own men.

The expedition gets under way. Hank and Bingo complain about its size and the slowness with which they travel, but Wayne seems content. The first night out, after they have pitched camp, he makes a play for Wanda, in a very casual and off-hand way. She repulses him haughtily, reminding him that he must keep his place as hired man. He shrugs indifferently and transfers his attention to her maid, with whom he has better luck until Wanda angrily separates them.

As they get into wilder country things begin to go wrong. Pack animals—assisted by Verner's crew—die, stray off, stampede, and are only recovered after hours' work. Hank, who knows something of the country, tells the others he thinks the guides are leading them astray. There are fights between Verner's men and the other natives in the caravan, and the others are driven into deserting. The country becomes wilder and wilder, the natives they encounter more and more hostile, often stirred up by Verner or his messengers. Verner conceals from Wanda and the three adventurers his intimacy with the country through which they are passing and sticks to his city-man-in-the-wilderness role.

The three ex-soldiers have continual trouble with their men, can keep their guides on the right route only by constant threats, and have to take turns standing guard at night. One night Bingo discovers Verner in friendly conversation—in the native tongue—with the unfriendly lama of a temple near which they are camping. Before he can tell the others, Verner has him killed, then sending away the last of their guides.

They go on. Wayne continues to play with the maid to infuriate Wanda. She tries to even things up by making a play for Verner, but quickly stops him when he gets too enthusiastic in private. Verner knows then that she is falling for Wayne. There is growing antagonism between him and Wayne, and between her and Wayne. Wayne pretends serene indifference to this, as to the rest of their troubles.

Few pack animals remain now, but Wayne insists that no matter what else is discarded, they must hang on to their machine guns and ammunition. He throws out most of Wanda's luggage, cuts Verner short when he protests. She is too proud to protest, too hell-bent on not letting him see how hard the journey is for her, and insists on leaving her maid behind in one of the villages they pass.

They come at length—travel-worn and bedraggled—to Wanda's mine and see that it is being worked. White men appear—not Wanda's engineer. Before Wayne can stop her, she rides up to the men and haughtily asks them what they are doing on her property. Verner rides after her, and then Wayne and Hank—some distance behind, since they had dismounted to set up their machine guns—but none succeeds in heading her off. When the men at the mine see Verner, one of them calls him a double-crossing so-and-so, and shoots him down. A battle starts. Wayne succeeds in getting the girl back, though Hank is shot while covering their retreat. Hank and Wayne set up their guns and finally clear out the mine, though Hank dies as soon as the battle is won. Wayne's remaining men have fled, as have all the enemy. He and Wanda are alone. He blames her for Hank's death, telling her if she had let them get their guns placed before stirring up the enemy they need have suffered no casualties. She breaks down, goes completely to pieces. Wayne relents then and soothes her tenderly.

They remain at the mine several days, recovering their strength. Then they begin the homeward journey, carrying as much provisions as they can, since there are no pack animals—theirs fled or were ridden away during the battle—and automobiles—of which there are several—are useless in the country through which they must pass. In spite of the hardships encountered, both find the return trip quite endurable, since they are now admittedly in love with each other. Presently they reach a village where they can buy horses and further provisions, and finish their journey without more trouble.

Home, the girl resumes the management of her business affairs; her lost haughtiness, imperiousness, begins to return. She and Wayne quarrel. He says this life isn't for him—he's going to run along and catch that Siberian train for Moscow and America. She angrily tells him to go if he wants, that he'll always be a tramp, etc., etc. He goes.

Next morning she comes to him—contrite—while he is loading his pack animals, begs him to stay. He says no; her life isn't his; she was swell when they were tramping, but he can't stand her manner when she is in her normal setting. She says all right, she'll go with him, tramping, just as she is. He looks quizzically at her, nods, saddles a mount for her. She gets on it and they head north. They ride along in silence a little while, he phlegmatic, she defiant, determined, then gradually begin to talk, recovering their former relationship. Presently, riding side by side, he puts an arm around her, kisses her. Their horses halt. He rubs his chin, looks back towards the town, looks sharply at her, grins, says: "Well, after all, if you'd promise honestly to behave—to stop being the Queen of Sheba—maybe we would be more comfortable back there." She laughs and promises. They turn and go back.

ON THE MAKE

Close-up of a railroad station newsstand. Gene Richmond, his back to the camera, is leaning over the counter talking to the girl in charge. His voice is blotted out by the combined sounds of hurrying feet, puffing locomotives, rattling trucks, clanging gates, distant cries of newsboys and taxi-drivers, and a loudspeaker announcing unintelligibly the names of cities for which a train is about to leave.

Widen shot to show two burly men standing on either side of Richmond a little behind him. They are typical police detectives. One looks at his watch, then taps Richmond's shoulder. "Come on, Richmond," he says, "your go-away's leaving."

Richmond straightens and turns, putting a couple of packages of cigarettes in his pocket. He smiles mockingly at the police detectives and says: "Boys, this is breaking my heart." He picks up his Gladstone bag.

One of them growls somewhat bitterly: "It'd've broke your heart a lot more if you hadn't had dough enough to fix it so you could leave town this way instead of going up the river with cuffs on you."

The other one says impatiently: "Come on. What are you trying to do? Miss the train so you can give the twist"—he jerks his head a little toward the girl behind the counter—"a play?"

Richmond chuckles. "That might be nice, too," he says. He turns his head over his shoulder to say, "By-by, baby," to the girl, then walks away from the newsstand between the two police detectives.

At the gate, Richmond produces his ticket, one of the detectives shows his badge, and they go through with him, the gateman looking curiously after them. They walk down the platform beside a train, past Pullman cars where porters are already swinging aboard. A few passengers are hurrying down past them. Train-hands are shouting, "All aboard." Richmond seems in no hurry and undisturbed by his companions' scowls.

Finally they reach the day coaches. One of the detectives jerks his thumb at the entrance to the first coach and growls: "And don't forget—the orders are 'out of town and *stay* out!'"

Richmond puts a foot on the bottom step as the train slowly starts to move and, holding on with one hand, his bag swinging in the other, smiles at the detective and replies: "I won't forget. And any time you bums are fired off the force for getting brains, look me up. I'll be running an agency somewhere—with ex-coppers working for me. Ta-ta! Give my love to the Chief." He climbs aboard.

The two police detectives stare after the departing train. One of them sighs as if relieved and says: "That's a good day's work. One crooked private dick like him can make more trouble than a hundred out-and-out thugs."

The other rubs a hand across his chin and shakes his head a little. "It's plenty of bad news for some other city," he says.

The first one shrugs. "That ain't our grief," he says.

They turn back toward the gates.

Close-up of a glazed office door on which a hand is lettering:

GENE RICHMOND
PRIVATE DETECTI

Enlarge to show painter starting to work on V, then inside to an unoccupied but furnished outer office (wooden railing fencing off space for visitors, three wooden chairs for them; one desk facing railing, another desk at other end of room, filing cabinet, wastebaskets, telephones, etc., all somewhat worn) and to a wooden door marked PRIVATE, and through this to a room where Gene Richmond is sitting at a desk, a cigarette in his mouth, looking narrow-eyed through smoke at a mannish looking woman of about 30 in mannish clothes who is seated in a chair beside the desk.

She is saying: ".... and, as I wrote you when I answered your advertisement, I've had experience in bookkeeping and general office work as well as stenography."

Richmond nods slowly, still looking narrow-eyed at her, and asks: "References?"

"Yes," she says quickly and begins to fumble with nervously clumsy fingers at her handbag.

Richmond looks interestedly at her fumbling fingers.

She brings out two letters of recommendation of the typical to-whom-it-may-concern sort, one on the letterhead of Wheeler & Nicholson, Chemicals, the other The Tidewater Manufacturing Corp., and gives them to Richmond.

He does not read the letters, but leans forward to snap on his desk lamp, lays the letters on the desk so the signatures are close together, and bends over them to scrutinize the signatures closely. The signatures are John G. Hart and Lewis Melville.

The girl looks at him with frightened eyes.

After studying the signatures briefly Richmond turns to her, smiling sardonically, tapping the letters contemptuously with the back of one hand.

She tries to banish the fear from her face.

"A pair of phoneys," he says. "You signed them yourself and made a bum job of it."

"Why, Mr. Richmond," she exclaims with all the indignation she can assume, "that—"

He interrupts her carelessly. "Come here and I'll show you, Miss Crane—so you can do it better next time."

Divided between the indignation she thinks it policy to assume and curiosity as to how he discovered what she had done, she slowly rises and moves nearer.

Richmond picks up a pencil and bends over the letters again. His manner is that of an expert good-naturedly pointing out the mistakes of a novice. "First," he says, touching the Hart signature with the point of his pencil, "this is written with a fine point, the letters slant forward, and the end letters"—he touches points A and B on the insert—"end with an upward stroke. This"—he indicates the Melville signature—"written with a heavy point, the letters slant backwards, and the final letters"—touching points C and D on the insert—"end bluntly. See what I mean? Everything just opposite. Another funny thing—none of the letters in the Hart signature appear in the Melville signature—the sort of thing you'd do if you weren't sure you could make the same letter different enough in each." He leans back in his chair and grins at her. "An amateur job—all those things too decidedly different."

He returns his attention to the signatures, saying: "Now let me show you something else." His pencil touches points E and F. "See those spaces. They're exactly the same as this," touching point G. "See the end of this *w* and the *i*"—touching point H—"and the end of the *v* and the *i*"—touching point I—"well, if you forget the dots they make *r*'s that are exactly like this one"—touching point J—"except they are written backhand instead of sloping forward."

He drops his pencil on the letters and rocks back in his chair, turning his derisive grin on her again. "Now isn't that funny? All the things an amateur would be likely to think about are different. All the others are alike."

She stares at him as if trying to make up her mind what attitude to take. He watches her amusedly for a moment, then asks: "Well, shall I call up the Messrs. Hart and Melville and ask them about it?"

She bites her lip, then lowers her head, her shoulders droop a little, and she says in a defeated tone: "There isn't any Hart, any Melville."

"You surprise me," he says with good-natured mockery. He regards her lowered face for a moment, then, indicating the letters, asks curtly: "Why these, sister? Too lousy a stenographer to get real ones?"

She raises her head indignantly, but immediately becomes spiritless again. "No," she says in a dull, hopeless voice, but speaking very deliberately, "but the only real ones I could give for the last five years would be no good. I've been in prison."

Richmond blows out cigarette smoke and nods slowly in the manner of one whose guess has been confirmed. "I thought I recognized the prison look," he says. Then he chuckles. "What'd you do? Stick up the Mint singlehanded? Anybody in your fix with nerve enough to walk into a detective's office—"

She interrupts him fiercely: "Nerve? It wasn't nerve, it was desperation. I'd try any—"

Now he interrupts her, and his smile is a sneer: "I know! I know, sister! Trying to go straight—your record against you—hounded by the police—I've heard it all before."

She, still fiercely: "Go straight? I'm reaching a point where I don't care what I do so I do something, don't care whether I go straight or—" Her voice is becoming shrill with hysteria.

He flutters fingers at her and interrupts her once more, in a half-serious soothing manner: "Sh-h-h! You'll wake up the office boy next door." Then his face and voice become altogether serious. "Sit down," he says, "and let's talk reasonably."

She sits down slowly, face and manner lifeless again.

He rocks comfortably back in his chair and asks in a friendly tone: "What'd they send you over for?"

She replies: "I was working for the president of an investment trust named Queeble. He was using the trust funds for his own speculations. I was his secretary and knew what he was doing, helped him. Both of us thought he was smart enough to get away with it. Well, he wasn't, and when he got 15 years I got what I got. Maybe you remember it. My name was Helen Crewe then. It's Helen Crane now." She recites all this with no emotion at all except some weariness, and when she has finished she sits looking expressionlessly at Richmond, as if expecting nothing, fearing nothing.

Richmond lights a fresh cigarette, leans back in his chair, and smokes and stares thoughtfully at the ceiling for a considerable while. Then he faces the girl again and says casually: "You can take your hat and coat off and go to work."

Her eyes widen. She stares at him in uncomprehending surprise.

He says: "I can use a secretary whose record shows she can do what she's told and keep her mouth shut. You say you want a job. Want this one?"

She rises eagerly. "Yes, sir! I don't know how to—"

He cuts her thanks short by handing her the two letters of recommendation and saying: "Bury these and make yourself at home in the outer office."

She takes the letters as if dazed and goes out.

Richmond watches her until she has shut the door, then makes a brief nod of satisfaction at the door, picks up a newspaper from his desk, squirms a little more comfortably into his chair, and begins to read. He looks up when Helen—without hat or coat now—opens the door.

"The man has finished lettering the door," she says. "He says it's five dollars."

He says carelessly: "Tell him we'll mail him a check."

"Yes, sir," she says and goes out, but returns almost immediately to say: "He says he wants it now, Mr. Richmond."

Richmond starts to frown, clears his face, and replies: "Oh, all right, send him in."

He puts his hand in his right-hand trouser pocket and brings out three crumpled paper bills and some silver, counting it surreptitiously in the shelter of the desk. When he has counted out five dollars there are only a few pieces of silver left. He shrugs philosophically and puts them back in his pocket.

The sign-painter comes in.

Richmond says cheerfully: "Five dollars? Here it is," and hands the man the three bills and some silver. Then, as the man says, "Thank you, sir," and turns away, Richmond says, "Wait—buy yourself a cigar," and gives the man a coin from the scanty remainder in his pocket.

The man grins, says, "Thank you, sir," again, touches his cap, and goes out, shutting the door behind him.

Richmond takes his few remaining coins from his pocket, looks ruefully at them, takes a deep breath, returns them to the pocket, and with a determined movement picks up the newspaper again. He turns briskly to the Personal column, runs his gaze down it, pausing momentarily at a couple of items having to do with missing persons, and then turns back to the news section of the paper. He skips all out-of-town items, reading only those having to do with local divorces, suits, crimes, scandals, etc. These he reads carefully, and spends a moment in thought after each before going on to the next.

He comes to one very small item tucked away in a lower corner of the page.

CHINESE SNUFF BOTTLE STILL MISSING

The valuable Chinese snuff-bottle
stolen last week from the residence of
Sidney F. Bachman, wealthy collector,
3661 Rennert Avenue, has not yet been
recovered. The police are working on
the theory that it may have been stolen
by a former Chinese servant.

Richmond stares thoughtfully at this item, pursing his lips, then his face lights up, he rises from his chair, thrusts his hands in his pockets, and walks twice up and down the floor, swiftly, smiling to himself. Then he snaps his fingers as if the idea he wanted had come to him, sits down again, and reaches for the telephone book. He finds Bachman's number and calls it.

"I should like to speak to Mr. Bachman," he says into the phone after a little pause. "It is about the Chinese snuff-bottle. . . . Thanks."

He drums cheerfully on the desk with his fingers while waiting for Bachman. Then: "Hello. Mr. Bachman?"

The other end of the wire. An extremely tall and bony old man with a tremendously bushy growth of white whiskers and no hair at all on his head. "Yes," he says excitedly. What is it? What is it?"

Richmond, very suavely: "This is Gene Richmond speaking. You probably know my detective agency by reputation—possibly we've—"

Bachman, impatiently: "Yes, yes! But what is it about the bottle? Have you found it?"

Richmond smiles at the preposterous "Yes-yeses" and continues in the same tone as before: "Certain information that may lead to its recovery has come into my possession during the course of certain other investigations we are making, and I—"

Bachman: "Yes, yes! Where is it?"

Richmond: "I'm sorry I can't tell you that, Mr. Bachman, and even the information I have may be worthless, but if I can see you I'll be only too glad to give it to you. I can't very well tell you over the phone. Shall I come out to your house?"

Bachman: "Yes, by all means, but what—?"

Richmond: "I'll be there in half an hour." He hangs up, pushes the phone aside, and rises. He puts on his hat and goes into the outer office.

Helen is standing looking out a window. She turns toward him.

He takes off his hat and makes a courtly bow. "Our first client," he says, "is a gentleman named Bachman, Sidney F., who's lost a bottle of snuff. You may open an account for him whilst I'm out gathering the sordid details." He bows again and goes out, leaving her staring after him.

He goes downstairs in an elevator and out to the street. A taxicab is standing a little distance from the office building entrance. He starts toward it briskly, puts a hand to the pocket his few coins are in, makes a rueful grimace, and runs for a passing street-car.

The front of a pretentious suburban home. Richmond goes up the steps and rings the doorbell. The door is opened by a stout manservant.

Richmond says: "Mr. Richmond. Mr. Bachman is expecting me."
The servant bows and stands aside for him to enter.

A room in Bachman's house. Richmond is seated. Bachman is standing in front of him, close, his bony shoulders high, his bearded face thrust down toward Richmond, his body bent into a question mark. He is demanding excitedly: "But what, exactly, is it you have learned?"

Richmond looks steadily into the tall man's eyes for a moment, then gravely replies: "Mr. Bachman, before I speak I must have your promise that you will divulge nothing of what I tell you to the police until I give you permission."

"But why?"

"I have my clients' interests to protect," Richmond explains smoothly. "As I told you, this information came to me while working on another matter. To have the police rush in with their usual clumsiness might spoil this other matter for my client. I cannot risk that."

Bachman becomes apoplectic with rage. "I am to suffer for your client!" he shouts. "I am to lose my most valued possession forever so some other man's—what was it?—interests are protected! What about my interests? I won't do it. I don't know your other man! I don't care about him! I want my bottle! You'll tell me or I'll call the police now and have them with their usual clumsiness force you to tell."

Richmond, who has been calmly looking at the angry man from under raised eyebrows, says coolly: "Go ahead—and then you and the police can try to guess whether what I tell is true or phoney."

An alarmed look comes into Bachman's face. "No, no," he says hastily, "I didn't mean that, Mr. Richmond. I was excited. I—"

"That's all right," Richmond says carelessly. "Now how about that promise?"

"How long—how long will it be before I can tell the police?" the collector asks in a wheedling voice.

Richmond's shoulders move in a little shrug. "I don't know. It depends on—" He breaks off with an impatient gesture. "Here's what happened, Mr. Bachman. I have an operative in—in an eastern city trying to locate some stolen property. It too is decidedly valuable. In the course of his investigation he had traced it to—a buyer of rarities, we'll say, but it developed that what had been offered to this buyer was not our article. My man, of course, paid little attention to the other article then—all he learned was that it was small, old, and Chinese."

"That is it!" Bachman cries. "That is certainly it! Who is this buyer?"

Richmond raises a protesting hand and shakes his head slowly. "As I told you, Mr. Bachman, I can't jeopardize my own client's interests by allowing the police or anyone else to come charging in, stirring things up, frightening—"

Bachman: "But you said this man hadn't bought your client's property. What difference does it make then?"

Richmond: "I said the thing we traced to him wasn't my client's. Because a false trail led to him doesn't necessarily mean that the true one won't."

Bachman, despairingly: "But, Mr. Richmond, you can't make me wait and wait and risk—" He breaks off as a thought comes to him. He holds out his hands in a pleading gesture and begs: "Suppose I too become your client. Suppose I engage you to recover it. Then you can handle it in your own way without fear of spoiling your other client's—"

Richmond, staring levelly at the collector: "I didn't come here to sell you my services. I came to give you what information I had."

Bachman, wheedling: "But you will handle it for me, Mr. Richmond? I'll pay you well. I'll—"

Richmond: "Besides, we've no assurance that the Chinese thing offered was your snuff-bottle; no assurance that we can find it anyhow. I don't know whether this person I mentioned actually bought it or not."

Bachman: "But you can find out. Will you, Mr. Richmond?"

Richmond, a bit reluctantly: "Well, if you wish."

Bachman grasps one of Richmond's hands and shakes it warmly: "Thank you, sir," he says. "You won't regret it."

Richmond, politely: "Oh, that's all right. Let's see, you'd better give me a check for, say, two hundred and fifty dollars to cover initial expenses."

Bachman, eagerly: "Splendid! Come downstairs and I'll make it out now."

Richmond rises. They leave the room together, one of the collector's long thin arms affectionately across the detective's shoulders.

Richmond's outer office. Helen Crane is sewing the seam of a glove. She puts it down as Richmond comes in from the corridor. He is all smiling cheerfulness.

"Did you open Mr. Bachman's account?" he asks.

Looking curiously at him, she replies: "There are no books to open it in."

"Tut, tut!" he says humorously. "We must get you huge stacks of books. Is there a piece of paper to jot things down on?"

"Yes, sir." She finds a sheet of paper and a pencil.

"Credit him with two hundred and fifty dollars on account," he dictates as she writes, "and charge him first with my taxi fare to his house and back, say a dollar thirty-five each way; then a telegram to New York, say three dollars and twenty cents—it should be a long one; and then a wire from New York, say a dollar thirty; and fifteen dollars a day from now on for the salary of an operative in New York. I'll let you know from day to day what the operative's expenses are." He starts toward his private office.

She clears her throat and says: "There's no typewriter, Mr. Richmond."

He halts and turns. "Tut, tut!" he says again. "We must get you one for each hand. Rent one this afternoon and we'll get what books you need and stationery and things." He goes into his office and shuts the door.

She stares thoughtfully after him.

Richmond's private office two months later. It is expensively furnished now, with thick carpet on the floor, pictures on the walls, etc. He, at an immense shiny mahogany desk, is writing a letter:

Dear Babe:

My first couple of months here have been prosperous enough to make me think I picked the right spot. Maybe you'd better put your other pair of stockings in a bag and come on down to get your share of the pickings. There are a couple of jobs I could use you on right now and—

He stops and looks up as the door opens. It is Helen Crane with a newspaper in her hand. "Did you see this?" she asks, advancing to his desk.

He turns the letter to Babe face down on his desk and looks at the portion of the paper she indicates with a finger. The headlines are:

STOLEN CHINESE SNUFF BOTTLE RECOVERED
POLICE ACCUSE BACHMAN BUTLER

Richmond smiles ruefully. "Too bad," he says. "He was good for another five hundred or so anyhow." He shrugs philosophically. "Oh, well, we didn't do so badly, at that." He runs a hand slowly over his hair. "Write him a letter of congratulations and enclose him a check for his unused balance of"—he pauses—"make it some odd amount like thirty-six dollars and forty cents." He grins. "We can give him that much back to make things look right. Fix up a statement of his account to show how it happened."

The girl is regarding him with worried eyes.

He pats one of her hands lightly. "This is a racket, my dear," he says lightly, "but you can get out of it any time you want."

She bites her lip, turns to leave his office.

He says: "I think I'll run over to Palm Springs for a couple of days' rest. You understand all the jobs we've on hand well enough to take care of the reports, don't you?"

"Yes," she says, "I—I hope you have a good time."

"Thanks." He returns to his letter as she goes out.

*   *   *

The sound of heavy surf in utter darkness. The darkness pales enough to let the white lines of breakers and the wet sand of a beach become barely visible. A motor boat is dimly seen coming through the breakers. Shadowy figures of men go over the sides of the boat and run it up on the beach.

From the complete blackness of the higher beach, the long white beam of a flashlight suddenly comes, to settle on the prow of the boat, on its painted name, *Carrie Nation*. The shadowy figures of men sink swiftly into the lower shadows of the boat's sides. From the side nearer the camera comes the report of a pistol and a small brief streak of light pointing at the flashlight.

The flashlight is tossed high in the air, spinning, its beam making slow eccentric patterns in the darkness. It falls to the ground and lies there, throwing a long thin triangle of light across the sand. Just beyond the light a man's body lies face down, motionless, on the sand. There is the sound of men's feet running away.

Next day. A middle-aged stout man, indignation written on his perspiring face, hurrying down the corridor of an office building. He stops at a door labeled GENE RICHMOND, PRIVATE DETECTIVE, wipes his face with a handkerchief, takes a deep breath, opens the door, and goes in.

The outer office is arranged as before, but it also is now furnished expensively. Inside the railing at the desk facing it, an office-boy of 15— freckled, his hair somewhat rumpled—sits facing the door, but his elbows are on the desk, his head is between his hands, and he is immersed in a book that lies on the desk. His eyes are wide and he is chewing gum rapidly.

Helen Crane is at her desk using a typewriter, but looks around immediately at the stout man. Then she speaks to the boy: "Tommy!"

The boy looks up at the man without taking his head from between his hands and says: "Yes, sir."

The stout man clears his throat. "I want to see Mr. Richmond."

The boy, automatically, as if speaking from habit: "Have you an appointment?"

"No." The man takes a card from his pocket and puts it on the boy's desk. "Is he in?"

The boy looks at the card. It reads: *Milton Fields, President, Star Portland Cement Corp.* The boy says: "I'll see. Have a seat." He turns his book face down on the desk—its title is *The Backgammon Murder*—and goes into Richmond's private office.

Richmond is smoking a cigarette and reading a newspaper. Tommy looks at him with obvious admiration. Richmond takes Fields' card, glances at it, tosses it on his desk, and, returning his attention to the newspaper, says: "Bring him in, Tommy." He puts the newspaper aside slowly when Fields is ushered in, smiles, says, "How do you do, Mr. Fields," and nods at a chair.

Fields sits down as Tommy, going out, shuts the door.

Fields says: "Mr. Richmond, three times in succession in the last few months we have been underbid on large contracts by another company—the same company—the Dartmouth Portland Cement Company."

Richmond nods attentively.

Fields continues, impressively: "I have reason to believe that one of my employees is supplying the Dartmouth Portland Cement Company with copies of our bids."

Richmond nods again, saying: "You want us to find out which of your employees?"

Fields shakes his head. "I know. I want you to get me proof. It is a young fellow named Kennedy, a clerk. I pay him thirty-five dollars a week, and I am told it is common knowledge in the office that he spends his week-ends in Caliente, is out every night gambling, running around with fast women."

Richmond begins: "Sounds likely, but maybe we'd better—"

Fields interrupts him: "He's the one all right. I want you to get me the proof."

Richmond looks thoughtfully at Fields, then says: "O.K. We ought to put two men on it. One to shadow him, one to get acquainted with him and pump him." He looks thoughtfully for another moment at Fields, who says nothing, and goes on: "They'll cost you ten dollars apiece—and expenses."

Fields says: "Very well, but I must have action—quick."

Richmond nods carelessly and presses a button on his desk.

Helen Crane opens the door and comes in, stenographic notebook and pencil in her hands.

Richmond addresses her: "Miss Crane, Mr. Fields will give you the name, address, description, and so on of a man he wants investigated." He rises slowly. His movements—like his words—are very deliberate, as if carefully thought out beforehand. He has the manner of a man too sure of himself to feel the need of trying to impress anybody. As he walks toward the outer office door he adds, casually, over his shoulder: "He'll also give you a check for say two hundred and fifty dollars to start with." He passes into the outer office, shutting the door behind him.

Tommy, looking around, tries to cram his book out of sight in a desk drawer.

Richmond smiles at the boy with good-natured mockery and asks: "Still keeping posted on how really good detectives work?"

The boy grins in embarrassment, then, in a burst of enthusiasm blurts out: "You'd make all these guys in the books look like a bunch of bums, Mr. Richmond." He drops his eyes, they look searchingly up at Richmond, his voice and countenance become ingratiating, and he begs: "Aw, gee, Mr. Richmond, I wish you'd give me a chance to—"

Richmond holds up a hand, palm out. "Stop it," he orders wearily, as if answering a familiar plea. "Stick around till you're grown and I'll send you up against all the thugs you want. Till then—see if you can get the result of the third race."

Tommy, crestfallen, reaches for the telephone.

Richmond goes over to Miss Crane's desk, lights a cigarette, picks up a small stack of unopened mail, and glances idly through it.

Tommy: "Not in yet, sir."

Richmond nods, drops the unopened mail on the desk again, and strolls back into his private office.

Tommy watches the door until it is shut, then draws his book out of the drawer, puts a fresh stick of gum into his mouth, and resumes his reading and chewing.

The inner office. Richmond is seated at his desk. Fields, standing, is handing a check to Miss Crane. She takes it, thanks him, and goes into the outer office. Fields picks up his hat from a chair. Richmond rises, holds out his hand to Fields, and, as they shake, says: "I'll keep in touch with you." He ushers him out through a door opening on the corridor, then returns to his chair and newspaper.

His telephone bell rings. Still reading the paper, he puts out a hand, picks up the phone, and says: "Gene Richmond speaking."

The other end of the wire, a luxuriously furnished library. A very dapper elderly man—rather prim-faced, white hair carefully trimmed and brushed, wearing nose-glasses with a black ribbon draped from them—is seated at a table, holding a telephone to his ear.

Standing close to him, head bent a little, watching and listening with a strained, frightened expression on a face meant by nature to be genial, is a man of 45. He is a little plump, a well-fed, well-groomed man, with a normally rather good-looking frank countenance. The hand in which he holds a cigar within six inches of his mouth is trembling, and his breathing is audible.

The elderly man speaks into the telephone: "Mr. Richmond, this is Ward Kavanaugh, of the law firm of Kavanaugh, Baker, and Kavanaugh. Can you meet me in my office at ten o'clock this evening?"

Richmond, his eyes still on his newspaper: "I can come over right now if you wish, Mr. Kavanaugh."

Kavanaugh: "No, I won't be back in the city until ten o'clock."

Richmond puts down his newspaper carefully. He purses his lips a little, but there is no other change in his face. He says: "Just a moment. I'll see if I'm free then." He puts down the telephone, goes to the outer office door, opens it, and says, in a quiet, matter-of-fact tone: "Have this call traced, Miss Crane."

He shuts the door again, puts his hands in his trouser pockets, strolls idly about his private office for a little while, then returns to the telephone. "Yes, Mr. Kavanaugh," he says, "I can make it."

Kavanaugh: "Thank you. At ten, then." He puts down the phone and turns his face toward the man standing beside him.

The man sighs, as if with relief, and puts his cigar between his teeth, but his face does not lose its strained, frightened look.

Richmond's office. He is reading the newspaper again.

Miss Crane comes in, halting just inside the door. "The call came from Herbert Pomeroy's residence at Green Lake," she says.

Richmond nods thoughtfully. "That's the stockbroker, isn't it?" he asks in the manner of one already knowing the answer. "That would be his country house."

Miss Crane: "Yes, sir."

Richmond: "See what you can dig up on him."

As she turns toward the door it opens and in comes a blonde girl of 23, pretty in a somewhat showy way, smartly dressed, carrying a small traveling bag. She has a breezy manner, an immense store of vitality.

Richmond rises, smiling delightedly, calling: "Hello, Babe."

As Helen Crane goes out, shutting the door behind her, Babe drops her bag, runs across the office to Richmond, throws her arm around him, and they kiss. She wriggles ecstatically in his arms, rumples his hair, pulls his head back by his ears to look at his face. "Gee, it's good to see you again, you no-good darling!" she says. She pulls his head down again, rubs her cheek against his, and begins scolding him happily: "What was the idea of leaving me to roost up there alone for two months before sending for me? Some other gal, huh? You two-timing scoundrel, and you waited till you were tired of her." She squeezes him tightly in her arms trying to shake him.

Richmond chuckles, frees himself, picks her up, and sets her on his desk. "Don't be such a rowdy," he says. He sticks a cigarette in her smiling mouth, puts one in his own, smooths his hair, straightens his tie while she holds a match to his cigarette and her own.

In the outer office Helen Crane is looking thoughtfully at the connecting door.

The inner office again. Babe crosses her legs, knocks ashes on the floor, and looks admiringly around the office. She is never still; a hand, a shoulder, a leg, her head—one is always in motion. "A nice flash you got here, Gene," she says. "In the money again, huh?"

He looks complacently at the expensive furnishings. "Not bad." He grins at her. "There's a penny to be picked up here and there in this town."

She laughs. "There always will be in any town for you," she says, "and a gal." She waves her cigarette at the connecting door. "But not that curio that went out as I came in?" she asks, and then, before he can speak, says: "No, I can't see you going for that. That's a novelty—you having a gal in the office that you wouldn't want to take home with you." She looks sharply at him and demands with mock severity: "You haven't reformed, have you, Gene?"

He shakes his head good-naturedly. "Lay off Miss Crane," he says. "She's a find." He touches Babe's uppermost knee with a forefinger. "I've got a job for you tonight, honey."

She pouts at him. "You mean you're going to put me to work right away? We're not even going to have this first evening together?"

"I'm sorry," he says, coming closer to put his hands on her shoulders, "but I've got to toil too. You know how things break in this racket. I want you to pick up a kid named Kennedy whose boss thinks is selling him out—make him—see what you can work out of him. Miss Crane will give you the dope."

Babe squirms petulantly under his hands, still pouting.

He pats her cheek lightly and reaches over to press the button on his desk.

Helen Crane, notebook in hand, enters.

Richmond addresses her: "Miss Crane, this is Miss Holliday, who will be working with us."

The two women acknowledge the introduction politely while sharply sizing each other up.

Richmond continues: "Miss Holliday's first assignment will be on the Fields job. Will you give her the particulars? She will. . . ."

FADE OUT

That night. Richmond at the wheel of a Cord roadster. As he parks near the entrance of an office building he looks at the clock in the dashboard. It is 9:55. He leaves the automobile, goes into the office building, looks at the lobby directory until he sees KAVANAUGH, BAKER & KAVANAUGH, 730, rides in an elevator to the seventh floor, and walks down the dimly lighted corridor to the lawyers' door. There is nothing in his manner to show he is on a serious errand.

He knocks on the door lightly, opens it without waiting for an answer, and goes into a reception room lighted only by one desk lamp. Ward Kavanaugh appears in a doorway across the room, saying precisely, "Ah, good evening, Mr. Richmond. It was good of you to come," coming forward with quick short steps to shake hands.

They go into Kavanaugh's office. Richmond takes off hat, overcoat, and gloves, and puts them on a chair, sitting in another large leather chair that Kavanaugh has pushed a little forward for him.

Kavanaugh sits at his desk, erect, adjusts his nose-glasses, then puts his fingertips together in front of his body, and, in his precise voice, says: "This matter upon which I wish to—ah—consult you, Mr. Richmond, is one of the—ah—greatest delicacy." He takes off his glasses and, holding them in one hand, looks sharply at Richmond. He is obviously somewhat flustered.

Richmond says nothing.

Kavanaugh puts his glasses on again, clears his throat, goes on: "One of my clients has unfortunately—or, rather, injudiciously—allowed himself to become involved—legally if not morally—in a somewhat—a decidedly—serious affair—" He jerks his head a little sharply at Richmond and concludes his speech quickly—"a crime, in fact."

Richmond is lighting a cigarette. His eyes are focused attentively on Kavanaugh's. He says nothing.

Kavanaugh takes off his glasses again and taps the thumbnail of his left hand with them, nervously. He says: "He—my client—is a man of the highest standing, socially and in the business world." He puts his glasses on his nose again. "Several days ago his bootlegger's— ah—salesman came to him and said he was going into business for himself, but had not a great deal of capital. He suggested that my client advance him a thousand dollars, in exchange for which he would supply my client—out of the first shipment—with—ah—merchandise worth much more than that at current prices." He takes his glasses off again. "My client is a man who lives well, entertains extensively. He had dealt with this man several years, satisfactorily. He agreed." He takes out a handkerchief, polishes his glasses and returns them to his nose.

Richmond smokes in silence.

Kavanaugh continues: "Unfortunately, in landing the first shipment from the rum-running ship—there was a—a serious accident. The bootlegger is now a fugitive from justice and threatens—if my client does not assist him—to—ah—involve my client." He takes off his glasses again.

Richmond asks casually: "How serious was the accident?"

Kavanaugh: "Very serious."

Richmond, still casually: "Murder?"

Kavanaugh hesitates, makes a nervous gesture with his fingers, says reluctantly: "A man was—was killed."

Richmond tilts his head back a little to look at a plume of smoke he is blowing at the ceiling. He says thoughtfully, unemotionally: "Your client is legally guilty, then, of first-degree murder?"

Kavanaugh, startled, begins a protest: "No, that's—"

Richmond quietly interrupts him, speaking as before: "The thousand to help finance the bootlegger makes your man an associate of the bootlegger's in the rum-running enterprise, maybe even makes him the principal and the bootlegger only his agent. Either way, rum-running's a felony and any killing done while committing a felony is first-degree

murder and everybody involved in the felony—whether they have anything to do with the actual killing or not—is equally guilty. It's a tough
spot for your man."

Kavanaugh puts his glasses on, and begins, unconvincingly: "It is,
as I said, a very serious matter, but I think you—ah—exaggerate the—"

Richmond shrugs carelessly, and in his quiet, deliberate voice says:
"Take him into court then."

Kavanaugh makes no reply to this. He puts his fingertips together
again and looks at them with worried eyes. Then he raises his head, looks
at Richmond, and asks: "Mr. Richmond, do you think that we—that you
could extricate my client from this—ah—affair?"

Richmond, casually: "Why not? It'll cost money, though. I wouldn't
touch it under twenty-five thousand down, and maybe it'll cost you a
couple of hundred thousand before you're through."

Kavanaugh protests: "But that's exorbitant!"

Richmond makes a careless gesture with the hand holding his
cigarette. "It's not so much"—he smiles gently—"for Pomeroy."

Kavanaugh's body jerks stiffly erect in his chair, his mouth and eyes
open, his glasses fall off his nose. "What? How?" he stammers.

"I detect things," Richmond says drily. "I'm a detective. That's
what you want, isn't it?" He puts his cigarette in a tray beside his chair
and uncrosses his legs as if about to rise. "Well," he asks quietly, "do I
go to work for you or don't I?"

Kavanaugh evades his gaze. "I'll have to—ah—discuss your—ah—
terms with Mr. Po—with my client," he says in confusion.

Richmond rises, says politely: "Right. Let me know as soon as
you can. The sooner we get going, the better." He holds out his hand.

Kavanaugh rises to take it spluttering: "Of course you understand
this is all in the strictest confidence."

"Certainly," Richmond says easily, "if Pomeroy hires me."

Kavanaugh goggles at him in consternation, stammering: "You
mean—?" He is unable to finish the sentence.

Richmond smiles coolly at the lawyer and tells him: "I'm a businessman. Like Pomeroy or any other businessman I use information

that comes to me in my line for profit. I'd rather get my profit out of Pomeroy, and I can promise him good value for his money, but if he doesn't want to play along with me—" He finishes with a shrug.

Kavanaugh draws himself stiffly erect. "That is blackmail, sir," he says in a somewhat pompously accusing voice.

Richmond laughs. "You've been reading the dictionary," he says with derisive mildness. His face and voice become hard and cold: "Pomeroy's in a sweet jam. I can help him or I can hurt him. Make up your mind." He turns and walks out.

That same night. The dashboard clock shows 11:30 as Richmond parks his car in a quiet street and gets out. He goes up the front steps of a large dark house set a little apart from its neighbors and rings the bell.

The door is opened by a plump youngish man in dinner clothes who says, "Good evening, Mr. Richmond," politely, and steps aside to admit the detective.

Richmond passes down the hallway to a room where there is a bar. He halts in the doorway to look casually at the occupants of the room, nods to a couple of them who greet him, exchanges a "Hello" with one of the bartenders, and goes on to another room, where there is a crap-game. He speaks to a couple of the players, watches the game for a moment, and then goes upstairs, through rooms where various games are in progress, repeating the same performance. Then he returns to the bar, has a drink, and leaves the house.

The dashboard clock shows 2:10 as he parks the car again in a shabby street of small stores, cheap hotels, etc.

He enters a small cigar store, says, "Evening, Mack," to the man in dirty shirtsleeves behind the counter, lifts a hinged section of the counter, and passes through an inner door set in one corner of the store behind the counter. He mounts a flight of stairs to another door, and goes through it into a large room where there is a bar, booths, tables, etc. Forty or fifty people are there, eating and drinking at tables and bar. They are a tougher lot than those in the other establishment.

He strolls casually almost the length of the room—speaking to an acquaintance or two—and sits down at a small table with a slack-jawed, sharp-faced man of thirty in cheap, showy clothes. "Hello, Barney," he says without warmth. "Been looking for you."

Barney's eyes move from side to side uneasily. "This is a hell of a place to get chummy with me," he mutters.

Richmond's shoulders move in an indifferent shrug. "This is a swell place," he says. "Nobody'll think you're a stool-pigeon with me meeting you in the open like this. Nobody can hear us. Make the right kind of faces while we talk and they'll think I'm trying to get something out of you and you're not giving me any." He leans forward, making his face sterner than his voice: "Which of the rum-running boys is in trouble?"

Barney's eyes move uneasily again. He mumbles: "I don't know what you mean?"

Richmond: "Scowl at me, you sap. Shake your head no while you give me the answer. Who's having to hide out?"

Barney obeys orders, while mumbling: "I don't know—there's three or four of 'em."

Richmond: "Which one that just went in business for himself?"

Barney, sneering contemptuously to carry out their play, though his eyes are still uneasy: "You mean Cheaters Neely?"

Richmond: "Who's he?"

Barney, shaking his head again from side to side: "Used to be with Big Frank Barnes. He—" He breaks off as a waiter comes up, blusters: "I don't know nothing, wouldn't tell you nothing if I did."

Richmond, to the waiter: "Scotch—some of that Dunbar's Extra."

Barney says: "Same."

The waiter goes away.

Richmond, making an ostentatiously threatening gesture with a forefinger, asks softly: "What kind of jam is this Cheaters in?"

Barney raises his voice angrily: "Go to hell!" Then, keeping the same angry expression on his face, he leans forward and says in a low rapid voice: "I only know what I heard third-hand. He's supposed to've had to blip a guy down the beach—undercover man for the narcotic squad, the way I hear it."

Richmond makes his ostentatious threatening gesture again. "Was he running dope too?"

Barney, sneering: "Must've had some with him."

Richmond scowls at Barney as if in disgust. One of his hands has brought a crumpled piece of paper money out of his pocket. He passes it to Barney under the table, then leaning forward as if uttering a final threat, says: "See what else you can dig up on it. Break away now."

Barney pushes his chair back and rises, swaggering. "Go jump in the ocean, you small-time dick," he says truculently in a fairly loud voice. "And don't come fooling around me until you got something on me. Nuts to you!" He puts on his hat and swaggers out.

Richmond, his face a mask, picks up the drink the waiter sets in front of him. Men at tables around him grin covertly.

The following morning. Babe Holliday is sitting in Richmond's chair, smoking and playing solitaire on his desk, when he arrives.

"Morning, beautiful," she says cheerfully.

He hangs up his coat and hat and turns toward her asking: "How'd you make out?"

She pushes the cards up together and laughs. "What a guy!" she says. "He took me to a movie and bought me a soda afterwards. Anybody thinks that kid ever saw any Caliente or any fast life is screwy."

Richmond looks quizzically at her. "You wouldn't let him fool you, would you?"

She laughs again. "You ought to spend an evening with him—for your sins."

Richmond sits on the side of his desk and takes out a cigarette. "What's the answer then?" he says.

She rocks back in the chair, and says: "Easy. He's been bragging down at the office, trying to make out he's a devil with the women and an all around man of the world. All kids do it some.

Richmond looks up from his cigarette. "Sure?"

Babe: "Yep. He did it to me in a mild way, but a couple of minutes of talking was enough to let me know he'd never been down to Caliente, or much of any place else. And it's a cinch he's got no dough. It's a bust, Gene."

Richmond nods. "Sounds like it. We'd better play safe by looking him up a little. Don't put in more than three or four hours on it."

"Oke," Babe says, rising. "My expenses last night were two and half for dinner and three dollars and eighty cents' worth of taxicabs."

Richmond smiles at her. "This isn't that kind of a job," he says. "Your expenses were two bucks for dinner and twenty cent street-car fare. Get it from Miss Crane as you go out."

"You cheap so-and-so," she says without ill-feeling, kisses him, and goes out.

He sits down to his morning mail.

Presently Miss Crane comes in. "The Andrews divorce comes up this morning, Mr. Richmond," she says.

Richmond looks up from his mail. "She pay us the rest of the money she owes us?" he asks.

"Not yet. She still says she thinks the expenses ran too high, but she'll pay it as soon as she gets a settlement from her husband."

Richmond returns his attention to his mail. "She'll have to try to get her divorce without my testimony, then," he says with quiet finality. "I'm not in this racket for fun."

Miss Crane says, "All right," and turns toward the door.

Richmond looks up from his mail again. "We're supposed to have two men working on that Kennedy kid job for Fields. We'll fake up their reports after I'm through with the mail. Better keep their expenses down around—say—eight or ten dollars a day apiece—at first."

Miss Crane nods and goes out.

Richmond's telephone bell rings. "Gene Richmond speaking," he says into the instrument.

The other end of the wire. Barney in a telephone booth. He says: "This is Barney, Gene. Happy Jones and Dis-and-Dat Kid were with

Cheaters that night, and a mugg I don't know anything about called Buck. I don't know if that was all of 'em."

Richmond: "Where are they now?"

Barney: "I don't know where they're hiding out."

Richmond: "Find out. How about the guy who was killed?"

Barney: "I guess he was an undercover man for the narcotic people, all right, Gene, but I don't know nothing about him. The newspapers just said an unidentified man. They left their booze there, but if they had any dope they took it with them when they scrammed."

Richmond: "Right. Let me know as soon as you pick up anything else." He puts aside the phone.

Two men are walking in sunlight across a broad, carefully trimmed lawn. One is Ward Kavanaugh, in a business suit. The other, in tennis clothes, is the man who stood beside Kavanaugh during his phone conversation with Richmond—Herbert Pomeroy. Behind them a large house—a mansion—is seen, with a broad driveway leading up to it, and beyond the house part of a lake is visible, with a couple of sailboats and a motorboat cutting across it.

The two men cross the lawn slowly, both looking down with worried eyes at the grass.

"But how did he find out *I* was your client?" Pomeroy asks.

The lawyer shakes his head. "I don't know, Herbert, but I dare say they have ways of keeping in touch with much that happens."

Pomeroy frowns and works his lips together. "If it weren't for Ann," he mutters. Then: "You still think I shouldn't give myself up and stand trial?"

Kavanaugh, gently: "That's for you to decide, Herbert. I still am afraid that a prison sentence is the best you could hope for."

They walk a little further in silence. Then Pomeroy: "And there's no other way out except to engage this Richmond?"

Kavanaugh: "I'm afraid not."

Pomeroy: "But if I do, will he get me out of the mess, or will he simply bleed me?"

Before Kavanaugh can reply a Packard sedan squeals to an abrupt halt halfway up the drive behind them. Both men turn around quickly.

A man gets out of the sedan, waves his hand cheerfully at Pomeroy and Kavanaugh, and starts across the lawn toward them.

"Oh, Lord!" Pomeroy gasps. "It's Neely!"

Cheaters Neely is a full-fleshed man of medium height, about thirty-seven, carelessly dressed in moderately priced clothes topped by a Derby hat. He wears horn-rimmed spectacles, has a jovial hail-fellow manner, and might be mistaken for a third-rate salesman. Three more men get out of the sedan and follow him. The first is Happy Jones, a lanky man of forty with a mournfully lined thin face and dark clothes that seem mournful because, needing pressing, they sag close to his thin frame. The second is Buck, a big beetle-browed, hard-jawed man of thirty with deep-set smoldering eyes. He wears a grey suit not quite large enough for him and a grey cap. The third is the Dis-and-Dat Kid, a hatchet-faced boy of twenty-two in markedly collegiate clothes. A cigarette hangs from a corner of his mouth. He has no eyebrows. His eyes and his fingers are in constant fidgeting motion.

Neely, having reached the two men who stand waiting for him, grasps Pomeroy's hand and shakes it warmly, as if sure of his welcome. "How are you, Pomeroy?" he asks heartily.

Pomeroy, dazed, allows his hand to be shaken, but says nothing.

Holding Pomeroy's hand, Neely turns to make with his other hand a wide gesture at his three followers. "I want you to meet my friends." He indicates each with a motion of his hand. "Mr. Black, Mr. White, and Mr. Brown. Boys, this is Mr. Pomeroy." He drops the stockbroker's hand and looks at Kavanaugh. "This your father?" he asks.

Pomeroy says stiffly: "This is Mr. Kavanaugh, my attorney."

Neely grabs the lawyer's hand and shakes it. "Pleased to meet you, sir," he says heartily. He turns to his followers. "Boys, this is Mr. Kavanaugh."

The boys look at Mr. Kavanaugh with blank eyes and say nothing.

Neely claps Pomeroy lightly on the shoulder, "Well, now that everybody knows everybody, what's new?"

Pomeroy winces, clears his throat, asks weakly: "Why did you come up here?"

Neely raises his eyebrows a little and his face takes on an affably questioning look. He jerks his head slightly toward Kavanaugh.

Pomeroy says: "Mr. Kavanaugh knows about it."

Neely beams on Pomeroy and on Kavanaugh. "That's fine," he says. He turns his head to beam on his followers. "Ain't that fine, boys?" he asks. "Mr. Kavanaugh knows all about it."

The boys do not say anything.

Neely returns his attention to Pomeroy.

Pomeroy repeats his question: "Why did you come up here?"

Neely pushes his Derby a little back on his head, hooks thumbs in the armholes of his vest, and says amiably: "Well, I'll tell you, Pommy. You know we were in a little trouble. Well, it got worse, and I said to the boys: 'Boys, Mr. Pomeroy is our friend and he's a respectable millionaire, and respectable millionaires don't ever get into any trouble except over women, so we'll go up and visit with him and get him to show us how he keeps out of it.'"

Pomeroy wets his lips with his tongue. "I—I can't help you," he says.

Neely claps him on the shoulder again. "Sure you can," he says jovially. "Don't worry. There's no hurry about it. We'll stay here and visit with you two or three days while you figure something out. The boys like your place." He turns his head over his shoulder to ask: "Don't you boys?"

The boys do not say anything.

Pomeroy looks despairingly at Kavanaugh. The dapper elderly attorney is rigid with anger and seems on the point of bursting into speech, but when he sees the three "boys" regarding him with coldly curious eyes, he coughs a little and subsides.

"Well," Neely says with good-natured decisiveness. "That's settled. How about putting on the feed-bag? We ain't had lunch yet." He puts an arm across Pomeroy's back and starts him toward the house, "A shot of steam wouldn't do us any harm, either."

Pomeroy allows himself to be guided back to the house. Kavanaugh hesitates, looks at the three "boys" who are looking at him, and trots along behind Neely and Pomeroy. The three bring up the rear.

At the house, Pomeroy opens the door and steps aside to let the others enter. Kavanaugh halts beside him. Neely and his three followers go in. Pomeroy puts his mouth to Kavanaugh's ear. "Get Richmond," he says.

Kavanaugh nods. He and Pomeroy go indoors.

Richmond's office. He is seated at his desk. Babe Holliday is rocking vigorously back and forth in another chair.

"There's nothing to it, Gene," she is saying. "The kid hasn't been away over a weekend for six months, and then only to his cousin's in San Francisco. And you can count the nights he's been out after midnight on the toes of your left foot. He goes to the movies and he reads, and that lets him out. I talked to—"

The telephone bell interrupts her.

Richmond speaks into the phone: "Gene Richmond speaking."

The other end of the wire. Kavanaugh crouched somewhat furtively over the telephone. His eyes dart toward the closed door. He speaks into the instrument in a low voice: "This is Ward Kavanaugh, Mr. Richmond. You may consider your terms accepted."

Richmond, quietly business-like: "Thanks. Where's Pomeroy? How soon can I see him?"

Kavanaugh: "He's here at Green Lake, but—"

Richmond: "I'll be up this evening."

Kavanaugh, looking fearfully at the door again, splutters: "But *they* are here too, Mr. Richmond!"

Richmond: "Swell! We can all gather around the fireplace and pop corn and tell ghost stories. I'm leaving right away."

Kavanaugh: "Are you sure you ought to—"

Richmond, reassuringly: "Just leave it to me." He puts down the telephone, stares thoughtfully at it for a moment, lips pursed, eyes dreamy and narrow; then his face clears again and he turns in his swivel chair to face Babe Holliday.

* * *

A formal garden beside Pomeroy's house at Green Lake. Cheaters Neely, Buck, the Dis-and-Dat Kid, and Happy Jones are walking in pairs down a path, looking around with manifest approval.

A girl of twenty-one comes up the path toward them. She is dressed in white and carries a tennis racket. She is lithe, beautiful, somewhat haughty. As she approaches the four men she holds her head high and regards them with disapproving eyes.

They halt, blocking the path. The Dis-and-Dat Kid's fidgety eyes look her up and down, ogle her, and he runs the tip of his tongue over his lips. Buck stares somberly at her. Happy Jones turns his back to her and pretends interest in the shrubbery. Neely grins amiably at her.

As they make no move to clear the path for her, she halts in front of them, regarding them haughtily.

Neely points a finger at the tennis racket and says, familiarly: "Hello, sister. How's the racket?" Then he laughs merrily at his joke.

The girl starts to speak, then bites her lip angrily, puts her chin higher in the air, steps out of the path, walks around them, and goes on toward the house.

The four men turn in unison to watch her.

"That's a pain in the neck," Buck growls.

The Dis-and-Dat Kid leers at the girl's back. "I'll take it," he says.

Happy Jones whines: "I like a woman with some meat on her."

Buck looks at Happy's thin frame. "You got a lot to give her," he says.

They retrace their steps to the house, going leisurely around to the back and entering through the kitchen, where the cook, a buxom middle-aged woman in white, is directing the activities of two assistants. She looks around indignantly as they come in.

They stroll through the kitchen in single file, looking around curiously. The Dis-and-Dat Kid spies a chicken on a platter. He picks up a knife, slashes off a drumstick and bites into it.

The cook, hands on hips, advances angrily, "Here! What are you up to? Clear out of here!"

Buck scowls at her. "Aw, go poach your kidneys," he growls. He leans over, tears the other drumstick from the chicken and stuffs half of it into his mouth.

They leave the kitchen through a doorway opposite the one by which they entered. Happy Jones pauses in the doorway to look back, amorously, at the angry cook.

The Dis-and-Dat Kid nudges Buck, points his drumstick at the sad-faced man in the doorway, sniggers, and says: "Ain't dat somepin'?"

They go through the pantry and dining room into a hallway, strolling idly, the Kid and Buck gnawing their drumsticks. In the hallway they see the girl in white again. Her eyes darken with anger when she sees them. She goes haughtily up the stairs. They stand and watch her mount the stairs. They keep their hats on.

She goes into a room on the second floor. Pomeroy and Kavanaugh are seated there. The room is furnished with elaborately carved, stamped, and brass-studded Spanish office furniture. There is a stock-ticker in one corner. Through an open door, part of Pomeroy's bedroom can be seen.

Kavanaugh rises and bows as the girl enters. Pomeroy says: "Hello, Ann. How'd the game go?"

Both men have put their best attempts at smiling unconcern on their faces for her.

She is still angry. "Father, who are those horrible men?" she asks.

He glances apprehensively at Kavanaugh, then smiles as carelessly as he can at his daughter and asks: "You mean those—" He finishes the sentence with aimless motions of his hands.

"Those four horrible, horrible men!" she says.

He smiles paternally at her. "They won't bother you, honey," he says. "And they'll only be here a couple of days at most. It's necessary that—"

She takes a step toward him. "A couple of days!" she exclaims. "They can't stay here, Father! We've people coming down tomorrow for the weekend—the Robinsons and the Laurens and—you can't have them here. They're horrible!"

Pomeroy puts out a hand to pat one of hers. "There, there!" he says soothingly. "Papa'll see what he can do. Perhaps it'll only be necessary to keep them here overnight." He looks at Kavanaugh for support, asking: "Perhaps, hm-m-m?"

Kavanaugh nods hastily, saying: "Perhaps. Perhaps."

"But why do you have to keep them here overnight?" Ann demands. "Why are they here at all?"

Pomeroy shakes a playful finger at her. "No prying into Papa's affairs, young lady," he says.

She screws her eyes up at him, wrinkles her forehead, asks, "Are they detectives or guards or something? Are you in some kind of danger?" She seems suddenly frightened.

"Sh-h-h," he says. "There's not a thing for you to worry about—word of honor."

She bends down to kiss him on the forehead. "And you will get rid of them?" she asks as she straightens up.

"Cross my heart," he promises.

She flashes a smile at Kavanaugh and goes out.

Kavanaugh sinks down in his chair again. The light goes out of Pomeroy's face. They stare at each other hopelessly.

A bedroom in Pomeroy's house. Happy Jones is lying on his back on the bed, hands clasped at the nape of his neck, staring mournfully at the ceiling. The Dis-and-Dat Kid is sitting on a window sill, looking boredly out at the grounds. Smoke drifts up from a cigarette in a corner of his mouth. Buck is straddling a chair, holding a glass of whisky in one hand. Neely is tilted back in another chair with his feet on the bed. He is wearing his derby; the others are bareheaded.

Neely is saying: ". . . and then I look at him again and I'm a son-of-a-gun if it ain't my brother."

Buck puts his head back and laughs heartily.

The Dis-and-Dat Kid turns his face from the window to grin crookedly. Then he leaves the sill, drops his cigarette on the floor, puts his foot on it, and asks: "What are we waiting for, Cheaters? For Happy to get bed sores?"

Neely pulls a watch from his pocket, looks at it, and sticks it back in. "I'm comfortable," he says amiably, "but if you guys are itching, all right."

Buck hurls his drink into his mouth without touching his lips with the glass, smacks his lips, and rises, saying: "I'm ready."

Happy gets up slowly from the bed, finds his hat on the floor, and puts it on. Buck puts on his cap, the Dis-and-Dat Kid his hat. They leave the room and go downstairs to the second floor in single file, Neely first, then Buck, the Kid, and Happy.

As Neely reaches the second-floor landing, he meets one of the maids. She looks at him and the others nervously and keeps as close to the far wall as she can on her way to another part of the floor.

Neely raises a hand. "Where's the boss?" he asks.

She pauses long enough to say hurriedly, "Mr. Pomeroy is in his office," and hurries away.

Happy looks sadly after her and shakes his head. "She ain't got the meat on her," he whines.

They go down to the room where Pomeroy and Kavanaugh are, Neely opens the door without knocking, and the others file in after him.

Pomeroy has been standing at a window, Kavanaugh is seated. Both try to conceal their alarm as they look around at the four men entering.

Neely, all smiles, says, "Howdy, gents," while Happy, the last one in, is shutting the door and leaning his back against it.

Buck strolls deliberately across the room and out of sight through the open bedroom door. The Dis-and-Dat Kid, fingers and eyes fidgeting, moves around the other side of the room, keeping himself turned slightly sidewise toward the stockbroker and his attorney.

Pomeroy and Kavanaugh exchange nervous glances. Pomeroy clears his throat and says: "Kavanaugh and I are still unable to see how we can be of any assistance to you—in—"

Neely stops him with an up-raised palm. "Don't you and Kavvy worry about that," he says amiably, smiling as if at a couple of younger brothers. "Us boys figured it all out. Didn't we, boys?"

The boys do not say anything. Kavanaugh and Pomeroy glance apprehensively at each other. Kavanaugh takes off his glasses and begins to polish them.

Neely says: "Stake us to get-away dough and we'll amscray.

Kavanaugh and Pomeroy stare uncomprehendingly at him.

Neely laughs. "Money," he explains, "and we'll go to read and write—powder out—blow—leave the country."

Pomeroy glances at Kavanaugh again, then asks hesitantly: "Ah—how much money would be necessary?"

Neely puts his thumbs in his vest armholes and rocks back on his heels, screwing his eyes up at the ceiling in good-natured calculation. "Well," he begins, "we'd have to. . . ."

Gene Richmond in his Cord roadster burning the road along the edge of Green Lake. Across the water the sun is going down. He turns off the road into Pomeroy's driveway, stops in front of the house, and gets out.

A man servant opens the door for him. "Mr. Pomeroy is expecting me," he says, "Mr. Richmond."

The servant takes his hat and coat, bows him into a reception room off the hall, and goes upstairs.

Richmond waits placidly until the servant has disappeared at the top of the stairs, then goes briskly up after him, reaching the top in time to see the servant entering Pomeroy's office. Then he moderates his pace and walks down the second-story hallway, arriving at the door just as the servant comes out. He says: "Thanks," politely to the man and goes in. The servant goggles at him.

The six men in the room—Buck is standing in the bedroom doorway now—stare at him.

He bows to Kavanaugh—"Good evening"—and then to the stockbroker, saying suavely: "Mr. Pomeroy, I suppose?"

Pomeroy returns the bow uncomfortably. He is sitting at the Spanish desk, the fingers of one hand on an open checkbook, the other hand holding a pen.

Richmond surveys the others meditatively, one by one, speaking as if to himself. "Cheaters Neely, of course," making a circle around one of his own eyes to indicate the spectacles; "and Happy Jones—that's easy," looking at the mournful man; "and Buck and I are old friends—remember the time I pulled you out of the sewer pipe up north? So you must be the Dis-and-Dat Kid."

Neely smiles pleasantly at Richmond and says: "You seem to know more people than know you, brother."

By then Happy has slipped behind Richmond to stand with his back against the hall door again. His right hand is in his coat pocket. Buck glowers at Richmond. The Kid's eyes fidget from Richmond to Neely.

Kavanaugh, speaking hastily, as if to forestall further conversation between Neely and the detective, says: "Ah—Mr. Richmond, we have just reached an—ah—amicable settlement." He adjusts his glasses to his nose with an air of relief.

Richmond looks with mild amusement from Kavanaugh to Pomeroy. The broker abruptly leans over and begins to sign the check.

Richmond takes two deliberate steps to the desk and bends to look at the check, and then, just as deliberately, puts out a forefinger and rubs it slowly across Pomeroy's incompleted signature, making an undecipherable dark smear of it.

Pomeroy rocks back in his chair in surprise.

The Dis-and-Dat Kid puts a hand to his right hip and takes a step toward Richmond's back. Neely catches the Kid's eye, smiles, and shakes his head. The Kid halts indecisively.

Richmond addresses Pomeroy carelessly: "That's a sucker play. Giving him money is what got you into this. You'll never get out that way."

Pomeroy starts to speak, but is interrupted by the Dis-and-Dat Kid snarling: "Who is dis mugg?"

Richmond slowly turns to face the Kid, smiles mockingly at him, and says: "Dis mugg is the only one that's going to be paid off on this job. The name's Gene Richmond, employed by Mr. Kavanaugh and

Mr. Pomeroy"—with the semblance of a bow vaguely directed toward them—"to shake you boys loose."

From the bedroom doorway Buck addresses Neely earnestly: "That's the truth he's telling, Cheaters. I knew him up north. There ain't no chance of anybody else turning a honest dollar with him around. Let's knock him off right now."

Richmond chuckles and turns to face Buck while Neely is replying good-naturedly: "We can always knock him off. Let's watch him do his stuff a while first."

Richmond turns to Neely: "Why don't you boys go out and pick some flowers and give us a chance to talk this over?"

"Sure," Neely says agreeably. "Talk your heads off, and maybe when you're through, Pommy'll write another check and maybe he'll make it bigger than that one." He turns toward the door. "Coming, boys?"

The boys follow him out, glowering at Richmond.

Neely puts his head into the room again. "We won't be far off if you want us," he says, "or if you don't." He shuts the door again.

Richmond lights a cigarette and addresses Kavanaugh gravely, deliberately: "Mr. Kavanaugh, you called me a blackmailer last night. Perhaps there was some justification for it. "My,"—he smiles faintly—"sales methods are somewhat high-pressure at times, but believe me when I tell you that I know I can straighten this thing out, and that I will if you and Mr. Pomeroy will simply let me handle it in my own way. It may not be a nice way, but this isn't a nice situation. But it isn't the first time a thing of this sort has ever happened. I've handled them before. It's chiefly a matter of deciding which of several possible methods happens to fit this particular case."

A large portion of their distrust has gone out of the two older men's faces while Richmond has been talking, and Pomeroy's face has become almost hopeful. But now he frowns hopelessly again and complains: "But I've got to get rid of them at once. There are people—guests—coming tomorrow. I can't have these men here."

Richmond laughs. "You'd rather go to San Quentin than spoil a weekend party?"

Pomeroy winces.

Richmond puts his hands in his trouser pockets and walks to the window and back to a chair and sits down. His manner is curt, business-like. "First," he says, "I'd like you to go over the whole thing from beginning to end, with every. . . ."

FADE OUT

Richmond, leaving Pomeroy's room, shuts the door, grins cynically at it, and starts down the hall. Buck steps out of another door and says: "Howdy, tin-star. Make out all right with the plutocrats?"

Richmond, with mock disgust: "They're a couple of sissies! I had a terrible time persuading them to let me have you boys killed resisting arrest. Where's Cheaters?"

Buck points a forefinger at the ceiling. They walk side-by-side to the stairs and go up to the bedroom where Happy is lying as before on the bed and Neely and the Kid are arguing hotly. All three turn to-ward the door—Happy rolling over on an elbow—when Buck, saying, "We got distinguished company," ushers Richmond in and shuts the door.

Richmond comes to the point at once, in an unruffled, matter-of-fact voice, addressing Neely: "What do you boys want to do? Do you want to crowd Pomeroy to the point where he lets me have you knocked off? Or where he goes into court with a lot of perjury and matches his reputation against yours—calling that thousand-dollar check a forgery?"

Neely chuckles. "You're full of cute tricks, ain't you? No, Richy, all we want is a get-away stake. That's little enough, ain't it?" he goes on persuasively. "Pomeroy'll never miss the dough, we'll get out of the country, and everything'll be all hotsy-totsy."

Richmond moves his shoulders a little and asks: "But what's in that for me?"

Neely stares at Richmond in surprise. The Kid says: "Well, I'll be—"

Buck growls fiercely: "See! What'd I tell you? Let this mugg hang around and we'll be lucky to get away from here without owing money!"

Neely recovers his voice. "What do you want?" he asks sarcastically. "A commission?"

Richmond dismisses that suggestion with a wave of his hand. "We can talk about that later," he says airily. "What I want just now is for you boys to stick around here, keeping out of people's way, not making any trouble for anybody, not riding Pomeroy, and I'll promise to take care of you."

They stare at each other in surprise.

Richmond steps back to the door. "And no matter what happens," he says, "don't let it frighten you into bolting."

He steps through the doorway and shuts the door. They all begin talking at once.

Night. Richmond is leaning on the back of a drawing-room chair, holding a partly filled cocktail glass in his hand. Pomeroy is seated beside a table on which there are glasses and a cocktail shaker. Kavanaugh is helping himself to an hors d'oeuvre from a tray a man servant is holding. There is no conversation; Pomeroy and Kavanaugh seem ill at ease.

Ann Pomeroy comes in, smiles at Kavanaugh, leans over to kiss her father's head, asking: "Am I terribly late again?"

Pomeroy rises to say: "Ann, this is Mr. Richmond. Mr. Richmond, my spoiled daughter."

Ann, smiling, goes to meet Richmond with her hand outstretched. He bows over it. She says, "I suppose they've been pretending they're starved waiting for me," takes Richmond's arm, and guides him toward the dining-room.

He smiles politely, but says nothing. His eyes gravely study her profile when she is not looking at him. Kavanaugh and Pomeroy follow them.

After dinner. Richmond and Ann come out of the house. He is bareheaded, smoking a cigarette. She has a shawl over her dinner dress. As they step down into a path leading to the formal garden, she takes his arm again and says gaily: "I know you. You're Gene Richmond. You're a detective. You found out who murdered Laura Gordon's Aunt Minnie in Portland. She told me about you."

He chuckles. "I remember," he says. "It was a janitor."

Ann: "That was years and years ago. I was in school."

Richmond: "That's right, I'm a doddering old man."

She laughs up at him.

Neely and his cohorts in the bedroom. They are playing stud poker on a card table. Neely, who is dealing, has most of the chips in front of him. Two cards have been dealt. Neely, looking at the cards he has dealt, says, "The king bets." Happy, who has the king showing, pushes out a chip. The Kid and Neely each push out a chip. Buck, the last man, says, "Folding a trey," turns his three of diamonds face down on his hole card.

He rises, yawns, stretches, and goes to the window. A tiny point of light shows through shrubbery down on the grounds, and then Richmond and Ann, walking slowly arm in arm become visible as they pass through an open space. Richmond's cigarette glows again.

Buck turns his head over his shoulder to tell his companions: "Sherlock's got the dame out in the bushes."

Neely pushes four chips into the center of the table: "Up a couple."

Happy pushes out four: "And a couple more."

The Kid turns his cards face down. "Ain't worth it," he says. He stands up, takes his coat from the back of his chair, puts it on. "Deal me out awhile," he says. He gets his hat and leaves the room, moving silently, unhurriedly. When the door shuts behind him, Buck grins at it. The others do not look up from their cards.

The garden. Richmond and Ann are seated on a bench some distance away. The Dis-and-Dat Kid moves silently toward them, going swiftly from shadow of tree to bush to hedge until he is close behind their bench. As he crouches there, ready to hear what they are saying, they rise and move on slowly. He follows, stalking them from shadow to shadow.

Ann is saying: "But what are you doing here if Father is not in danger?" She raises her voice a little, tensely. "He is. I know it. I can feel it. It's those four horrible men. I've felt it ever since they've been here."

Richmond smiles at her earnestness. "I can understand your not liking them," he says.

"Liking them?" she repeats, and shudders. Then, both hands on his arm, peering up at his face, she asks: "You are here on their account, aren't you?"

"Part of my business here is with them," he admits, "but your father is not in danger, there is nothing for you to be afraid of. Believe me."

The Kid, moving into the shadow of a tree, startles a cat, which goes hastily up the tree, its claws rasping against the bark.

Ann clings to Richmond, her terrified face twisted around toward the noise, gasping: "What is that?"

Richmond, his arms around her, looking down at her, paying no attention to the noise: "Nothing to be afraid of. You're trembling." He strokes her upper arm with a soothing hand.

The Kid is flat against the tree, out of their sight. His eyes shift from side to side. He is breathing silently through his mouth.

The girl slowly extricates herself from Richmond's arms, though she continues to hold one of them. She looks around uneasily, "Let's go back to the house," she says.

Richmond nods. They go back, arm in arm, the girl now and then glancing apprehensively around. The Kid follows them back—from shadow to shadow.

In the library they find Pomeroy, alone; Ann kisses him, says, "Good night, Father," then holds out her hand to Richmond. "Good night, Mr. Richmond."

He bows and says, "Good night," as she leaves the room. Pomeroy, impressed by his daughter's ready acceptance of Richmond, smiles at him more cordially than heretofore and says: "Smoke a cigar with me." He opens a box on the table beside him.

Richmond says: "Thanks. Where's Kavanaugh?"

Pomeroy: "Gone to bed. He wants to catch the early train back to the city."

Richmond: "Swell." He goes over and shuts the door, then takes a seat facing Pomeroy. "It's just as well to keep him out of it as much as we can."

Pomeroy draws his brows together a little. "I don't understand you," he says a bit coldly. "Mr. Kavanaugh was my father's best friend, has been almost a second father to me. He is, in my opinion, the best lawyer in—"

"I know," Richmond agrees evenly, "but like a lot of top-notch lawyers he's probably never been in a criminal court in his life. All he knows about civil and corporation and this and that kind of law's not going to help you here, Pomeroy—not even criminal law. We don't need law, we need tricks. And maybe we'll be doing Kavanaugh a favor by sparing his conscience knowledge of some of the tricks we'll have to use. If we need legal advice, I've got the man for you—he hasn't looked into a law book for twenty years, but juries don't hang his clients."

Pomeroy winces at the word "hang," then nods doubtfully, partly convinced.

Richmond rises. "I think I'll get some sleep." He looks down at Pomeroy. "Kavanaugh told you I wanted twenty-five thousand dollars down, of course. Will you phone your office in the morning and have them send the check over to my office?"

Pomeroy nods again.

Richmond says, "Thanks. Good night," and goes out.

A corridor. The Dis-and-Dat Kid steps swiftly through a doorway and shuts the door. Richmond comes into sight, passes the door behind which the Kid is standing, opens another door farther down, and goes into his bedroom.

The Kid comes out, looks up and down the corridor, and goes quietly to another door, putting the side of his face to it, listening while his eyes and fingers fidget.

Inside the room, Ann Pomeroy, in night clothes, is brushing her hair, humming, smiling as if pleased with her thoughts.

The Kid listens for a while, then takes a deep breath, exhales it, grins crookedly, licks his lips, and goes away.

Richmond, beginning to undress in his bedroom, takes a typewritten piece of paper from his pocket and looks thoughtfully at it, pursing his lips.

It reads:

Herbert Pomeroy.
> Age 45.
> Widower.
> One daughter: Ann, 21.
> Residence: Pasadena & Green Lake.
> Major Partner Pomeroy & Co. Stocks and Bonds.
> Large timber holdings Northern California.
> Director: K.C. & W.R.R.; Shepherds' National Bank;
Pan-American Inv. Co.
> Bank Accounts: Shepherds'; Sou. Trust Co.; Fourth
Nat'l Bank.
> Large real estate holdings vicinity Los Angeles.
> Reputed worth $10,000,000 to $12,000,000.

Richmond's finger, traveling down this list, hesitates longest at the fourth item and the last.

He returns the list to his pocket and continues undressing.

The next morning. Richmond's roadster is standing in front of the house. He comes out of the house just as Ann rounds the corner.

She looks at the car and at him and asks, somewhat dismayed: You're not going away?"

"Just to the city for a few hours," he assures her. "I'll be back this evening."

Her face brightens. She gives him her hand, saying: "Be sure you are."

"It's a promise," he says as he gets into the car.

She waves at him from the steps as he rides swiftly away.

An unclean, shabbily furnished housekeeping room. The bed is not made. There are dirty dishes, an empty gin bottle, glasses, cigarette butts on an unclothed deal table. In one end of the room a bedraggled youngish woman in a shabby soiled kimono is frying eggs on a small gas stove on the drain-board beside a sink. Barney, in pants, undershirt, and stocking feet, is sitting on the side of the bed.

"Aw, stop bellyaching," he says irritably. "I told you I got a trick up my sleeve that'll have us sweating against silk when I pull it off, but I need two-three days more to get set. I—"

The woman turns around, snarls at him: "I heard that before. You ain't got anything up your sleeve but a dirty arm. I'm sick and tired of having to bring in all the dough while you lay around and—"

There is a knock at the door.

They look at one another. Barney rises from the side of the bed, glances swiftly around the room as if to see that nothing is visible that should not be, and goes to the door. "Who is it?" he asks.

"Richmond."

"All right." Barney opens the door.

Richmond comes in saying: "Hello, Barney. Hello, May."

The woman nods without saying anything and turns around to her eggs.

Barney shuts and locks the door, saying: "Set down."

Richmond remains standing. He has not taken off his hat. "What's new?" he asks.

Barney's eyes move sidewise to focus sullenly on May's back. Then he steps closer to Richmond and mutters: "They had the junk all right—ten pounds of C. They delivered it to Rags Davis." He puts a hand to the lapel of Richmond's coat, "Keep me covered on this, Gene," he begs. "I wouldn't last an hour if—"

With a gloved hand, Richmond removes Barney's hand from his lapel.

"I'll keep you covered, Barney," he promises. "Where's Rags' hang out now?"

"Sutherland Hotel—five eleven."

Richmond nods, asks: "Got anything else? Find out who the guy they killed was?"

Barney shakes his head, then says: "But he was a narcotic under-cover man, all right."

Richmond: "State, city, or federal?"

Barney: "I don't know."

Richmond says: "Stick around. I may want to get in touch with you today or tomorrow." He turns toward the door.

Barney touches his elbow. "Slip me a piece of change, Gene? I'm kind of on the nut right now."

Richmond takes two bills from his pocket, gives them to Barney, says, "Don't forget to earn it," drily, and goes out.

The woman at the stove turns around, looks contemptuously at Barney, spits noisily on the floor between them and says: "That's all you're good for—ratting!"

Barney has finished locking the door. He takes a step toward her, snarls viciously: "Shut up! I'll pop a tooth out of your face!"

The woman, frightened, begins to scoop the eggs out on plates.

Richmond goes to his office. Tommy jumps up from his book to open the gate for him, saying: "Good afternoon, Mr. Richmond."

Richmond says, "Hello, Tommy," leans over to look at Tommy's book, says humorously, "*The Murder in the Telephone Booth*—good Lord, what next?" rumples the boy's hair, nods to Miss Crane, saying, "Will you come in for a moment," and passes into his private office.

He hangs up his hat and coat and sits down at his desk.

Miss Crane comes in with some papers in her hand, also her note-book and pencil. She seems nervous, her face strained.

He is looking through his mail. "Anything new?" he asks without looking up.

"No," she says. Her voice is a trifle hoarse. "Here are the reports of the two men we're supposed to have working on the Fields job."

He takes the papers from her, runs his gaze over them rapidly. "Swell," he says as he hands them back to her, "but if you make the one that's supposed to be shadowing Kennedy—what do you call him? Harper?—watch his house until after the street cars stop running we can add taxi fare to his expenses."

She says, "All right," and goes out with the reports.

He picks up the telephone, says: "Get me Joe King, Narcotic Agents' Office in the Federal Building."

He reads his mail until the telephone rings. Then, into the instrument, still looking through his mail: "Hello, Joe; this is Gene Richmond."

The other end of the wire—a grey-haired man with a strong-featured, keen-eyed, clean-cut face. "Yes, Gene?"

Richmond: "I want to swap some information with you."

King: "Yes?"

Richmond: "Was the fellow they killed down the beach the other night one of your men?"

King's eyes narrow. He says: "I thought you wanted to swap. I didn't know you just wanted to *get* information."

Richmond: "Well, if he wasn't, say so, because then nothing I can say will be any good to you."

King, after a moment of thinking, replies: "All right—suppose we talk as if he were."

Richmond pushes his mail aside and gives all his attention to the telephone: "Fair enough. Know who killed him?"

King, softly: "Yes."

Richmond draws his brows together a little in disappointment. Before he speaks King is saying: "I'm hoping what you can tell me is where they are now."

Richmond's face clears. A faint smile lifts the corners of his mouth. "I'll be able to, Joe," he says, "inside of three days."

Joe King says: "That'll be—"

Richmond: "Have you got enough on them to swing them for the job?"

King: "I've got enough to hold them on while I get the rest."

Richmond: "Would it help to know the dealer they delivered the junk to, and what they delivered?"

King, keeping his interest from showing in his voice, but not in his face: "It wouldn't hurt any."

Richmond: "Ten pounds of cocaine to Rags Davis. He's living at the Sutherland Hotel, room five eleven."

King: "Thanks, Gene."

Richmond: "Have I held up my side of the swap?"

King: "You have."

Richmond: "Good. Now I want to ask a favor."

King, cautiously: "What is it?"

Richmond: "If you pinch Davis, just tell the papers he's being held as a dealer—keep the killing angle out of it until we've got the others."

King: "That's no favor—we're playing it that way ourselves. We haven't gone in for any publicity on the murder." He pauses, looking sharply at the phone, then asks casually: "How do you get in on this, Gene?"

Richmond, easily: "Oh, it's just an off-shoot of another job I've been working on. Let me know how you make out with Rags, will you?"

King: "Yes. You're sure of him, are you?"

Richmond: "Absolutely."

King: "Right. Thanks."

Richmond: "O.K."

They hang up.

King scowls thoughtfully at his telephone as he pushes it back, then picks up another phone and says: "Come in will you, Pete."

A hard-mouthed man of forty in quiet clothes comes in.

King addresses him: "Gene Richmond's got a finger in this Neely business somewhere."

Pete makes a mouth, rubs his chin with a thumb, says: "That's un-nice."

King: "He just phoned, promised to turn Neely and his mob up inside of three days, said they had ten pounds of coke that night and delivered it to Rags Davis."

Pete scowls, says: "There's a lot of things I'd rather have than Richmond messing around. What do you suppose his angle is?"

King shakes his head. "Too hard for me. Might be anything—that's got money in it. Better send somebody out to try to keep tabs on him. You and I'll go up against Rags."

"Try is right," Pete says glumly as he moves toward the door.

Gene Richmond's private office. He is standing shaking hands with a small middle-aged man dressed in neat, conservative clothes, and is saying: "We'll find him. Don't worry about it. Things seldom happen to youngsters of that age."

The man says, "Thank you, Mr. Richmond, thank you, sir," as if very much relieved. Richmond smiles and ushers him out through the corridor door.

Richmond returns to his desk and pushes the button. Helen Crane comes in.

"This man who was just in—Wood—wants us to find his fifteen-year-old kid—ran away yesterday. There's no occasion for secrecy. The police can do more than we can. Get in touch with them; they'll do their usual routine broadcasting, telegraphing, and so on." He picks up a piece of paper. "Here's the kid's description and the rest of the dope." He picks up a check. "I took fifty dollars from him. Charge him with one man's time till the police find the boy or he comes home."

Helen Crane takes the paper and check with a trembling hand. He glances curiously at her, but goes on in the same business-like tone: "This Pomeroy job is getting a little ticklish. I could wind it up now, but I think I can swing a big-money angle by holding off a day or two. But I'd better tell you that Neely and his crew are up there—at Green Lake—so in case— Let's see. I'll either phone you or be here twice a day. If I don't—you'd better turn in the alarm—to Joe King and the sheriff's office up there. It's best to—"

Her agitation has increased to such an extent that he cannot ignore it. "What's the matter, Helen?" he asks.

Her lips are quivering. "I don't want to go to prison again," she wails.

He rises, puts an arm around her, attempts to soothe her. "Sh-h-h. Nobody's going to prison. I know what I'm doing and—"

"That's what Mr. Queeble used to say," she moans, clinging to his lapels, "and both of us went to prison." Tears are running down her cheeks now.

The door opens and Babe Holliday halts in the doorway, her eyes large. Neither of them see her.

Richmond is stroking Helen Crane's shoulder and back, speaking softly to her: "There's nothing to be afraid of, but if you're that frightened, why don't you quit. You're all right and—"

Babe, who has recovered from her astonishment by now, advances swiftly into the room, saying angrily to Richmond: "Let her alone! She's not your kind!" She puts her arms around Helen, leading her toward the door, murmuring: "There, there, don't cry. He's not worth it."

Helen moans: "It's not his f-fault. I'm just a silly fool."

Richmond stares at them. Bewilderment and amusement are mixed in his face.

Babe, having deposited the weeping girl in the outer office returns and shuts the door.

"Aren't you a pip!" she says angrily. "Can't you let anything in dresses alone?" Suddenly her face and voice change, and she goes into peals of laughter that is merry and without rancor. "Good old On-the-Make Gene," she laughs. "He takes his fun where he finds it, no matter how queer they are." She affectionately takes his face between her hands and kisses him on the mouth.

The telephone rings. Richmond, grinning half-shamefacedly at Babe, wipes his face with a handkerchief, goes to the phone, and says: "Gene Richmond speaking."

The other end of the wire. King in a hotel lobby phone booth. He says: "This is King, Gene. You sure Rags is our baby?"

Richmond: "I was there at the birth."

King: "Well, we've been pushing him around for an hour and a half and haven't been able to crack him."

Richmond: "Search his place?"

King: "Frisked it from floor to ceiling, found nothing."

Richmond's eyes narrow. He purses his lips, then says: "Bring him over here. I'll take him apart for you."

King, somewhat skeptically: "Thank you, kind sir. I'll bring him." They hang up.

Richmond addresses Babe: "You'll have to scram, sister; company's coming."

"Oke," she says. "What are you doing tonight?"

Richmond: "I've got to go back to Green Lake."

Babe nods: "Pomeroy's got a daughter—two to one."

Richmond: "So has old man Holliday."

Babe nods again: "But old man Pomeroy's is newer to you."

Richmond chuckles, rises, kisses her, and says: "We'll go to dinner tomorrow night. How are you making out with the ancient Johnston? Got nearly enough on him for his wife's divorce yet?"

She dangles the end of a string of beads at him, saying gaily: "I've got this."

He scowls at her half-seriously. "That's not what you're being paid for. What good's Mrs. Johnston's divorce going to be to her if you leave him nothing to pay alimony with?"

"I couldn't guess," she replies, kisses him again, says, "Dinner tomorrow," and goes out.

He puts his hands in his trouser pants, rattles change, walks slowly to the outer-office door, opens it, puts his head through, and addresses Tommy: "Get Barney on the phone—tell him to come over right away. Show him in as soon as he comes."

Tommy says, "Yes, sir."

Richmond withdraws his head and shuts the door, looks doubtfully at the floor for a moment, shrugs a little, says in an undertone, "That's his hard luck," and goes back to his desk.

Joe King rides in an elevator to the fifth floor of a better class hotel, goes to room 511, takes a key from his pocket, unlocks the door, and enters.

Pete is sitting tilted back against the wall in a chair close to the door. A dandified slim man of medium height, perhaps thirty years old, is sprawled, cross legs straight out, in an arm-chair smoking a cigarette. The room shows signs of the narcotic agents' intensive searching. Both men look at King with calmly inquisitive eyes.

King speaks to the dandified man with the cigarette: "Come on, Rags, we're going visiting."

Rags smiles mockingly, says, "Don't care if I do," gets up, takes his hat from the bed.

Pete brings his chair down on all fours and gets up. He leaves the room first, then Rags, then King. They walk toward the elevator with Rags between the two narcotic agents. Neither of them touches him.

Richmond's private office. He is seated at his desk. Rags sits as before in a wooden arm-chair. King is half sitting on, half leaning against Richmond's desk, facing Rags. Pete is lounging against the wall beside the outer-office door.

Rags, gesturing lazily with a cigarette, is saying: "I've been nice to you boys, but you can't expect me to sit around like this forever. What are we waiting for; what are we going to do?"

King says: "You're more comfortable here than in a cell, aren't you?"

Rags: "Uh-huh—only my lawyer and a bond-broker can get me out of a cell before I begin to get tired of it. If that's where we're going, let's go."

King looks at Richmond. Richmond looks at his watch, opens his mouth to speak, but stops when Tommy opens the outer-office door for Barney.

Barney takes a step inside the office, sees Rags, blanches, and starts to turn back. Pete puts his left hand on Barney's left forearm, steps behind him, and pushes him a little farther into the room. Tommy, wide-eyed, shuts the door slowly, staring through the narrowing opening.

Barney turns his terror-stricken face from Rags to Richmond and begins to babble despairingly: "You promised you'd keep me covered, Gene! You told me you'd—"

Rags laughs mockingly. "Ever know a copper that'd give his stool-pigeons anything but the worst of it?" he asks Barney. His voice, like his face, is calm, but when he glances down at his hands he sees they are tightly gripping the arms of his chair, and the backs of his hands are dotted with sweat. Casually, to avoid the attention of the others, he forces his hands to relax and moves them slowly to his thighs, turning them backs-down so his trousers mop up the moisture.

Richmond, coldly: "Sorry, Barney. You'll have to talk. We'll protect you."

Barney: "But you promised you'd—"

Richmond: "I know, but it can't be helped. Tell these gentlemen how you know Neely took the stuff to Rags."

Barney puts both hands out pleadingly to Richmond and seems about to fall on his knees. "I don't know nothing, Gene," he cries. "Honest to God, I don't! I was just guessing!" His voice rises in a wail: "He'll kill me! He'll kill me, Gene! You can't make me—"

Rags smiles evilly and says: "It doesn't look like you're going to live forever, and that's a fact."

Barney cringes.

King addresses Rags curtly: "Shut up!" He leaves the desk, takes Barney by the lapels, pulls him close, and growls: "Come through. He's not going to be anywhere where he can hurt you—if you talk enough to let us put him and keep him out of your way."

Richmond: "You've got to go through with it now, Barney. He knows you've squealed. Make a clean job of it and we'll give you all the protection you need. If you don't—we'll have to turn Rags loose. You know what kind of a spot you'll be in then."

Barney stares past King at Richmond for a long moment, then at King, at Pete. The last trace of hopefulness goes out of his face, leaving it dumbly defeated. His body becomes limp. "All right," he says lifelessly, "he's got another room on the same floor of his hotel under another name where he keeps the stuff—in sample trunks. He's. . . ."

Pete has moved around behind Rags' chair, watching the dealer sharply. Richmond and King listen attentively to Barney.

Half an hour later. Barney, standing in the center of the floor, has just finished answering the last question. Rags, sitting as before, is staring thoughtfully at his feet. Pete is leaning on the back of Rags' chair. King is half sitting on, half leaning against the desk again. Richmond is smoking a cigarette.

King and Richmond look at each other. The narcotic agent says: "That does it, doesn't it?" His voice is faintly tinged with satisfaction.

Richmond nods gravely.

King, jerking a thumb at Barney, addresses Pete: "Take him down and book him as a witness."

Pete leaves the back of the chair, taps Barney on the arm, and says: "Come on."

Barney looks pleadingly at King and Richmond, begins: "You'll take care of me? You won't let—"

King nods curtly. "We'll take care of you. Go ahead."

Pete takes Barney out.

King turns to Rags, asking quietly: "How do you like it now?"

Rags raises his gaze from his feet, smiles bitterly, replies in a voice just as quiet, though rueful: "It's not so hot." He stops smiling. "Well, you've got it all. What are you waiting for?"

King: "Got any suggestions?"

Rags looks thoughtfully at King, at his feet, then up at King again, and asks evenly: "You don't think I had anything to do with bumping off that guy at the beach, do you?"

King leans forward a little and says persuasively: "Maybe we won't think so if you don't fight us too much."

Rags grins ruefully: "I'm pleading guilty to the rest of it," he says. "You got me cold."

"That's sensible," King says, rising. "Let's go."

King and Rags go out.

Downstairs, in the office building lobby, an inconspicuous looking man is loitering. He and King exchange significant glances as King and his prisoner pass.

The inconspicuous looking man is still in the lobby when Richmond leaves the building a few minutes later, and follows Richmond out.

Richmond gets into his roadster. The man following him gets into a black coupe farther down the street, and follows the roadster.

Richmond turns two corners, runs through a parking lot from one street to another, tilting the car's mirror to watch the coupe following him, drives half a dozen blocks and then down into the rear entrance of a garage under a large apartment house, out the front, through an alley, and away swiftly up a broad boulevard.

The man in the coupe waits awhile in the rear of the apartment building, then goes into the garage, looks around, questions one of the attendants, makes a gesture of chagrin, and goes away.

The dining room in the house at Green Lake. The Pomeroys and their guests are rising from the table. There are seven guests besides Kavanaugh—three men and four women—all young and gay and fashionably dressed. As they leave the dining-room, laughing and talking, the sound of an automobile comes from out of doors. It is dark outdoors.

Ann Pomeroy makes vague, somewhat incoherent, excuses and goes to the front door. Richmond is getting out of his roadster. She runs down the steps to him. "Oh, I'm glad you're back!" she says impulsively.

He looks curiously at her, asks: "Why? Has anything happened?"

She is suddenly embarrassed. "N-no," she stammers. Then she puts a hand on his arm, says earnestly: "I *am* glad you're back. Father—I made Father tell me the—everything. You can help him, can't you?"

He pats her hand. "Certainly," he says. "There's nothing to worry about. Nothing's happened today?"

Ann: "No—except the youngest one of those four horrible men—wherever I go I either see him or have the feeling that he's watching me." She shivers, moves close to Richmond. "I'm not—I don't think I'm very brave. I'm afraid, Gene!"

Richmond puts an arm around her. "Sh-h-h," he says soothingly, "it's coming out all right. I wish your father hadn't told you."

"I made him," she says. "Are you sure it's going to come out all right?"

"Absolutely," he replies as they ascend the stairs.

The Kid steps out from behind a bush and scowls sullenly at their backs.

The bedroom where Neely and the others were seen before. Happy is lying in his usual position on the bed. Neely is sitting on the foot of the bed, wearing his hat. Buck is at the table, pouring himself a drink.

The Kid comes in, shuts the door, and says: "Richmond's back."

Buck suddenly slams his full glass into a corner of the room and wheels on Neely. Happy swings his legs over the side of the bed and sits bending tensely forward, a hand behind him: his face remains as usual. The Kid crouches with his back to the door, his right hand swinging near his hip.

Buck is speaking in a hoarse, strained voice: "Listen, Cheaters, I got enough of this hanging around waiting for somebody to pull the ground from under our feet. What I say is let's go down and put a rod against this Pomeroy's belly and either collect or leave him looking at the ceiling. And I say let's do it right now."

Richmond opens the door, but does not enter the room. He looks mockingly from one to another of them. They maintain their positions, turning only their heads toward him. While selecting a cigarette from a package in his hand, he tells them casually: "There'll be news for you in the morning paper. Don't let it excite you too much. Just sit tight and Uncle Gene will pull you through."

He shuts the door and goes down to the room where the Pomeroys and their guests are. All except Ann and a slim dark-haired boy in dinner clothes are playing bridge at two tables. The boy and Ann are sitting on a sofa by the fireplace. When she sees Richmond she makes a place for him beside her, patting it and smiling at him. He goes over to her and sits down. The dark-haired boy's smile is polite rather than cordial. The three of them laugh and talk, though nothing they say can be heard above the chatter at the tables. Gradually, as they talk, Ann turns on the sofa to face Richmond more directly, until her back is almost squarely turned on the dark-haired boy, and by then he has almost been excluded from the conversation, neither Ann nor Richmond seeming to remember he is there. He pouts, then gets up somewhat angrily, and moves off to watch one of the bridge games. They do not seem to notice his going. Several of the card-players look at them with politely moderated curiosity.

A closer shot of them as she stops laughing, glances around to see they cannot be overheard, and says very seriously: "You weren't just trying to keep me from worrying when you said everything would come out all right?"

Richmond: "I honestly wasn't, Miss Pomeroy. I—" He stops, looking questioningly at her, as she frowns. "I called you Gene out there," she says severely.

He smiles apologetically, says: "I wasn't just trying to keep you from worrying, Ann."

She laughs.

He continues, seriously now: "A lot happened in town today—in our favor. It—"

"What happened?" she asks.

He smiles and shakes his head. "Nothing I can tell you. This is nasty business. I'm having to do things I don't like to talk about—especially not to you."

She puts a hand on one of his, says softly, earnestly: "You're doing them for me—for Father and me. I ought to be forced to hear what you're having to do."

He says drily: "I'm getting paid for it. I'm a hired man doing his job."

She puts both hands on his and corrects him tenderly: "You are a friend—savior."

He looks around in embarrassment, sees that the bridge games have broken up and some of the players are coming toward them. He rises with evident relief.

Later that night. The guests are saying goodnight and going up to their rooms. Pomeroy and Ann are left alone in the room. He sits on the sofa facing the fireplace and stares at the fire while finishing his cigar. Ann goes over to him and sits on the arm of the sofa beside him, putting an arm around him, leaning her cheek on his head.

Presently she asks: "Do you like Gene Richmond, Father?"

Pomeroy takes the cigar from his mouth, frowning a little, and says slowly: "I don't know, honey. I don't think I do."

Ann: "Why?"

Pomeroy, still speaking thoughtfully: "I've a feeling that he's not too scrupulous, that perhaps some of the things he does in his work are—"

Ann, quickly: "But he's doing them for us, Father!"

Pomeroy turns his head and looks at her. "Yes, that's so," he says slowly.

As he continues to look at her, her face flushes and she averts her eyes.

He asks: "Do you like Gene Richmond, Ann?"

She looks at him and says: "Yes."

*   *   *

Outside. Richmond, smoking a cigarette, is strolling along a dark path toward the house. On the grass beside the path, twenty feet behind, the Kid is following him silently. The Kid's right hand is in his bulging jacket pocket. As they approach a part of the path made especially dark by sheltering bushes, the Kid quickens his pace, closing in, and when Richmond reaches the dark spot, the Kid jumps him. Nothing can be seen but two indistinguishable moving figures in the light of Richmond's cigarette. There is a distinct sound of a fist hitting flesh, once—then footsteps running away. Richmond's face can be seen as his cigarette burns brighter with an inhalation, and he resumes his stroll toward the house. He opens the front door, light flooding him, turns to look at the dark grounds, snaps the butt of his cigarette into the darkness in a long arc, glances at the knuckles of his right hand with a faint smile, and goes indoors, shutting the door.

The Dis-and-Dat Kid leaves a sheltering tree, scowling toward the door, putting a hand tenderly to a side of his jaw. Then he looks around. A lighted kitchen window catches his eye. He goes down and looks in. Happy is seated at a table eating a piece of pie, drinking milk. Across the table, the buxom cook is seated, her face broad and smiling, talking coquettishly, though the Kid cannot hear what she is saying.

He starts to grin crookedly, stops grinning and puts his hand to his face again, and leaves the window, vanishing in the darkness.

A cheaply furnished, but very clean and orderly, bedroom. Helen Crane is sitting at a dressing-table mirror brushing her hair. Her eyes are wide, moist, and frightened. Her lips are moving. She is saying: "I don't want to go to prison again," over and over to her reflection in the glass as she brushes her hair.

*   *   *

Pomeroy's house. Richmond is standing with his back to the fire talking to Pomeroy and Ann, who sits as before. He is addressing Pomeroy: "It's better for you not to know what I'm doing. As I told Miss Pomeroy—"

"Ann," Ann says.

Richmond chuckles. "As I told Ann," he goes on, "a lot I've had to do hasn't been nice, wouldn't be nice to listen to. You can take my word for it that things are shaping up much better than I expected. A few more days should see you in the clear. But it's enough for me to have the dirty details on my conscience—that's my job—without having you worried with them.

Pomeroy: "You really feel you're making satisfactory progress?"

Richmond: "Oh, yes."

Pomeroy looks at his daughter. She snuggles closer to him and says impulsively: "I'm sure Gene's right—about our leaving everything to him—trusting him." She looks up somewhat proudly at the detective, then asks: "You don't have to go to the city again tomorrow, do you?"

He nods. "Yes—it all centers there."

She makes a face at him.

He speaks to Pomeroy: "I'll need some money, cash, five thousand. A man who gave us some valuable information will have to be shipped abroad. His life isn't worth a cigarette if he stays here, and his killing might drag the whole story out in the open. Will you have your office send the money over to mine in the morning?"

Pomeroy says: "Yes. Is there anything else?"

Richmond says: "No."

Pomeroy rises, says, "Well, I'm off to bed, then," kisses his daughter, says, "Good night, Richmond," and goes out, leaving Richmond and Ann together.

The corridor outside the girl's bedroom door. The Kid stands with his ear against the door, listening. A clock somewhere in the house strikes four faintly. The Kid opens the door, goes in, shuts the door, crosses to the bed, looks down at the sleeping girl, moves cautiously around the room, looking into bathroom and dressing room, then goes out.

Next morning. Richmond alone at table eating breakfast. He rises hastily as Ann comes in. They exchange good-mornings, sit down, and she asks earnestly: "*Must* you go to the city today?"

He smiles, says: "Must."

She does not smile. She leans toward him and says in a low, strained voice: "I'm afraid, Gene. I'm afraid—awfully. Don't go."

He tries to soothe her: "I don't think there's anything you really need to be afraid of here. It—"

She: "I'm not afraid when you're here, but when you're gone it's awful. Even if there are a lot of people here—if you're not here I'm afraid."

"Go with me," he suggests.

"I can't—not with these people here."

"Swim, play tennis, keep on the jump," he advises her; "don't let yourself stop and think. You'll be all right."

"I'm afraid," she repeats.

"There's nothing to be afraid of," he assures her, smiling cheerfully. "Your father shouldn't've told you anything." He continues jestingly, trying to laugh her out of her fears: "And I'll bring you a bag of gumdrops and a doll and a new ribbon when I come back this—"

She is not to be turned from her point. She comes quickly around the table, puts her hands on his shoulders and whispers desperately: "Don't go. Don't leave me—dear."

He rises, upsetting his chair, takes her in his arms, and kisses her, but when she looks questioningly at him afterward, he shakes his head and says earnestly: "I've got to." His eyes brighten as he thinks of an unanswerable reason. "You were there when I told you about the man we'd have to get out of the country, or at least as far away as we can."

Ann: "Yes."

Richmond: "Well, it may be a matter of life or death for him—my going to the city today."

Ann, impulsively: "It was selfish of me. You must go, of course."
She comes into his arms again.

Richmond in his roadster riding toward the city, whistling happily.

Neely holding a spread newspaper in his hands. His cohorts hanging
over his shoulders as they read a news item headed:

DRUG DEALER HELD
John ("Rags") Davis Arrested
in Downtown Hotel

They breathe heavily, and when they have finished they look at
one another in consternation.

Richmond enters his outer office, acknowledges Tommy's and Miss
Crane's greetings, and asks: "Did Pomeroy's office send anything over
for me?"

Miss Crane says: "Yes, sir," and hands him a thick envelope. She
is obviously holding herself tightly in hand.

He tears it open, takes out a sheaf of hundred-dollar bills and asks:
"Anything else turn up?"

Miss Crane: "Barney's been phoning every hour or two since late
yesterday. He seems very excited."

Richmond nods. "Get him on the phone for me." He goes into
his private office, hangs up hat and coat, sits down at his desk, counts
off ten of the hundred-dollar bills, folds them, and puts them in a vest
pocket. The balance of the bills he stuffs into his wallet.

The telephone rings. He picks it up, says: "Gene Richmond speaking."

The other end of the wire. Barney at a wall phone in the hall of
his rooming house, his eyes looking fearfully around as he speaks in a

harsh whisper over the wire: "For God's sake, Gene, do something for me—get me away from here before they croak me! They're after me, Gene! I got to blow! They'll croak me sure! Give me some dough— enough to get away with—Gene! You got to! You got me into this! You got to get me out! You got to, Gene! Please! Please! For God's sake!"

Richmond: "If you'll turn off the monologue long enough to listen, I'll tell you I've got a thousand bucks for you."

Barney, hysterically relieved: "Have you, Gene? Will you—"

Richmond: "Where are you?"

Barney: "Home."

Richmond: "All right. I'm on my way over with it." He hangs up the receiver in the midst of Barney's profuse hysterical thanks.

Richmond puts on his hat and coat, says, "I'll be back in a little while," as he goes through the outer office, rides down in an elevator, and leaves the office building, going afoot. He walks along without any especial signs of haste, stopping once or twice to look in a shop-window, enters Barney's rooming-house, and goes up to his room. When he knocks on the door it swings open. Barney is lying on the floor, face up. There is a dark spot on his coat over his heart. He is dead.

Richmond, scowling thoughtfully, touches his chin with fingers and thumb, then kneels beside the dead man, feels his hand and wrist, rises, looks around the room, goes out to the telephone in the hall, drops in a coin, and says: "The police. This is an emergency call." Then: "A man is dead in room two sixteen at thirteen hundred and nine South Whitfield Street. Yes—murdered."

He goes back to the dead man's room, goes in, and shuts the door. Standing there, looking at the dead man, waiting for the police, he slowly takes the ten hundred-dollar bills from his vest pocket, straightens them out, and stuffs them into his wallet with the others.

Joe King's office in the Federal Building. He, Pete, and Richmond are there. They silently wait until two men bring in Rags Davis.

Rags smiles at them, saying: "Afternoon, gents."

King nods at a comfortable chair. "Sit down, Rags," he says.

Rags sits down.

King asks: "Got cigarettes?"

Rags, amused: "Yes, thanks." He takes out a package of cigarettes and puts one in his mouth, feeling in his pockets for matches. One of the men who brought him in holds a light to the cigarette. Rags blows smoke out, says: "Thanks."

King smiles at Rags, says in a friendly voice: "Tell us who killed Barney, Rags."

Rags laughs. "Somebody finally cut that rat down? That's just swell!"

King, in the same friendly voice: "Who did it, Rags?"

Rags: "I wish I knew, King. I'd like to send him a little present."

Pete takes a slow step toward Rags, says good-naturedly: "Aw, stop kidding. Who did it?"

Richmond hunches his chair a little nearer Rags. . . .

The clock on the wall moves from four o'clock to nine o'clock.

Rags is now sitting under a strong electric light. His collar is loosened, his necktie askew, and there is perspiration on his face. His faint grin has more weariness than mockery in it. He shakes his head wearily from side to side.

"That's a lie!" King says hoarsely. He wipes his neck and cheeks with a damp handkerchief. "There's a dozen ways you could get word out."

Pete, in shirt sleeves, puts out a hand and raises Rags' face roughly. "You got word to Slim and he turned the trick." His voice is hoarse as King's.

Rags: "No."

All the men in the room except Richmond are disheveled, but he seems tired as the others. One of the other men begins firing questions at Rags.

King looks questioningly at Richmond, who looks significantly at the clock and makes a hopeless gesture with his hands.

King interrupts the questioning. "Take him away," he orders.

Two men take Rags out. The others clump wearily in their chairs. Nobody speaks.

Richmond in his bathroom, shaving while carrying on a conversation with Babe Holliday, who is sitting crosswise in an easy chair in his living room, leaning against one arm, legs dangling over the other. She is asking: "And is this Ann Pomeroy really as beautiful as she looks in her pictures?"

He goes to the bathroom door, razor in hand, and looks at Babe under wrinkled forehead. "You been looking her up?" he asks incredulously.

She swings her legs and laughs. "Yep—back-number newspaper society pages. I'm a gal that does things about her curiosity. Is she that good-looking?"

He shrugs and goes back to his shaving. "She's not bad to look at," he says after he has removed most of the lather from his chin. He scrapes the other side of his face and then goes to the door again. "Can you keep a secret?" he asks, and then without waiting for her to answer, "I think she's the big one."

Babe laughs. "It's probably her old man's dough that's the big one."

He grins good-naturedly, says: "Maybe—but I find myself forgetting that sometimes."

She pretends amazement. "Then it *is* serious!" She looks at her watch. "Are we going to dinner or breakfast? It's after ten o'clock."

As she starts back toward the bathroom the telephone bell rings. He answers it: "Gene Richmond speaking."

The other end of the wire. Kavanaugh, disheveled, frantic, crying: "They've taken Ann with them! We didn't know she was gone till we found the note! They left an hour ago, but we didn't know they had her. We thought—"

Richmond drops his razor: "Shut up and answer questions! Did they go in their car?"

Kavanaugh: "Yes!"

Richmond: "What did the note say?"

Kavanaugh: "That since Pomeroy wouldn't give them money—They had made a final demand just—"

Richmond: "Shut up! Took her as a hostage?"

Kavanaugh: "Yes, they—"

Richmond: "Which way did they go?"

Kavanaugh: "Toward the city. We—"

Richmond: "Did you phone sheriffs along the way?"

Kavanaugh: "Yes, and Pomeroy and the others have gone after them. They may—"

Richmond: "They got away about an hour ago?"

Kavanaugh: "Around nine o'clock, I'd say. We saw—"

Richmond: "Anything else I ought to know?"

Kavanaugh: "No, except maybe—"

Richmond slams the receiver on the hook, whirls into his bedroom and begins getting into the rest of his clothes while shouting, "Come here," to Babe.

She is already there.

"Get pencil and paper," he snaps.

She gets them. While putting on his clothes he dictates a description of the three men and the girl, and a description and the license number of the Packard car. "Phone King of the federal narcotic department, the police—they abducted her—left Green Lake around nine o'clock—headed this way," and he dashes out, leaving the door open behind him.

He goes downstairs half a flight to a leap to the basement garage, gets into his car, heedlessly bangs fenders of other cars getting out of the garage, and roars up the street with pedestrians and other cars hurriedly getting out of his way.

Various shots of him leaving the city, dashing madly along country roads.

Then he rounds a bend and comes upon half a dozen cars standing in the road, blocking it, with men moving among their lights. He slams on his brakes barely in time to keep from running into the nearest car, and is out of his roadster before it has quite come to a halt.

In the light of one of the cars Ann is standing with her father. She leaves him immediately to run to Richmond, panting: "Oh, it was horrible! I thought you'd never come." She clings to him, weeping softly.

Richmond soothes her with his hands while looking around.

Neely, the Kid, Buck, and Happy are standing in a row, guarded by half a dozen hard-faced deputy sheriffs.

King and Pete are standing together, looking speculatively at Richmond, but before he can express his surprise at finding them there ahead of him, Pomeroy comes up and says: "I'm going to make a clean breast of it, Richmond, and take the consequences. When I think of the danger my cowardice put Ann in"—he swallows, puts his lips hard together, then says—"I'd rather be tried for a dozen murders."

"Sh-h-h," Richmond says pleasantly. "You're in the clear on that now."

King and Pete quietly move nearer, listening to Richmond.

Richmond is explaining to Pomeroy: "The man they killed was a narcotic agent. They were running dope. You hadn't anything to do with the dope—no jury could be convinced you had and the killing is tied up with that end—not with the liquor end. You're all right."

Ann raises a suddenly happy face to him, crying: "Oh, Gene," kissing him and then going to kiss her father.

King nudges Pete and they approach Richmond. He says: "Hello! How'd you boys get here ahead of me?"

King, drily: "We were on our way to Green Lake and happened to run into this party. A crazy dame that says she works for you came in right after you left tonight and told us the boys were up at Pomeroy's. She told us a lot of interesting things in between telling us she didn't want to go to prison again. That got to be kind of tiresome, but the rest of it was all right—about you knowing all along Pomeroy was in the clear and just stringing him along getting all the money you could. She said some things about some of your other jobs, too, and as soon as the doctors get her mind cleared a little we're going to have—"

Ann, her eyes cold, her head high and imperious, steps between King and Richmond, facing Richmond. He looks levelly at her.

"You did that?" she demands in a pitifully strained voice. "You left us at the mercy of those men for days; you kept Father in fear of disgrace, prison, the gallows; you let this"— shuddering—"happen to me—all so you could get more money out of him?"

Richmond's eyes fall. "I wasn't sure enough," he begins to mumble. Then he raises his head again and his voice becomes coldly composed. "I'm in business for money," he says evenly, "just as your father is and—"

She turns and walks away from him. He looks at Pomeroy, who stares back at him with bleak contemptuous eyes. He looks at King.

King shakes his head with an assumption of regret. "Always on the make, aren't you, Gene?"

Richmond has recovered all his composure. He grins cynically and replies: "Maybe you boys like working for your lousy little salaries. I'm in the game for money. Sure, I'm always on the make."

King shrugs. "Lousy little salaries is what we get, but we can sleep at night."

Richmond chuckles. "I lie awake a lot with my conscience," he says mockingly. He looks around. "Well, there doesn't seem to be anything for me to do here. Night." He turns toward his roadster.

King touches his shoulder, says, "Uh-uh, Gene. We've got to take you in and book you. You know—there are formalities to go through with."

Richmond, unruffled, nods. "You'll let me stop at a phone on the way in and get hold of my lawyer, so he'll have bail arranged by the time we get there?"

King: "Sure—we're not being rough with you." He looks around. "Let's go. Pete and I'll ride with you." He raises his voice to call to one of the men over by the prisoners: "Harry, we're going in with Richmond."

A voice answers: "Right."

They crowd into the roadster, Richmond turns it around, and they ride toward town until they come to a cross-roads drug store. They go into the store together. Richmond enters a glass telephone booth, while the two narcotic agents loiter in sight, but some distance away, at the cigar counter.

Richmond calls a number, asks for Mr. Schwartz, and when he gets him says: "Schwartz, this is Gene Richmond. . . . Yes. . . . I'm in a jam and I want bail arranged. . . . I don't know exactly, better arrange for plenty. . . . Right, in about an hour. . . . Thanks."

He calls another number and asks for Mr. Keough. The other end of the wire—a newspaper office. Richmond says to Keough: "Hello, Keough—this is Gene Richmond. I've got a story for you. We've just picked up four men on charges of rum-running, dope-smuggling, murder, and abduction of Ann Pomeroy. Is that news? . . . Right. . . . No, I didn't make the arrests myself, but they were made by narcotic agents and local deputies on information supplied by my office, so give me a good break on it. . . . Right. . . . Now here are the details. . . ."

FADE OUT.

The next morning. In Richmond's outer office Tommy, alone, is wide-eyed over the front page of a newspaper wherein Richmond's feat is described in glowing terms. Tommy looks admiringly up at Richmond as he comes in and says, "Good morning."

Richmond glances at the headlines in passing with a faint smile.

"Gee, you're smart, Mr. Richmond," Tommy blurts out.

Richmond rumples the boy's hair and goes into his private office. He shuts the door behind him and leans back against it wearily. His smile is gone. He pushes his hat back and mutters: "Gee, I'm smart! I got thirty thousand dollars and will probably have to go to jail or at least blow town, where I could have had ten million and the one woman that's ever really meant anything to me—maybe." He touches his forehead with the back of his hand and repeats, "Gee, I'm smart!"

The telephone-bell rings. He goes to it. "Gene Richmond speaking," he says with mechanical suavity. "Oh, good morning, Mr. Fields. No, nothing new yet. . . ." He looks thoughtfully at the phone, then: "It might be wise to place another man in the Dartmouth Cement

Company's offices and see what we can get from the inside. . . . Yes, I'd advise it. . . . All right, I'll do that."

He hangs up and presses the button on his desk. Tommy opens the door, says, "Miss Crane hasn't showed up yet."

Richmond blinks, then laughs. "That's right," he says. "That'll be all."

Tommy shuts the door.

THE END

APPENDIX:
THE LOST
SPADE

COMMENTARY

This collection closes with the beginnings of Dashiell Hammett's only known unpublished Sam Spade story. In 1932, Hammett published three original short stories featuring Spade—"A Man Called Spade" and "Too Many Have Lived" in *The American Magazine* and "They Can Only Hang You Once" in *Collier's*. He'd needed the income. Despite the critical success of his first four novels (including *The Maltese Falcon*) and screen-story assignments with Paramount and Warner Bros., Hammett was broke by late 1931. He ran through money or gave it away as fast or faster than he earned it. Ben Wasson, the literary agent Hammett shared with drinking buddy William Faulkner, had encouraged him to return to short-story writing and Hammett obliged. The Sam Spade stories he submitted were hardly serious efforts, however. Two are rewrites of early *Black Mask* tales and the third unimpressively thin. Although Hammett was willing to capitalize on the popularity of his celebrated detective, he seemed reluctant to bring much vigor to the project. He'd set his sights higher.

"A Knife Will Cut for Anybody" had its genesis in this period, when Hammett was torn between cranking out quick crowd pleasers and struggling to meet his own literary ambitions. The story is set in

San Francisco, with reappearances by *The Maltese Falcon*'s Lieutenant Dundy and Detective-sergeant Polhaus. The scene of the crime, however, closely mirrors the main floor of the building at 133 East Thirty-eighth Street in the Murray Hill district of New York where Hammett lived in a rented apartment. The address appears on headings of both Hammett's aborted first draft of *The Thin Man* and an unfinished novella titled "The Darkened Face." And, in fact, "Knife Will Cut" and "Darkened Face" are two versions of the same tale.

Hammett, it seems, was so pleased with the setup he'd invented for his fourth Spade story that he opted to repurpose the narrative into a more substantial work. He anticipated twenty-five thousand words, replaced Spade with a Continental Detective Agency operative named Fox, changed the nationality of the victim from Argentine to German, and shifted the locale from the West to the East Coast. His draft typescript for "A Knife Will Cut for Anybody" was abandoned and eventually made its way to the antiquarian marketplace and the safekeeping of a savvy collector—a writer and Hammett enthusiast. Hammett's incomplete novella, in contrast, was cached among his "keepers" and is now preserved in his archives at the Harry Ransom Center in Austin.

While Hammett lightly expanded and developed his revised crime narrative, the text of the original draft is offered here. It is both a tribute to Sam Spade as America's seminal hard-boiled detective and a singular opportunity for readers to enjoy a bittersweet sample of a great, untold story.

A KNIFE WILL CUT FOR ANYBODY

When Samuel Spade knocked on the door it swung open far enough to let him see the mutilated dead face of a woman. She lay on her back on the floor in a lot of blood and a red-stained hunting-knife with a heavy six-inch blade lay in blood beside her. She was tall and slender, her hair was dark, her dress was green: her face and body had been hacked so that little beyond this could be said about her.

Spade breathed out sharply once and his face became wooden except for the alertness of his yellow-grey eyes. He flattened his left hand against the door and slowly pushed it farther back. The fingers of his right hand, held a little away from his side, curved as if they held a ball. He glanced swiftly to right and left, up and down the ground-floor hallway in which he stood, then into as much of the room as was visible from where he stood.

The room was wide, and open double doors made it and the room behind it one long room. Grey and black were the predominant colors and the furniture, modern in design, was obviously new.

Spade went into the room, walking around the dead woman, avoiding the blood on the floor, and saw in the next room a pale grey telephone. He called the San Francisco Police Department's number and asked for Lieutenant Dundy of the Homicide Detail. He said: "Hello, Dundy, Sam Spade. . . . I'm at 1950 Green Street. There's a woman here's been killed." He listened. "I wouldn't kid you: somebody's made hamburger of her . . . Right." He put down the telephone and made a cigarette.

Lieutenant Dundy turned his short, stocky back to the corpse and addressed Spade: "Well?"

Two of the men—one was small, one very large—who had come in with Dundy were bending over the dead woman. A uniformed policeman stood at attention near one of the front windows.

Spade said: "Well, the Argentine Consul hired me to find a Teresa Moncada, for her family or something." He nodded at the dead woman. "Looks like I did."

"This her?"

Spade moved his thick, sloping shoulders a little. "What you can see of her fits the photo and description they gave me. There's a fellow at the consulate who knows her. I phoned him to come over. He ought to—" He broke off as the men who had been examining the dead woman stood up.

The smaller man—he had a lean dark intelligent face—wiped his hands carefully with a blue-bordered handkerchief and said: "Dead an hour, I'd say. This knife all right."

Dundy nodded. "You found her?" he asked Spade.

"Yes. The street-door was open, so when nobody answered the bell I came on in and tried this one, and there it was. There wasn't anybody else here. Looks like there's nobody else in the house. I rang both upstairs-flat bells, but no luck. Another thing, there's no clothes here except her hat and coat there on the chair, and there's nothing in her handbag except about twenty bucks, lipstick, powder, and that kind of stuff. That's the works."

Dundy's lips worked together under his close-clipped grizzled mustache. He was about to speak when a grey-faced man wearing a wide-brimmed black hat stuck his head in at the door and said: "There's a fellow says his name's Sanchez Cornejo here wanting to see Spade."

"That's the fellow from the consulate," Spade told Dundy.

"Send him in."

The man at the door stepped aside and said, "O.K., come on," to someone behind him.

A very tall, very thin young man appeared in the doorway. His glossy black hair, parted in the middle, was brushed smooth to his somewhat narrow head. His face was long and dark, his eyes large and dark. He wore dark clothes and carried a black derby hat and a dark walking-stick in his hands.

He dropped his stick when he saw the woman on the floor, his eyes opened to show whites all around the irises, and blood going out of his face left it a dingy yellow. "*Virgen santísima!*" He went down on one knee beside her. Then he mumbled something to himself and stood up again. Color began to come back into his face. He bent over to pick up his stick.

Dundy, scowling suspiciously at him, asked, "You're Sanchez Cornejo?"

Cornejo winced a little, as if at the Lieutenant's pronunciation of his name, and said, "Yes, sir."

"You know Teresa Moncada?"

Cornejo began to tremble. He opened his mouth, but no sound came out. He nodded his reply.

"This her?"

Cornejo dropped his stick again and jumped nervously when it clattered on the floor. His dark eyes were wide with bewilderment. "*Si*—yes, sir," he stammered. "Of course."

"Sure?"

The dark young man had recovered his composure. "Yes, sir, I am," he said with conviction.

"Right. Come on back here." Dundy led the way into the next room. He waved a stubby hand at a metal chair and the young man sat down. "Now give me what you've got."

Cornejo stared at the detective. "I do not understand."

Spade sat on the corner of a table near Cornejo. "What you know about her," he explained. "I'm Sam Spade, a private detective. Your Consul, Mr. Navarrete, hired me to find her and told me you knew her. That's how I happened to run into this and call you."

The young man nodded several times. "I understand. Señor Navarrete had the kindness to tell me." He smiled at Dundy. "Please excuse my not understanding. I will tell you all I know."

"All right." Dundy's face and voice responded in no way to the young man's smile. "Do that little thing."

Cornejo moistened his lips and looked uneasily at the Lieutenant.

Spade's manner was more friendly. "How long have you known her?"

"Three years. That is I met her three years ago in the house of her uncle and guardian, Doctor Felix Haya de la Torre, in Buenos Ayres, but I have not seen her for quite a year and a half—" he swallowed "—until today."

"An orphan?"

"Yes, and supposedly the second wealthiest woman in our country." He frowned earnestly. "That is why her uncle was so afraid—so anxious to find her. You see, she did not like her uncle, and she resented his perhaps too careful guardianship, and so when, on her twenty-first birthday last August, she came into control of her estate and was her own mistress, she left his house."

"And came to America?" Dundy asked.

"To North America? No, not immediately, but her uncle thought her too young and inexperienced and too wealthy to be quite safe alone and considered it his duty to continue to watch over her in spite of her objections." Cornejo shrugged. "As I say, she resented that, and last month she, with a distant cousin, a Camilla Cerro, disappeared, presumably coming here and assuming fictitious names."

Spade nodded. "This flat was rented under the name of Thelma Magnin."

"Yes?" Dundy said. "Well, Cornejo, or whatever your name is, who killed her?"

The young man's voice and eyes were steady. "I do not know."

"Who'd have reason to?"

"I do not know."

"Who'd get her dough?"

"I beg your pardon?"

"Her heirs?" Spade explained.

"Oh! I don't know. Her uncle and his sons Federico and Victor are her nearest relatives, but she may have made a will, of course."

Dundy scowled at Spade. "What do you think?"

"Nothing yet."

Dundy looked at Cornejo thoughtfully, surveyed him deliberately from head to foot, and turned to Spade again. "I guess we're safe in calling it a spick job. They like knives."

Cornejo's face flushed. He said stiffly: "A knife will cut for anybody, I believe. That knife is not—"

Spade, grinning wolfishly, interrupted the young man. "How do you know she was killed with that knife?"

Cornejo stared blankly at Spade.

Dundy growled: "All right. What does this other girl, this Camilla Cerro, look like?"

Spade, still grinning, said softly: "I bet she looks more like that girl lying in there on the floor than Teresa Moncada does."

Dundy said: "What?"

Cornejo opened his mouth as if he were trying to say something, but no sound came out. His face was ghastly with fear.

Spade said: "Though they must look something alike or he wouldn't've tried to pass one off as the other when he found we'd guessed wrong."

The young man could speak now and did, very rapidly, so that his accent, barely noticeable before, became more pronounced. "It is true. It is true that they look somewhat alike, I mean, and I may have made a mistake. It may be Camilla Cerro and not Señorita Moncada who was killed. I have not seen them since a year and a half ago and—"

Spade said, "Tch, tch, tch," reprovingly and asked: "How do you suppose I found this place?"

"I don't know."

"By shadowing you."

The young man lowered his head and stared miserably at the floor.

Detective-sergeant Polhaus—a burly carelessly shaven florid man—appeared in the doorway. "All through with the body. Want it anymore?"

Dundy's attention did not waver from Cornejo. Only a corner of his mouth moved slightly. "No."

Polhaus left the doorway and his cheerful voice came in from the other room. "All right, boys, pack it out."

AFTERWORD

Dear Reader,

It seems we've now seen the last of Dashiell Hammett's original Sam Spade stories (albeit unfinished) and almost certainly the last "new" collection to be pulled from his typewriter and rescued from his archives. Are you surprised? Are the stories what you expected? I hope in some ways they are surprising, that they suggest images of my grandfather that you wouldn't have anticipated based on previous publications or biographies or popular conceptions of the father of hard-boiled detective fiction.

My grandfather was sixty-three when he told a *Washington Daily News* reporter that he'd stopped writing when he discovered he was repeating himself. "It is the beginning of the end when you discover you have style," he claimed. But that was a throwaway line as much as a genuine reflection on his experience. As this collection—and his body of work as a whole—demonstrates, Hammett had both exploited and resisted stylistic expectations since his earliest days as a writer.

He is best remembered by way of his five crime novels, but even there his protagonists range widely. The Continental Op was a no-nonsense gumshoe who went blood simple in Montana and chased clues, cons, and ghosts in California; Sam Spade juggled love, lust, pragmatics, and justice in his City by the Bay; Ned Beaumont tested the bounds of camaraderie and family in an ersatz Baltimore; and Nick Charles drank and partied and solved for problems in New York City and beyond. Hammett created all those characters, their supporting casts, and conflicts out his own pied life experience. It would be a mistake, however, to constrain my grandfather's story to the familiar. *The Hunter*'s rare works offer fresh glimpses into Hammett and his shifting worldview—as a reflective, enigmatic man who toggled between poverty and wealth, west and east coasts, and pulp-, book-, and film-writing careers.

Both as Hammett scholar and granddaughter, I'm fascinated by the glimmers of biography that surface in this collection. "Faith" is set north of Baltimore, not too far from where Hammett spent his youth, in the kind of riverside terrain where he would have enjoyed fishing or hunting. The half-dozen or so San Francisco stories reflect his early married life, laced with familiar place names from the 1920s: Ellis Street, where John's Grill and my grandparents' first apartment was located; Larkin, the site of the all-important public library; Market Street, home to Samuels Jewelers and the Flood Building, with the Pinkerton's offices in suite 314; Polk, running between city hall and the Civic Center; the Embarcadero and the Ferry Building, both critical to San Francisco's waterfront mischief. "On the Make" and "On the Way" come later, with echoes from Hammett's experiences in the Los Angeles basin in the early 1930s, where he worked for Hollywood's studios and met Lillian Hellman. Life and relationships were complicated there. Places, then, evoke life history, tie fiction to fact, and provide an essential baseline.

"Monk and Johnny Fox" and "Action and the Quiz Kid" go on to suggest some of Hammett's lesser-known interests, as well as the more disreputable sections of New York that would have attracted Hammett during his Manhattan stays. My grandfather was a boxing enthusiast of long standing, who respected the kind of toughness required to train for and participate in orchestrated slugfests. Years after he invented Monk and the Kid, he was thrilled to meet Joe Louis, who visited Anchorage as part of a USO program. "I like him," Hammett said. "He doesn't have a lot to say, but he is far from being anybody's dope." We know, too, that Hammett enjoyed baseball and listening to games on the radio—so perhaps he followed the career of young Joe DiMaggio, who'd played ball in San Francisco before moving up to the Yankees in 1936. Certainly DiMaggio's honorable mention in "Action" was no accident. And, like Action, Hammett would have been tempted to put some money on the game. My grandfather liked to test his luck on sports, cards, and the ponies, to his occasional misfortune. In sum, he wrote what he knew, as an ex-detective and as an engaged and observant human adventurer.

It's a rare privilege and opportunity to look backward into Hammett's life by way of his unpublished and little-known works. He, who rarely saved anything, saved these, which survive as both fiction and artifact. The files at the Harry Ransom Center at the University of Texas in Austin are a mother lode for Hammett scholar-detectives. They preserve the real deal—smudges and chips dating back to the mid-1920s, drafts on the backs of old letters or on both sides of cheap brown paper. Money was tight in those days. Chapter outlines and character descriptions. Penciled edits in Hammett's careful rounded script. Whole sections crossed out or reworked. Headings that list addresses, sometimes revised as he moved from apartment to apartment, the earliest ones earnest and complete as he tested the marketplace, the later ones just a title—or not even that—with little concern for impressing future editors. Shifts in typewriters and formatting and from pulpy pages to good, hard stationery. Hellman's hand in places. And, if you look carefully, clues to Hammett's ambitions.

For researchers, editors, biographer, and granddaughter, archival visits are irreplaceable, near-religious experiences, ripe with potential for new discoveries. "Faith" is a case in point. The typescript is twelve letter-sized pages, produced in Hammett's characteristic tidy manner, with only a smattering of autograph emendations. Page eight seems at first glance the same size as the others, though the text runs a little farther down the page than its mates. A second look reveals roughly an inch of the sheet folded back at the bottom. Closer examination turns up Hammett's paste job, so neatly worked that it's nearly imperceptible.

He'd added exactly three lines to the middle of the page: "That's when I began to know for sure that it was God after me. I had sort of suspected it once or twice before—just from queer things I'd noticed—but I hadn't been certain. But now I knew what was what, and I wasn't wrong either!" Feach's declaration doesn't move the plot forward or change the trajectory of the narrative, but it illuminates a driving tension between truth and delusion, rationality and religion, a thematic point important enough to Hammett that he'd fit it precisely into the existing tale. It was a tell, an indicator, a clue.

Careful readers of Hammett's fiction can almost always find a line or two keyed to each story's central concern—a job or duty, a choice, or a question of human nature. Sometimes, perhaps, he himself pointed to them. Along the edges of his typescripts there are occasional markers, scratched in at critical points. In "The Cure" it runs alongside a line about courage not being a "damned thing but a habit of not dodging things because you're afraid of them." In "Nelson Redline" it accompanies a passage about men who refuse to conduct themselves according to acceptable and predictable rules. Were these Hammett's marks? Was he consciously developing a grand literary or epistemological scheme? There is no proof, of course, but the idea makes sense in the light of Hammett's biography and bibliography.

My grandfather may have started his writing career as a means to keep food on the family table, but he was too smart and too ambitious to stop at a paycheck or to be satisfied with whodunits, no matter how well-crafted they might be. His best work succeeds in the ultimate literary twinship: entertaining stories that explore important aspects of the human experience. Walter Huston called him as a genius: "Someone who sees things in a way that illuminates them and enables you to see things in a different way." My grandfather was more modest about his creative capacities, but they were clearly substantial. He was in many ways an everyman's philosopher whose intellect and life experiences synthesized in a talent to transform important, even complex, issues into storylines that were both digestible and insightful.

Hammett once confessed to his daughter Jo that he never knew what to say to people who asked what his next book was about. "What the hell else is there to say except maybe that it's about people?" he wrote. And that's true enough. Whether crime stories, mystical extravaganzas, cynical romances, or hard-boiled dramas, the stories are always more about the characters—their conundrums and choices—than about plots or puzzles. Hammett's narratives serve up no simple tonics. As he said, "I only write 'em. . . . It's up to the readers to try to figure out what in the name of God they're about, if anything."

The stories in *The Hunter* come to the marketplace some fifty-two years after Hammett's death and, while they are published without his consent, the collection has been closely considered by the Hammett family and trustees. We believe *The Hunter*'s stories deserve to be published, read, and included in the greater Hammett canon. We believe that they complement Hammett's better-known fiction and complicate and extend the legend and life story of their author. They're stories about people, as Hammett said, and it's up to today's readers to discover for themselves the tales' significance as artifacts and their meanings as entertainment or art. Maybe, as Huston suggests, they'll help you see the world in a different way. What more could any writer ask?

J.M.R.